You
Wouldn't
Dare

Also by Samantha Markum

This May End Badly

You Wouldn't Dare

Samantha Markum

WEDNESDAY BOOKS
NEW YORK

Published in the United States by Wednesday Books, an imprint of St. Martin's Publishing Group

www.wednesdaybooks.com

The Library of Congress Cataloging-in-Publication Data is available upon request.

ISBN 978-1-250-84678-5 (hardcover)
ISBN 978-1-250-84679-2 (ebook)

First Edition: 2023

10 9 8 7 6 5 4 3 2 1

For second families everywhere,
but especially for mine—
the Barrons/Houghs

You
Wouldn't
Dare

Chapter One

JAQUES
All the world's a stage, and all the people merely
players.

(THE BAND enters noisily.)

BAND MEMBER 1
So you're in the band?

JAQUES
Am I what?

BAND MEMBER 1
In the band.

JAQUES
No, I am not. I am a guest at this wedding.

BAND MEMBER 1
Then get off the stage. The only players here are in
the band.

*(THE BAND strikes up instruments. Orchestra commences
discordant music playing.)*
—Act 1, Scene 1, *Midsummer Madness*

I get the text when Maybelle and Susanna are in a particularly nasty argument about Maybelle's "lost" invitation to

the Christmas costume party. Susanna has the wild, wide-eyed look on her face that always prefaces a meltdown. I'm poised with a chip halfway to my mouth and my heartbeat ramping up for the inevitable screaming match when my phone buzzes, lighting up on the coffee table.

> **MOM**
> Will you be gracing your job with your presence today? Or am I paying you to lie on the couch and watch Proper Southern Ladies?

I glance around the living room, briefly wondering if I need to check for hidden cameras, before I jump up from the couch, shutting off the TV and tossing aside the remote.

> **ME**
> I'm halfway there!

> **MOM**
> I'll believe it when I see it.
> It being you. Here. In 3 minutes.

I'm already out the door, shoving my feet into my ugly nonslip sneakers and grabbing my bike from where it's leaning against the front porch. Milo would kill me if he knew I didn't lock it up last night. My beach cruiser is baby pink with hundreds of glued-on shells and cheap craft-store gems, a glittery basket, and a cute little bell. The whole thing sparkles in the sun like a disco ball. I decked it out myself during an extremely boring winter two years ago, and Milo followed up with the world's most boring Christmas gift: a lock that spends more time looped uselessly around our porch rail than around my bike.

Piper and Junie's Café and Curios is normally a four-minute

ride from our house, but I push my bike far beyond what anyone would call cruising speed to cut my time. Not even the ocean breeze drifting over the island is enough to cut through the thick Florida heat, and heavy strands of blond hair, increasing in volume with every additional second spent out in the humidity, stick to my sweaty neck.

"This is interesting. Running late?" a familiar voice calls as I screech up to a stop sign. The biggest pain is adhering to traffic laws on my bike, but Sheriff Abadiano would definitely give me a ticket if he saw me run a stop sign or try to ride on the sidewalk, and then Milo would gloat about it. *Sidewalks are for pedestrians. Traffic laws are for anyone on wheels, even bikes.* He's a horrific rule follower—probably a side effect of being the sheriff's son, and especially Sheriff Abadiano's. Milo says his dad, the island's first Latine sheriff and a Colombian immigrant, can't leave any room for criticism. Everything is by the book, to the letter. White Coral Key might be a laid-back island, but there are a ton of vacation rentals around here, and those non-resident owners have a lot of sway—and worse, a lot of money.

"No," I pant, already drifting through the deserted intersection.

Graham stands on the other side of the street, leaning against a pickup truck with the NEIGHBORHOOD HERO logo on the doors.

"What would make you think that?" I ask as I wipe the back of my hand across my forehead. A great look for me, I'm sure. But it's *just* Graham. How I look doesn't matter, because we are *just* friends. Tentative, maybe, but still friends—after months of hard work, on both our parts.

"You always say you don't bike hard enough to sweat," he says.

3

"I'm turning over a new leaf. It's a hardworking one. I'm really dedicated to being on time."

I'm only slightly comforted seeing that Graham is as much of a mess as I am—his NEIGHBORHOOD HERO T-shirt is streaked with something black, maybe grease or dirt, and his dark hair is rumpled and damp. His tan skin glistens with sweat. But even though he's probably on his last job of the day, or close to it, he still looks good, which should honestly be a crime.

Neighborhood Hero does odd jobs all around town—hanging pictures and patching holes, unclogging toilets and sinks and showers, delivering groceries and takeout and toiletries. Any random task, any time of day, someone's on call at Neighborhood Hero.

Behind Graham, his boss, Rita, a sturdy woman with a thick, wild pixie cut and deep brown skin, exits the house. "Good to go!" she calls, jingling the keys to the truck. She holds a bucket in her other hand, and as she loads it into the bed of the truck, she nods to me. "Hiya, Junie. Late for work?"

I push off the concrete. "I don't know why everyone keeps saying that!"

Graham's laugh follows me, warm in my ears, all the way to the end of the street, until I turn the corner and leave him far behind.

P&J's waits at the end of the road, painted pink and purple and yellow and blue, string lights dangling from the roof overhang and yard art, iguanas and fish and flip-flops and palm trees, tacked up on the walls. I pedal into the gravel parking lot behind the restaurant and lean my bike up against the back of the building.

When I screech to a stop inside the bustling kitchen, Mom is standing at the back door with her hands on her hips. It's probably the only definition her ankle-length sack dress has seen all day. She could be three toddlers standing on top of one another under that thing, and no one would know.

"That was more than three minutes," she says.

"You set me up for failure." I realize I forgot my apron at home, so I lean into Mom's office to grab a spare. It's a small tragedy. Mine is pink with hand-painted white daisies all over it, but this one is plain, boring black.

"You were already late, Juniper Nash," Mom says. "You set yourself up for failure."

"What's the point of being the boss's daughter if I can't push the rules?" I ask as I head toward the café, hoping to lighten the mood. The kitchen is open to the dining room, and I can see every table is full, with a few groups milling about waiting for a table to clear.

Hanging overhead are mismatched chandeliers—some made of plastic gemstones, others of old silverware and soda cans, one of shells and sea glass. Among the chandeliers are yard ornaments, birdcages, a bicycle, disco balls, and paper lanterns. Separated from the dining room by big, hand-painted screens is our consignment shop. The shop itself is mostly full of work by local artists—paintings, trinkets, clothes, and jewelry. The biggest sellers are the sculptures, some small and made for coffee tables, others life-size or larger, all whimsical and gorgeous and made by Mom's best friend and my godmother, Hal.

"Ah, yes, nepotism. Our crowning achievement." Mom catches me by my apron strings. "Hey, listen. You're supposed to be here to train Tallulah, remember?"

I bite back a groan. Mom has been dating Tallulah's dad, Paul, for almost two years, but Tallulah and I have managed to keep our lives mostly separate. As in, I mostly don't go to their house, and she mostly steers very clear of me. It's even easier at school, where we're separated by a grade and share no classes. Now that she's working at P&J's, I not only can't avoid her, but I have to train her. Personally, I think I've been a paragon of patience. In the last week, I've watched her argue with a tourist over heating up a scone, forget to put out the WET FLOOR sign when mopping up a dropped coffee, and spill lettuce off the side of someone's salad and try to put it back with her bare hands. My only comfort is knowing she makes me look like I'm fantastic at my job by comparison. Tallulah and I aren't playing in the same league. At this point, I'm not even sure Tallulah's playing the same game.

"I had to send Mac out to cover for you," Mom says. "Go put him out of his misery. He's probably traumatized."

I spot Mac clearing a table for a group of tourists, his expression tight and nervous. He looks even paler than usual.

Angela, who runs the counter of our consignment shop, says Mac is one of those guys who peaked in high school. She showed me pictures of their group when they were my age, and Mac was always with a different girl and wearing a killer smile. It's only been six years since they graduated, but the Mac I know has a receding hairline and the tired, sunken eyes of a twenty-four-year-old with two toddlers. The only girl I've ever seen him associate with is his wife.

As for Angela, she retained all her cool-girl energy. She makes her own clothes, can talk to anyone about anything, and is a member of a local roller derby team, Intoxiskated, which means she often clocks in with new bruises blotting her dark skin. She says they're her badges of honor. Her derby name is Angela Death, which is a huge contrast to the sunny, approachable vibe she has at work. To us, she's Everybody's Friend Angela.

My friend Lucy says Angela is her dream girl. She doesn't know if she wishes she could date her or be her. I suspect it's a little of both—especially since Lucy took up roller-skating a couple years ago.

"Thank God you're here," Mac says when he sees me. I feel a little rush of satisfaction, even though I know it's less about me being me and more about me being *anybody* to save him from the dining room. I don't even have a chance to respond before he's ducking past, making a beeline for the kitchen.

Tallulah, who's delivering two plates to a small table in the back, shoots me a flat look. "Oh, you're here." She doesn't sound relieved—just pissed off, which is kind of what I consider her baseline. She's wearing an oversized tie-dyed T-shirt that says CLIMATE CHANGE IS REAL on the front and a pair of tattered jean shorts, her legs long and bronzed from the sun. Mismatched socks peek out of her clunky nonslip shoes, one clearly cut higher than the other. Her pastel mermaid hair is tied back in a braid, flyaways secured with old-school butterfly clips. The hair is what got her fired from her job at the grocery store last week—a handbook violation.

It pains me that Tallulah looks so much cooler than she actually is. If she didn't treat me like slime, she might be the kind of person I'd enjoy hanging out with. As it is, there's only so much damage my ego can take.

I glance back to appeal to Mom, but she's already gone. Mom always works the opening shift, because breakfast at P&J's is the most chaotic, though you'd never know that from looking at this late lunch crowd. People stream in all through the morning for a Piper Abreheart Special—Mom changes it every day—and a coffee from Moonface, P&J's resident psychic barista. In the afternoons, it's Isaac and Elden running the kitchen, and Mac washing dishes with machinelike speed.

7

I miss last summer, when afternoons at P&J's meant me and Rooney. But thinking about it feels like pressing a bruise. For Graham, it probably feels even worse—like phantom pains after an amputation.

I swallow down a rush of guilt.

"Junie," Isaac calls from behind the counter, "we've got orders up!"

Elden laughs. "Come on, Superstar, show us those skills you're so proud of."

You'd never know Isaac and Elden are brothers from looking at them. Isaac is buff, tan, and clean-cut. He looks like a Marine, or someone who plays one on TV. Elden is soft like a teddy bear, pale from spending most of his time indoors, and has a long ponytail. But despite being slow-moving in life, Elden is a whip in the kitchen. He works almost as fast as Mom does, and together, Isaac and Elden are unmatched.

I try to calm the rowdier tables with free drinks and fresh-baked cookies. I say hello to some of the locals and manage to nab two of the Klingman kids hiding under a table.

I attempt to give Tallulah pointers as we work, but she's in a sour mood, so after about an hour, I give up and let her fend for herself.

I'm in the kitchen unloading a dish bucket when I hear the crash. It sounds like one of the chandeliers has fallen, but when I skid out into the café, I see it's our glass water dispenser, which survived my butterfinger tween years, seven tourist seasons, and the Klingmans' six children. I once saw Bryce Klingman, at age five, lift up Savannah Klingman, at only two, to dispense her own water. Moonface said she had a vision of the whole thing toppling onto the two of them, completely unrelated to her psychic abilities—just common sense.

Leave it to Tallulah to finally take it down.

"Okay, I need everyone behind the lemon tree, please. Back it up, people." I look at Tallulah. She's standing over the shattered mess, looking stunned. "What happened?"

Tallulah turns without a word and walks off.

I stare after her, jaw somewhere around my knees.

"Watch out, Little J." Mac emerges from the kitchen with a broom and dustpan, the WET FLOOR sign tucked under his elbow.

Behind him, Isaac and Elden are watching Tallulah as she makes her way to the back door. I step gingerly over the broken glass and follow, sticking my foot in the door before it swings shut behind her. I lean against the doorjamb, listening past the rustling palms and cars crunching on the road. It only takes a few seconds to realize that she's on the phone with my mom.

"I didn't want to work here anyway," she says. "Just tell my dad I'm a total screwup, okay? Trust me, he'll believe it." There's a pause, and then Tallulah snaps, "Let Juniper Nash tell him then. She'll have no problem. She'll probably be thrilled."

I let the door drop.

It's not like Tallulah and I are friends, or even friend-adjacent. I know she thinks I'm a vapid airhead who'd be late to her own funeral. But I didn't know she thought of me like *that*—someone happy to see her fail.

I should be relieved to be rid of the deadweight, but instead I slouch through the rest of my shift, feeling both guilty and annoyed about the whole thing.

Our little beach cottage sits on the canal, last house on the right. Standing in the kitchen, it's a clear shot out the back windows to the small dock across from ours, where Milo spends most nights with his telescope.

The house is dark and quiet when I let myself in, and I remember Mom had a date with Paul tonight. Exhausted, I collapse on the couch to watch the rest of the *Proper Southern Ladies* episode I had to abandon this afternoon.

I'm half asleep, with a melting pint of ice cream on the coffee table, when Mom floats in from her date. She has a dopey smile on her face, and her gaze drifts over the room like she's only half-present.

"You look totally blissed out," I say, sitting up. "You weren't doing *the drugs,* were you? Let me check your eyes."

She sinks onto the chaise across from me with a laugh, letting her blond curls down from her bun. "No, I wasn't doing *the drugs.* I'm just happy."

"That's suspicious," I say. I was expecting the lecture of the century about being nicer to Tallulah and my responsibility to train her, but it looks like this afternoon's disaster is the last thing on Mom's mind.

She sits up and turns to face me, seriousness creeping into her expression. "I have something to tell you, Jujubear."

I check her hands, but there's no ring, which sends a rush of relief through me.

It's not that I'd be mad if Paul proposed, but it's a strange thought. He's my mom's first serious boyfriend in my lifetime. She and my dad were never married and broke up before I was born. Dad lives out of town and rarely gets to visit. So, despite the two years I've had to acclimate to Paul's presence, it's still weird to have a man around, even part-time.

Plus, I've always thought getting engaged or married before you've lived together is a little risky. What if he has bad sleeping habits? Or always forgets to put the toilet seat down? Or—

"Paul and I have decided that now would be a great time to move in together."

I should have seen that coming.

I sit up. "What?"

"You only have a year left before college, and we both think it's a good idea for you and Tallulah to have that time to bond under the same roof." She folds her hands in her lap, suddenly looking prim, very unlike my usual laid-back, hippie-dippie mom. "Marriage is the logical next step, but we want to try cohabitation first."

It's so bland and technical that I know she's quoting Paul, who is Mr. Logical. I mean, the man's a doctor, for God's sake.

"Um, okay," I say after a minute of processing. "Cool."

I feel slightly less than cool about it, but I'm trying to relax. Maybe living together will make the whole Paul thing a little less weird for me, especially before he becomes my stepdad—the words *logical next step* ping around in my head.

Acting happy is easy, though, when Mom looks this excited. She smiles like she can't believe what she's hearing. "Cool?"

"Yeah. I mean, it'll be a little strange at first, but . . . I'm not a total dork, Mom. I figured this would happen eventually. It makes sense that we should all live together now, before . . ." I trail off, not wanting to jinx it. I have to actually *get into* college before I start talking about going off to it. Otherwise, I'm just being presumptuous. It could very easily be Spoonbill Community College and an extra two years at home for me. I'm realistic enough about my grades to recognize that. Which could mean *three* years living under the same roof as Tallulah.

Unless she gets into college. But from what I know of

her dedication to school—which is limited, since she's a year younger than me, but still—I doubt that'll happen.

I glance at my bedroom and wonder how Tallulah and I are going to make that work. I already sleep on a twin-size bed because my room is so small. We'll probably have to un-install my ceiling fan to fit bunk beds or something.

I have a trundle, but I doubt she'd go for it.

I bet I'll have to redecorate, too. I can't imagine she'll be a fan of the vintage Broadway posters on my walls, or of how my furniture sparkles from the glitter I tossed in when I repainted it all two summers ago. I bet she'll especially hate the heart-shaped mirror that hangs over my dresser.

Absolutely nothing in my bedroom—including its primary resident, me—feels Tallulah-approved. A year in there together sounds like a prelude to the apocalypse, but three? I'd rather try my luck in the ninth circle of hell.

Maybe this is the kick in the ass I need to pull my grades up. People love a comeback story, right? It'll make for a great personal essay.

> *Dear Florida State,*
> *Please let me in, I'm absolutely begging you. Three years with this girl might lead to murder, and I'm too soft for prison.*

If I'm being completely honest, the thought of sharing a room with Tallulah makes me feel a little sick, especially after the disaster this afternoon and learning her real opinion of me. But I don't want to ruin Mom's excitement. I'll voice my worries later, when it won't kill her smile that's so bright, it could power the whole house. I almost have to shield my eyes to look at her.

"*Cool.* Okay," Mom says with a delirious little laugh. "I thought I'd have to do some serious convincing. I wrote up a list of points during dinner." She holds up her phone, flashing the screen at me. The page is filled with writing.

"Okay, that's a little dramatic!" I laugh. "I'm not totally unreasonable."

"Oh, of course not," she says, and I shoot her a look that I hope conveys how little I appreciate the sarcasm in her tone.

I settle back into the couch. "Want to watch the newest episode before bed?" I ask, my finger hovering over the remote.

Mom cozies into the chaise and says, "I know you already watched it without me." I blanch, and Mom arches her no-bullshit eyebrows at me. "Yeah, you thought you were slick. And don't think you're off the hook for what happened today."

I groan. "I was hoping your good news gave you amnesia."

"You need to be nicer to her, Juniper Nash."

"All I did was ask her what happened!" But it's an old argument. Mom is constantly asking me to be nicer to Tallulah. As if *I'm* the problem here. Tallulah decided she didn't like me from basically the moment we officially met. I knew of her then—everyone did. Even as a freshman, I heard about how she was pulled out of school halfway through eighth grade. Her mom had died in a drowning accident while Tallulah was visiting her in Clearwater. Her parents were long-divorced, and Tallulah spent her summers with her mom. But after her mom's death, even though Tallulah was back in White Coral, she was homeschooled and rarely seen in public. We didn't even meet until our parents were starting to get serious.

I tried to be nice to her right off the bat during that first dinner—takeout from Vittoria's, this delicious Italian restaurant on the mainland. I offered her one of the meatballs from my spaghetti—even though Vittoria's is so expensive, Mom and I almost never eat there—and I was really excited about my dinner. But Tallulah just sneered, "I'm vegetarian," and went back to her mushroom ravioli. Then I made a joke about her dinner being a little insensitive to Toad from Mario and how I was calling PETA on her, and Tallulah launched into a lecture about how I was perpetuating the belittling of vegetarians, and how PETA isn't even an ethical charity, and then we all had to sit there awkwardly eating our dinner while she pulled up stats to back up her case. And Mom thinks I'm the one she needs a bullet-point argument for? Tallulah is a one-person debate team.

It never got any easier after that. I thought it was a response to her dad dating—that she hated Mom and me equally. But even though she isn't super warm and fuzzy with Mom, she's still nice. She talks to her like a human being, at least. I think she even smiled at her once.

"She was embarrassed, Juju. Try to be understanding," Mom says now, as though this is a perfect excuse for Tallulah being so vile in response to a simple—and understandable!—question after she destroyed our water dispenser.

But I'm running out of energy to argue. Today was exhausting, and no matter what I say, Mom will just insist I be the bigger person.

"I convinced her to come back, and she'll be on mornings with me for a while," Mom continues. "You'll get Darius."

I do a little cheer, pumping my arms in the air.

Mom's no-bullshit eyebrows make another appearance. "And then they'll switch back, and as the one with seniority, you'll need to be responsible for her."

My cheer dies a swift death, and I slump against the arm of the couch. "Please, no more responsibilities."

"Think of it as *your* training," Mom says. "Once you graduate high school, you'll have a lot more on your plate."

"Woof." I pick up the remote and click *start over* on the newest episode. "Okay, can we just immerse ourselves in the drama of rich people already? I'm definitely not emotionally mature enough for this conversation yet."

"Mature up," Mom says. "The future is coming."

I make an exaggerated barfing noise, and Mom laughs. As I sink into the couch and the show starts up, I try not to imagine Tallulah in my place next year, Mom laughing at her jokes while the two of them watch TV.

I'm *definitely* not emotionally mature enough for that.

Milo's Mullet Fan Club
Today 10:46 PM

ME
B I G NEWS Y'ALL

LUCY
Good news or bad news?

MILO
Is it that your bike got stolen because you didn't lock it up at work?

ME
Oh shit
I didn't think you'd notice that

MILO
I didn't.
You just sold yourself out.

GRAHAM
That's embarrassing

ME
Oh damn
Ok well! Moving on
Idk how to say this so I'm just gonna go for it
My mom and Paul are moving in together

LUCY
😵

GRAHAM
💍?

ME
Not yet
But mom says it's the step before 💍
Or Paul says and mom quotes: "logical next step"
I wanted to tell you all in person but how could I
wait eight hours for morning????

LUCY
How do you feel about it?

MILO
You do seem surprisingly chill . . .

.

ME
Idk. Mom happy = Junie happy??

LUCY
Full debrief tomorrow? West beach at Hyacinth at
10?

Chapter Two

FAIRY 1
It's a wedding! A celebration of love! A joining of
families!

PUCK
(Mischievously.) Lord, what fools these mortals be.
—Act 1, Scene 3, *Midsummer Madness*

In the morning, Milo and Lucy text that they're already at
the beach catching early waves, and it's no shock to anyone
that I'm the last to arrive. West Beach at Hyacinth Road
is the island's dog-friendly beach, and Milo's dog, Cosmo, is
down in the water, bunny-hopping in the tide. Out in the
surf, I spot Milo and Lucy on their bodyboards.

Graham is stretched out on a beach towel, one arm slung
over his eyes, head propped on his sketchbook—Graham's
greatest secret that none of us have ever seen, not even Lucy,
which is a huge deal. We're allowed to see his quick sketches
and art class work and the little napkin drawings he does,
but the sketchbook is off-limits.

He's got a bit of a farmer's tan from his days sporting his
NEIGHBORHOOD HERO T-shirt, but a few hours in the sun
will make him golden brown all over. He's Filipino on his

17

mom's side, but his dad is extra pale—even whiter than I am, and I'm so white I have to apply sunscreen twice an hour in the summer. Graham tans well and tends to burn only across his nose and high on his cheeks, a perfect sun-kissed pink, like he belongs in a VISIT FLORIDA ad.

"Hey," I say, dropping my bag and unfurling my towel beside his. When he doesn't respond, I nudge his bare rib cage with my toe. It seems safe, but his skin is warm, and my cheeks burn twice as hot as I force my gaze to his face. "Are you dead?"

He lifts his elbow to squint up at me and yawns. He sits up, shaking his hair out of his eyes. "Hey." He groans and rubs his hands over his face. One hand is ink-stained as always, and his nails are painted sky blue, the pastel bright like summer.

I try to breathe through the kaleidoscope of butterflies set loose in my belly. The sight of his painted nails always brings on a rush of memories—of kisses and roaming hands and the thrill of sneaking around.

Last summer, when Milo was busy with his now-ex, Marissa, and Lucy with hers, Zephyr, Graham and I were left to our own devices. He didn't have a job then, so he spent a lot of time hanging around Piper and Junie's while I worked, or meeting me after community theater because he was bored. On my days off, we'd spend long hours at the beach, or hiding out in his house or mine, watching TV and sitting in the stream of the air-conditioning.

We were at the beach when the game started. Truth or Dare, though it should have just been called Dare. A dangerous game for two people who treated the entire world like one big dare. There was nothing too far or too high for Graham and me. It was the reason we needed Milo and Lucy there to rein us in and keep us from doing something wildly stupid.

At first, it was small stuff, like letting me bury him in the sand, or drawing a giant dick on my back in sunscreen so I'd have to walk around with it for a few days—all the immature things our friends would never let us get away with. Me: doing a drop-in at the skate park, even though I don't know how to skateboard. Graham: riding my pink, sparkly bike around for a day. Covering myself in temporary tattoos of his choosing. Letting me paint his nails.

The last one stuck. Some tourist girl at P&J's told him it looked hot, and he came over to pick through my collection to test out other colors.

I was vibrating with jealousy by then. After half a summer spending all my time with him, I was starting to see something in Graham I hadn't before. That he was cute, and he made me laugh, and sometimes when he touched me, I'd feel it through my whole body. At night, I would think about how his hands had felt helping me put on all those temporary tattoos, or the way his finger had traced the outline of a dick on my back, and it felt so stupid. Like, that can't be sexy.

And yet.

"This is so dumb," I said as we riffled through my nail polish, pulling out colors he liked—light blue, dark purple, black, orange. "One girl tells you painting your nails is hot, and that's all it takes? You're just painting your nails from now on?"

Graham shrugged, not looking up from the box of nail polish. "Do I need a reason?"

I scoffed. "I guess not. But if all you wanted was some girl to say you look hot, I could've said it."

Graham leaned back, tilting his head at me. "I wouldn't waste a dare on something like that."

"You wouldn't have to dare me."

The words left my mouth before I could stop them—before I could think.

And then it was just me, Graham, and a staring contest. The kind he's so good at—the kind that will make you squirm before you cave and blink.

But this time, Graham looked away first. His gaze dropped to my mouth, and I licked my lips in anticipation.

Graham swallowed, his throat moving with the effort. "Truth or dare?"

He was giving me a choice—an out. Not *truth or dare,* but *no or yes.*

My heart thundered in my chest as I took what I knew would be the most dangerous risk of the summer. "Dare."

Graham lifted his eyes, and the staring contest continued, right up until our mouths met. As soon as I closed my eyes, the tension left his body.

We ended up making out on my floor until my back ached and my lips felt bruised. When Graham pulled away, his mouth was swollen, his hair a mess, and his shirt wrinkled. We didn't talk about it, just went back to picking out nail polish, and then he left. I barely slept that night.

The next morning, I noticed a hickey on my neck, just below my ear. I spent half an hour trying to cover it with makeup but gave up when he texted me, asking me to come over. I thought it was going to be a gentle letdown, and at least the hickey would embarrass him. And I wanted him to feel as embarrassed as I did, because I'd liked it. But clearly the whole thing had freaked him out, and I was about to get the *Hey, we should just forget that happened and stay friends.*

I would agree to forget it if he wanted, but I wasn't happy about it. And I could fake it, but I wouldn't forget, not really. I'd be thinking about it for the rest of the summer, maybe the rest of the year—the rest of my life. That kissing Graham Isham sent tingles throughout my entire body, and I wanted to feel it again, badly.

When I got to his house, his parents were at work. I'd barely toed my shoes off in the entryway before Graham had his arms around me, leaning me into the front door.

"Oh," I squeaked, and Graham froze, his head snapping up. He started to release me. "Sorry, I thought—"

"No, I want to."

His eyes found mine. We were so close, I could smell the spearmint on his breath. "You do?"

I hesitated, embarrassment creeping up. "I mean, if you do . . . ?"

"God, yeah," he said on a breath, and then he kissed me.

"Just—one—thing," I said between kisses, pulling back with a gulp of air.

Graham nodded. "Anything."

I tapped my finger against my neck, and he followed the movement, his eyebrows arching up when he saw the badly concealed hickey.

"Shit." A laugh hissed out of him. "Sorry." He put his hands on my face, brushing his thumbs over my cheeks. "I'll be gentle this time."

My knees turned to water. I wrapped my arms around him, hanging on tight to stay upright.

Later, as I rubbed an ice cube over my mouth to ease the redness before work, Graham and I agreed to keep this between us. I don't remember who suggested it, just how I felt relieved that we were on the same page. I wasn't ready to explain this to Milo or Lucy or, God forbid, my mother. And we had no idea what we were doing, so the last thing we needed was our friends weighing in. They'd either try to hyperanalyze our feelings themselves like a type-A power duo, or worse, try to kill whatever this was before it started. Not that I thought they'd do it on purpose, but I could imagine the panic they'd put Graham and me into by over-thinking every possible terrible outcome.

I told him I knew someone who could give me a good alibi. No one would ever know.

But I made a deal that tied us to a sinking ship, and when it capsized, it took us down with it. In the wake, acting normal around Graham is an exhausting feat.

"You fell asleep?" I ask him now, exhaling a soft laugh. "How long have you even been up?"

His expression pinches in annoyance. "When the baby's awake, we're all awake. All through the night. Every two hours."

It's like setting off a bomb in the center of my warm, fluttery feelings. Guilt ratchets up into my throat and lodges there. My face burns in a way that has nothing to do with complicated feelings or the late morning sun. Now my feelings are decidedly simple: shame and regret.

From the look on Graham's face, he didn't mean to say it, but there's no rewinding.

The way Graham and I avoid talking about his new half brother, Owen, is almost painful. We skirt around the subject like it's poison ivy growing into the road of our conversations. We talk about his father even less. And Rooney . . . it's like she doesn't even exist when Graham and I are together.

As for my feelings, I took care of those months ago. All

that remains are the dregs, like tea leaves stuck in the bottom of a cup.

"But hey, who needs sleep, right?" Graham says, his voice lighter, like we can dispel the awkwardness by sheer force of will. "I got to play *Omen* at three a.m., and they've got all kinds of badass stuff you can only get at that time of night. They call it Dead Hour."

"Of course they do," I reply with a grimace.

Omen: Darkest Night III, a horror role-playing video game, is Graham's latest obsession. I don't pretend to know anything about the games he's into, but this one features demons and ghouls and necromancers, which is a word I never thought I'd use. It's basically a nightmare in RPG form.

He shakes his head at me. "You just don't understand the magic of *ODN*."

"A real tragedy," I deadpan, grabbing my sunscreen from my bag. I start spraying it on, and Graham splutters, waving his hands around his face.

"Hey, what the hell! You don't spray that stuff *into* the wind!"

"My bad," I say as I finish up and toss the bottle onto my blanket.

Graham shoots me a glare before flopping back onto his towel, head thudding dully against his sketchbook. I strip down to my swimsuit and start toward the water, adjusting my hat over the mass of frizz that is my hair. As I put distance between us, what's left of the awkwardness between Graham and me stretches, then pops like a bubble. When I get back, we'll both pretend nothing was said and happily move on with our lives.

Even though I'm upwind, Cosmo must smell me. His head whips around, tail wagging. He's knee-height and stocky, with ears that point up when he's excited, and has mostly white fur with big brown spots. He bounds up the sand and crashes into my legs, sending me sprawling, licking my face with such vigor that he knocks my hat off.

When he finally runs off, I lie there and catch my breath, eyes squeezed closed against the burning sun as I reach around for my hat. I can't find it, but it doesn't matter, because a shadow falls over me, dripping water. I squint one eye open.

"Have we figured out yet why my dog loves you more than me?" Milo asks, reaching down to help me up.

"Because I'm pretty."

He makes an insulted sound. "I'm pretty."

He's more boyishly cute than pretty—floppy dark hair, deeply tanned skin, and lots of freckles. His face is the only soft thing about him, though; the rest of him is six-two basketball player who is very serious about his conditioning. From the neck down, he's all hard planes and lean, roped muscle.

"I'm prettier," I say.

"And you've been sneaking him food off your plate for the last three years," he says, dusting off my hat and plopping it on my head.

I plaster on an innocent smile. I thought I'd been sneaky, but as usual, Milo's got my number.

Behind him, Lucy glides in on her bodyboard and drags it out of the surf. She flashes me a smile, pink braces glinting in the sun. Her rope braids are piled atop her head in a massive bun, and sea water shimmers on her dark skin.

"Morning, Junie," she says as she nears us. "Nice of you to be late, since we're all here because of you."

"Yeah, that was my bad. I snoozed my alarm one too many times." Six too many times, really. But they don't need to know that.

24

Lucy snorts, heading up the sand toward Graham. "I think I speak for everyone when I say you seem surprisingly chipper after this news about your mom," she says as we follow her.

"I mean, it'll suck sharing a room with Tallulah, but it's only a year."

"Sharing?" says Graham. "I didn't know there were houses on the South Shore that only came with two bedrooms."

"Well, yeah, *their* house has four bedrooms, but . . ."

All at once, it clicks. The way my friends are looking at me, and how nervous Mom was to tell me. Not because she knows Tallulah and I aren't friendly, and not because she's worried about us sharing a bedroom.

But because Paul and Tallulah aren't moving to the North Shore. Of course not.

"Oh my God," I say, my whole body going slack with shock.

"Ah," Milo says, eyeing me with worry. "She just got it."

My gaze snaps to him. "You all . . . figured that out?"

"It was my first thought," Milo says, the only one brave enough to admit it aloud. But the look Graham and Lucy exchange tells me they thought the same thing.

There's a long stretch of silence as I process what they're saying. Then Lucy says, "Junie? Are you okay?"

"I just—I think I need to talk to my mom?" My throat is tight with tears. "Yeah, I need to talk to my mom." I grab my flip-flops and run toward the street.

"JN!" Milo shouts after me. "Wait a sec!"

As soon as I'm clear of the sand, I slip on my flip-flops. They slap against the pavement as I sprint toward P&J's, breathless from the combination of physical exertion and nerves. My hat flies off, and I have to double back to grab it, clutching it in my sweaty hand as I run.

This can't be happening.

It shouldn't be a big deal, moving. The North and South Shores of White Coral Key are only a few minutes' drive away from each other, bisected by a central area we call No Man's Land, where we do things like grocery shop and go to school. But even though we're all one island, our two shores are worlds apart—the South Shore our tightly buttoned, wealthy lady, and the North Shore our quirky, vintage freak.

Mom and I are North Shore people, always have been, from the day we arrived—Mom heavily pregnant with me, and me, so excited to get here, I put her into labor three weeks early. My early arrival is the reason a tourist in town for a car show found her half sitting on a juniper bush at the edge of our former mayor Dot Slip's yard and already in labor, and how I was almost born in the back of his antique Nash Rambler on the way to the hospital. Now, Mom and I attend the car show every year in honor of my birthday.

I was supposed to be named Isla, but Mom had to tell the story to so many people—the nurses, her doctor, Dot, Hal, the Barajas sisters—she had the words stuck in her head. Juniper bush, antique Nash Rambler. *Juniper Nash.* It's one of the North Shore's favorite stories—the new girl and her baby. It made us staples in town, like the people who'd welcomed us to White Coral—Hal, who approached Mom when she first got off the bus that very hot summer, and Dot, who let Mom move into her guesthouse, and Maria Oliver, the Barajas sister who gave Mom her first job at Ollie's, which would eventually become Piper and Junie's. Our entire life together has been defined by this place.

"Mom!" I yell as I burst into the kitchen at P&J's. "Mom!"

"Juniper Nash Abreheart!" Mom cries when she sees me standing there in nothing but my swimsuit and flip-flops. I'm so sweaty, my thighs are chafing. "What in the—what in the world! Get—go! No open-toed shoes in this kitchen; you know better, and where the hell are your clothes? Out, out!"

She hustles me right back out the way I came.

"Mom, listen." I grab her arm as the door swings shut behind us. "Are we— Did I—"

Her expression flicks from annoyed to concerned. "What's the matter? Are you okay? Here, sit." She plunks me down in the metal folding chair where Isaac vapes during his breaks and crouches in front of me. "Breathe, Juju. Breathe. Tell me what happened."

I gulp down air and ask, "Are we moving in with Paul and Tallulah?"

Her brows lower in confusion. "Well, yes. That's what we talked about last night."

"But *we*," I say, smacking my hand against my chest. "Are *we* the ones moving?"

"Ah." Her expression softens with understanding. "I see. Yes, we'll be the ones moving."

"But that's not fair!" My voice cracks, and my throat aches. "Why should we have to be the ones who move?"

She gets this loose smile on her face, the one she always uses when she's nervous or at a loss for words.

"It's your dream house," I remind her. "I thought we'd live here forever. Piper and Junie's is here. My friends are here. *Milo* is here."

Since I was five years old, I've never been farther from Milo than the width of the canal that runs between our houses.

And before that, we were in daycare together almost every day. Our moms have been trading babysitting favors, extra groceries, books, and gossip for as long as I can remember, even before we were just a shout across the canal. When Milo's parents found out their behind-neighbors were moving, they told Mom before the house went on the market—that's how we ended up living in our house at all.

Milo is tied to every piece and part of me. It's not even that I don't want to be separated from him, it's that I don't know *how* to be separated from him. I thought the first time I'd have to would be college. Now it's come knocking early, and I want to dead-bolt every door and hide with my hands over my ears.

Mom smooths her hand over my hair. "I know, Juju. I know. But dreams change. Now my dream is for all of us to live together, no matter what the house is like. I know this is a big deal for you—I get it. I should have been clearer last night." She sighs, leaning forward to rest her forehead against mine briefly. "Listen, it's only four miles away. You can bike that in twenty minutes. You'll make it up here in no time."

It's not about how long it'll take. It's that the North Shore is our home, and I don't know how to explain that it feels like a part of me. We aren't South Shore people, with their nice cars and too-large houses and fancy jobs across the bay. We don't belong there.

But I can't find the right words, which is why, as I start to lose the battle with my tears, I simply say, "People are gonna call us snobs."

Mom lets out a surprised laugh and pulls back. "What the hell are you talking about?"

I shoot her a reproachful look. "That's what they say! The

South Shore is for snobs, and Paul isn't doing us any favors by being a doctor."

Mom chuckles. "Oh, the drama."

"That's not funny," I say, wounded.

Mom sighs, shaking her head with a small smile. "I know you're upset. If our house was a little bigger, maybe—"

"Tallulah can sleep on my trundle. It's only a year."

Mom puts her hands on my cheeks. "I'm sorry. It sucks, I know. But I'm really excited to move in with Paul. Can you do it? For me?"

I swallow thickly.

She brushes her fingers under my eyes. "Juju?"

I sigh, shrugging. "I mean, I guess."

"You guess?"

I nod.

Mom takes a deep breath and straightens. "I'll have to take what I can get." She glances toward the door. "I need to get back inside. Are you gonna be okay? You can come in and go straight into my office if you want to hang out while you calm down."

I wave her off. "I'm okay. I left my friends at the beach." Mom seems reluctant to leave me, but I give her what I hope is a reassuring smile. "I'm good, Mom."

"We'll talk later," she says. "We can start thinking about how we'll decorate your new room! You'll like that."

She looks so hopeful, I don't have the heart to crush her, so I smile wider and nod. "Yeah, I was thinking we could wallpaper it in *Thunder from Down Under* posters."

She barks out a laugh. "You are deranged, child of mine."

The back door swings shut behind her, and I sag in the folding chair. My hands are shaking.

"Quite a performance."

I close my eyes. I should have known.

When I turn, I wonder how I even missed her in the first place. She's hiding out between the storage shed and the back of the kitchen, in the tiny slip of space where we keep broken furniture and old decorations we need to get rid of.

She's got a cigarette between her fingers, and she takes a long drag. It's a stark contrast to the NO PLANET B hat she wears over her pastel hair.

Paul pretends he doesn't know Tallulah smokes, but there's no way he misses the way she reeks. I try not to judge—she's been through hell since her mom died. But it's not the nineties anymore; we all know smoking kills. She started up even with all those anti-tobacco advertisements shoved in her face.

One night, when the four of us were watching TV together, I paused under the guise of grabbing a snack while on a particularly gruesome commercial showing the accelerated aging effects of smoking tobacco, hoping Tallulah's vanity would get the best of her. If anything, that just made it worse. I caught her smoking in the shadows outside only an hour later, and I swear she was smiling.

I glare at her. "Thanks, but I'm not interested in performance reviews. I do it for my love of the craft."

"I'm sure you do." She takes another drag and steps out into the light. "But you know us South Shore snobs. We can't keep an opinion to ourselves."

My eye twitches.

"I'm not exactly thrilled about this either, you know," she says. "Working together was bad enough."

I agree, but her honesty chafes. "What did I ever do to you?"

30

"Oh, come on, Juniper Nash. You and I both know I'm not the snob between the two of us." She crouches to put out her cigarette on the concrete and tosses the butt into the dumpster.

Then she disappears back into the kitchen, leaving me stunned and angry in the parking lot. I'm peeling myself from the metal chair when my friends round the corner of the building, and the quiet tears from my conversation with Mom come rushing back tenfold.

I'm sobbing by the time they reach me, and Milo gets to me first, dropping his bodyboard at my feet so he can wrap me up in a hug.

"Oh no, it's a Juniper Nash Cry Fest," he says gently. This joke started long ago, back in elementary school when I was known as Crybaby Junie, a nickname that stung even in its unoriginality. Milo's solution was to cheer me up whenever I looked like I was about to cry, with a joke about how the Juniper Nash Cry Fest was coming to town, and he hoped they'd have frozen lemonades or a carousel or something else very typically carnival. I thought he'd drop it once the nickname died, but he's been making the same joke since we were eight, and of course Lucy and Graham have caught on by now.

"I hope they've got a Ferris wheel," Lucy says, wrapping her arms around us. She smells like coconut and tangerines and sea water. They're both sun-warmed, closing me in on both sides. Cosmo nudges between us, his fur soft against my knees.

"Stop trying to cheer me up. I'm just a big dumb idiot, and you were right." I blubber on Milo's shoulder, wetting his T-shirt even further with my tears and—let's be real—snot. "We're moving to the South Shore. I'm so stupid."

"No, you're not," Lucy says. "You're not stupid, Junie. Not at all."

I sniffle, pulling back, and catch Graham's eye. He lingers behind Milo, my beach bag slung over one shoulder and our towels under his arm, his skateboard clutched in his hand. As soon as we lock eyes, his gaze flicks away, and he moves to set my things on the chair.

Graham and I haven't hugged in nearly a year. I shouldn't be surprised that he won't hug me now, no matter how much it stings.

"Oh, and then!" I flip back around to look at Milo and Lucy, trying not to think about the awkwardness between Graham and me. "Tallulah Breeman called me a snob. Me, of all people, a snob!"

Milo rubs my back. "That wasn't very nice of her."

"Right?" I lean down to scratch Cosmo behind the ears. "I'm no snob, right, Cosmo?"

Cosmo takes this opportunity to lick my face.

"She just doesn't know you well enough yet," Lucy says, ever the optimist. "But now you'll be spending more time together, and she'll get to know all your best qualities."

"Like what?" I ask, because it wouldn't hurt to hear something nice about myself right now. But my heart gives an anxious little jump when Graham moves closer, his arm nearly brushing mine, and I momentarily forget I'm waiting for a compliment.

Then a pickup truck rolls by on the street and honks. "Nice rack!" the driver shouts out the window. The passenger cheers.

"Oh geez, that's great," I say, reality crashing in at hyperspeed. Milo makes a shocked noise from the back of his throat and moves to block me from their view. *"There's* something to like about me."

Without hesitating, Graham lifts his arm and flips them off.

I laugh, grabbing his wrist and pulling his hand down. "Stop. What are you gonna do if they come back and try to start something?"

Graham shrugs. "Let the big, beefy boy handle it." He reaches over and smacks Milo on the shoulder.

"Nice," Milo says. "That sounds about right—the two of you dragging me into trouble."

I let out an affronted noise. "Excuse me! I didn't do anything except have a nice rack."

When Graham's gaze slides pointedly away, I feel a small rush of embarrassment.

I don't know why I said it. Maybe because Graham and I have always treated our friendship like a game of chicken, leaving Milo and Lucy to rein us in. This is how things used to be, before—well, I guess before he became intimately acquainted with my nice rack.

In hindsight, I should probably try thinking before I speak.

Milo's cheeks burn bright red as he says, "Jesus, JN, come on."

Lucy laughs. "Here, you want this?" She digs into my bag and holds out my shirt.

I thank her and pull my clothes back on. They stick to my sweaty skin.

Milo slaps my hat onto my head. "Keep that face out of the sun. We don't need you getting burnt the first weekend of summer."

I throw my head back in dismay and nearly lose my hat

again, catching it with one hand clamped against it. "See? What am I gonna do next summer when you're not here to remind me to wear sunscreen and put on a hat and use my bike lock?"

"I'll still be here to remind you of all that, JN." He chuckles and puts his arm around my shoulders, pulling me in.

"Yeah, but four miles." I groan and lean my head on his shoulder. "A nightmare. We don't even have cars."

"I don't even have a license," Lucy says brightly, like it's some kind of achievement.

"I thought you were turning over a new leaf," Graham says to me. "A real hardworking one. The kind where you sweat when you ride your bike."

I point at him. "Is this bullying? This feels like bullying."

He laughs, his dark eyes brightening. "That's what you said yesterday! A real hardworking leaf."

I shake my head in faux disgust. "I can't believe you're using our limited time left together to make fun of me."

Graham hangs his head with a groan, and I feel a rush of satisfaction. Clearly the boob joke was too soon, but that doesn't mean normalcy is off the table. We can do this—the surface stuff, the funny stuff. Maybe if we keep doing it, the rest will come back, too.

"Can we get ice cream?" Lucy asks, looking at Milo.

Milo glances around. "Am I the dad here or something? Do I have to give permission?"

I shake my head at him. "If this is just a ploy to get us to call you *daddy,* it's not gonna work."

His face turns so red, I'm afraid his head might shoot off into space.

Lucy screeches as she grabs my arm, her smile wide and bright. As she pulls me toward the General Store, our laughter echoing down the street, I'm hit with a thought that sends a shot of anxiety through me.

I will miss this.

From: Katherine Liu
To: All
Subject: Special Election and Community Theater
Mailing List: <wckhs.all.dramaclub>

Hello All,

I hope you're enjoying your summer so far. While I hate to interrupt your fun-having with anything other than community theater, I have a necessary announcement.

As you all know, we had our election for next year's officers during the last week of school. The results were as follows:

President: Jessica Kotke

VP: Sophie Keller

Treasurer: Tyler Broginski

Secretary: Thomas Piat

As of today, Jessica has withdrawn from White Coral Key High School and thus, resigned as president.

We will hold a special election when the new school year begins. Those already holding office are not eligible to run.

For the rest of you, your participation in community theater bears *no* weight on your eligibility, but I always encourage you to volunteer. We're putting on *Midsummer Madness* and our first meeting is tomorrow night at 7 p.m. at the Schooner Park Amphitheater. Auditions this weekend. Bring your singing voices.

> Sincerely,
> Katie Liu
> Drama Department
> White Coral Key High School

From: Sophie Keller
To: Junie Abreheart
Subject: Funeral planning

OUTDOOR community theater? In FLORIDA? When we have a perfectly good EMPTY theater???? Will we die this summer or nay?

From: Junie Abreheart
To: Sophie Keller
Subject: RE: Funeral planning

She died the way she lived: sweating her ass off for her love of the craft. I hope you all remember me fondly.

From: Sophie Keller
To: Junie Abreheart
Subject: RE: Funeral planning

As if we could remember you any other way!! Sooooo you running for prez?

From: Junie Abreheart
To: Sophie Keller
Subject: RE: Funeral planning

You have to ask?

Chapter Three

OLIVIA
We need these flowers fixed *now,* fairy! I am meant to
be wed in mere days!

PUCK
A cake, now flowers. I think this wedding has
more holes than you can fill. Your ship is sinking,
bride-to-be.

OLIVIA
It's these guests of mine! They wreak havoc. Please,
fairy—

PUCK
(Feigning reluctance.) Fine, fine. We'll fix your flowers.
Let us come to your party, and I'll put a girdle round
about the earth in forty minutes if I must.
                              —Act 1, Scene 5, *Midsummer Madness*

When we take our seats in the Schooner Park Amphitheater,
the plastic burns the back of my thighs, and sweat immediately begins to pool in every crease, crevice, and roll on my
body. The sun is just high enough in the sky that it's still an
open-flame kind of hot, rather than the nighttime's stifling-
sauna kind.

Miss Liu, our drama club advisor and community theater

director, stands perfectly still onstage while she waits for everyone to settle. *Everyone* might be too generous. The group is small, and the word *ragtag* comes to mind when I glance over the volunteers gathered.

After Miss Liu mentioned *Midsummer Madness* in her email, I'm not feeling super confident. *Midsummer Madness* is a pretty big ask of any community theater, but especially with our current turnout. It's a twenties-era Shakespearean musical in which different characters from Shakespeare's plays attend a wedding. Montagues and Capulets are rival bootleggers double-booked for the wedding and get into a violent fight during the rehearsal dinner, the groom's sister has to pose as him during the ceremony after he goes missing, and fairies drug the guests during the reception, resulting in a kind of acid-trip dream number before Titania, the fairy queen, comes to set everything right, happy ending tied in a neat bow.

"I am aware," Miss Liu says from the stage, with the flourish of someone who desperately misses the spotlight, "that outdoor theater in Florida may seem cruel and unusual, but outdoor theater is where drama began. This summer, we get back to our roots."

Beside me, Sophie Keller has a tiny fan plugged into her phone, and she alternates pointing it at herself and at Peter Choi, who sits on her other side. Her free hand is entwined with his, and I imagine it's a nightmare of palm sweat.

Sophie is the only daughter of Reba Keller, of the law firm Keller & Barnett. "We'll get you off!" is their famous motto. It's one of the most-played commercials in our area, so everyone who owns a TV knows it. Calls of "Hey, Sophie, are you as good as your mom at getting me off?" followed her through middle school, right up until the end of eighth grade, when she started dating Peter, who is Mayor Choi's son. Peter isn't what I'd call a great enforcer, but he has a lot of social sway. He's one of those nerdy top dogs, even though he's only on student council and looks like he'd wear a suit to school. (He mostly wears khakis and polo shirts, which isn't much better.)

Sophie and Peter are what you'd call a power couple. If their power is never being apart. Like now—Peter isn't in Drama Club, but he'll participate in community theater for Sophie's sake. It's definitely not for his love of the craft.

Meanwhile, I couldn't have dragged my friends here if I had them on leashes. Other than the six drama club members who have shown up and Peter, we've only managed to pull in the same five locals who always turn up for community theater.

Annie Engel, who is long retired, sits near the front, dabbing her forehead with a handkerchief embroidered with her initials. Lou Strey, who works at the North Shore's only auto shop, lounges a few rows behind me, beside Hourig Papazian. She works in the school office, and I've had to get more than one late pass from her. She's friendly enough for someone who has borne witness to my chronic tardiness.

The last members of our sad-looking team are Carl, a bartender from Driftwood—one of the nicer restaurants on the island—and his boyfriend, Jed Loveland, who owns Jed's Gym. Carl is on the shorter side and whip-thin, always with his longboard under his arm. Tonight, it's propped against the theater seat in front of him. Jed looks like he just fell off the cover of one of those bodice-ripper novels—shirt with one too many buttons undone, lazy smile, jaw cut by the hand of God.

"Now, I hate to be the bearer of bad news," Miss Liu says, even though I've seen her pass out detention slips at school with a look of glee, "but our turnout tonight doesn't look good. I'd been hoping to put on *Midsummer Madness* this year, but if we don't end up with more volunteers, we won't have enough people to fill the principal roles, let alone the ensemble. That may mean we need to pick a smaller musical."

Sophie groans. "Not *Little Shop of Horrors* again."

"I trust our Drama Club members present will be looking for additional volunteers before auditions this weekend," says Miss Liu. "Bring your friends, your family; grab any tourists who are here for the summer. Community theater is open to anyone, and don't forget about backstage crew. We have plenty of space to fill."

She spends the next twenty minutes going over logistics, auditions, and the practice schedule. Then she tucks her clipboard under her arm, claps her hands once, and says, "Dismissed. I'll see you all back here at the same time Saturday for auditions."

"My ass is sweating," Sophie complains as we head for the parking lot. She turns her butt toward me. "Are my shorts wet?"

"I could have checked," Peter says, tugging on her hand.

She shoves him. "I don't want you to see my butt sweat!"

"You're good," I say after a cursory glance at her shorts.

Sophie tucks herself under Peter's arm, even though it's hotter than the surface of the sun out here. I swear, the soles of my flip-flops sizzle on the blacktop of the parking lot.

"Hey, Junie, you should get Milo to help out. Maybe he could get some guys from the basketball team to join," Sophie says as we climb into Peter's car. I wince as the leather seats burn the backs of my legs. It's so hot in the car, I get goose bumps.

Peter blasts the air, which comes out blazing hot but quickly cools thanks to Peter's car being both expensive and brand-new. "I doubt they've filled all their community service hours," he says. "This counts for a lot."

Sophie twists around in her seat. "I know community theater doesn't affect your eligibility in the special election, but it'd carry a lot of weight with the rest of the Drama Club. You'd be saving us all from another rousing rendition of *Little Shop of Horrors.*"

I frown. "There're only six members participating, including me and you. Will that even matter in the long run?"

"Yeah, because there are only twelve people in Drama Club with the graduating seniors out," Sophie says. "You've got two secured votes, obviously. Me and you. But you get the other four? That's half the club tied down. There's no way someone else could secure the entire other half. Plus, you pull in enough volunteers, you get in good with Miss Liu, and she's got sway."

I hesitate, thinking of how much groveling I'll have to do to get Milo to agree.

She leans between the seats, her green eyes bright. *"Imagine"*—she throws her hands up, like she's showing a marquee—"your college apps, with Drama Club president at the top of your extracurriculars." She takes an exaggerated whiff of air. "It smells like the difference between acceptance and rejection to me. How about you?"

"She makes a good point," says Peter. "Officer positions look nice on your college apps. They show you've got drive, leadership skills—"

"A personality," Sophie cuts in. She turns back around in her seat and reaches for Peter's hand. I'd feel a lot safer if he'd drive with both hands on the wheel, but since I'd be on my bike if not for the two of them, it feels weird to ask. "That you're someone people actually like."

"Getting volunteers shouldn't be hard once they realize this maxes out their community service hours," Peter says. "Miss Liu should be advertising that on the flyers, but she'd rather get people for their *devotion to the theater.*" He pulls a face that I catch in the rearview mirror. Clearly the idea disgusts him.

"I guess it can't hurt to try," I say with some reluctance. I don't have the heart to tell them it's not my extracurriculars that'll be making or breaking my college apps; no one will care if I have a personality or not when I can't pull an A in any subject but drama.

The truth is, drama is the only thing I've ever been good at. Not passably good like I am at school, or decently good like I am in my job at Piper and Junie's, but actually, seriously good.

It started with those little-kid plays in elementary school, where everyone gets a part, and all roles are equally important. It's where I learned that my ability to cry on command, affinity for voice imitation, and comedic timing were valuable talents. After watching my friends play sports and make it onto honor roll and draw perfect replicas of cartoons we watched on TV, I'd worried there wasn't anything out there for me. But then I got the role of Dorothy in our third grade mini-production of *The Wizard of Oz,* and at our first rehearsal, when I squeezed my arms around Graham in his dog costume and ad-libbed the line "Wow, Toto, you're bigger than I remember," everyone laughed, and I knew I'd found it. My thing.

After that, I took my role onstage very seriously. Mom

even has a video of me throwing my arms up and rolling my eyes on performance night when the boy playing the Scarecrow forgot his line for the second time.

Of course, that boy was Milo. We're reminded every time we enter Graham's house, where his parents have a shot from the video framed in their entryway—Graham gazing wide-eyed at me, Milo, red-faced, looking offstage for help, and me in my blue-checked Dorothy dress, staring straight into the camera with a look like, *Can you believe this guy?*

I'm sure that'll be his first argument when I try to convince him to do community theater. He'll lord it over me the way he does everything, because Milo has never once in our entire lives given me a break.

And even though Drama Club president might be what makes or breaks my acceptance to Florida State, my gut says winning the special election isn't worth giving Milo something to hold over my head.

I'm halfway up the front walk after Sophie and Peter drop me off when my phone buzzes in my pocket.

DAD

A rush of excitement tears through me, and I sit on the front steps as I answer.

"Hi, Dad!"

"Hi, baby," he says. "How's it going?"

His voice is deep and round, like he's always on the verge of laughter, and he has a Southern drawl earned growing up in the Florida Panhandle. He and Mom were high school sweethearts, which is about the extent of my knowledge of my parents' lives before White Coral Key. I've never been to their hometown, and the only ties I have there now are my mom's parents. They've been estranged since Mom left for White Coral, nineteen years old and seven months pregnant. I've tried asking my parents about it, but I get the feeling the one thing they agree on is shielding me from that part of their lives.

"I just got home." I stretch my legs out and lean back on the step above me. "What are you doing?"

"Not much. Where were you? Out with those hooligan friends of yours?"

I grin. "No, I was at community theater. My *hooligan friends* wouldn't come near the amphitheater if their lives depended on it."

"Pretty sure your hooligan friends could use some structure to their summer."

"Yeah, you try telling them that."

He snorts.

"No, really, I need more volunteers," I say with a laugh. "Think you could convince them?"

He groans like he's stretching. "Sure, I can use my intimidation tactics."

I consider my dad, who looks like an extra from a biker gang TV show with his tattoos and sun-weathered skin from working all his odd construction jobs. With a name like Damon Slade, he even sounds the part. But the truth about my dad is that he spends his free time watching alien conspiracy videos and sci-fi shows, listens to old-school blues music, and drives a beat-up truck that's as old as I am.

"Perfect," I say. "But you'd have to actually *be here* to do that."

It's a tired conversation, not even worth calling it an argument. Dad doesn't come around very often. He moves a lot, following jobs, and he rarely has time to visit. The last time I saw him in person was more than a year ago.

Which is why I'm surprised when he says, "Well, it won't be in time to save your play."

"What do you mean?"

"My job's finishing up," he says. "They offered to keep me on for the next one, but my boss is a real dick."

This is old hat for Dad—all his bosses are dicks.

"So I thought I could come see you in a couple months. Stay a week. I'm moving out that way for the next one—they're putting up a resort in Emerson."

"Wait, what?" My heartbeat kicks into double time. "You're gonna be working in Emerson?"

Emerson is a rich beach town on the other side of the bay. I heard about the resort from Dot, who says it'll be a massive eyesore on the other side of the water. White Coral has Dot to thank for our no-resort mandates. We have a lot of rentals, but razing houses to put up a huge condo building or hotel is strictly forbidden on the island. It keeps us quaint, which is how we like it here.

I can hear the smile in Dad's voice as he says, "Yeah, I'll be out there for about a year on that one."

A year of Dad. It's a bright spot in what I've begun to think of as my dark senior year. I'll be living on the South Shore and sharing a bathroom with Tallulah, but *my dad will be here.*

"*Dad,* that's awesome! I'm so excited, oh my God!" I let out a hysterical little laugh.

"I'll come around in August as soon as this job's over," Dad says. "Be there for your birthday. How's that sound?"

"You could come the week before! The musical's right before my birthday—you could be here for both!"

Dad chuckles. "Alright, I like that. I'd love to see you onstage."

He's never seen me perform live. I've sent him videos of

my school plays but having him there in the crowd would be so much bigger. More special. The thought sends a rush of exhilaration through me.

"It'll be so good! I promise, you'll love it! It's called *Midsummer Madness*—it's really funny."

"Okay, text me the date, and I'll put it on my calendar."

When we hang up, I throw my hands up and squeal in delight.

The front door swings open behind me.

"What the hell are you doing?" Mom asks with a laugh, leaning against the doorjamb.

I scramble to my feet. "Dad's coming!"

Her smile freezes on her face. "What? Now?"

"No, in August! For the musical!" I rush past her into the house, practically skipping. "He's gonna stay for my birthday!"

Mom turns, shutting the door behind her. "And where's he staying?" she asks, her voice gentle enough that it gives me pause.

I twist around, leaning against the back of the couch. "With us. Where else?"

Mom stares at me. "Juju, we'll be in the middle of moving. The whole place will be packed up. I'm selling off a bunch of furniture. Where will he sleep?"

"He can have my bed. I'll sleep with you."

She looks unconvinced.

"Mom, come on, it's *Dad*."

Mom tries to smile, but it looks more like a grimace. "It's so typical of him to assume he can drop in on us without even talking to me."

I can't keep the wounded look off my face. "You don't want him to come?"

Mom's expression falls. "Of course I want him to come. I'd love for him to be here for your play, and for your birthday."

I widen my eyes hopefully. "So . . . ?"

Mom rubs a hand down her face, weary but clearly caving. "So . . . I guess I'll sleep with you for the week, bed hog."

I toss her an affronted look. "I am not a bed hog!"

"You are too!" She heads back to where she was sitting on the couch. "In fact, you better bring your own blanket, because I'm not sharing."

"Mom! This is how you treat your only child?"

"Yes," she says, and laughs at my insulted expression. She clicks the TV back on, and *Proper Southern Ladies* begins to play.

"You're watching without me!" I shriek, throwing myself onto the chaise.

Mom chuckles. "You're not the only one who can cheat in this house, Juniper Nash."

I settle in. "They keep flashing back to Blake and Maybelle's vow renewal every time they fight."

"The producers love the drama," Mom says. "But we all knew that vow renewal was the kiss of death for them. Maybelle deserves better."

Maybelle is having dinner with her family, and her husband, Blake, is annoyed about some party she wants him to go to. Their daughters, who are both in middle school, look miserable.

"I think he's still cheating," I say. "I bet they announce their divorce by the end of the season. I wonder if McKenna and Kayleigh will miss family dinners, or if they'll be relieved."

Mom is silent for so long, I look over to make sure she's still awake. But as soon as I see her calculating face, dread pools in my stomach.

"No," I say. "Whatever you're thinking, please, no."

Mom smiles, pausing the show as she turns to face me. "Family dinners sound nice, don't they?"

I know immediately what she means. Paul, Tallulah, Mom, and me all gathered around the table sharing stories about our days.

"Not really," I say.

"I have a great idea for how you can repay me for letting your dad stay here."

I gape at her. "This feels like one of those traumatic child-of-divorce things."

"Your dad and I were never married."

"It's the symbolic divorce."

Mom nods thoughtfully. "Hmm. Then I guess this could be one of those traumatic child-of-divorce things, yes."

"Mom!"

She laughs. "I'm kidding, Juju! You won't be traumatized. I'm just thinking we should have dinner with Paul and Tallulah twice a week until we move."

"I'm thinking the opposite. Let's enjoy our time alone together until we're all forced to share a dinner table."

She shoots me a disapproving look. "That's not very nice."

"But Mom, I'm already so busy this summer. I have work and community theater—"

"I'm sure there are two nights a week you can spare." She claps her hands. "This is a great idea. I'm texting Paul."

"Tallulah's gonna hate it."

"You don't know everything about Tallulah. And this will be a great opportunity for you to get to know each other better."

Somehow I know Tallulah will hate that part most of all.

Chapter Four

VIOLA
I have a grand idea—simply grand! I will walk down the aisle in my brother's place.

OLIVIA
And you and I will marry?

VIOLA
No one will know the difference.

OLIVIA
God will know the difference!

VIOLA
Unless He's planning to get your unruly guests out of here, you'd better trust in me before God.

(OLIVIA *pauses to think.*)

OLIVIA
Though this be madness, there is method in it.
—Act 2, Scene 13, *Midsummer Madness*

My jewelry box is filled with more coins than accessories, but they're mostly only good for small wishes—a few euro coins, state quarters, and Canadian nickels. Pretty much anything

samantha markum

that's ended up in the register at Piper and Junie's by accident.

The Wishing Fountain doesn't demand coins based on value but on how likely you are to see one in the wild in White Coral Key. Foreign currency can fetch a substantial wish. The ten yen coin I fish out of my collection isn't worth much monetarily, but it should grant me the favor I'm about to ask. At least I hope so, because I already used my rarest coin to pass my physics final last month. I got an A, and I didn't get an A on a single physics assignment all year; so goes the power of the Wishing Fountain. The ten yen is all I've got left, unless I want to buy something from Mrs. Bloom's rare coin jar at the General Store. But I don't have the kind of scratch for that, and I can't let Milo see me making a wish. He'd refuse to help me simply to be difficult.

I just have to get past Milo's stubbornness. Then it's *Midsummer Madness,* Drama Club president, one last great summer spent with my friends before I'm shipped off to the South Shore, and, most importantly, my dad in the crowd, watching me perform live for the first time.

We're in the special part of the afternoon when the sky turns dark gray, and we can bet on rain for at least a few minutes. The Florida Summer Special. I pedal my bike toward Bayfront Park, the long slip of grass in front of the beach on the eastern side of the island. People do a lot of fishing on the pier there, and the playground is always crawling with grubby-handed kids and their exhausted babysitters.

The plaque in front of the Wishing Fountain gives no instructions or history, but a warning: BAD LUCK FOLLOWS THOSE WHO STEAL FROM THE WISHING FOUNTAIN.

I've heard tourists laugh about it, but every local knows someone who stole from the Wishing Fountain and got their due. Some of the dumber kids from school will dare each other. A couple of years ago, a kid in the grade above me stole a bunch of coins out of it, and two weeks later, his parents shipped him off to military school with no explanation. Last summer, I heard about a tourist who stole a coin, got in her rental car, and immediately backed into a lamppost. My mom even told me a story about a guy who used to work in the kitchen at Ollie's—before it was Piper and Junie's—who stole out of the fountain and lost his sense of smell immediately after. He only got it back when he returned the coins he'd taken and added a few extras.

The Wishing Fountain giveth, the Wishing Fountain taketh away.

I find the tossing spot—a bronze square on the pavement with a shooting star embossed on it—and toss the ten yen.

Please, please, Wishing Fountain, let Milo agree to help me with community theater.

Thunder rumbles overhead, and the wind whips my hair across my face. I glance around quickly, looking for dropped coins, and give a little jig when I notice a penny glinting on the concrete. I study it closely to make sure it's common— I'd hate to waste a rare penny on a regular wish—then toss it in.

And please make sure it doesn't rain today.

I hop on my bike and cruise into town, grinning as the wind settles and the sun peeks through the clouds. I take the side entrance into the General Store, where Mrs. Bloom, the owner, sells drinks and baked goods from the counter. The store is stocked with overpriced toiletries, sunscreen, and snacks, mostly for tourists. The store and ice-cream shop are connected by a wide doorway covered with a beaded curtain that *shick*s pleasantly as people come and go.

At the counter, I order a sweet tea from Mrs. Bloom. Her sweet tea has magic powers—it can put anyone in a good mood. And I'm hoping if Milo is already in a good mood, this will put him in an even better one. It certainly can't hurt.

"This is suspicious," Milo says as I push aside the beaded curtain and step into the ice-cream shop. It's empty, the front door swinging shut with a merry jingle as a family of tourists heads out.

I gasp in offense. "I'm just bringing some sweet tea to my absolute best friend in the entire world."

"No, thanks. I don't like drinks with strings attached."

"What makes you think there are strings? This is stringless!" I dance the cup across the ice-cream case and put on my best Pinocchio voice. *"I'm a real boy!"*

Milo stares at me.

I shake the cup at him. "See? No strings. No obligations, no favors. Just a good old-fashioned—"

"Bribe," says Milo.

My laugh comes out too high and shaky. "What could I possibly be bribing you for?"

"Oh, I don't know. You had community theater last night, so I'm assuming I'm about to hear your bid for me to save you from *Little Shop of Horrors* again."

I stare at him. "Who called you?"

Milo smirks.

Lucy. I should never have asked her first, but I was keyed up after talking to my dad, and I wanted to give her time to work her magic on Graham. Even though the four of us are a group and rarely separate, we've always been a set of pairs— Lucy and Graham, Milo and me. Lucy is a year younger than us, but her dad and Graham's work together at the biggest accounting firm on the island—Isham, Bayonne & Waugh. Like Milo and me, Lucy and Graham have been together basically since birth. Even though Graham was always in Milo's and my periphery, our group didn't form until the tail end of elementary school, when the four of us were on the same Field Day team. Our friendship formed the way most do at that age—effortlessly. One day we were separate pairs, and the next, every playdate was for four.

I'm not brave enough to ask Graham myself. And being Lucy's best friend means he'll do stuff for her he'd never consider doing for me—especially not after what happened with Rooney.

I tried the Wishing Fountain on that one, too. In the fall, right after our blowup fight, I bought a Swedish ten krona from Mrs. Bloom for thirty dollars. It was the rarest coin she had in her collection, and when I tossed it in, I wished, *Please put my friendship with Graham back to normal.*

But maybe even the Wishing Fountain can't fix the damage done when you help your coworker cover up her affair with an older married man. Especially when it turns out he's the father of one of your best friends. Especially when she was covering for you, too.

The worst part wasn't just that I'd been involved in Graham's dad's affair, but how I'd involved Graham by extension. And he'd had no idea.

After Graham and I agreed to keep what we were doing between us, I'd gone to Rooney. I needed a cover story, something I could use that wouldn't involve my mom. It wasn't uncommon for Graham to go unaccounted for, but radio silence from me would be read as an SOS.

And Rooney was happy to make an even trade. "How about a little quid pro quo?" she said when I asked her. We were in the back of Piper and Junie's during a lull, cleaning the counter and lining clean food baskets with paper.

"No, thanks. I love seafood, but I draw the line at tentacles."

Rooney stared at me. "What?"

I blinked back. "Huh? What, what? You said squid."

"I said *quid*. Quid pro quo? I scratch your back, you scratch mine?" At my blank look, she scoffed. "God, what are they teaching you in school these days?"

I smiled. "Nothing right now. It's summer vacation."

Rooney rolled her eyes and nudged me with her elbow, and I dropped the basket I was holding. As I set it aside to be washed again, Rooney said, "I was hoping you could do the same for me. Cover for me when I'm with my new man."

Rooney always put it like that—*my man*. She never said *boyfriend*.

It made me think of Graham, and what I'd call him if someone asked. The thought of saying *my boyfriend* sent fizzy, zinging feelings through me, like someone popped a can of soda in the center of my chest.

I swallowed down my giddiness long enough to apply some logic to Rooney's question. "Why do you need me to cover for you?" I asked with a smile. Then, leaning in, I added quietly, "Is he a celebrity? An ex-con? An FBI informant hiding out in a small Florida town while he waits for a mob boss to go to trial?"

"You watch too much TV." Rooney pushed me away, laughing. "He's just not exactly single. *Yet*."

I frowned. "Wait, so he's cheating?"

Rooney shot me a look. "Don't say it like that. He's not happy, and he's planning to end it. At this point, he's already emotionally removed even without me, so what's the difference?"

I bit my tongue, because a sharp note I hadn't heard from Rooney before had entered her tone. It was the first time she'd made me feel like a kid, like I couldn't possibly understand her sophisticated adult relationship.

"Can't Angela cover for you? Why do you need me?"

Rooney rolled her eyes. "Come on, Junie, you know Angela." She shot me a smile that made me feel like I was in on a secret. It soothed the sting of her earlier tone. "She's so black and white about everything. She wouldn't get it. Besides, you're like my baby sister! Sisters always cover for each other!"

Rooney is an only child like me, and I loved that she called me her baby sister. It made me feel like I was connected to someone in a way I'd never experienced before. Like we had an unbreakable bond.

So I agreed, because the fizzy feeling had intensified at the thought of sharing secrets like this with Rooney. Of being *in* on her life. And it worked out, because I got my cover story in return—movie nights and drives to the mainland and nights Rooney fell asleep on my couch.

When everything blew up later, it was the worst kind of mess. Because I didn't know that while I was sneaking around with Graham, Rooney was sneaking around with his dad.

After Rooney found out she was pregnant and confronted Macauley Isham at his house in front of his family, Graham's entire world imploded. His mom, Joy, who had been working with Macauley at the same CPA firm long before his name was on the door—before they were married, and Graham wasn't even a distant daydream—left her job of twenty years.

It wasn't only the embarrassment of facing her coworkers or seeing Macauley every day, but according to Graham, his dad was vindictive after the separation. Joy refused to move out right away, and Macauley wasn't happy about putting Rooney up at a hotel while he worked out what to do. Graham said it wouldn't have taken long for his dad to find a reason to let Joy go from the firm, backing her into a corner where she *had* to leave the island. Especially once he removed her from his healthcare plan, which he somehow managed as both her husband and her boss. As a type-one diabetic, Joy is dependent on having a job with healthcare.

"Sneaky and underhanded and sick," Graham said after his mom found out. He was furious about all of it—the injustice of his mom's health situation, and his dad being the looming threat that could pull out what little security she had left from under her at any moment. She'd given up becoming a CPA to raise Graham, supported Macauley throughout his entire career, and dealt with the humiliation of being cheated on, all so he could hurt her further by taking away the few vital things she had left—her job, her health insurance, and, when she finally left town, her son.

Days after she was dropped from his health plan, Macauley filed for divorce. But by then, it didn't matter who filed first—Joy was already packing up and planning to move to Jacksonville, where her father and the rest of her family lives. It wasn't only for the support and help getting back on her feet, but her sister had called with a job opportunity Joy couldn't pass up for anything.

Not even for Graham.

I'm not sure which blowup was worse—the one between Graham and his dad when the affair first came out, or the one between Joy and Graham when she begged him to leave with her and he said no.

When we asked Graham why he didn't go, he was confused why it was even a question. "Obviously I stayed for you."

I tried not to let it send my heart into overdrive. He meant the collective *you*—the three of us, his friends. Looking at me when he said it didn't mean he meant me specifically.

I especially couldn't let myself think he meant it that way after what I'd done.

"And for school," I said. "Obviously. Junior year is the most important year of high school. Moving right now could derail your whole life."

To which Graham responded, "My life's already been derailed."

My shame was suffocating, but I stayed quiet as the dust settled over the following months. School started. Graham and I stopped meeting up, like nothing had ever happened. He had more important things to worry about, and I was too filled with guilt. I wasn't sure I'd ever be able to be alone with him again.

I don't know what I was hoping. That he'd never find out, or that I'd have more time to explain. But as the months drifted by, the window for a confession narrowed, then closed completely.

It had been three months when we were at Lucy's after school one day, talking about Thanksgiving break and midterms and Milo's first basketball game of the season.

Graham was quiet, but that wasn't unusual then. He was picking at his nail polish, a chipped forest green. I was watching him—I was *always* watching him—so I saw the moment he realized. His face changed, his mouth going slack and his eyebrows arching up.

And he looked at me, asking the question I absolutely could not lie about: "Did you know?"

I swallowed down my instinct to run. I knew before I even

answered, from the way his expression turned pained and I could see the agony there, that he didn't need me to say it.

"I'm sorry," I whispered, because I'd been carrying my shame for months, and being sorry was all I knew.

"You're sorry." His voice was leaden, the way it often was after his parents split, but there was something else beneath it, like rushing water behind a thin barrier of ice. Then the months of quiet anger Graham had been holding back just . . . broke.

"You're sorry for *what*, Junie?" he asked, his jaw wound so tight, he was talking through his teeth. When I didn't respond, he filled in the blanks. "Please tell me you didn't help her."

I sucked my lips between my teeth. "I'm sorry," I repeated, quieter, like my voice was trapped somewhere deep in my chest.

His expression turned fierce, his cheeks going splotchy red with anger. "*Stop saying that.*" I reached for his arm, but he wrenched away, his expression furious and betrayed and—the absolute worst—wounded. "I knew something was off. I knew you were acting weird, and I've been the idiot sitting here waiting for you, and—I can't believe I convinced myself you liked me."

I could feel the wide-eyed, dropped-jaw look Lucy and Milo were exchanging as they tried to catch up to this new reality.

"I *do* like—"

"Don't say it." Graham's voice was ice-cold as he cut me off. My breath stuck at the sound. "Don't lie."

I didn't know which was more important—convincing Graham that I did like him, so much it ached sometimes, or that I hadn't known the extent of what I'd helped Rooney do.

58

Sometimes I wonder if I made the wrong choice in what I said next.

"I didn't know—I didn't know it was your dad."

Graham's eyes narrowed. "But you knew it was *someone*. Someone else's husband. Someone's else's dad." I could tell the second he said it how much the word *dad* pained him.

"No!" There was a desperate hitch in my voice as I tried to backpedal. "She just said he wasn't single yet, but he would be!"

Graham's face twisted, and that's when his eyes filled. Lucy reached for him, her face soft and sad, her eyes filling, too. She's always been a sympathetic crier, especially when it comes to Graham. That he'd pulled away from me but not her as she wrapped her arms around him sent a razor-edged feeling through me, so sharp it hurt to breathe.

"I didn't know," I tried again when Lucy shot me a tight look that said lines were being drawn and sides picked. "I had no idea it was him. I swear. I didn't even know he was married."

"He didn't have to be married," Graham said, swiping his wrist across his eyes. "You knew she was cheating with someone, somehow. It could've hurt anyone, and you didn't just let it happen. You *helped*." He swallowed hard, the corners of his mouth tight, like he was holding back fresh tears. "You helped her *ruin my life*. And I helped you do it."

He staggered to his feet, covering his eyes with one hand as he started to cry, and his voice cracked as he delivered the final blow. The words I still think about. The ones that live in a hollow part of my chest.

"I've spent weeks sitting here wondering why you pulled away when I needed you, but of course—right—it was never about me. It was about you and your guilt. You never thought about me at all."

I'd never seen Graham like that before. He'd always been the funny one, even when things got serious. He was good for a joke and lightening the mood. It was like watching an actor drop character. Things were suddenly so different, and I didn't know then that even when things got better, they would never be the same.

He stormed out after that, and Lucy followed. Milo and I went home.

Neither of our friends ever asked for details about what had happened, but it didn't matter. They knew without being told.

Graham and I avoided each other for a week before I got up the courage to call him. I didn't want to make him see me, but I wanted to apologize, and to explain that I understood and how sorry I was. He apologized, too, even though he didn't need to. I deserved everything he had said. I probably deserved worse. And maybe that's what I got. Because we never talked about last summer, or how I abandoned him, or what we might have felt for each other. It got swept up like everything else, tied up and tossed out so we could move on.

I made the wish after that, but seven months later, things still aren't back to normal. Either it was a coin wasted, or the Wishing Fountain is taking its sweet time with fulfillment.

"Come on, Milo, it's my last summer on the North Shore, and plus—plus—" I struggle to say it, because Milo isn't my dad's biggest fan. My dad is a bit like me—a space case. Milo has been there every time my dad forgets my birthday, or gets a new girlfriend and stops calling, or flakes on a visit. Milo thinks my dad doesn't grovel enough when he messes up.

He watches me now, his eyebrows arching up.

I set the sweet tea on the counter and nudge it toward him. "My dad's coming."

His expression changes from hard obstinance to frustration. "Dammit, JN."

"But it's not just about that! If we can save the musical from *Little Shop of Horrors,* I might have a real chance at Drama Club president!"

He frowns. "I thought you already lost to Jessica."

"I don't appreciate your use of the word *already.*"

He makes a choking noise. "But you did!"

"Jessica's out. New school." I lean toward him and lower my voice. "I heard it's drugs, but you know I hate to spread rumors."

He rolls his eyes. "Right. So, Drama Club president and your dad. You really know how to state a case."

"And don't forget, this is my last summer on the North Shore. I want to make it count."

He shoots me a look. "This isn't your last summer on the North Shore. You'll be up here every day next year."

"But it's the last one where I'll be living here! I want it to be special. I want to end on a high note, all of us doing something together again—me, you, Lucy, Graham—"

"I don't know about Lucy, but Graham will not be there. Guaranteed."

I feel that one like a physical blow. "Right."

Milo winces. "You know what I mean. Not because of you."

"Nah, it's because of me."

Milo looks uncomfortable. An unfortunate side effect of the weirdness between Graham and me is how it's affected our friends. For the most part, we ignore it. Graham and I made shaky amends, supergluing our friendship back together like shattered pottery. But it's misshapen now, and we can all see the cracks.

"Maybe you could work your magic on Graham, too," I say, feeling the world's tiniest spark of hope. An idea pings to life in the back of my brain—that maybe a summer doing community theater will fix what I broke. If the Wishing Fountain won't do it, I'll make it happen myself.

Getting Milo's help certainly wouldn't hurt.

I think Milo senses the idea because his eyes narrow. "You're expecting a lot from me on this, aren't you?"

I hold out my hands, widening my eyes innocently. "I just thought, since you're so beloved—"

"Uh-huh."

"—and on the basketball team, whose cup runneth over with boys looking to fill their community service time cards—"

"I see what you're getting at, and the answer is n—"

"—and I'll owe you *such a huge favor,* God, Milo, you wouldn't even believe the size of the favor I'll owe you."

He stops at that, his mouth curling into a small smile. "A favor?"

"A huge favor. Monumental."

Milo considers this. "Expiration date?"

I silently curse. I was hoping to hit him with that later, but Milo knows all my tricks. "Three months."

He snorts. "Don't insult me, JN. Non-expirational."

"Absolutely not. One year. Final offer."

Milo laughs. "You're not exactly in a place to negotiate. If I say no, you're screwed, and we both know it. Non-expirational level-five favor, or I'm out."

Defining the value of a favor is difficult. The way beauty is in the eye of the beholder, the value of a favor is in the eye of the purchaser. I would never call a weekend of doing Milo's chores for him a level-four favor—it'd be level two at most—but I would if it were Lucy, whose family does a full spring cleaning once a month. In the same way Lucy would never call giving me choosing rights on movie night a level-three favor—that's a one or, on a bad night, maybe a two—but Graham would call it a four if I made him sit through *Into the Woods* again.

But even though Milo defines the cost of the trade, it's never stopped me from attempting a compromise.

"Level *five*? Asking your b-ball bros to volunteer in a musical isn't exactly a level-five favor! Level five would be if I was asking you to help me get rid of a body! This is level four at most."

"After the humiliation that was *The Wizard of Oz*?" He gives me a look.

"I *knew* you'd bring that up."

"That's what happens when you traumatize a kid in his formative years. Level five, non-expirational." Milo glances at an invisible watch. "Offer expires in thirty seconds."

"That's not fair!" I squawk.

Behind me, the door swings open with a jingle, and a gaggle of people stream in. They're all kids from school, wearing clothes haphazardly over their bathing suits and tracking in sand.

I'm momentarily distracted, until I glance at Milo and he taps his invisible watch.

"Fine," I whisper sharply. "Level five, non-expirational. Pass me the scissors."

Milo grins as he slides a pair of scissors and a marker across the counter. "Pleasure doing business with you."

"Hi, Milo," says Cora Kalisch as she approaches the counter. "Busy today?"

He shrugs. It's his pretty-girl shrug. That *aw schucks who me* half-shoulder thing he does. "Earlier, yeah. Not so much once those clouds rolled in."

I pull a face as I clip a piece of fabric off my favorite purple shorts. "Tourists love to dip in the water but hate to get wet," I say as I slide the scissors back across the counter. The tourists have no way of knowing, of course, that I secured them a beautiful beach day.

I scribble *5N*—level five, non-expirational—and my initials—*JNA* with the *A* turned into a star—on the snipped fabric and drop the marker in the cup by the register.

Our friends have been trading favors like currency for as long as I can remember. It started with Milo and me, watching our moms trade peaches for Parmesan cheese, one book for another, a night of babysitting for a bottle of wine. We traded toys, snacks, the rights to the TV remote, and anything else we could think of. It didn't take long for that to catch on in our friendship with Lucy and Graham, where it evolved into trading homework, gossip, fibs, and favors.

For a while, using our memories got us by. But the summer after seventh grade, I tried to pull a fast one on Milo—convincing him I hadn't used the level-one favor he'd sold me for all my turns on Graham's Nintendo one afternoon. Really, I'd already used the favor to get him to buy me a Kitchen Sink Sundae from the General Store. But then my bike got a flat while we were in town one day, and I tried to reuse the favor to get Milo to fill the tire for me at the bike shop, which is still run by Castor Clemmons, the meanest man on the North Shore.

Milo was suspicious, but Graham was the one who remembered—recalled in detail that I'd made Milo get me extra hot fudge because, according to Graham, "You said he owed you, remember?"

That day, Lucy devised two rules: expiration dates, so we can't play with each other's memories, and signed tokens that cannot be replicated. And like a golden ticket, tokens are re-collected in the end, to make sure they can't be reused. It's the reason I have a closet full of clothes with triangles of fabric cut off the hems and sleeves, and a shoebox filled with re-collected favor tokens hidden in my dirty laundry hamper.

"Take it before I change my mind," I say to Milo now, passing the fabric across the display case.

Milo grabs it and tucks it into his pocket while Cora eyes us. "What's up with you two?"

"Just securing some community theater volunteers." I turn and lean against the case, grinning at Vince, who was last year's Drama Club president. "Vince, you'd make an excellent Duke Orsino."

Vince smiles. "Sorry, Junie, no luck. I leave for school August first. But I'll put the word out that you need volunteers."

"You're an angel amongst mortals."

"It's the least I can do for my new successor," he says.

"Oh, you heard about Jessica?"

"Yeah, lucky break for you."

"We'll see. I still have to win the special election." I turn back to Milo, who's fully distracted by Cora, giving her that pretty-girl smile and batting his extra-long lashes. Girls eat it up, especially ones who have been eyeing Milo for weeks the way Cora has.

"I'll see you later," I say to him, tapping the counter. "Auditions are in two days."

Milo whips his head around to look at me. "Two days?" he bleats. "I have *two days* to convince them?"

I put on an innocent smile, backing toward the door, and give him a thumbs-up. "I believe in you."

He picks up the sweet tea and takes a swig. "And you tried to tell me this wasn't a level-five favor. I don't know why I expected fair play from you."

"Don't forget to talk to Graham," I say as I slip out the door.

Milo's Mullet Fan Club
Today 9:21 PM

ME
Auditions at 7 tomorrow don't forget

GRAHAM
This is an interesting text. No idea why you're telling me.

MILO
He'll be there

GRAHAM
No I won't

LUCY
Ugh. Are we really doing this?

**Junie named the conversation
"White Coral Best Actors Club"**

GRAHAM
No!!!

LUCY
I guess we are
See you at 7

GRAHAM
I won't be there
Hello?
I'm not coming I'm serious
HELLO?

Chapter Five

ORSINO
What is the matter with those two?

*(Side-stage, BENEDICK and BEATRICE fight
animatedly.)*

JAQUES
Ah, I hear there hasn't been a day of peace since their
wedding. There's a skirmish of wit between them.

ORSINO
There's a skirmish of something—good God, someone get that butter knife from her!

—Act 1, Scene 3, *Midsummer Madness*

"Why so glum, sugarplum? You look positively radiant out
here in nature's glow."

Graham glares at me from his seat in the amphitheater
as he flips his sketchbook shut and stows it in his backpack.
He's wearing a pair of jeans rolled at the ankles and a T-shirt
that looks too big on him. His feet are propped on his skateboard while he idly rolls it back and forth. His fingers are
ink-stained, and his blue nail polish is chipped off almost
completely.

He's the first one of my friends to arrive. I've been here

twenty minutes already, organizing snacks and lukewarm water bottles. I'm not sure who's more surprised—me that Graham showed up, or him that I'm not only on time, but early. Especially since I came straight from P&J's, where I was blessedly relieved of working with Tallulah in exchange for Darius from the morning shift. He didn't seem quite as thrilled to work nights as I was to have him there.

Apparently sour attitudes are a theme of the night, if Graham's glower is any indication.

I lean over the row in front of him, my hands braced on the back of the seat, attempting normalcy. If the universe is going to give me a chance to fix things this summer, I'm not going to waste it.

"Don't be such a sourpuss," I say, forcing lightness into my voice. "You're getting community service hours, and you get to spend more time with your friends. That's what we call a win-win."

"I don't think you and I share the same definition of a win-win."

I slide forward, bracing my forearms on the seat, my hands hanging over the edge. "I'd think my sparkling company is more than enough."

He rests his elbows on his knees and smacks his open palms against mine, making my skin tingle. "What are my other options?"

We hold a long, unblinking staring contest that feels like the worst kind of dare. Naturally, Graham wins, because I am a coward.

I head back to the stage where I'd set up the snacks, grabbing a bag of Doritos and a water bottle, and lob both into his lap. He catches the chips but misses the water bottle. It smacks his thigh before he gets a hand around it, saving more important places from imminent doom. He loses his skateboard in the process, and it rolls down the row until it curves and bumps into the leg of one of the seats.

Graham glares up at me. "That wasn't very nice."

"Just delivering your prize."

"You aren't gonna sit with me?" he asks as I wander away.

"Not with that attitude," I call back. The truth is, I'm *so* grateful he's here, but I have no idea how to show it. I should be trying harder, but being alone with Graham feels loaded. Maybe in a month I'll be able to push aside everything that's happened between us, but until then, I need Lucy or Milo around as a buffer.

Besides, I'm too anxious to sit. Between Graham and auditions and the fact that I haven't heard from Milo yet, it feels like bees are buzzing in every inch of my body.

I check my phone, and the buzzing intensifies. We're getting dangerously close to the start of auditions. Lucy shows up, barefoot and clutching her roller skates, right before Miss Liu takes the stage.

Lucy is still wearing her shirt from Hot Dough, the donut shop in town where she works. She pulls her sandals out of her bag and slips them on as I ease into the seat next to her. On her other side, Graham sulks while crunching on his Doritos. As soon as she's settled, Lucy shoves her hand into the bag and steals a few. Graham lets her without protest, but when I reach across her lap, he holds the bag away from me.

"After you tried to maim me?" he says, leaning around Lucy to give me a look like he can't believe I'd have the audacity. "I don't think so."

"Don't ever let anyone tell you you're not meant for the theater, Graham," I say. "That dramatic performance was Oscar-worthy."

He makes a big show of eating the last chip and crumpling the bag in his hand.

Lucy takes stock of the crowd. "Where's Milo?"

I check my phone, which confirms Milo is officially late. "No idea. He hasn't texted me back."

She snorts. "Probably too busy sucking face with Cora Kalisch and lost track of time."

I rear back in my seat. "Doing what with whom?"

"It's not nice to gossip," says Graham.

We ignore him.

"Didn't he tell you?" Lucy asks. "He hung out with her yesterday, and I saw her lurking around the General Store this afternoon when he was working."

My gasp comes out big and overdramatic, probably a result of being in the amphitheater and consumed by the spirit of the stage. "He *hung out* with her?"

"Here we go," Graham says, shaking his head.

I lean around Lucy to stare at him. "Did you know about this?"

Graham shrugs, which means he did.

I shouldn't be surprised. Graham and Milo spent a lot of time together over the last year. Whenever Graham and his dad would have a particularly bad fight, Graham would retreat to Milo's for the night—sometimes a few nights. Milo's parents were always happy to have him, and Graham's dad was happy to be rid of him.

It was strange to share my best friend with someone else, but it's not like I could complain. I'm not great at sharing, but even I recognized that Graham needed Milo more than I did (and by extension, Milo's parents, who filled a gap Graham was missing with his parents gone—one physically, and one emotionally). And I owed him at least that much, after everything I'd done.

In the end, it worked out better for me, anyway. Being at Milo's so often is part of what brought Graham and me back together. I was always around, and our friendship began to naturally heal—at least in a way. Like a bone that wasn't exactly set right.

The first night we really spoke, just the two of us, was at Milo's after Graham had a bad blowup with his dad. It was the weekend after the school called Macauley to talk about Graham's name request—that he be listed on his teachers' rosters as Graham Napalan, his middle name and Joy's maiden name, even if his transcripts still said Graham Isham.

His dad was furious. But he underestimated Graham, who has been known to have bouts of stubbornness, where the harder you want him to do something, the more he'll do the opposite.

In the end, Graham won. Even when the administration refused to list him the way he wanted, he convinced every single teacher he had to call him by Napalan instead of Isham.

I don't think it's even because he hates his last name. But he wanted to win, and despite the way he floats so carelessly through life at times, Graham is surprisingly competitive.

"I can't believe Milo is about to get a girlfriend and didn't tell me," I say, aiming for that light place between joking and truly annoyed. "He's in so much trouble."

"You can berate him when he gets here." Lucy glances around the auditorium. "No Tallulah yet, either?"

My head empties. "No Tallulah where?"

"Here, obviously. I told her she should come and do

something like costumes." She twists around, scanning the back rows. "She can do the alterations at home, so it won't interfere too much with work, but she still gets to hang out."

"Lucy, *why*? Why would you do that? Where did you even see her?"

"I caught her at Piper and Junie's a few times. I've had the early shifts at work this week, so I've been in for breakfast." Lucy eyes me as she faces forward. "What's with the face?"

"I was gonna say I didn't know you two knew each other, but if you knew her that well, you probably wouldn't have invited her."

"Don't be mean," she says admonishingly. "Tallulah and I have a bunch of classes together, and we're in the same testing group. Bayonne," she points at herself, then away, "Breeman."

Since she and Tallulah are in the same grade, it shouldn't surprise me that they see each other at school. But Lucy was sophomore class president last year, and Tallulah probably spends more time sneaking cigarettes behind school than attending class. I can't imagine they have much in common.

"So you're saying you *should* know better," I say.

Lucy gives me a little shoulder shove. "Come on, be nice."

"Yeah, Junie, be nice," Graham says, mocking and superior as he leans around Lucy to look at me again. He's perked up considerably at the possibility that I'll be as miserable as he is now.

"I'm always nice. It's Tallulah who's sour all the time. Talking to her is like eating a Warhead—the longer you do it, the worse it gets."

"You make her sound evil," says Lucy. "She's gone through a lot, that's all."

"Lucy, you don't have to adopt every stray because you feel bad," I say.

Lucy scowls at me. "That's not what I'm doing. Don't say it like that."

"I'm just saying, if you invited Tallulah, you're taking responsibility for her."

"That's fine with me," Lucy replies, a hard edge in her voice as she shoots me a prim look.

I stare at her a little too long, surprised. But then Miss Liu starts her pre-auditions speech, and my stomach knots up tighter. I glance toward the parking lot, my fingers drumming on my thighs.

Graham sighs, leaning over Lucy's lap to whisper, "Hey, stop freaking out. If he said he'll be here, he'll be here."

And he's right—Milo shows up when Sophie is halfway through her rendition of "Memory" from *Cats*. And even though he's trying to quiet his group, it's a fruitless effort. No one is paying attention to Sophie anymore. Even Peter is distracted. Judging by Sophie's reddening face, she knows it.

From what I can see, Milo managed to recruit five guys from the basketball team, three terrified-looking freshmen from the Space Science Club, and two girls who, judging from the way they're hanging on a pair of basketball guys, are girlfriends.

When he finds me, he slips into the seat beside mine, ears red, and whispers, "Sorry we're late. When I told the guys they'd have to sing in their audition, a bunch abandoned ship before I could tell them about working backstage." He nods to where Sophie is finishing up. "I think Will is pulling for Benedick, though? I didn't even know he could sing, but he's pretty good."

I want to give him a hard time, but I'm up after Sophie,

and the audition nerves have set in. My singing voice isn't spectacular like Sophie's or some of the others in Drama Club, which is why I'm auditioning with "Look at Me I'm Sandra Dee" from *Grease,* because if nothing else, I can capture Stockard Channing's flair.

I end up getting a few laughs during my performance, which really swells me up with pride—until Derek Johnson from the basketball team gets up and sings the theme song from *Sponge-Bob,* which has everyone howling with laughter and takes the wind right out of my sails.

But I should be grateful. In the end, between the community volunteers and Milo's group, we have a chance at a decent ensemble and main cast, with more than enough people to work behind the scenes. That includes Tallulah, who shows up at the end and volunteers to help with costumes.

As soon as I see her chatting with Miss Liu, I shoot Lucy a murderous look.

She meets it with an innocent smile and tickles her fingers under my chin. "Don't frown, Juniekins. This is gonna be fun, remember? That's what you told me when you forced me to come."

I don't have a reasonable argument, and she grins because she knows she's got me beat. Behind her, Graham looks smug with her victory. I hate when they tag-team me. It makes me itchy with jealousy, because even though I have a best friend, too, I feel more like the messy little girl Milo has been forced to drag along than his equal.

"I'll be emailing the cast list and practice schedule in the next few days," Miss Liu calls from the stage as Tallulah joins our group. "If I don't have your email, come up and give it to me before you leave."

Milo heads toward the stage, and I follow. "Lucy said you hung out with Cora yesterday."

He glances at me, a blush burning his cheeks. "Oh yeah?"

"Yeah." I nudge him with my elbow. "Why didn't you tell me? Two weeks ago, you called me from Chipotle because you couldn't decide if you wanted carnitas or chicken. You choose dating Cora to be the time you stop asking my opinion?"

"We're not dating. We just hung out."

"That sounds like one of those hookup code words I don't understand."

He exhales a laugh. "It's not. We hung out, the way you and I hang out."

"I doubt it was the way you and I hang out." I shoot him an incredulous look. "Tell me honestly. Did you lay those lips on her?"

He puts his hand on the top of my head and forcibly turns my face away. "Stop it."

"Look, I know I haven't dated anyone in a while"—read: two years, because I certainly can't count last summer and Graham—"but I know how the game works, kind of."

"Kind of," Milo repeats with a laugh, ruffling my hair.

"So, should I start working my magic on her? Make sure your new girlfriend doesn't hate me like your last one did?"

Milo frowns. "Marissa didn't hate you."

Marissa hated me. Milo likes to pretend like it never happened, but she definitely hated me. She probably still hates me. But she hurt Milo's feelings when she dumped him right before prom, so it's safe to say I hate her more.

"But maybe," he says reluctantly, like he doesn't want to admit I might be right, "it wouldn't hurt for you to put in some effort with Cora. Just in case. Come to the bonfire at her house tomorrow? Play nice?"

"I always play nice." I frown. "But I've got family dinner with Paul and Tallulah tomorrow." I shoot Tallulah a glare over my shoulder, like it's her fault we're stuck doing this. She's chatting with Lucy and looks completely unaware of my existence.

"Bring her," says Milo. "Could be the ticket to getting out of dinner, or at least getting out early."

I swing around to stare at him in horror. "*Bring* her? My nemesis? To a bonfire? So, what, she can push me in?"

He laughs. "She's not your nemesis, JN. Come on, be the bigger person. You two can get to know each other away from your parents. And if it's a nightmare, at least you're not stuck sitting at a table with her."

I grimace. "I hate when you make sense."

Mom picks me up from my shift at Piper and Junie's for our first family dinner. The drive to the South Shore is a short one, but as soon as we pass the Publix and the fast-food chains, we reach the Whole Foods that marks the end of No Man's Land, and then it's like driving on a different island altogether.

The South Shore's main drag is a four-lane road lined with fancy corporate shops and bisected by a median of tall palms. It's essentially an outdoor mall that ends in a roundabout with a park in the center that has always felt deeply unsafe to me considering how few people understand how round-abouts work. The area is always packed with tourists who seem to forget that a Pottery Barn in Florida is the same as a Pottery Barn in Indiana. If I had to list all the reasons why the South Shore sucks, the crowd outside the Cheesecake Factory would top it.

As we pull into the U-shaped driveway, I'm struck anew by how much I loathe Paul's house. Before, it was just a simmering dislike—the way you feel about seeing an ugly shirt. But now it's an ugly shirt I'm required to wear. On picture day. Memorialized for everyone to see, forever.

It's done in that typical Floridian Spanish style you see on new construction, with a two-car garage and a pillared entryway with no porch. I try to imagine parking my bike in the driveway or sitting on the front step with a glass of iced tea, and both images are subtly horrifying.

Even though we're moving in soon, Mom rings the doorbell, which just cements the feeling that this place is Not Ours.

Paul answers the door looking a complete mess. His dark hair is rumpled, and there's a streak of black on his cheek. I smell smoke and do a quick check to make sure he's not on fire.

"I was trying to grill," he says as we come into the house. "Hi, Junie."

I wave, peeking past him to assess the damage. Their front door looks directly out the back windows onto the deck, where I spot a grill they didn't have last month. He probably bought it to impress Mom, but Paul isn't much of a cook, and I'm not convinced he's ever used a grill before. Which is a little nerve-racking when propane is involved.

But I guess if he blows up the house, at least we won't have to move in.

"Save me," he says to Mom, motioning to the back door.

Paul is surprisingly hapless for a doctor. I don't know what he's like at work, but I've seen him forget his glasses are propped on his head, accidentally leave the house with a carton of oat milk in hand and his keys sitting in the fridge, and ask Mom if she'd seen his phone so he could enter something into his calendar while talking to her on that very phone. I sincerely hope he just uses all his brain juice up at work, that he isn't the type of person who pulls a *whoopsie daisy* on his patients.

Inside, the house isn't exactly cozy, but it's a home. Most of the art on the walls are photos of Tallulah or Tallulah and Paul together, and a line of her school pictures march up the staircase wall, from her gap-toothed kindergarten photo to her bland, nearly imperceptible smile from sophomore year picture day.

The house is mostly clean but lived in, with Tallulah's shoes piled by the door to the garage and a few dishes in the kitchen sink. There's a whiteboard calendar on the wall with Paul's schedule scribbled on it, along with emergency numbers, and a magnet in the shape of a pizza slice pins a couple of twenty-dollar bills to the fridge.

Tallulah isn't downstairs, so while Mom and Paul are outside, I make myself comfortable on the couch and pull up *Proper Southern Ladies* on demand. I'm caught up on the original—Montgomery, though it is sacrilege to call it *Montgomery* and must always be referred to as *the original*—but I'm three episodes behind on Savannah, so I may as well entertain myself.

As the Savannah ladies are boarding the party bus that will take them to the harbor for their casino cruise, I hear a disdainful snort behind me.

"Wow, way to support the patriarchy."

I whip around. "Excuse me? *Proper Southern Ladies* is a show about women produced by a woman."

"Just because it's made by women and about women doesn't mean it's feminist." Tallulah leans on the back of the couch, glaring at the TV. "Look, even the title—what's *proper*? Rich? So, we only care about rich people?"

I hit *pause* and twist around on the couch to face her. "It's a show about people of a specific lifestyle."

Tallulah smirks. "Rich white women doing rich white women shit."

"There isn't a single iteration of *Proper Southern Ladies* where they're all white."

"Just most of them," Tallulah says.

"That's patently untrue, and you'd know that if you'd ever watched."

Tallulah turns up her nose. "I don't need to watch."

"Do you normally form your opinions without educating yourself on the material?" I ask, giving her a bland smile. "That won't do you any good in college. You should consider my wisdom, you know, as your elder."

Tallulah rolls her eyes and turns away, stalking across the kitchen. "If we don't eat in the next ten minutes," she says, maybe not specifically to me but to the room, even though I'm the only one in here, "I'm gonna be a different person."

"Don't threaten me with a good time," I call after her as I press *play*.

Our first family dinner goes about as well as can be expected.

First, Paul burns Tallulah's seitan steak on his new grill. Mom, who has plenty of experience turning around a bad situation in the kitchen, manages to save the non-vegetarian steaks, but Tallulah is incensed. Probably hangry. If she's a tiger on a regular day, now she's a tiger whose dinner was put in front of her and pulled swiftly away. Apparently that was the last seitan steak in the house. Sitting across the table from her as she wolfs down leftover tofu chow mein from her lunch, I feel distinctly unsafe. Like if I make eye contact, she'll decide *I'm* dinner and bite my head off in one go.

I guess that's why I find this moment to be the perfect time to say, "So, there's this bonfire up on the North Shore tonight. I was thinking maybe Tallulah and I could head out early and meet my friends?"

I'm making good on my promise to at least invite her. If she's in too terrible a mood to say yes, well, darn, at least I tried.

Tallulah nearly chokes on a chunk of tofu, spitting it back into her bowl. "Tallulah could meet who?"

I bat my eyes at her. "I thought you might want to come, but no pressure." My voice is so light and casual, I barely recognize it.

Mom must feel the same, because she shoots me a suspicious look. "I don't know, Juju. I'd like it if you stuck around here tonight."

"I thought the beaches were closed today anyway," Paul says. "They had a huge infestation of jellyfish washing up this week."

This is the only major downside to White Coral Key. Bottle Beach, which is the northernmost point of the island, has hundreds of messages in bottles wash up every year, some lost in time, others in different languages. It's one of our bigger tourist attractions and has something to do with the currents and the wind and the location of our island in relation. The downside is the same currents and wind also bring in large groups of Portuguese man-of-wars.

"If the beaches are closed, I'm sure the sheriff has already shut your party down," Mom says.

"It's a private beach, and it's on the bay side, not the west side. They've hardly got any man-of-wars over there." I fold my hands together like I'm praying. "Come on, Mom, everyone's going."

"I'm not going," says Tallulah.

"Well, I just invited you, so it's not because you can't—it's because you won't."

"Actually, this might be a good idea," Paul says. "Tallulah could drive Junie up and hang out for a while."

"Dad," Tallulah protests. She doesn't throw her voice into a higher register, so somehow this doesn't come out sounding like a whine, the way it always does for me when I try to appeal to Mom.

Maybe I should start taking notes.

But whether she's whining or not, Tallulah's objection doesn't sway Paul. "Come on, Mush, you were just saying you don't know anyone up there. This could be a great opportunity to get to know some of Junie's friends."

It always surprises me that Tallulah seems to lean into her nickname from her dad—Mushroom, thanks to a particularly bad bowl cut she got when she was a toddler, memorialized in many photos around the house. She seems like the type who'd hate any form of affection, but she has a soft spot for her dad. She's clearly about to cave on the bonfire. I think she doesn't like to disappoint him.

I smile at her from across the table, my hands folded under my chin. Spending more time with Tallulah was not on the agenda for my last great North Shore summer. But at least once we get there, my friends can act as a buffer—it would be what Lucy deserves after inviting her to community theater.

"Okay, if you think it's a good idea," Mom says to Paul, her expression softening. She glances from Tallulah to me. "You two have fun."

Chapter Six

Lights up on art deco hotel. MONTAGUE BOOTLEGGERS are gathered with best man DUKE ORSINO, who has arranged the wedding alcohol. The Montagues carry crates of alcohol into the hotel.

ORSINO
(To himself.) Gin, gin, and more gin.

(SEBASTIAN, the groom, enters.)

SEBASTIAN
Orsino, you've outdone yourself.

ORSINO
As long as you like a Gin Rickey.

SEBASTIAN
Well, you know what they say. Sweet are the uses of adversity.

—Act 1, Scene 1, *Midsummer Madness*

Cora lives in one of the bigger houses on the North Shore, a beachfront stilt house with a wraparound deck. The house is dark, and Cora's car is the only one in the driveway. Tallulah follows me down the path that winds around the side of the house.

I shield my eyes against the setting sun, which is just now touching the water, casting everything pink and gold. The beach is crowded with people from school, mostly gathered in clumps a good distance from the bonfire. It's not quite cool enough yet to brave the heat.

Lucy's ex-boyfriend Zephyr and his small group stand off to the side with a cooler full of beer. As Tallulah starts in their direction, I call, "Hey, where are you going?"

"To make this night manageable," she replies, her voice low and serious.

I watch her go as I head toward my friends, who are sitting with Cora. "Well, I brought her," I say as I drop down between Milo and Lucy. It puts me directly across from Graham, who watches me as he takes a long pull from the can of beer in his hand. "For better or worse. Probably worse."

"That was nice of you," Lucy says, narrowing her eyes at me in suspicion.

"You *would* think that," I reply. "I'm surprised you didn't invite her yourself. You weren't shy about asking her to join the musical."

"You were the one begging for volunteers!" Lucy argues, her jaw dropping.

"You couldn't have invited someone off the street? Like, any other single person in this entire town but her?"

"This is literally the last time I help you with anything," Lucy says with a laugh, leaning to the side so she can kick me in the thigh.

"Hey, no fighting," Milo says.

"Yeah, why should we argue when we know the real person to blame for tonight? It was Milo's idea for me to bring her," I say, nudging him with my elbow. "To get out of family dinner early."

Milo frowns. "That's not exactly what I said."

"Oh, really?" I shoot him a faux-confused look. "That's what I heard."

"You, hearing what you want to hear? I'm shocked," he says flatly.

I give an exaggerated gasp. "*Moi?*"

Cora giggles. "I'm just glad you made it, Junie," she says, leaning around Milo to smile at me. Her blond hair is twisted into an artfully messy braid, and she's wearing a cropped tank top with matching shorts, white-and-pink striped, showing off her perfect summer tan. Her legs are folded up like a pretzel, long and thin but strong. Cora is a volleyball player. Side by side, she and Milo look like they belong on a pamphlet for the White Coral Key High School athletics program.

"Oh, me, too," I say, stretching my legs out in front of me. "Especially after Tallulah's dinner got ruined. It felt like I was risking it all sitting at that table with her. At least here, I have a better chance of survival."

"Especially since she'll probably be drunk soon," Graham says, staring over my shoulder. "She just grabbed a beer directly out of Zephyr's hand, and I think she's planning to shotgun— Oh, yep, there she goes."

I turn right as Tallulah puts the foaming can to her mouth and starts sucking it down. Zephyr whoops.

"I'm sure she's fine," I say mildly.

Lucy gives me a pleading look, but when I glance pointedly away, she turns it on Graham.

He groans, shooting a glare in my direction, which I ignore. "Fine, I'll go get her." He shakes his beer can. "I'm empty anyway."

"Saint Graham," I say as he gets up.

He raises his eyebrows. "You don't hear that often."

I grin. "Maybe only slightly more than Saint Junie?"

"I doubt anyone's ever said Saint Junie," Graham says.

"Hey, that's not true," says Milo. "She's the Patron Saint of Dramatics."

I point at him. "That's right. Just say my name three times in a row, and then it's showtime."

Graham snorts. "Okay, Beetlejuice."

"More like Bloody Mary," says Milo.

"Hey!" I protest, shooting a beseeching look at Lucy. "Defend me!"

She holds up her hands. "I'll ask my mom to pray for you."

Graham laughs. As he walks off, I settle.

It feels good to joke with Graham. Getting back to normal has felt like swimming against the current, but maybe I've been doing it wrong. Maybe it's like getting caught in a riptide—I'm supposed to stop struggling and let the lighter stuff drag me back to the shore of normalcy instead.

Cora and Milo are talking quietly to each other, all mooney-eyed and smiling. Their hands are entwined in the sand.

"Do you feel like we're interrupting?" I whisper to Lucy.

"Absolutely like we've crashed a date," she murmurs.

I'm grateful when Graham returns a minute later, even as he says, "She told me to fuck off."

"Oh, so it's not only me she hates," I say. "It's everyone."

"Sorry, she actually said, 'Tell Juniper Nash to fuck off and I'm fine.'" He does a pretty good impression of Tallulah's husky smoker's voice.

I frown, glancing in Tallulah's direction. "Hmm. That's rude."

My gaze snags on Zephyr. He's telling the group around

him some animated story, hands flying. Then he steps backward and falls over his cooler, ass into the sand. The whole crowd erupts in laughter.

Tallulah doesn't crack a smile. She's too busy going to town on her beer. Her second? Third? How many has she put away while I wasn't looking?

Not my problem. Just because I brought her does not make me her babysitter.

A while later, when Lucy and I have nearly finished off the sparkling water she graciously shared with me and Graham has nursed his second beer to empty, someone calls, "Hey, Cora, where's your guitar? Play something for us."

When I look over, I'm surprised to see it's Sloan, who lives on the South Shore. I know she and Cora are friendly, but summer is different on the island. It's strange to see someone from the South Shore up at a North Shore party.

My gaze strays toward Tallulah, who has been completely absorbed into Zephyr's group. She's staring at Sloan with the dumbfounded look of someone who's just been sucker punched.

Sloan and Tallulah were once the kind of inseparable best friends who automatically paired up in class without even sharing a look, who decorated each other's lockers for birthdays and holidays, who you never saw in town without the other.

Tallulah's mom died in the year she and I were at different schools—me, a freshman, and Tallulah, in eighth grade. When our parents started dating, she was still being homeschooled, but it wasn't until she came to our high school that I realized she and Sloan were no longer a unit.

I always found it strange. I'm sure watching her mother die changed Tallulah in ways I can't even imagine. But no matter how hard it might be, or how much they'd try to resist, I could never abandon any of my friends that way. I know I looked at Sloan differently after their friendship ended so abruptly—a lot of people did. But maybe it's different when you're living it. Maybe what happened, and how it changed Tallulah, weighed on Sloan, too.

Cora's laugh draws my attention back to her. "Okay, okay," she calls, getting to her feet. "Let me run inside and get it." She looks down at Milo and her smile widens. "Wanna come? You can see my room."

Milo scrambles to his feet. "Yeah," he says, a little breathless. "For sure."

I twist around to watch them go. They're nearly out of sight when I see her reach back and take his hand.

"Scandalous," I say as they disappear.

"They're cute," says Lucy. "Kind of like an ad for hot high schoolers. Like, they could definitely be in one of those cheesy shows where sixteen-year-olds own their own businesses and run biker gangs or whatever."

I snort. "Yeah, I could see Milo running a biker gang."

"Sons of Asteroidery," Graham says with a grin.

Lucy and I groan in agony.

"Joke jail," I say, pointing at him. "Joke jail. Immediately."

Someone whoops down near the water, and I turn. A group of people are stripping down to their underwear, tossing clothes away from the tide as it rolls up over the sand.

"Oh good," Lucy says, her voice a little shaky. "Night swimming. Always a good idea when beer is involved."

With the sun fully set, the only light on the water comes from the moon and the fire as three people plunge into the water, scream-laughing.

I glance at Graham. Last summer, he would've been all over night swimming—even with the beaches closed from the man-of-wars. But tonight, he shakes his head with a wry smile. "Idiots."

I try to hide my surprise as I glance away, and my gaze snags on Tallulah. She's standing at the cooler, watching the swimmers splash into the water with dread on her face.

"Someone's gonna get hurt," I say absently, taking in her apprehensive expression.

Tallulah catches me looking, and her face shifts to anger. She chugs the rest of her beer, crushes the can in her fist, and stomps over. "This is boring," she says fiercely. "I'm going home."

"Hey, *no.*" I jump up and grab her arm. "Uh-uh."

Lucy sits up on her knees, holding her hands out. "Tallulah, why don't you sit with us?"

Tallulah barely spares her a glance. "No, thanks. I want to go home."

"You can't drive like that," I say, my hand still on her arm to keep her steady. She's swaying enough that I'm sure she's had more than the two beers I can confirm she drank. She probably had double that.

"I'm not *driving.*" Tallulah shakes me off and tosses her beer can into the trash bag someone set up. I hope they're planning to sort and recycle. "I'll walk."

I follow her. "You can't walk four miles. You can barely stand! Besides, it's not safe."

"What? Afraid I'll get kidnapped?" She wiggles her fingers at me, her eyes wide and her smile like something from a horror movie. "*Ooooh,* scary."

"Tallulah, I'm not kidding." I smack her hands away.

She seems to sober a bit, and her smile loosens as it turns sardonic. "I'm sure they'd throw me right back anyway. It's not like I'm a prize catch."

"Did you hear that?" a voice booms from behind me. "Tallulah Breeman thinks she's a catch and release!"

Zephyr has drifted over, probably to try to butter Lucy up. She broke up with him after Valentine's Day, deciding he was too immature, almost directly after they slept together for the first time. Despite the breakup, she says it was pretty romantic—that he brought freshly cleaned blankets to cover his truck bed and he was really sweet to her.

I'm not sure if Zephyr isn't over her yet or if he's just bored. We deal with a limited dating pool on the island, and I don't think Zephyr has too much pride to beg Lucy to take him back, at least for the summer. But whatever plan Zephyr had coming over here, he abandons it for some new and terrible idea. I can see in his eyes that whatever he has in mind, I'm not going to like it.

I point a finger at him. "Don't."

He ignores me. "You know what we have to do with a catch and release, right?" He grabs Tallulah around the waist and hauls her off her feet.

"Put me down!" she screams, kicking her legs. Braden, Zephyr's moronic best friend, grabs her ankles.

"Hey, stop it!" I pull roughly at Zephyr's shoulder. "Let her go!"

He shrugs me off easily, and I stumble back. "We gotta release her, Juniper Nash. That's how it goes."

They lurch toward the water, swinging a screaming Tallulah between them. I run after them, grabbing Zephyr's elbow.

"Don't, don't! Stop it!" My voice is strained from the effort of holding on to him. "Zephyr, you cannot throw her in!"

"Hey!" Cora calls, running down the sand with her guitar in one hand, Milo at her side. "What the hell are you guys doing? I could hear you all the way up at the house! I have neighbors, you morons!"

Hands reach past me, and suddenly Lucy has her elbow crooked around Zephyr's neck. She yanks him back so hard he makes a garbled choking sound and releases Tallulah. She slams shoulder-first into the sand. Graham knocks Braden out of the way and reaches down to help Tallulah to her feet, but she wrenches away from him and runs directly into me. When I stumble back from the force, Milo catches us both. Tallulah is shaking all over. I hold on to her tightly.

"You two are fucking idiots," Lucy snarls, shoving Zephyr away. She doesn't have to say what we're all thinking: that Tallulah's mother drowned in the ocean, and Tallulah watched it happen, and you can't just throw someone into the water in the dark, especially after something like that.

Tallulah must hear what Lucy doesn't say, because she jerks out of my arms and charges up the beach, stumbling in the sand.

"Tallulah!" I turn to Milo, panicked. "She still has her keys."

Graham appears at my side. "It's fine, I've got it." He shoves Milo toward Cora. "You stay."

Graham motions for me to follow as he turns and sprints up the beach.

Milo glances from me to Cora, who's still standing there with her guitar in one hand. His mouth hangs open, like he doesn't know what to do.

"Junie, let's go!" Graham shouts from up the beach, where he's caught a thrashing Tallulah.

I can't wait for Milo to decide, so I pat his arm before sprinting after them.

When I reach Graham and Tallulah, she's sobbing and trying to yank her arm out of his grip. He catches her free hand, holding her while I shove my hand into her pocket and grab her keys. She gets an arm loose and tries to elbow me in the face. I manage to dodge it, but she catches Graham in the stomach. He groans, his face paling.

"I'm so sorry," I say to him as we pull her toward the car.

"I'm fine," he grunts.

When we get the back door of her car open, Tallulah resists being shoved inside, holding on to the doorframe with a white-knuckled grip. It takes us five minutes to get her into the back seat and to put on the child locks so she can't make a grand escape.

"You really don't have to come with me," I say to Graham as we settle in the front. He looks exhausted.

Tallulah makes a snuffling, whining noise and slumps in her seat. "I really hate you. I should never have come tonight. I knew it was a mistake. I'm *such* an idiot." She wipes a hand over her face, smearing mascara in every direction.

She leans up to wrench open the center console and pulls out a pack of cigarettes and a lighter. Her hands are shaking so bad, she can't even get the flame up. Graham snatches the lighter out of her hand. She throws the unlit cigarette at him.

"Somehow I think you'll need my help getting her inside," he says. "I can walk home from your place."

Graham and I haven't truly been alone together in almost a year, and last time was a very different vibe. Tallulah might be here as a buffer, but what happens after we get her in bed? My nerves start sparking like live wires.

I put on a bright smile and try for normal, hoping he can't sense what I'm thinking. "Milo totally owes you. Wingman of the year, or what?"

If Graham feels any of the weirdness between us, he doesn't show it. He slouches in his seat and yawns. "Yeah, well. He needs all the help he can get. The guy has no idea how to prioritize."

I frown. "What does that mean?"

Graham coughs. "Nothing. Never mind."

Tallulah begins to laugh, a high, hysterical sound that pierces like a needle. "You two are so fucking boring, I can't stand it." The laughter turns into keening, and then she's crying again, but with that big, scary smile on her face. "Just take me home."

I watch her in the rearview mirror, then turn around to face her. "Tallulah, you know I can't do that."

She kicks the back of my seat.

"Stop it." I whip around to start the car. "I'm not itching to spend more time with you, either, but you'll never sneak into your house and past your dad like this."

"He doesn't care."

"Somehow I find that hard to believe, and I'm not risking my ass just so you can sleep in your own bed. You're staying at my house."

"You think you can sneak past your mom?"

"Yes," Graham says before I can. "Junie's room is closest to the front door."

He's right—it ends up being almost too easy. Mom isn't even home yet, and the walk from the front door to my bedroom is four steps.

As I shove Tallulah into my bed, I hear the fridge open and shut. I'm slipping her sandals from her feet and narrowly avoiding a heel to the chin when Graham reappears with a water bottle, cracking the seal and then reclosing it gently. He sets it on my nightstand, then turns and rummages around in the hall closet right outside my bedroom, returning with two Advil.

It's strange, having him back in my bedroom. My friends have been in my house since our fight, but we never hang out in my room. Graham hasn't stepped foot in here since last summer.

I wonder sometimes what would have happened if we'd had more time. If Rooney hadn't been a factor and Graham's family hadn't fallen apart. If I hadn't played a part in it. Would I have slept with him? *Probably,* I think, which is embarrassing when Graham won't even so much as hug me now.

But what's more embarrassing is the follow-up. *Would we have dated?* It's worse, because I think we would have. I was on the brink of wanting just about everything from Graham. It's nothing I haven't thought about before, but it feels extra dangerous now, in my house, when we're about to be truly alone for the first time in months.

I shake the thoughts from my head as I fluff my quilt over Tallulah. She quickly pushes it off, her long legs tangling in it.

Graham drags the little trash can from beside my desk to the side of the bed, then sets a hand on my back, which makes me jump.

I don't know what my face must look like, but Tallulah catches it all, her blue eyes gleaming in the light from my window. Her gaze flicks from me to Graham to the arm he has extended between us. She watches his hand fall back to his side.

Then she rolls over and buries her face in my pillow, streaking makeup across the pillowcase. My insides shrivel.

"This is the worst," I mutter to Graham as we leave the room.

"Just think, you can have these fun sleepovers all the time when you live together," Graham says lightly as I follow him onto the porch.

I gape at his back. "Oh my God, why would you say something so horrible to me?"

He chuckles. "Make sure she sleeps on her side."

I shut the front door behind us. "Trust me, I'll be checking on her once an hour. The last thing I need is Tallulah dying on my watch. She'd probably haunt me out of spite."

"We'll be on basically the same sleep schedule then," Graham says. "The newborn method."

I freeze. "Oh."

He stops on the stairs, turning to peer up at me in the dark. I didn't switch on the porch light, so I'm relying on the glow of the moon to read his expression.

"Sorry," he says with a humorless laugh. "I don't know why I keep doing that."

"You don't have to apologize to me," I say quickly.

Graham blows out a breath, turning away. I think he's about to leave—strand this conversation before we touch on anything important. But instead, he sinks down onto the porch stairs.

I must stare at the back of his head for too long, because eventually he reaches over and pats the empty spot beside him.

"Yeah, I do," he says as I sit, leaving a healthy amount of space between us.

"No, you *really* don't." I lean forward, wrapping my arms around my knees. "I just want you to be my friend again."

He sighs, tipping his head back. "Jesus, Junie, we're still

friends. God." A laugh has hooked into his words, but it sounds more shocked than amused. "I thought we did this already."

The exhaustion in his voice sends guilt ricocheting through me.

"We did!" I say, my voice hitching up. "We are. I didn't mean it like that. I just meant that I want it to be the way it used to be."

Graham hesitates. "The way it used to be."

I look over in alarm. "Not—not like that. Before that."

He huffs out a nervous-sounding laugh. "Right. I wasn't assuming . . ."

"Of course not."

He turns his head, his gaze piercing. "I want that, too. To go back to normal. But you gotta stop avoiding me, Junie."

"I didn't mean to avoid you."

His mouth hitches up in a half smile. "Yeah, you did."

"I've been trying to give you space, or—or respect your boundaries, or whatever."

"Well, respect them a little less," he says, his smile wider but a little unsure. "Because you're making me feel like an asshole."

"That's not what I was trying to do. You're not an asshole. *I'm* clearly the asshole."

"You're not an asshole," says Graham. "You did a bad thing, but . . . I get it, okay? She took advantage of you. Made you think you were friends, and used you to get away with it. I've lived with her awhile now—I get how she works."

Rooney moved into Graham's house almost as soon as Graham's mom moved out. Angela, who was Rooney's roommate and best friend, was furious about what Rooney had done, especially that she involved me. I never told her or Mom how

I'd lied for Rooney—never told anyone, really, except when Graham confronted me. But after a summer of ice cream and life talks and movie nights with me, it was easy for everyone to figure out that none of it had happened—that for Rooney, "hanging out with Junie" meant seeing Macauley Isham.

Angela and Rooney had a huge fight about it, and days later, Rooney was gone. She'd moved out of her apartment with Angela, and she never came back to P&J's. But no one expected she'd actually move in with the Ishams—or what was left of them.

"She's one of those people who can make you feel special, just by giving you attention," Graham says. "It's hard not to like her, and that's from me. I can't imagine what I would've done for her if I'd been you."

It's true that Rooney made me feel special. So special, she probably could have convinced me to do anything for her.

There was only one moment last summer when I hesitated. Rooney had bailed on Angela's roller derby matches a couple times to hang out with "me" instead, and Angela was giving me the third degree about what we had been doing. I thought she might have suspected something. I got worried about her figuring it out, and then telling my mom, so I tried to back out.

"Oh, don't be a big chicken," Rooney teased when I told her. "Angela's just jealous because she knows how close we are. She's probably worried I'm replacing her, but that's not even possible, because you could never be *just* my best friend. You're like my little sister. That's why I know I can rely on you for this stuff, because this is what sisters do for each other."

It was such a new feeling for me, being treated like someone who could be counted on. Everyone else either treated me like a kid—a kid they loved, but a kid nonetheless—or, in the case of my friends, someone messy and kind of a liability.

But Rooney never treated me like that. And when she called me her little sister, it created all these big, warm, fizzy-pop feelings inside me. Like most only children, I've always wondered what it'd be like to have a sister. Rooney was the epitome of what I imagined a big sister would be like—someone cool and fun, who made me feel like I could do anything. And she's like the sun—when she shines her light on you, you want to turn your face toward it.

I forgot how the sun can burn.

Looking back, it feels like I had Stockholm syndrome. It's embarrassing to think about how much I loved her, and how little she cared about me.

The most shameful part of all is that she could have roped me in with the simplest of threats. Sometimes I wish she'd just said, "If you stop helping me, I'll stop helping you." At least if she'd been terrible, I could admit I did it because I wanted Graham that badly. She didn't have to make me love her. I would have kept covering for her, just to keep him to myself.

"Don't give me too much credit," I say to Graham now, my voice quiet and my face hot. "It wasn't only because of Rooney. I wanted to do it for me, too. Because I wanted . . . Because we were . . ."

"Because you couldn't resist me," Graham says lightly, grinning over at me.

I shove him, grateful for the dark to hide what I'm sure is a bright red blush. It's the first time either of us has said something openly about last summer. Normally we skirt around it like one of our many conversational land mines.

"Look, it was gonna happen either way," Graham says. "My dad wasn't fooling anyone with those happy hour networking events—like we were supposed to believe it was for anything other than scoping out girls closer to my age than his. If it hadn't been Rooney, it would've been someone else."

"But that's not the point. It's not about what he did—it's about what I did. And how I handled it after . . ."

"Yeah, I gotta say, that sucked," Graham says, words skittering out on a laugh that isn't really a laugh. I can hear the hurt, covered up with a little bit of a joke, some lightness in his voice, frosting spread over the cracks in a cake. "It sucked a lot when you first did it. It really sucked when you kept doing it."

I blink at him, realizing the truth. That the way I've acted with Graham all these months, avoiding being alone with him and tiptoeing through every conversation, was never for him. When everything came out last year, I pulled away out of guilt, and he called me on it, and I remember exactly how he sounded when he said it. Like that was the worst thing I'd done. *I've spent weeks sitting here wondering why you pulled away when I needed you.*

I apologized, but what was that apology worth when I never stopped pulling away?

"I'm sorry. I totally abandoned you. I—I *keep* abandoning you. Giving you space you never asked for so I don't ever have to do the hard stuff. *God,* I don't know how you're so nice to me."

"Because I can forgive everything else if you'll be here for me now," he says, like I can erase what I did with something so simple—just being his friend.

I feel the tears crawling up, and Graham must sense

they're coming from my changing expression. "Oh no, not the Juniper Nash Cry Fest."

I sniffle, waving him off. "Don't joke around. I'm being serious."

"I am, too. I'm really hoping they have a ring toss. I want to win a goldfish that'll die in a week."

"That's actually a myth," I say, crying harder. "Goldfish are supposed to have a really long life span, but people don't know how to take care of them!"

Graham slides closer. "Geez, okay, okay, I'm sorry I brought it up."

"Stop apologizing to me." I press the heels of my palms into my eyes, my chest constricting tightly.

Graham huffs out a laugh. "No." He grabs my wrists, tugging my hands from my eyes. "Come on, Junie, stop crying."

"I don't deserve an apology; I never did. You were right about everything. What I did was selfish, and how I handled it was worse, and I'm *still* screwing up. You should hate me." My voice cracks over the word *hate* like even my body doesn't want to admit it. "No one would blame you. I'd blame you least of all."

Graham's expression tenses as he cups my face in his hands. "Hey. Stop," he says, brushing my tears away. "I don't hate you. My biggest regret with us is that I made you think I could."

It feels like everything around us has stilled, the night quieting, like it's holding its breath to see what will happen next.

And then Graham leans forward and wraps his arms around me.

The last time Graham put his arms around me, he had

me pressed up against the back of the half-pipe ramp at the skate park after everyone had gone home. That was two days before Rooney showed up at his house and everything was ruined. I couldn't stomach trying to touch him after, knowing what I'd done—even when he needed it. Not to make out, but to be held.

"I'm sorry," I say, pressing my face into his shoulder. "For what I did, and kept doing, and for making you reassure me when it's, like, the last thing you need to be worried about."

"Don't tell me what to worry about," he says, his hand drifting up and down my back. The rhythm calms my wild heartbeat, and I wonder if he does this with Owen—rubs his back when he's fussy.

Considering how much I've cried tonight, it's not beyond the realm of possibility that Owen and I have a lot in common right now.

It should feel dangerous to hold on to him this long. But I don't want to let go, and Graham doesn't seem to want to, either.

I shift slightly when my back starts to ache, and when my bare leg brushes his, all those warm, shooting-star feelings I've tried to suppress go racing through me. And I don't know how to deal with that, or how to keep it off my face, so I say, "Welcome to Prickle City. I haven't shaved my legs in a few days."

It's like taking a hammer to the tension. Graham laughs, and the discomfort of the last seven months shatters around us like broken glass, tiny shards glinting in the moonlight.

We pull away, and it feels like this could be natural for us—hugging between friends. We can get back to what we were. Graham lounges back on the step behind us, and I mirror him. Our elbows overlap, and we nudge each other, fighting for space.

"You look really fucking scary right now, by the way," Graham says after a while.

"What?" I croak, shooting up straight. "Why?"

He holds up a hand, showing me the black streaked against his thumb. "Raccoon eyes."

I swipe at my cheeks, glaring at him. "Thanks for the heads-up."

He grins. "You're welcome." Then he checks his phone and grimaces. "I should get home."

"Must be nice," I say as we stand. "You get to go home, and I have to stay here with the drunk demon."

Graham chuckles. "Owen could out-demon Tallulah any day. You haven't heard him scream."

I still feel the twinge of remorse, but its hold on my heart is looser. Like maybe one day Graham will mention his younger half brother, and I won't feel any guilt at all.

"Hey, what did you mean earlier?" I ask as Graham heads down the steps. "When you said Milo doesn't know how to prioritize."

"Ah." Graham groans, like he was hoping I'd forget. "It's no—"

"If you say *nothing,* I will wring your neck."

"Sorry, I'm not really into that kind of thing," he says lightly.

"Graham."

"God, fine. Because Milo tends to put you before everyone else, and it makes girls feel bad."

"Oh."

His eyes flick up to mine, but it's dark enough that I can't read his expression. "And it reminds them that everyone's just waiting for you two to get together."

The heaviness of Graham's stare almost makes me look away. *Almost.* We both know what a loaded statement that is.

Graham shrugs, holding up his hands. "You asked."

I watch his retreating back until he reaches the end of the street and I can no longer see him.

Everyone's just waiting for you two to get together.

I wonder if that includes Graham. If maybe it always has.

Chapter Seven

PUCK
We'll fix these flowers, but for a price.

OLIVIA
What should you want from us for something so small?

FAIRY 1
We fairies do love a party.

OLIVIA
You want to come to the wedding?

VIOLA
(*Pulling Olivia aside.*) Absolutely not. We can't allow it—they'll wreak havoc.

PUCK
(*Dramatically.*) O deadly sin! O rude unthankfulness!

OLIVIA
Oh, please don't cry! You can come—you can all come! Just fix these flowers, please, I beg you.

VIOLA
(*Breaking the fourth wall, to the audience.*) Let it be known I said this was a very bad idea.
                    —Act 1, Scene 7, *Midsummer Madness*

samantha markum

Mom has never been the lecturing type, but as Tallulah and I sit at the kitchen table while she rails at us about the dangers of underage drinking, it strikes me that she's not half bad at it. She's just angry enough that she sells it, and disappointed enough that we feel bad.

Well, I feel bad. I don't know what Tallulah is feeling. Probably the steady knock of her brain against her skull.

When Mom got home last night, nothing could hide the sound of Tallulah retching from behind my bedroom door. My only comfort is knowing Tallulah feels like white-hot garbage this morning. It's only fair when I'm getting read the riot act, too.

"I should have known when you texted me about Tallulah staying over that it was too good to be true," Mom says to me. "I had a bad feeling about that party, and I was right."

I can't even defend the party after what happened with Zephyr. Tallulah got blasted all on her own, but the party *was* a disaster. Mom doesn't know the half of it.

"And now you've both put me in this terrible position where I decide your fate," she continues, dropping into her chair at last.

"To be fair, I wasn't drinking, and you've always decided my fate," I say, reaching for the chive-and-onion cream cheese.

Mom fixes her laser-point gaze on me, and I shrink back in my seat.

While I slump there, stomach growling, I add my bone-liquefying hunger to the list of things that are *all Tallulah's fault.*

"If I don't tell Paul about this, then I'm sending the message that it's okay for you to act this way, and I'm taking away his right to parent. But if I do tell him, I'm sure this

104

will be a red mark on my record with you until you're about twenty-seven and can understand why I had to do it."

Tallulah rubs her temples.

Mom picks up her coffee and takes a generous gulp. She should be at P&J's right now, but she had Elden cover for her so she could be here when Tallulah woke up.

I've been awake for ages, trying to figure out if I'm in trouble, too, or if it's just Tallulah. I mean, really, all I did was make sure she got home safe and had a trash can to throw up into. I should get a medal.

"Not to mention I have to tell Cora's parents that she had alcohol at this bonfire."

I jerk up. "Whoa, Mom, no. *No.* You can't tell Cora's parents about this."

"I know you don't understand how parenting works yet, Juju, but I have to. I'm the adult here. Someone could have gotten hurt last night. What if one of those kids drove home?"

I picture Zephyr's truck and Sloan's Mini-Cooper parked outside Cora's house. Had Sloan been drinking? Did someone take Zephyr's keys?

"Zephyr Gaines brought the beer," I say. "Cora had nothing to do with it." I'm not sure this is strictly true, but I'm not feeling all that generous toward Zephyr.

Mom looks unsure.

I get up and wave Mom toward the kitchen, away from Tallulah, though I'm pretty sure she's fallen asleep sitting up.

"Mom, you can't do that to Tallulah," I whisper when we're far enough away. "If the Kalisches tell Cora you told them about the drinking, everyone will know it's because Tallulah got caught. She already has a hard time making friends."

Mom glances toward Tallulah. She has her head on the table now.

Definitely asleep again.

"Okay," Mom says at last. "I'll talk to Zephyr's parents. But there's no getting around the Paul issue. I have to tell him."

I breathe a sigh of relief.

Then, remembering I'm perhaps not on the chopping block but still very near it, I pull that breath right back in. "So, am I in trouble?"

Mom eyes me. "How long has that been beating to get out?"

"Only about ten hours."

"Were you drinking, Juniper Nash?"

I put my hand over my heart and hold the other in the air. "Hand to God, I was not. I drove Tallulah's car here, and I'd never drink and drive."

Mom watches me for a long time—too long. I see the moment her gaze shifts from observing to calculating, and I start to feel itchy.

"Mom?"

Her mouth curls into the kind of bland smile I've come to associate with bad things. It's the same smile she got when she suggested family dinners.

"Oh no," I mutter as she returns to the table. I follow, a fluttery, panicked feeling in my stomach.

"Okay, Tallulah. You're gonna stay here for a few hours while you work through that hangover—"

"Mom, she's not hearing you right now." I use one hand to lift Tallulah's head, and she blinks blearily at us.

Mom lets out a weary sigh. "Are you listening, Tallulah?"

Tallulah grunts.

"Okay. You're gonna stay here and sleep off that hangover. I expect you at P&J's for your shift this afternoon. I'm taking your keys with me, so don't get any clever ideas. After work tonight, you and I will go to your house and talk to your dad, and maybe he'll be amenable to the idea I have of how you can make up for your behavior last night."

Tallulah nods slowly. "Okay. Anything else?"

Mom seems surprised that there's no argument. Obviously parenting me has scarred her. "Well. No. I guess not."

Tallulah pushes back from the table and stumbles to my bedroom. She shuts the door behind her, and I hear the creak of my ancient bed. I imagine she face-planted into my pillows again.

I hope—but not too hard—that she doesn't smother herself in there.

"An idea of how she can make up for her behavior?" I raise my eyebrows at Mom. "Why do I feel like this is about to end badly for me?"

Mom smiles. "I think it'll be very character building for you."

"I have enough character," I say. "I'm *full* of character. Just ask my drama teacher."

Mom picks up her coffee and drains it. As she sets her mug in the sink, she says, "Keys, please."

I finish slathering chive-and-onion cream cheese onto my now-cold toasted bagel. Then I get up from the table and go to the couch, where I stashed Tallulah's keys under one of the cushions I slept on.

As I hand them over to Mom, I swear she looks impressed.

When she leaves to run some errands, I head out to the dock. Milo is out there, hosing off his family's small fishing boat while Cosmo runs back and forth, snapping at the stream of water.

Milo shuts off the hose and calls, "Morning." His voice is

rough with sleep, and his hair sticks up wildly. "How's Tal-lulah?" He picks up one of Cosmo's toys from the dock and flings it into his backyard. Cosmo charges after it.

"Sleeping it off. She threw up most of the night."

He winces. "I'm sorry I didn't go with you. I should've been the one—I mean, you know I'm not normally like that."

I flap a hand in his direction. "Not even worth an apology. Graham and I had it under control. He practically carried her inside for me."

Milo hesitates. "So . . . you and Graham . . ." He trails off, like he isn't sure where to go next. I can tell he wants to know how things went but doesn't want to acknowledge that things were ever off in the first place. Lucy's method the last seven months has been to throw Graham and me together, where Milo's was to not acknowledge any of the weirdness and hope it would disappear on its own.

Eventually, he settles on: "You two were . . . okay?"

"Yeah," I answer, my voice like a whistle. I clear my throat and try for a tone more suited for human ears. "We actually— We talked. I think things will be . . ." I release a breath, and it whooshes out of me as if I've been holding it for the last seven months. I smile. "I think we're good."

Milo's relief seems to mirror my own so perfectly that I feel a prick of guilt. I knew the weirdness between Graham and me was weighing on us all, but I never considered that it might weigh heavier on Milo and Lucy than anyone else— that the burden to keep things normal had fallen on them.

"Nice. That's good to hear," he says, shaking out the kinks in the hose. Cosmo abandons his toy and returns to bite at the rubber while Milo quietly scolds him. Milo unearths an-other toy from beneath a shrub and hurls it into the yard.

Cosmo bounds after it, and Milo turns back to me. "But I still should've gone with you. It was pretty uncool of me."

I shoot him an exaggerated sympathetic look. "It's okay, Space Boy. Being uncool is sort of in your nature. I mean, look at your interests." I wave a hand at the telescope folded up against the wall outside their sliding glass door.

His expression flattens in annoyance, and he points the hose's spray nozzle at me, a silent threat.

I hold up my hands, backing away. *"Besides,"* I continue, "I know you were just blinded by love." I widen my eyes and bat my lashes at him. "Cora's very pretty."

Milo's face reddens.

I grin. "So, how was the tour of her bedroom?"

The red deepens until his light brown skin looks sunburnt. "Juniper Nash."

My jaw drops. "I'm being *two-named*? So, you're telling me you got to second base."

He goes a shade of red I'm pretty sure has never been documented before. He flicks on the hose, arcing a spray of water across the canal. I squeal as I dart away, laughing wildly as I retreat inside the house.

Of all the inexplicable things on White Coral Key, Dot Slip's garden might top the list for sheer strangeness. Like most gardens in Florida, it grows year-round—but unlike other gardens, which are bound by the laws of soil and climate and sun exposure, Dot's garden can grow anything, anytime. And when you cut it away, it grows back fast—sometimes overnight.

No one has an explanation for it. When you ask Dot, she just smiles and says, "The garden must know I'm not a patient person."

In the center of the overgrown garden is Dot's house—a two-story beach cottage with a screened-in porch and a second-floor balcony. Dot often sits on the balcony like a queen overlooking her kingdom. Behind her house, mostly obscured from view by the main house and the garden, is a small guesthouse—my first home in White Coral.

Dot is the closest thing I have to a grandmother. My mom is estranged from her parents, and my dad lost his mom before I was born. His father lives in Miami and has never shown any interest in knowing me.

But in the same way I don't need aunts because I have Hal and the Barajas sisters, I don't need those other grandparents because I have Dot.

For better or worse.

She stands in the middle of her garden, her hands on her narrow hips. Her skin is sun-weathered tan, and her gray hair is long and twisted into a thick braid. She doesn't look much like the stereotypical grandmother, and she's got the personality of a honey badger. In her khaki shorts and work boots, she looks like she's about to lead a hike up a mountain rather than a short trek from her house to Piper and Junie's down the road.

It's Market Day, which means the shop at the front of the café is being restocked, with artists hand-selling their work. Mom hosts Market Day a few times throughout the summer, and Dot always takes it as an opportunity to unload flowers from her garden. We sell Dot's flowers year-round at P&J's, but she can really clear away a chunk of overgrowth on Market Day, when tourists flock to the café in droves.

"Watch those thorns," she says in her gruff voice as I manhandle a bundle of roses. "I keep telling you to wear your gloves. You can catch a nasty infection from a rose thorn."

I grimace and slide on my gloves, my hands instantly beginning to sweat.

"Okay, roses, marigolds, periwinkles, sunflowers," I call to her as I check the collection in my large basket. I've been here for an hour already, helping her cut away pieces of her garden. "Where are the peonies?"

"In the buckets by the gate," she says, rolling her wheelbarrow past me. I glance toward the gate and spot three buckets of water, where the peonies are soaking upside down to get rid of the ants. "Grab them on your way out. And push this thing, would you?" She drops the wheelbarrow without warning, and metal clangs against the stone path that weaves through the garden.

I sigh as I straighten from where I'm crouched beneath the rosebush. By the time I get the peonies from the buckets and push the wheelbarrow out onto the sidewalk, Dot is halfway to P&J's.

"Why are you in such a rush?" I shout, pausing to brush my fingers over the juniper bush at the edge of the yard.

"Because we're running late!" she calls back.

I groan as I heft the wheelbarrow higher and begin to run.

Market Day is swinging into action when we arrive. I struggle to get the wheelbarrow through the front door while Dot barks instructions at me. By the time Angela abandons the line of customers at the counter and comes to help, there's a backup of people behind me. Inside, a line stretches all the way through the café, and I spy Mom running food to help Darius while Moonface works the register.

In the shop, Dot's first display is already full of her regular stock, but a second one has been set up without us. Dot being the former mayor and most loved person on the island has its perks.

Hal is perched on a table in the corner with her smaller sculptures, her bare feet dangling over abandoned sandals. Her hair is tied up in a scarf, dark curls spilling out the front and across her forehead. She's wearing a big blue apron over a pair of orange floral overalls and a white T-shirt. Her dark skin is streaked with old clay and paint, which must mean she was working either through the night or early this morning. She and Moonface share a little bungalow a few blocks away, and the entire backyard is Hal's outdoor studio.

Hal's corner of the shop is always well stocked, but her sculptures sell fast. She doesn't necessarily need to be here to hand-sell her work, but I think she likes participating in something so very White Coral as Market Day.

"Right on time," Hal says as we approach. "They just got here."

When I realize she's speaking past me, I glance over my shoulder and drop the wheelbarrow in shock. One metal leg lands on my foot, and I yelp.

"The line was long," Tallulah says as she stalks past me and sets two cups of Mom's morning raspberry tea on the table next to Hal. Tallulah's pastel mermaid hair is pulled into a messy bun, and she's wearing a pair of loose jeans with the knees cut out and a cropped T-shirt over a bikini top. "And I was talking to Piper about how bad plastic cups are for the environment. There's zero reason to use plastic when there are so many alternatives nowadays."

"What . . . ?" Distantly, I'm aware of Dot saying something to me, but I'm so hyperfocused on Tallulah, it's like the rest of the café has faded into a different realm. "Why are you here?"

Tallulah turns, stabbing her paper straw into the lid of her tea. She shakes the cup so the ice clacks against the sides. "Serving my sentence. Why are *you* here? Nothing better to do on a Sunday?"

"Because she enjoys our company," Hal says, and reality comes screaming back in with her words. "Don't worry—you will, too, eventually. Pretty soon, we won't be able to tear you away from Market Day."

Tallulah rolls her eyes. "Yeah, right."

Dot smacks me in the exact center of my back. "Get the wheelbarrow out of the way before someone trips and kills themselves on it." While I was busy gaping at Tallulah, Dot finished unloading the flowers, and the wheelbarrow now sits empty.

Tallulah leans against the table, watching me over her cup. "Your mom decided this would be a great punishment for getting drunk at the bonfire. Coming into work three hours before my shift so I can volunteer at Market Day. My dad agreed because he's a suck-up."

I glare at her. "That's rude."

She continues like I haven't spoken. "I figured you'd be stuck here for aiding and abetting my crime, but it sounds like you do this for fun. Which I guess is punishment enough." She takes a sip of her tea.

I plant my hands on my hips. "You know what—"

"Juniper Nash!" Dot barks. "The wheelbarrow!"

I grit my teeth and turn away to grab the wheelbarrow. I spin it around and nearly take out a man passing by with an armful of take-out containers.

"Sorry!" I call as he hurries away with a frown.

I struggle to get the wheelbarrow out the door, holding

up the line until Angela groans loudly and shouts, "Tallulah, for the love of God, help her!"

Which is how Tallulah and I end up arguing at the entrance for three minutes while people start to lose their vacation cool, crowding around us to get in or out of the café.

"If the fire marshal sees this, we're toast," I say.

"Why did you even bring it inside?" Tallulah demands, finally yanking the front of the wheelbarrow through the door. We spill out onto the sidewalk, and people stream out behind us like ketchup loosed from a clogged bottle. "God, I should've never gone to that stupid bonfire with you. I should've just let my dad look sad and pathetic about it. I'm fine watching you struggle, but I don't want to be involved."

As I park the wheelbarrow outside, I whip my head around to glare at her. "You know, I invited you to that bonfire as a gesture of goodwill. You don't have to throw it in my face because you couldn't handle yourself. I was trying to be nice."

Tallulah snorts her derision. "No, you weren't. You invited me because you knew it'd *look* like a gesture of goodwill, and you didn't want to miss a party."

I press my lips together, my jaw clenching so tight, it aches.

Tallulah's eyebrows twitch in satisfaction, and she stalks back inside.

"That was intense."

I slump, turning toward Lucy as she glides up on her roller skates.

"Sounds like she's got you all figured out," she adds, grabbing my arm so I can pull her along to the front door.

"She thinks she does," I say as I tug her into the café.

Lucy pushes off, sailing past me across the polished concrete floor.

"Lucy Bayonne, I told you no skates in here!" Angela calls after her. "We've got breakables!"

"Sorry, Angela!" Lucy pauses at a table, leaning her butt against it as she slips off her skates. "But I have to practice if I want to join Intoxiskated in a year!"

Angela rolls her eyes, the corner of her mouth lifting in a half smile. "I don't care if you turn eighteen early. We don't take high schoolers."

But Lucy isn't deterred. "Hey, everyone makes exceptions eventually."

"Not us," says Angela.

Lucy shrugs, a haughty look on her face. "We'll see about that when I'm the best skater in the county."

Angela snorts. "Oh lord, you've got long way to go!"

Lucy's expression sours. "She has no faith in me," she says to me as she takes her sneakers from her bag and pushes her feet into them.

"She's a naturally skeptical person. I'm sure if anyone can change her mind, it's the unyielding Lucy Bayonne."

Lucy gives a little bow. When she straightens, her eyes brighten as she spots Tallulah standing with Hal. Tallulah's expression doesn't quite change, but her gaze sharpens with something like apprehension.

"Hi!" Lucy says, bounding over to them. She pauses at Dot's flower display. "Oh wow, Dot. These peonies are gorgeous."

Everyone loves peonies. They're fluffy and delicate, and they look great in a vase.

"Take some," Dot says, because of course she does. Dot's

display in the shop barely pays for itself. She always ends up giving half her stock away, just to be rid of it.

"Really?" Lucy reaches out and smacks the back of her hand against Tallulah's arm. "Help me pick."

"Oh, um." Tallulah hesitates and— Wait, is she blushing? "Okay?"

Some days more than others it's extremely obvious Tallulah isn't accustomed to regular social interactions. She seems surprised that even Lucy, a certified golden retriever, would be kind to her.

While they pick through the selection, I collapse into the single folding chair beside the display. I don't like watching Tallulah socialize with my friends.

"Get up, lazy," Dot says, smacking my leg with one of her gardening gloves.

I jerk up and glower at her. "Lazy? I've been up since eight helping you, and I was on time!"

"For once," Dot says, which is fair. I'm usually at least ten minutes late. Something about leaving the house with enough time to make it somewhere evades me. I usually find myself leaving at the same time I'm supposed to be wherever I'm going. It's my worst habit, though not too terrible a sin when everything on the North Shore is a ten-minute-or-less walk from my house.

I'll probably have to get it together when I live on the South Shore and things are farther away. My stomach sours at the thought.

Dot smacks my leg again. "Up, Juniper Nash. Lounging around all day is just preparing for the casket. You've got to suffer a little so you know you're alive."

I drag myself to my feet. "Aren't I suffering enough?" I ask, motioning to Tallulah.

"Not as much as I am," Tallulah says sweetly.

Lucy gives me a warning look. I notice she doesn't use it on Tallulah, which feels massively unfair.

"You two," Hal says from her table, where a passing couple has paused to admire a small sculpture. "What are you gonna do when you're living together? Will it be World War Three at all times?"

"I'm more of a Cold War kind of person," says Tallulah.

I don't know the difference, so I wisely choose not to speak.

"You'll exhaust yourselves eventually," Dot says. "Siblings always do."

"That's true," says Lucy. "Even Ruby and I can't stay mad at each other too long. And as you know, my sister is demon spawn."

I nearly drown on dry land. "Excuse me? We aren't siblings."

Hal shoots me an amused look. "Just a matter of time, Junie. Most only children dream of having siblings. Didn't you two ever want a sister?"

I stare at Hal, then Tallulah. She looks equally horrified.

Sisters.

Right when I was getting used to the idea of living with her, someone had to throw that word into the mix.

Because of course I dreamed of having siblings growing up. I envied Lucy with her older sister, Ruby, even as hostile as their relationship could be, and the Klingmans with their six kids. I wanted an older sibling to look up to, or a younger sibling to take care of. It's the reason I so eagerly jumped at the chance to be close with Rooney.

The universe *would* fulfill that dream by giving me Tallulah. The quintessential wish with strings attached. I'll get a sibling, sure. But she hates everything about me, and we'll probably never get along, no matter how many play practices or shifts at P&J's or Market Day mornings we share together.

"Sure," I say to Hal, my voice flat. "This is a dream come true."

Tallulah turns away and flips me off behind her back.

Chapter Eight

BENEDICK
Shall I compare thee to a summer's day?

BEATRICE
(Fanning herself.) If it's *this* summer's day, you're a dead man.

BENEDICK
Why, my precious wife, do you not find the weather agreeable?

BEATRICE
That depends. How close are you feeling to heat-stroke?

—Act 1, Scene 4, *Midsummer Madness*

From: Katherine Liu
To: All
Subject: Audition Results
Mailing List: <wckct.all.tdc>

Hello everyone,
Here are the results of the auditions for *Midsummer Madness*.

Olivia: Sophie Keller

Sebastian: Abe Rivera

Viola: Camila Lopez

Duke Orsino: James Soltenberg

Beatrice: Junie Abreheart

Benedick: Will Heinbach

Puck: Ireland Tuohy

Orlando: Ted Neuberger

Rosalind: Selena Morales

Jaques: AJ Dayal

Rosencrantz: Jed Loveland

Guildenstern: Carl Bilstein

Wedding Planner: Hourig Papazian

Queen Titania: Annie Engel

Duke Senior / King Oberon: Lou Strey

Fairies / Midsummer Players / Montagues and Capulets / Ensemble: Lucy Bayonne, Derek Johnson, Harrison Tsing, Vanessa Jordan, Lydia Kochani, Elizabeth Naidoo, Jamil Bukhari, Peter Choi

Crew: Jodie Ladhoff, Joel Gonzalez, Milo Abadiano, Alana Ornstein, Graham Isham, Tallulah Breeman, Bridget Gutschke, Porter Wallace

I've attached the rehearsal schedule to this email. Please be on time.

> Sincerely,
> Katie Liu
> Drama Department
> White Coral Key High School

From: Junie Abreheart
To: Sophie Keller
Subject: Smoochies to your new beau

On a scale of one to plotting someone's death, how jealous is Peter that you're going to be smooching Abe Rivera?

From: Sophie Keller
To: Junie Abreheart
Subject: RE: Smoochies to your new beau

On a scale of one to plotting someone's death, how jealous am I that you get to kiss Will Heinbach?
(Don't tell Peter I said that . . .)

"You don't look so good," I say to Milo when he collapses beside me in the grass. His face is red, his T-shirt soaked with sweat.

We're at rehearsal, and the sun is just dipping below the horizon, finally blessing us with some much-needed relief. My face aches from the way I've had my brow furrowed all evening. Even with my sunglasses, the glare of the sun was relentless.

"He's not good. He's dying," Graham says as he flings himself down on my other side. "We all are. If I fall asleep, don't wake me. I'm hoping the Grim Reaper will come to relieve me from this mortal plane."

"You could always give up stage crew—"

"I love the sound of that," says Graham. "I quit."

"—and join the *cast*," I finish, an edge in my voice as I reach over to smack his arm. "You're not quitting."

"If I had to sing onstage, your next social event would be my funeral," he says without opening his eyes. "In fact, don't cut your losses yet. I'm not sure I'll survive the night."

While most of the cast was participating in the first read-through with Miss Liu, Jodie Ladhoff, our stage manager, had the stage crew hard at work prepping the set. Milo and Graham have been hauling huge pieces of wood and buckets of paint down from Jodie's truck for the last half hour.

"You need water," Lucy says, climbing to her feet. She tosses her copy of the script atop mine in my lap. "I swear, the two of you wouldn't survive a day without me."

I shoot Graham and Milo a haughty grin. It's rare that I'm excluded from the you'd-die-without-me lecture. "Yeah, *some of us* are self-sufficient."

"I meant you and Graham," Lucy calls over her shoulder.

"Wha—what!" I twist around to glare at her retreating back. "What did I do to deserve this kind of treatment?"

"Well, JN, some of us are self-sufficient," Milo says, his mouth stretching into a pleased smile.

"I don't like that you treat being lumped in with me as an insult," Graham says. He motions to the script in my lap with an anemic wave of his hand. "Could you fan me with that thing if you aren't gonna read it?"

"Hmm, what'll you give me?" I ask.

He sits up to make a swipe for the script with surprising speed for someone who was just claiming to be on the brink of death. I snatch it out of his reach, holding it above my head. Graham glares at me, and I make an exaggerated sad face.

"Ice cream," he says. "Two scoops, *plain* waffle cone. One week."

"I prefer a cup."

"Deal." He holds out a hand, and I pass him the pen I've been using to make notes in my script. Graham scribbles *1–1W* and his initials on a corner of Lucy's script, then tears it off and passes it to me.

He collapses into the grass and closes his eyes again.

I tuck the favor token into my pocket. "See how easy that was?" I lean over and fan his face with both scripts because I'm feeling generous. I glance over at Milo to see how he's faring and startle when I notice he's watching us.

He raises his eyebrows at me, glancing pointedly at Graham. I smile.

"This is a sight," Lucy says as she returns, arms laden with four cold water bottles from Miss Liu's cooler. She passes one bottle to Milo, and he cushions it under the back of his neck, groaning with relief.

"You're meant to drink it," Lucy says kindly.

"This is better," Milo replies.

I watch him, sprawled in the grass, long limbs stretched out and his shirt riding up. I twist my mouth up on one side, considering. I do wonder sometimes why Milo has never affected me the way everyone thinks. Objectively, he's very good-looking. He's dated a lot, so he's clearly appealing to the masses. But whatever button he pushes for everyone else must be broken in me.

"Thanks," I say to Lucy as she drops a water in my lap. The cold bottle on my leg draws my attention back to the present. As my gaze slides away from Milo, it snags on Graham, who is watching me through narrowed eyes.

My heart kicks up at the look on his face. *Is that jealousy?*

"You're slacking," he says, jerking his chin at the script in my hands.

Ah. Right. Of course not.

"You said to fan you." I sit back and flip open my script. "You didn't say for how long."

Graham's eyes widen. When he realizes I'm right, he collapses into the grass again. "*No,*" he says in agony.

I smile sweetly. "I think I'll have one scoop of strawberry and one chocolate. Or cotton candy and mint chocolate chip. I can't decide."

"You could've warned me," Graham says to Milo with a look of betrayal.

"Hey, it was your turn to lose to the Queen of Loopholes," says Milo. "Besides, you know how vindictive she is. If I'd warned you, it'd be me next—she'd make sure of it."

I give a dramatic gasp, placing a hand on my chest like I've been wounded. "I can't believe you'd say that about me."

"I'd say it twice." Graham sits up and swipes my water bottle from my lap.

"Hey!" I reach for it, but he smacks my hand away. Then he cracks it open and dumps half of it over his head. "Graham!"

He chugs the rest, then picks up his own bottle, holding a hand out to ward me off when I reach for it. He takes a long swig, his Adam's apple bobbing several times as he downs it. Water drips from his wet hair. My gaze follows a drop as it rolls down his jaw.

Graham finishes the second bottle in one go, then falls back into the grass with his eyes closed.

"Quite a performance," I say, watching his chest rise and fall rapidly as he recovers. "Are you sure you don't want to join the ensemble? I'm sure there's room for you."

He holds out a thumbs-up. "I'm good."

"Stage crew seems a lot harder," Lucy says thoughtfully. "I'd rather sing than pick up a hammer."

"Some would say your singing is like being hit with a hammer," says Graham.

She reaches over and smacks his arm. "I'm not that bad!"

The rest of us groan.

"You're all assholes," Lucy says, laughing despite herself.

"Don't worry, we're getting our punishment for it. We have to build a train," Milo says, finally sitting up to drink his water. He takes a few gulps, then belches into his sleeve before swiping his forearm across his mouth. "A *train*."

"Just think of it as conditioning," I say. "Keeping fit in the off-season."

"I don't have an off-season, and I don't want to be fit," says Graham.

"Between this and your new job, I don't think we'll be able to stop you." Lucy reaches over to squeeze his bicep and squeals in mock delight.

Graham's face is already red from the heat, but he flushes deep crimson as he shakes her off. His gaze skitters to me and then Milo before he tilts his head to look at her.

"Stop, you'll embarrass me in front of my new friends," he says, smirking in the direction of the stage, where a few guys from the basketball team are lounging, along with Alana Ornstein, Porter Wallace's girlfriend. A freshman from the Space Science Club, Jamil Bukhari, is hanging on the edge of the group, chattering away to Joel Gonzalez.

"Oh no, poor Joel. Jamil's got him," I say. Jamil is not known for being brief in his storytelling. When I went to the Space Science Club holiday party last year, he caught me for fifteen minutes showing me pictures of an eclipse his cousin in San Francisco took on his phone. It required some of my best acting skills to seem impressed.

"I mean, I'm sure he's used to listening to someone wax poetic about the moon after being on a team with you all these years . . ." I stretch my leg out to nudge Milo with my foot, and he catches it in both hands.

"Hilarious," he says flatly. He yanks my foot hard, and as my butt slides across the grass, I topple backward into Graham. My head lands on his stomach, and he lets out an *oof* of surprise.

"Sorry," I say to Graham as I aim a light kick at Milo's side. He whacks my foot away like it's an annoying insect and scoots out of reach.

"Fine," Graham says, his voice strained. "Only my appendix. Nothing important."

"That's on your other side, dear," Lucy says.

"Oh good, so my spleen," says Graham.

"And this is how we know Graham learned nothing in anatomy last year," Milo says with a laugh.

"Sorry, I just got a traumatic internal injury from someone's rock-hard head," Graham says, nudging the back of my head with his knuckle. "It must be affecting my brain function."

I shoot him a glare, and he grins.

I catch Lucy glancing between us, her gaze hopeful. But this is the light stuff with Graham. We've been pulling off this kind of behavior all year. Surface stuff has been easy. It's the conversational land mines that are a problem.

But I know the hopeful look in Lucy's eyes mirrors my own.

"Damn, do I need to go save Joel?" Milo asks, glancing toward the stage, where Jamil is still talking and Joel is looking around for an escape. "I don't want to save Joel. He beat my ass in a pickup game yesterday." He chugs the rest of his water, crushing the plastic in his hand.

"I'll go," I say, getting to my feet. "I need another water, anyway." I shoot Graham a pointed glare, and he responds with a twinkling smile.

When I reach the group by the stage, they all toss me various greetings. One benefit of being friends with Milo is that I'm peripherally known by the entire basketball team, though I've never hung out with them. Now that I'm alone, I feel my bravado slipping, so I try to put on a brave acting face. If there's one thing my time in Drama Club has taught me, it's how to fake it through a social situation.

"Hey, it's my lovely wife!" Will calls as I approach. My nerves ease.

Will was cast as Benedick, the other half of a warring married couple. I play Beatrice, his wife. We spend most of the play accidentally ruining different wedding events, like when Benedick hires a group of bootleggers, the Montagues, to bring in alcohol, not knowing the best man, Duke Orsino, has already hired their rivals, the Capulets. This mishap results in a brawl between bootleggers that ends in the wedding cake being smashed.

Will was surprisingly good during the first half of the read-through. I'm kind of worried he'll outshine me. It doesn't help that he's good-looking in that athletic kind of way. He has a strong jaw and a wide forehead, floppy blond hair, and light skin that's already golden from days spent at the beach. He looks like he could play a lifeguard on TV.

"Hello, darling husband," I say with a little flair, just to get some laughs out of the group. "How's everyone feeling? Filled with a love for the theater yet?"

"Filled with agony," Joel says, half turning from Jamil like I'm a walking escape hatch. Joel is the shortest guy on the team, closer to my height, which has always made him feel more accessible than the others. I gravitate toward him automatically. "This is worse than conditioning."

"No way. Conditioning with Coach Ehrich is pure torture," Porter says, waving his free hand at Joel. His other hand is clasped in Alana's. They're one of those couples that never seem to separate.

"You only think that because your girlfriend isn't allowed at conditioning," Harrison Tsing says from where he's perched on the edge of the stage.

"At least I have a girlfriend," says Porter.

Alana backs him up by reaching into the snack bag of chips they're sharing and lobbing one at Harrison.

Will ducks in front of him, catching the chip in his mouth. He whoops in celebration, banging his chest with his fists. "Did y'all see that?"

I notice Jamil inching away. The rest of the kids from the Space Science Club are still gathered onstage.

I take pity and grab a bag of chips from the snack pile. "Jamil?" I say, holding it up. "You want anything?"

He waves me off. "I had cookies."

"I'll take one," Joel says, holding up a hand.

I toss it to him, but it goes wide so he has to snatch it out of the air.

"The reflexes of an athlete," I say to Jamil.

Jamil laughs.

"Junie, you're such a great host," Alana says with a grin, hanging on Porter's shoulder now. He feeds her a chip, and she crunches on it happily.

"Just showing my appreciation," I reply. "I don't think I've actually told you all how grateful I am that you showed up for this."

Will smirks in Milo's direction. "Who could say no to that face? Besides, my dad had to cancel our Cabo trip, so I didn't have anything better going on."

I smile. "Nice. Always glad to be last choice."

Will grins. "Abadiano also seemed super desperate."

"Really?" I try to suppress my pleased smile.

Will and Porter exchange a glance.

Alana elbows her boyfriend. "Don't."

Joel peers into his chip bag, looking overly interested in its contents, while Harrison stares down at his phone. Jamil smiles at me like a puppy who has no idea what's going on.

Then Derek Johnson wanders up, eating a pickle in a bag. He's trailed by Vanessa Jordan, his girlfriend.

"Looks tense over here," Derek says, grinning like he can't wait to say whatever just popped into his brain. "What's the dill?"

Joel busts out laughing. "What the hell? Where did you get that?"

"I stopped at Publix on my way here. They've always got 'em in these juicy sacks in the deli."

"*Juicy sacks,*" Vanessa repeats in disgust, glancing up briefly from her phone.

Derek grins and tips the bag so he can drink the pickle juice.

I cringe. "Okay, I can't watch that. I have to go."

"What's the dill, Junie?" Derek calls after me while they all laugh. "*What's the dill?*"

Lucy glances up as I drop beside her in the grass. She eyes me. "What's the dill?"

"He's got a pickle." I pause, grimacing. "That's not a euphemism. Don't ask."

When Miss Liu calls that our break is over, we all climb to our feet except Graham.

He remains very still in the grass.

"Graham?" I nudge his foot with my own. "Let's go."

"Tell her I'm dead."

Chapter Nine

Lights go up on the forest, where SEBASTIAN sleeps on the ground while PUCK crouches beside him.

SEBASTIAN
(Still half asleep.) Hmm, Olivia? Or are you an angel that wakes me from my flowery bed?

(PUCK leans over him, grinning.)

SEBASTIAN
(Waking fully.) GOOD GOD! Who are you?
— Act 2, Scene 10, *Midsummer Madness*

"Why."

The word leaves my mouth so fast, I don't even have time to tack on a question mark.

"Hi, Junie," Paul says, stepping in from the front porch with a duffel bag slung over one shoulder.

"Hi. Um, what's with the bags?" I ask.

Mom ran out to grab takeout from the Chinese restaurant in Emerson, but she didn't warn me to expect guests.

"Could you pick up your jaw before someone trips over it?" Tallulah asks as she shuts the front door behind her. She swings her backpack off her shoulder, and it nails me in the stomach—not hard, but enough that I grunt.

"Oops." I can't tell from the flat, deadpan tone of her voice if it was an accident or not.

"Mush," Paul says, a light warning.

Probably not an accident, then.

Tallulah ignores him, disappearing down the hall to drop her bag in my room—for some unfathomable reason that does not align with the reality in which I'm living.

"Sorry to drop in on you," Paul says, setting his duffel by the chaise. It's the closest he can set it to Mom's room without putting it inside. Even though Paul has slept over before, I think he's hesitant to make it so blatant that he'll be sleeping in my mom's room tonight.

I suppress a shudder. We're pro-sex in this house, but I don't know if I'll ever be comfortable thinking about my mom . . . having . . .

I'll just save that kind of emotional maturity for my twenties. Maybe my thirties.

Judging by the look Tallulah gives me as she passes by me again, I should just be worried about *making it* to my twenties or thirties.

She opens the fridge and freezes. "Plastic water bottles?"

Paul sighs. "Mush, come on."

Tallulah whips around to glare at him. "Dad, we're a beach community! Do you know how much water bottles make up the plastic waste that ends up in the ocean?"

"No, but I'm sure you'll tell us," I say.

Tallulah shuts the fridge and turns to glare at me. "I know you like to be super flippant about everything, but there's no Planet B. We get one shot here." She reaches up to rub her forehead. "Just . . . tell your mom not to buy bottled water anymore. I'll get you reusable bottles. You can keep them in the fridge so they're always cold."

I blink at her.

She huffs a breath out through her nose. "And when you finish the ones you have, save the bottles and give them to me—don't put them in the regular recycling."

"Why, are you making a nest?"

She narrows her eyes at me. "Because there's a company making sustainable footwear using recycled plastic bottles and old shoes, and when you donate personally, they use your materials to make shoes for people in need."

I swallow. "Oh. Okay, cool."

When I glance at Paul, he's suppressing a proud smile.

"Sorry I'm late!" Mom calls as she comes through the front door, arms laden with two big paper bags. "They were packed tonight."

"A little warning next time?" I whisper as I take one of the bags from her.

"Sorry, Juju, I forgot," she says absently, setting her bag on the kitchen counter. She goes to kiss Paul, and Tallulah and I busy ourselves unpacking dinner. If there's one thing we agree on—and it really is probably just one thing—it's that watching our parents kiss is weird and kind of gross.

"We're having the house sprayed for bugs," Paul says to me. "We do it every year around this time. Normally we stay in a hotel, but your mom thought it'd be fun if we stayed with you this year."

From the pinched expression on Tallulah's face, she's thinking the same thing I am. *Fun* is not the word we'd use.

"For how long?"

"Juniper Nash," Mom says in warning.

"What?" I look up from the container I've popped open—crispy eggplant—and pass it to Tallulah. "I'm just asking!"

"Too long," Tallulah mutters as she serves herself some vegetable lo mein.

"Only one night," Paul says, slipping past me to grab his own dinner. He passes another container to Mom. "We'll be out of your hair tomorrow morning."

"You're not in our hair," Mom says, reaching around me to squeeze his arm. Trapped between them, I shoot a panicked look at the table, where Tallulah has already claimed a seat. Her grin is pure evil satisfaction as she pops a piece of eggplant into her mouth.

If they lean around me to kiss, I will absolutely lose it.

Mom must sense it, because she nudges me with her hip and then moves to my other side, putting herself between me and Paul.

I escape to the table. And because Tallulah looks far too smug, I reach over and spear a piece of eggplant on the end of my chopstick. "Let me try that."

"Hey!" she protests, but I've already eaten it.

"Yum. Thanks."

Tallulah rolls her eyes so hard, I'm not sure they'll return from the back of her skull.

"Hey, what's it look like in there?" I ask. "A big empty cavern?"

She turns her chopsticks and pretends to stab out her eye in frustration.

"Juju, enough," Mom says as she and Paul join us at the table.

I put on an innocent face as I twirl a bite of noodles onto

my chopsticks. "Hey Tallulah, wanna make a bet? Whoever finishes dinner first gets to sleep in the bed, and loser takes the trundle?"

Tallulah stares at me. "Bet?" She makes a face like she smells something bad. "No, thanks. Why would we do that?"

"I figured you'd want a chance to sleep in the bed tonight," I say, reaching over to swipe a piece of sweet and sour chicken from Mom's plate.

"I thought you'd be a generous host and let your guest sleep in the bed anyway," says Tallulah.

I bark out a laugh. "That's funny."

Mom clears her throat. "I think that'd be nice of you, Juju."

I whip around to stare at her, betrayed. "What?"

Mom's expression is admonishing as she says, "It's one night."

"Exactly!" I motion to Tallulah. "She'll be fine on the trundle for one night!"

"It's fine," Paul says, waving Mom off. "Junie shouldn't have to give up her bed just because we dropped in on you."

Mom frowns, glancing from Paul to me. Her expression doesn't change, but her gaze is pleading.

I purse my lips and point my chopsticks at Tallulah. "Or you could earn the bed, fair and square. You already had a head start."

"And you've been busy eating off everyone else's plates," Tallulah replies. She takes a few bites of eggplant until her cheeks bulge.

I respond with a heaping bite of beef chow fun and nearly choke on a particularly large piece of scallion. I feel it slither all the way down my throat.

As I'm taking gulps of water to wash it away, my phone buzzes on the table.

DAD

"Pause!" I say, pointing at Tallulah. "I have a call."

"No," Mom says, grabbing my phone. "We're eating dinner."

I turn a beseeching look in her direction. "Mom, come on. It's Dad!"

"No, Juju. You're not available right now." She silences the buzzing and sets my phone at the end of the table. "It's rude to take a call during dinner."

"But what if it's about August?" I say. "What if he's trying to make a plan or something?"

"Plans can wait. Nothing is so urgent that he has to speak to you right this second."

I clench my teeth, frowning as I turn back to my meal.

"August?" Paul asks when the silence stretches on too long. "Is your dad visiting, Junie?"

I swallow another bite of my dinner, nodding quickly. "Yeah, he's coming for the musical and my birthday."

Paul chuckles. "Well, if he's trying to get a room in peak season, it might be more urgent than you think," he says to Mom.

She blanches.

I frown, glancing between them. "He's staying here. With us."

Now it's Paul's turn to blanch.

When I glance at Tallulah, she's watching us all with an unreadable expression. Her gaze lingers on her dad.

Then I realize that while I've been distracted, Tallulah has cleared her plate. She dabs her napkin delicately against her mouth, her eyes narrowed in satisfaction.

"Enjoy the trundle," she says primly.

"Don't be a sore winner," Paul says to her with what seems like a forced smile.

Mom hesitates, then says, "I forgot to tell you."

Paul gives a small shake of his head, a signal. His expression isn't angry, or even upset. But I can tell he doesn't want to talk about it at the table.

I feel a rush of guilt, even though I have nothing to feel bad about. I didn't do anything wrong.

After dinner, we clear away the trash and wipe down the table. Tallulah announces she needs a shower.

I grab my phone, nearly tripping over my feet to get to the back door. "I'm going to call Dad back!"

As I curl up on the porch swing and lift my phone to my ear, I notice Milo out on his dock. I'd wave, but he has his eye firmly fixed to his telescope, and I know he's a hundred million miles from Earth right now.

Milo wants to work for NASA at the Kennedy Space Center. It's an extremely Milo kind of dream—the biggest space job he can get without going to space himself, and close enough to home that he'll be able to visit his family often. He's nothing if not perfectly practical.

I listen to the ringing on the other end of the line until Dad's voice mail picks up, the generic, robotic voice telling me he's not available.

I wait outside for a while, not wanting Mom to know. I want her to think it was a nice, long conversation. That Dad doesn't only call when it's convenient for him.

When I creep back inside, everyone is gone. I hear the shower running in my bathroom—Tallulah. Mom and Paul are in her room with the door shut.

As I tiptoe past, I hear whispers from inside.

". . . to tell you. I'm sorry."

"It's okay."

"It's not," Mom says. "You should have been my first call after she told me he was coming. I'm just used to doing everything on my own, and when stuff like this happens—I didn't think."

If Paul answers, it's too quiet for me to hear.

"You have nothing to worry about. Trust me, I have no lingering feelings for Damon. I've watched him break my daughter's heart too many times for that to even be a possibility. He's a big, self-centered child. Everything is everyone else's fault, and everyone is out to get him. He does this every time—gets her hopes up and then crushes them, leaving me to deal with the fallout."

"You think he won't come?" Paul asks, sounding surprised.

I bite my lip. *He will. He's coming.*

"I'd bet the house on it."

I can hear the smile in Paul's voice as he says, "Which house?"

"Oh, yours, obviously."

"*Ours,*" Paul says meaningfully.

They both get quiet, and I shuffle away from the door. Then I slip back outside and head down to the canal, counting out deep, calming breaths.

"Hey, Bigfoot," Milo says from across the water. He leans away from his telescope to peer at me in the dark. "What's with the stomping?"

"Nothing." I sit heavily at the edge of our dock and wrap my arms around my legs. I can't tell Milo about this conversation. He'd only agree with my mom.

No one has any faith in my dad but me. To them, he bails every single time. And maybe he does have stuff come up a lot. But he's made it a few times, too. They don't remember the times he came through, though. I'm the only one who remembers those, because to me, they meant the world.

Which means I'm the one who has to keep believing in him.

"Can I sit out here with you?" I ask. "I'll be quiet."

Even in the dark, I can see Milo's frown. "Of course. Are you okay?"

I swallow hard. "I'm fine. I'd just rather wait to go back inside when I know Tallulah will be asleep."

"Tallulah?"

"Oh yeah. It's one big happy family sleepover at the Abreheart house."

Milo makes a low humming noise. "You can stay out here as long as you want. I'll probably be out here all night. I'm hoping to see the June Bootids."

I snort. "June Booty? That's not what that telescope is for, young man."

I can hear the eye roll in his voice as he says, "It's a meteor shower—a weak one, but there might be a burst. You never know. The last one happened before we were born."

"So you'll just sit out here and wait and hope you see something?"

"It's all about patience," Milo says, returning his eye to his telescope.

I lie back on the boards and peer up at the sky, and I wonder what he's seeing.

When I wake in the morning, Tallulah is curled in my bed with the quilt pulled over her face. I can only see her mermaid hair splayed across my pillow. We had an argument before bed, when I came in and turned on the ceiling fan.

"I can't sleep with that on," she complained, going to the wall to flip the fan off.

"If you're cold, put on more clothes," I said, turning the fan on again. "I have sweatpants you can borrow."

Tallulah glared at me. "I'm not *cold*. I have sensitive nasal capillaries. I can't have all that air moving around—it dries me out, and I'll get a nosebleed. You want your sheets ruined?"

"I'll risk it." I cupped my hand over the switch, waiting patiently until she gave up and climbed into bed. She pulled the quilt over her head and didn't say another word.

She can never find out that I did, in fact, get cold in the night.

I adjust my T-shirt as I sit up, yawning. My hip aches from sleeping on my side atop the hard mattress. I can't remember the last time someone slept on this thing—probably four years ago, before Milo had his growth spurt. As soon as his feet started hanging off the end of the trundle, we moved our sleepovers to the living room. Though the couch isn't much better for him.

I glance at Tallulah, trying to judge whether she's awake. She snored like a middle-aged dad when she was drunk, but she was quiet last night, so it's hard to tell.

I roll slowly from the trundle to the floor, wincing when the metal creaks under my weight.

Tallulah doesn't stir.

I slip out of the room and close the door softly behind me, shoulders loosening with relief as soon as I'm in the hall. I'm finishing up in the bathroom, mouth minty fresh and face slathered in sunscreen, when I hear a noise from the other side of the house.

I stick my head out of the bathroom, frowning. The noise comes again, a pulsing buzz that sounds like a drill.

I check the clock on the stove as I pass through the kitchen. It's a little after nine, which means Mom is at P&J's, and I distinctly remember Paul mentioning that he had to work in the morning.

I follow the noise into Mom's bathroom, freezing in the doorway. I blink at the lime-green NEIGHBORHOOD HERO T-shirt and dark, messy hair in front of me. The French doors that open to the side of the house from Mom's bathroom are flung wide, letting in the balmy morning air. The doors lead to the outdoor shower, which Mom has used almost exclusively since she had it put in five years ago.

I note with a sour taste in my mouth that Paul's house doesn't have an outdoor shower.

Graham has his back to me, kneeling in front of one door as he drills a screw into a shiny, new hinge.

When the noise stops, I say, "Graham?"

He startles, twisting to look at me. Sweat drips down the sides of his face, his hair damp. He swipes it from his jaw with the back of his wrist.

"Hey," he says, a little breathless. He swallows, setting the drill aside and easing off his knees to sit on the tile. He groans, stretching his legs out the door so his feet hang on the stone walkway that leads to the shower. "Shit, that feels good."

My brain momentarily short-circuits.

Graham doesn't seem to notice as he sprawls back on the floor. "This job is killer. I feel like I've aged twenty years in the last four months."

I blink rapidly as my brain comes back online. "Aren't you supposed to be supervised when you're in someone's house? For safety?"

It's uncommon to see him without his boss, Rita, or one

of the other Neighborhood Hero employees. Rita Delgado is the wife of White Coral Key's real estate king, Tony Delgado, and she started Neighborhood Hero on a whim a few years ago. She's a Barajas sister, so drumming up business wasn't much of a chore—until she had so much business, she had to hire on help. Graham got the job in the spring, just before school ended. He's spent the last few weeks doing all their outdoor jobs on his own, or working on a team for the indoor jobs, since he can't do in-home jobs on his own until he turns eighteen in April.

"Usually, yeah. But it's your mom, so Rita made an exception." Graham turns his head to look at me, brows lifting. "Why? Am I in danger?"

My gaze slides over him—the lean muscles of his arms, the way his shirt has ridden up, the cut on his shin. My heart picks up speed.

No, but I might be.

Graham must sense we're heading into previously charted yet dangerous territory, because he sits up, hunching over his knees as he picks up the drill.

I linger, watching as he finishes.

When he reaches up to swing the door back and forth, testing the hinge, my gaze drops to the place where his shirt has pulled up, his bicep flexing with the movement.

"Why are you just standing there?"

I yelp, whirling to stare at Tallulah. She stands in the middle of the bedroom, rubbing sleep from her eyes.

"Jesus!" I gasp out, clutching my heart. "Make a noise once in a while!"

Tallulah drops her hand and rolls her eyes.

"Morning, Tallulah," Graham calls from the bathroom.

She leans around me to peer in at him. "Oh. Hey."

She doesn't seem surprised to see him, but I can't tell if it's because she expected him, or because this is her baseline. I've never seen Tallulah look surprised at anything. A comet could be hurtling toward Earth to destroy us, and she'd watch the news footage with a bucket of popcorn and a bored expression.

"Lucy's here," Tallulah says. "You didn't hear her knocking?"

I frown, turning toward the living room. "No."

"She said to tell you she brought a maple bacon."

Graham lurches to his feet.

"Absolutely not, this one's mine," I say when we get caught in the bathroom doorway.

Graham boxes me out with his shoulder, but he only makes it a few steps across the bedroom before I grab his shirt, yanking him back and propelling myself forward. He catches me around the waist, swinging me to face the opposite direction as he trips through the bedroom doorway into the living room.

I bodycheck him into the chaise, and he tumbles onto the cushions as I sprint around the armchair and make a dive for the doughnut box, searching for the hottest of commodities, the rarest of rare doughnuts, the golden ticket to Hot Dough heaven—the maple bacon. People wait in line outside Hot Dough every morning just to get one.

I barely register Lucy standing in her banana-print socks and Hot Dough T-shirt as I tear open the box of doughnuts.

But Graham has recovered and caught up to me. His arms slips under mine, and he tries to knock my hands away from the box, but I get my fingers around the lone maple bacon of the bunch before he can reach it. As soon as I have it in hand, I let him push me out of the way.

Graham whips around when he realizes he's lost, but I'm

already sinking my teeth into the doughnut. It's still warm, and I have to resist the urge to close my eyes. It is *perfect*.

I ward Graham off with one hand as he tries to reach for it, flitting around me like we're playing basketball and I'm about to make a shot. His arms flap wildly as I wolf down the doughnut. When there's one bite left, he finally loses it and grabs my wrist. His mouth closes over the last piece, his teeth scraping my skin and his tongue sliding between my fingers.

I jerk back in surprise, my fist clenching so hard, my nails bite into my palm. My fingers are sticky with frosting.

Graham swipes a thumb over the corner of his mouth, his eyes narrowed on me. My brain fills with a hundred memories of the feel of his mouth and that warm, molten look in his eyes.

I turn away, my face heating.

"We could have shared," Graham says from behind me.

I let out a high-pitched laugh that's bordering on a hysterical screech. "Yeah, right!"

I'm hoping no one notices the shake in my voice, but when I glance at Lucy, her gaze is flicking between Graham and me like a tennis match. When she settles her stare on me, I feel a flush of embarrassment.

After a moment, she plasters on a smile and turns to Tallulah, who is biting into a purple doughnut with yellow frosting. "Do you like that one? The lemon lavender is usually the only one we have left after we sell out, but it's my boss's favorite, so she won't take it off the menu."

"I like anything lemon," Tallulah says.

"Is it because you have so much in common?" I ask, reaching past Lucy to grab a half-smushed French toast doughnut. I pluck a pecan from the top and pop it into my mouth before taking a bite. "Sour and acidic?"

"Full of health benefits?" Lucy counters, shooting me an arch look.

I pull a face. I didn't realize I was friends with the Tallulah Defense Squad. I'd love to know where the Juniper Nash Defense Squad is, but somehow they're never around when Tallulah tries to deliver a death blow.

Lucy turns her back to me, and I can hear the smile in her voice as she addresses Tallulah again. "Strawberry cheesecake is my favorite. You should try it." She picks up the only strawberry cheesecake doughnut and breaks it in half, offering a piece to Tallulah.

Tallulah looks wary, but she accepts it. "Thanks."

Graham bites into a dulce de leche doughnut, which has cinnamon sugar on the outside and is filled with gooey caramel. Caramel spills out, dripping onto his T-shirt, and he groans.

"Whatever," he says around a mouthful of doughnut. "Probably won't be the worst thing I get on this shirt today." He lifts his shirt to lick the caramel off, and I get a brief flash of tan skin.

I see Graham shirtless all the time at the beach. I'm not about to be knocked on my ass by the sight of his torso.

But I turn away, because it feels a little safer.

"Hey, why'd my mom hire you to fix the doors?" I ask him as I pass half of the French toast doughnut to Lucy as a peace offering. She takes it, though she doesn't look entirely pleased. "I know they squeak, but she never really cared."

When Graham doesn't answer, I glance over my shoulder at him. He still has his head down, studying the caramel stain on his shirt. "Uh, well, she said she wanted to fix them before the house goes on the market."

Right. Because we're moving. My body goes cold, and the swift internal temperature change makes me feel suddenly ill.

Graham glances up at me, looking worried. "You okay?"

I take in a deep breath. "Yeah, I'm fine."

Lucy and Graham exchange a look. Tallulah watches me with a scary kind of intensity.

I glance around the kitchen, and it hits me, maybe for the first time for real, that I'm leaving this house soon. Not for college, but for something permanent. I won't be able to return and sleep in my childhood bedroom.

We're moving out, and we aren't coming back.

I take another breath and hold it. I don't want to freak out in front of Graham and Lucy, and definitely not in front of Tallulah.

I'll save the tears for when I'm alone.

There really isn't time for sentimentality anyway. Not when Lucy suddenly yelps, "Oh my God, Tallulah, you're bleeding!"

My head snaps around. Sure enough, Tallulah has blood leaking from her nose. It drips onto her pink T-shirt, leaving bright red stains.

I feel woozy. "Oh no."

Lucy jumps into action, tearing paper towels from the roll by the sink. "Oh my God, oh my God, don't move! Or—I don't know—tilt back? Tilt back! Or is it tilt forward?"

Graham catches my arm as I sway. "If I pass out, don't let anyone take a picture of me," I say to him.

Tallulah grabs the paper towels and tilts her head forward, glaring at me. "I got it. This happens to me a lot."

"Oh, please tell me this is because of the ceiling fan," I say, turning to rest my forehead against Graham's shoulder.

Tallulah makes an outraged sound. "I told you I have sensitive nasal capillaries!"

I tilt my head up to look at Graham. "You're absolutely sure she didn't punch herself in the nose while I wasn't looking?"

"Junie," Lucy says in warning. Behind me, I hear the sink flip on.

Graham rubs my back lightly, his other arm tight around my waist. "You want to sit?"

"Sure." I start to slide.

"This is an interesting choice." Graham grunts, tightening his hold on me. "I meant in the chair."

"Oh, right." My voice is barely a whisper. I'm distantly aware that I'm pressed against him and still in my pajamas, no bra. But it's a little too distant for me to care. Plus, it's nothing he hasn't felt before.

My stomach turns. "I might barf."

"Do not," Graham says sharply as he sits me in the chair.

I sprawl, my head lolling back. Graham grabs a water bottle from the fridge and crouches in front of me as he cracks the lid.

"Don't you get tired of carrying girls around this house?" I ask. "First Tallulah, now me . . ."

"Never," he answers, offering me the water. He meets my gaze as I lift the bottle and take a sip. The water makes a cold slide down my throat, and Graham keeps his fingers poised on the bottom, ready to catch it if my hands fail. His nails are painted orange. They remind me of little Halloween pumpkins, and I smile.

"What?" he asks, a grin pulling at his mouth.

I shake my head.

"Tell me." His voice is firm but playful, and he squeezes my knee in a ticklish spot. I snort out a laugh, my leg jumping.

He catches my calf before I can knock him over. The palm of his hand sears my skin, chasing away the wooziness and the giggles until all that's left are my stupid, silly feelings.

I take another gulp of water, and I only feel a small wave of nausea as it settles ice-cold in my stomach.

Graham keeps his eyes on me, settling into a staring contest. When I blink first and snap the thread, his gaze returns to normal as he checks his phone. "I gotta head out."

"Shoot. Me, too," Lucy says as he disappears back into Mom's room. "My break's almost over." She finishes cleaning up a spot of blood from the counter and tosses the paper towels into the trash.

I grimace. "Straight from that carnage back to the doughnuts? I can't even *think* about food right now."

"Blood doesn't gross me out," Lucy says lightly as she heads for the door and grabs her skates. "If it did, I couldn't join Intoxiskated. Do you know how many skinned knees I've had to deal with learning how to roller skate? And that's just on my own. Once I'm on a team, it'll be brutal." Her smile is bright as the sun, like she can't wait to be absolutely pummeled.

"Oh, is there blood involved in roller derby?" I ask, my voice faint. "I had no idea."

Graham chuckles as he reappears with his toolbox, and I feel warm satisfaction slide through me.

Tallulah eyes Lucy as she finishes wiping her face and neck clean. "You want to do roller derby?"

"Yep!" Lucy beams at her as Graham opens the front door, letting them both out. "I plan to be the first high schooler to join. I have an early birthday, so I'll be eighteen in a little over a year. Then I get to skate with them until I leave for college. I've got a whole plan."

Tallulah looks impressed, which isn't something I'm used to seeing from her. It's kind of freaking me out.

"Hey, where's Milo?" I ask as Lucy and Graham start down the front steps.

"I texted him," Lucy says, "but he didn't respond."

"I think the better question is, where are Lucy's shoes?" Graham asks.

Lucy tosses a grin at him as she hops down the walkway in her socks. "I left them at work."

"That's actually not the better question," I say.

"He's probably still asleep. Or grounded," Graham answers as he follows Lucy to the Neighborhood Hero truck parked in the driveway.

I gape at his back. "*Grounded?* Grounded for what?"

"He got caught sneaking out last night. Or sneaking in, I guess."

"Scandalous," Lucy says with a giggle, rounding the front of the truck to the passenger side. Like most things between Graham and Lucy, the conversation about driving her back to work was silent and imperceptible. "I bet the sheriff loved that."

I leave the front door hanging open behind me as I move to the top of the steps. "How do you know?"

"He was texting me on his way home," Graham says as he sets the toolbox into the truck bed. "But he stopped texting back when he got there."

"Wait, wait. When I saw him, he was planning on being on the dock all night looking for some meteor shower. What did he sneak out for?"

Graham stops and turns, the driver-side door hanging open behind him. The look he gives me is pointed and knowing.

"Oh," I say, realizing. "To see Cora."

He gives me a quick finger-gun, then turns and hops into the truck. As he rolls the window down, Lucy leans across him and shouts, "Enjoy the doughnuts! And be *good*, Junie!"

I put a hand on my chest. "Who, me? I'm a perfect angel!"

I hear them laughing as Graham eases out of the driveway. Which is pretty insulting, if I'm being honest.

Chapter Ten

SEBASTIAN
I don't understand. Why remain married when all
you do is fight?

BENEDICK
If we didn't fight, we'd be bored.

ORSINO
You sound quite the fool, Benedick.

BENEDICK
Let me be that I am, and seek not to alter me.
—Act 1, Scene 6, *Midsummer Madness*

Miss Liu is blocking a scene between AJ Dayal, who plays
the melancholy Jaques, a comic-relief character who mostly
spends his time riling up different members of the ensemble;
and Sophie Keller, who is easily the best performer in our
group, which is why she plays our lead, the bride, Olivia.

AJ is a couple years older than us, but he was never in
Drama Club, even though he's really good. He's always done
community theater, though, because his mom is the music
director. She'll join rehearsal in a few weeks; right now, she's
at the indoor theater with the orchestra, learning the music.
I'm deeply jealous they get to practice in the air-conditioning.

I'm standing offstage with Camila, who plays the maid of honor, Viola; and Will, my partner in terror throughout the musical. He's studying his script intently. He's showing real promise as a musical actor for someone who, up until this point, has only shown promise at shooting three-pointers.

We're coming up on the scene where Will and I accidentally ruin the bridal party's flowers during a particularly nasty argument. What the characters don't know is that the real culprits are Rosencrantz and Guildenstern, two ghosts who don't know they're dead, who were led to the wedding by the mischievous fairies.

"Will is so hot," Camila whispers to me, her mouth so close, I feel her breath all the way in my ear canal. I grimace, shrugging her off.

"Yeah, sure," I respond, my voice quiet. "I guess."

Camila leans around me, blinking dreamy eyes at him. She's just one of several people in the cast who aren't immune to his floppy-haired, easy-grin charm.

"Hey, Will, think you'd ever join Drama Club?" Camila asks. "You're really good."

I try to shush her, but she ignores me.

Will considers her question with a thoughtful look that seems very exaggerated. "I don't know. Depends how many girls I'd get to kiss in the next one."

I pull a face. "Don't be gross."

"Ooh, Junie. Is my wife jealous?" He shoots Camila a playful look.

"Yeah, massively jealous," I say, glancing down at my script. "Hey, Camila, you're about to go on."

I'm sweating more than usual from the stress. I'm trying to be a responsible member of the Drama Club in my push to get voted president during the special election, but it's hard when Camila wants to stand here and joke around. I'm about to look bad by association, and that's the last thing I need. I was already ten minutes late to rehearsal today, which earned me a real stink eye from Miss Liu.

"Okay, Camila, I'll think about it," Will says, tossing her a wink. "Just for you."

She looks like she might actually swoon, and when her cue comes, she practically floats onstage.

I glance at my script. I've been following along, and we're at the part where Camila brings in the bride's ruined bouquet. The fairies will follow, Puck leading the way to make the bride an offer to fix the flowers if the fairies are allowed to attend the wedding. They'll eventually get the groom, Sebastian, played by Abe Rivera, drunk and whisk him off to Fairyland, leaving Viola, his twin sister, to step into his shoes during the ceremony so as not to delay. The bride and groom are *very eager* to be rid of their noisy, often violent guests.

Midsummer Madness is a difficult piece, because it relies on so many guests being onstage at the same time, and the ensemble fills the roles of fairies, the players from *A Midsummer Night's Dream* as the wedding band, and the Montague and Capulet bootleggers who will not stop trying to stab each other. But the chaos is part of the hilarity, especially with the ensemble. At one point the fairies change into the *Midsummer* players' costumes right onstage, and at another, Rosencrantz and Guildenstern wander into Fairyland only to encounter Montagues and Capulets hastily fitting themselves into fairy costumes.

Once Camila is out of earshot, I whisper to Will, "Maybe you could tell everyone you're joining Drama Club just until we have the special election, and then you can drop. You'd be one more vote for me, and that wouldn't hurt."

"Oh no, does my wife have a popularity problem?" He waggles his eyebrows at me. "Want me to work on 'em for you?"

"Yeah, Camila specifically would be a big help, actually." I'm only half kidding. I think Will can tell, because he laughs and goes back to his script, killing any chance of this becoming a real favor.

"Why does it sound like you're up to no good?"

I spin in surprise to face Milo. "Oh. Hello. No, I'm a paragon of innocence. Just reading my script." I flap the script at him for effect.

Will pretends to cough into his fist. "Liar."

I glare at him. "Listen, we don't need to take our marital problems offstage."

"Okay, I'll say it then," Milo says, coming up beside me. "Liar." He drops a sweaty arm across my shoulders, and I shudder with wild exaggeration.

"Ew, ew, gross." I duck away from him. "Why are you so disgusting?"

Milo lifts his shirt to his nose and sniffs. "It's just sweat. It's hot out here, JN. What do you expect?"

I dab delicately at my sweaty forehead. "You look like you went into the shower with your clothes on."

Milo gives me a look. "So you're thinking about me in the shower is what you're saying."

"I'm vomiting," I say. "I'm vomiting right now. In my mouth."

Milo holds up his hands. "You said it, not me."

"Listen, it's rude to be so familiar with me when my husband is *right here*." I motion to Will. "Please respect our marriage, even if I did try to stab him with a fork at dinner earlier."

"You almost got me for real," Will says. "You put a lot of force behind that stabbing motion."

samantha markum

"Oh, I'm sorry, dear." I reach up and pat his cheek. "I don't know my own strength."

"Maybe we should switch if you're so strong," Milo says. "I bet I could play a simpering wife, and you can go haul around set pieces for Jodie." He clasps his hands behind his back and bats his eyes at Will.

Will laughs.

"You haven't been watching if you think that's how my character acts." I kick him lightly in the shin, and he makes a big show of grabbing it and jumping around.

"That's really more like it," Will says, nodding at Milo's leg. "She's brutal."

"Sounds like there might not be much acting involved," Milo says, reaching over to ruffle my hair until it hangs in my face.

"This is defamation," I say through the curtain of tangles that hang in my eyes. "I'll sue."

"Hey, speaking of untrue things," Milo says, putting an arm around me to lead me away from Will as he lowers his voice, "remember, you don't need to scheme to win this election. Just keep being responsible and present when they need you, and you'll get the votes."

I scowl. "Easy for you to say. All that stuff comes naturally to you."

Milo won't have any of the problems I will getting into college. He's in the top 10 percent of our class, is president and founder of the Space Science Club, and is likely to be named captain of the varsity basketball team next year. I'm barely scraping by, and right now, Florida State feels like a distant dream. Of the colleges in Florida, it's one of the most competitive. I don't have the GPA, so I need something that sets me apart.

Just thinking about college makes me feel itchy.

"Besides," I add, avoiding Milo's gaze so he doesn't see the panic beating to get out, "I really need to get better at being on time if we want to talk about me being present."

"You're present when you're here. That's what counts." I don't point out that I'm the opposite of present right now, off whispering with him. "You don't need to play dirty to win."

"It sounds shitty when you say it like that."

"That's because it is shitty. And it won't make people trust you."

I huff in annoyance. "You could let me off the hook one time, you know."

"Someone's gotta hold you accountable; otherwise, you'll run wild."

"Why does it always feel like you're playing my babysitter?"

"Stop acting like a baby, and I won't have to."

I gasp like the star of a soap opera finding out her dead husband was alive all along.

Miss Liu spins around and glares at us. "*Junie,* please don't disrespect your fellow cast members like this." She shakes her head. "I expected better from you."

My whole body goes hot with embarrassment.

"Sorry. Sorry, everyone. It won't happen again." I hold up my hands in apology, then shoot a glare at Milo as I inch away from him.

Graham stalks out from backstage, swiping his hand through his sweaty hair. It sticks up wildly, and his face is flushed. He has a big bandage on one elbow and another on his chin from a fall he took on his skateboard. His T-shirt is soaked with sweat, clinging to his torso.

I try very hard not to notice. My gaze slides immediately to the floor.

"Dude," Graham says, grabbing Milo by the back of the collar, "if you ditch me in that sweatbox one more time—"

"Sorry, sorry," Milo says with a laugh, twisting in Graham's grip. "I'm coming."

Graham gives me a look. "Aren't you supposed to be the responsible one now? You better not let him slack off anymore."

I snort as he drags Milo away, disappearing backstage.

When we showed up today and found out a couple of the AC units weren't working backstage, he called up Rita from Neighborhood Hero, and the two have been tinkering for most of the evening, free of charge. Milo has been playing assistant.

It's a little strange to see Graham like this. For our entire friendship, it's felt like we were the kids with Milo and Lucy playing parents. We've always been the late risers, the inappropriate joke-makers, the ones ready for a dare or a risk that would make our friends groan or threaten to leash us. And even though Graham still has the spark that makes him quintessentially Graham, there's something new. A steadiness I'm not used to seeing.

"*I don't know why you insist on*— Ah, Junie," Will says.

I turn, startled. "Huh?" Then I realize—I missed our cue. We're supposed to walk onstage arguing, as Benedick and Beatrice always do. Will was on cue, but I wasn't, leaving me standing in the wings and Will three steps ahead of me.

"Junie!" Miss Liu barks. "Please pay attention."

I wince. "I'm so sorry." I rush onstage, peering down at my script to see where we are. I've lost the scene, and I realize with distress that we're two pages ahead of where I was last reading.

Miss Liu sighs, and it pierces like it's barbed.

"Sorry," I say, glancing around at my castmates. "It—It

won't happen again." I flush, realizing I made the same promise only a few minutes ago, and it did, in fact, happen again.

Sophie waves me off. "It's hot. Your brain's probably boiling. Maybe we need a break."

Miss Liu's mouth pinches. "Let's finish this scene, and then we'll take a short rest."

I nod, shooting a grateful look at Sophie.

We're nearly done with the scene when I hear a whoop from backstage, and we all falter.

Graham appears in the wings a moment later, leaning out onto the stage to give us a thumbs-up.

Miss Liu beams. "Wonderful."

When Graham's gaze flicks to me, I mouth, *Thank you.*

His grin softens, and he nods, ducking his head.

And my heart gives a violent and traitorous thump.

"Did you just have that lying around at home?" I ask Tallulah, eyeing the tape measure in her hand. It's the soft kind, used for measuring hips and waists and shoulders, and Tallulah has it hanging around her neck like some kind of professional tailor.

As I step onto the aerobic deck we're using as a fitting platform, Tallulah shoots me a look. "Miss Liu gave it to me. From the costume department at school." As always, Tallulah's words are clipped, her sentences short like she's forcing out every word, and each extra detail is an inconvenience.

We're in one of the rooms backstage, the window unit blasting cold air thanks to Graham and Rita's emergency repair two nights ago. Though the noises it's making haven't convinced me the unit will last until opening night.

It's our first day measuring for costumes, and Lucy lounges in one of the dressing table chairs close by, her hands folded on her stomach. "I think I'm most excited about the costumes. I wasn't super thrilled to do this, but it's cool that I get to wear the flapper dress and the fairy costume and the wedding band outfit." She bats her eyes at Tallulah. "Can you make my band outfit extra cute? Like, can I have a fun little vest?"

The corner of Tallulah's mouth twitches with a smile. "Sure. With sequins?" She finishes measuring my chest and makes a note in her book.

Lucy squeals, kicking her legs. "Oh my God, *yes*! Make it really sparkly. I want to look like a freaking disco ball up there."

"It'd be very typical Lucy to outshine everyone, even from the ensemble," I say. "The greatest overachiever of our generation."

Lucy picks up a crumpled piece of paper from the dressing table and tosses it at me. "Rude."

"It's basically a compliment," I say as I step down. "Better than an underachiever. I could be calling you the greatest loser of our generation."

"That title's already taken," Tallulah says as she marks something down in her notebook.

When neither of us responds, she looks up, taking in our matching looks of confusion.

"By Zephyr Gaines," Tallulah says.

Lucy scoffs in mock outrage. "Listen, you two are gonna make me feel bad about myself if you keep calling my ex a loser."

"We can't fault you for your savior complex, Luce," I say.

Lucy scowls at me for real now. "I don't have a savior complex."

I laugh. "You absolutely do! You think you can fix everyone."

Lucy gets a freshly sucked lemon look that reminds me a lot of Tallulah's most sour expression. "I don't try to *fix* everyone. That's a really mean thing to say, Junie."

I jerk back. "I wasn't—I didn't mean it like that."

"I don't know how you meant it then, because it makes me sound pretty elitist."

Tallulah clears her throat. "Hey, Lucy?" She looks surprised as Lucy's name leaves her mouth, like she didn't intend on saying it. Her mouth flattens into an irritated line, but I don't know if it's with us or herself. "You're up. We need to be fast."

Lucy steps past me, the tense lines bracketing her lips a dead giveaway that she's barely holding together her bright expression. "You don't need to wait for me," she says to me. "I'm sure you have a scene to run through before practice is over."

I gape at her. "Lucy—"

"You should go." She waves me off. "Seriously."

I must hesitate too long because Tallulah jumps to her rescue. "Go," she says to me. "I need you to send in whoever's next."

And because I don't know what else to do, I listen.

My texts to Lucy after practice go unanswered. When I haven't heard from her by late next morning, I head to her house armed with homemade strawberry cheesecake cupcakes and an apology.

It's hard to upset Lucy, but I definitely stepped in it last night. Even though we have rehearsal again tonight, I don't want to wait that long. Lucy is the strong, dependable heart of our friend group. Knowing I've upset her had me tossing and turning in bed all night, until I had to retreat outside to get some fresh air around two in the morning.

Milo was out on his dock with his telescope.

"I'm a jerk," I said as I sat down across the canal, the water quiet between us.

Milo leaned back from his telescope. "You're not a jerk. A jerk wouldn't apologize." He peered over at me, his expression a challenge. "But you always apologize when you mess up, right?"

And I do. So here I am, ready to apologize.

Lucy's family lives in a stilt house a few streets over from the center of the North Shore. I climb the stairs to the front porch with my cupcake carrier in my arms.

Lucy answers the door, dressed in her Hot Dough T-shirt.

"Hi," she says, sounding wary but also relieved.

I hold up the cupcake carrier. "I brought a gift."

Her sister, Ruby, appears behind Lucy, her eyes wide. "Cupcakes? For us?"

"For *me*," Lucy says, shooting a glare in her sister's direction.

Ruby gives Lucy a sharklike smile. "Until you leave for work, sure."

Lucy scowls. The only time I've ever seen Lucy act anything less than a perfect angel is with Ruby. Side by side, they look almost nothing alike. Ruby is tall and thin like their mom, with natural hair grown long and fluffy, and a 70s hippie vibe. Right now, she's wearing a pair of heart-shaped pink glasses and a striped tube top with high-waisted shorts.

Lucy is shorter with wide hips and strong shoulders like their dad. She always wears her hair in whatever style will keep it protected from the saltwater, so she can bodyboard without having to worry about it. She's the master of cute things, with a bedroom full of stuffed animals won from carnival games and claw machines, and she journals almost obsessively, so her desk is a treasure trove of markers, calligraphy pens, stickers, and washi tape. The only thing in Lucy's bedroom that feels out of place is the Gators flag on her wall—a gift from her dad when they went for homecoming last year. It's his alma mater, and he's really pushing for Lucy to go there, though she swears that's where the legacy ends—she will *never* become an accountant.

But even though they have almost nothing in common and often don't get along, Ruby was the first person Lucy came out to after Graham. Ruby even knew before me or Milo.

Lucy pushes the screen door open. "Come on. We can talk in my room."

I slip off my sandals in the entryway before following her.

Inside, the house is sweltering. Lucy's parents keep the thermostat at a stifling eighty degrees or more, and it always feels a little humid and still inside their house. Lucy has an oscillating fan in her room that has been my lifeline for so many years, I turn it on without looking as I step through her bedroom door.

I do a quick scan of her room and spot a plate of her grandmother's tablet pistache—peanut candies—on her nightstand. Contraband in the Bayonne household, where they aren't allowed to eat in their bedrooms. Technically that makes the container I'm holding contraband, too.

"Give my love to my dentist," I say, making a beeline for her nightstand. I've completely forgotten my purpose here with thoughts of sugary goodness melting in my mouth.

Lucy puts an arm out to block me. "Mémé made those for *me.*"

Lucy's grandmother moving here from Miami has been the best thing to happen in the Bayonne house—mostly for my stomach. She used to own a Haitian bakery there, but she retired and sold the business last year before moving in with Lucy's family.

"I thought people with siblings are supposed to be good at sharing. I'm bad at it, but I'm an only child. My bad habits are a product of my situation."

"If you were related to Ruby, you'd get it," Lucy replies, taking the cupcake container from me. "So, what's the occasion?" She sets the container on her desk and pops it open. She pulls out a cupcake and unwraps it as she bites a heart-shaped slice of strawberry from the top.

"A bribe," I say, remembering why I'm here. "Apology cupcakes. I don't really believe you want to fix people, Luce. I just—I meant you see past people's flaws."

"Look, it's fine if you want to joke with me like that when it's us," Lucy says as she licks frosting from her braces. "But I don't want you to joke like that in front of other people. I don't want people to think I'm only nice to them because I'm—I'm collecting strays or have a savior complex or whatever. That's not what I'm doing."

"I know," I say quickly. "It was a bad joke. I know you just see the good in everyone. I mean, *literally* everyone, when we consider you even saw the good in Zephyr. But I'm sorry for joking about it like that. Really. I think it's a good thing you are the way you are."

Lucy twists her mouth up on one side, considering. Then she takes a big bite of the cupcake and nods. "Thank you."

I wait a beat, watching her cross the room to perch on her bed, motioning for me to follow. As she finishes off her cupcake, she drags a fluffy pink pillow into her lap. I can't imagine putting anything unnecessary on my body right now. It's so hot, I want to crawl out of my skin and go skeletal.

"Tallulah sticking up for you, though," I say, shooting her a sideways look as I take a seat beside her. "That was . . . new."

Lucy purses her lips. "Mm-hmm."

"I guess I didn't realize you two were so close."

"She was just being nice."

"I didn't know she was capable."

"Junie," Lucy says, a warning in her voice.

A sharp noise of outrage catches high in my throat. "What? Have you not heard the way she talks to me?"

Lucy's expression softens. "Maybe if you're nice to her, she'll be nice to you."

"I was never rude to her to begin with. She's the one who started it!"

"So then you be the one to end it. At least try. Be the bigger person."

"Why does everyone keep telling me to be the bigger person? Do I have to be nice to someone who's been nothing but rude to me just so I can say I took the moral high ground?" I cross my arms and give a little huff of irritation. "I don't want it. I want the low ground."

"It's not about taking the moral high ground," Lucy says. "It's about making things easier on yourself next year. Do you really want to be doing this whole nasty drama when you're living together?"

I scowl. I don't even want to think about living with Tallulah. "Sorry, do I need to start giving you this lecture every time you fight with Ruby?"

Lucy glares at me. "That's different. Ruby is evil."

"So is Tallulah!"

"Not even in the slightest. Someone who cares as much about the world as she does has to have a big heart."

"Hey, I have a plenty big heart," Ruby says as she shoves open Lucy's bedroom door.

Lucy picks up the fluffy pink pillow in her lap and hurls it at her sister. "Stop listening at my door, demon spawn!" she roars.

Ruby chucks the pillow back, but she must have terrible aim, because she nails me in the face instead.

I fall back on the bed dramatically. "That's it. She's killed me. Murder."

"Wow, Junie, what a relief you found your way to the theater," Ruby says as she snags a cupcake from the container on the desk.

"Ruby! Those are mine!" Lucy launches from the bed, chasing Ruby to the door. Ruby makes it out with a cupcake in each hand, and Lucy locks her bedroom door behind her.

"You're really selling the whole sisterhood thing," I say, propping myself up on one elbow. "Seriously, it seems like such a joy."

Lucy glares at me. "Ruby is an anomaly. She could make the pope swear."

"I could make the pope do a lot more than that!" Ruby calls through the door.

"Ruby!" Lucy bangs her fist against her door. "Get away from my room!" She turns back to me, her rage face falling away to a more serene expression. "I'm gonna kill her one day."

I shake my head. "I feel like you're missing a super vital point of your argument."

"Listen," she says, moving to grab another cupcake, "just because I give advice doesn't mean I have to take it. But you should listen to me anyway. Tallulah has been through a lot—way more than you or I can even imagine. At least try to get her to meet you halfway."

Bringing up Tallulah's mom is the best play. It's easy to forget what she's been through when she's so prickly. But maybe that's why she is the way she is—because all she's done is lose the people closest to her, from her mom dying to her best friend abandoning her.

I scowl at Lucy. "Don't try to guilt-trip me."

She holds up a hand in surrender. "Fine," she says. "I know you need to come to it on your own anyway. It'll be a much sweeter victory for me that way." She takes another bite of cupcake and grins, pink cake smeared across her braces.

I flop back on her bed. "Whatever you say, daydream believer."

Chapter Eleven

(BOOTLEGGERS grab for each other, tussling violently. The unseen PUCK sneaks between them, putting out a foot. A BOOT-LEGGER is tripped at the ankles and topples into the table. The wedding cake splats onto the floor, destroyed.)

(WEDDING PLANNER wails.)

WEDDING PLANNER
(Pointing at the Montagues and Capulets.) Oh, you wretched fiends! A plague on both your houses!
—Act 1, Scene 4, *Midsummer Madness*

I'm on my way home from Lucy's when the dark gray sky opens up and releases a deluge that makes me glad I'm not riding home with the cupcake carrier. It was difficult enough to keep it balanced on my basket when the sky was a cloudless bright blue.

I pedal hard on my bike, rain slicking down my face and into my eyes. I nearly skid out on the wet pavement as I veer down a side street, heading for Piper and Junie's, which is closer than home. I shove my bike into the rack at the front of the restaurant and barrel through the front door, feet sliding around in my wet flip-flops.

Angela is leaning over the consignment counter, peering

into the dining room with a pinched look on her face when I come inside.

"What's wrong?" I ask, pausing at the counter to wring out my hair. "You look constipated."

Angela glares at me. "You have such a charming way of speaking, Juniper Nash. Has anyone ever told you that?"

"Not that I can remember." I grin and blow her a kiss, heading toward the café to get something warm to drink. Now that I'm standing in the AC blast, I'm shivering.

Tallulah freezes in the center of the dining room, watching me warily.

"Hey, Junie," Angela calls after me, "you may want to give those shorts a good tug."

I flush hot all over as I yank my soaked shorts down. They've ridden so far up, I'm surprised I didn't feel them in my colon.

Tallulah eyes me. "I have some extra clothes in my car if you want to borrow them."

I stare at her in shock.

She clears her throat loudly and proclaims for all the world and God to hear, "Though why you wouldn't just go home, where your own clothes live, is beyond me."

I gape at her, then gesture wildly in the direction of the front door and the monsoon beyond. "It's *raining*."

Moonface appears behind Tallulah, holding a steaming mug. "Well, are you gonna stand there all day, or come in and have a seat?" She holds the mug out to me, and there's a heart in the foam.

I smile. "Thanks, Moonface. Where's Isaac?"

"We switched shifts. I had a thing this morning."

I don't ask what the thing was. Sometimes with Moonface, it's better not to know.

As I follow Moonface into the café, I notice the big table in the back is full. I spot Cora's best friend, McKayla, right away, and Zephyr's telltale bleached-white hair. Zephyr's best friend, Braden, and Milo's ex-girlfriend, Marissa, are both there, sitting close together. She has her hand on his thigh, and his arm rests across the back of her chair.

I force myself to hold back my judgmental side-eye. Braden is Milo's opposite in almost every way—blond and gangly, no academic drive, and if he has any athletic ability, he's only ever used it to skateboard with a sheet tied around him like a cape during a tropical storm. The one thing they have in common is a penchant for run-ins with the sheriff—Milo over breakfast, and Braden pretty much any other time.

There are others with them—Anisa, our school's star swimmer, and Vince, of former Drama Club president fame, along with his boyfriend, Nick. Nick's sister, Bea, is there, too, and some of her friends from cheerleading.

"What's going on?" I ask Tallulah, taking a sip of my coffee. I splutter in surprise—there must be three shots of espresso in this mug.

Moonface, who has returned to her spot behind the register, gives me a bland smile.

"Nothing," Tallulah says, but there's a waver in her voice that makes me pause.

She sounds . . . vulnerable. Which is deeply unsettling, considering Tallulah's scale runs from tolerating to mildly perturbed to annoyed to irritated to furious. I've never heard her sound anything like this.

I push past her into the dining room.

The big table is loud, and they've got tons of plates and empty cups. Just as I come in, Zephyr lifts out of his seat and calls to Tallulah, "Hey, server girl, could I get a refill?" He holds up his empty mug.

I stare at him. "It's self-serve."

He must not have noticed me standing near her, because Zephyr looks surprised. But instead of backing off, he doubles down. "We're *thirsty,* Juniper Nash. You know, it's a real *dry* summer."

The table titters.

Oh, I get it. They're mad because Zephyr got in trouble for bringing booze to Cora's bonfire.

I look at Tallulah. "Are they giving you trouble?" I ask her quietly, feeling protective for some stupid reason. It shouldn't matter to me what anyone says to Tallulah. She's neither my friend nor my responsibility.

But when she doesn't meet my gaze, my blood boils.

It occurs to me that if Lucy ran the universe, this is exactly what she'd throw at me. It feels almost by design that this would happen right after the conversation we had. But I know from the fury coursing through me that whatever I'm about to do, Lucy would not approve.

I shove my mug into Tallulah's hands and head into the kitchen.

"Your *shoes,*" Moonface says, following me.

I ignore her as I grab a tub for dirty dishes from the sink.

Mac looks up in surprise. "Hey, Junie, I didn't know you'd be in today."

"I'm not." I shove the bin under my arm and look at Moonface. "You're letting those nitwits heckle our employees?"

Moonface gives me a long look. "I wanted to kick them out ages ago, but Tallulah said to leave it, so I left it."

I blow my rapidly drying—and frizzing—hair off my

forehead. "Well, I've never listened to her before, so I don't know why I'd start now."

I head back into the dining room, the bin under my arm.

Tallulah stands in the middle of the room, eerily quiet and wide-eyed.

I stalk over to the big table and start gathering up the empty plates. "Well, guys, thanks so much for coming in. We truly appreciate your patronage. Let me get these plates out of your way. Anisa, how's your mom? I saw her the other day at the General Store buying a pregnancy test. That's awesome—congrats. I've always wanted a sibling. Hey, I heard your dad comes home next month, too. God, a whole year with Doctors Without Borders—he's so brave."

I shove a few plates into the bin.

"Hi, Vince. Glad I bumped into you. Remember that guy I saw you with at Driftwood last week? What a prince. What was his name again? Gregg? Super cute."

Nick whips around to look at Vince. "Gregg with two Gs?"

They descend into a whispered argument.

I grab a few more plates and work my way around the table. "LeAnne, great to see you. Looking luminous. All those skincare products I saw you slipping into your purse at Target a few months ago must be doing their work."

I pause at the end of the table and level Zephyr with a look. "Zephyr Gaines, my favorite of Lucy's exes—mostly because it means I can call you her ex. You know, I keep thinking, I just love the bleach job." I flap a hand in the direction of his hair. "It really does wonders to disguise your receding hairline. You probably won't have to shave it off to camouflage the balding until you're at least twenty-three."

I put my free hand on my hip and grin at them. "Now, Tallulah's a little new to P&J's, but I hope you'll treat her as nicely as you've always treated me. Coffee's in the carafe. Feel free to grab some to-go cups on your way out—on the house." I wrinkle my nose and wink at them, putting the last few plates in the bin before hefting it. I start to head to the kitchen.

When I'm a few steps away, I can't help myself and glance back. "Oh, and Marissa? You've really traded up." I indicate Braden with my free hand. "You two are so well-matched."

When I turn around, Tallulah looks like she's been punched in the gut. She follows me to the kitchen and hands me my coffee before walking straight outside into the pouring rain.

I glance into the dining room as the big table clears out.

Vince comes up to the counter, red-faced. I assume he's grabbing a to-go cup, because only he would be so brazen.

But he glares at me and snarls, "You will *never* be Drama Club president. Not if I have any say in it."

My stomach bottoms out, but I try to keep a cool face. "Get fucked, Vince."

As soon as they're gone, Moonface begins to clap. "Bravo, my dear."

The back door bangs open and Tallulah slinks in, damp from the rain. She shoves a bundle into my arms and stomps past me.

Clothes. Rain-spattered, but mostly dry. The shorts look small—they'd have to be if they're Tallulah's—but they're drawstring, so I cross my fingers for luck.

I go into Mom's office to change, and when I come back out, the rain is pounding even harder. My flip-flops squeak against the floor.

Briana Klingman, the oldest of the Klingman kids and an incoming freshman, stands at the counter with three of her siblings, all rain-soaked. These three are varying middle school ages, a pair of them twins. I have a distinct childhood memory of being bullied by the twins once, even though I'm several years older than them. They're terrifying, dark-eyed demon children with deceptively innocent gap-toothed smiles. Even now, they give me the shivers.

"Hey, Junie," Briana says. "We just saw Milo at the General Store. He gave the kids way more samples than they needed. They're hyped on sugar. I thought some real food might bring them back down."

I glance at her siblings. They all look flushed and wild-eyed, but the twins extra so.

"Good luck with that." I glance over to where Tallulah is clearing a table, this little smile on her face, like she's actually having a good time.

I don't think I've ever seen her smile so genuinely.

I'm distracted enough that the twins must sense a moment of weakness. I take one step forward at the same time one of them sticks out a foot, and I catch it right on the ankle. My damp flip-flops stay glued to the floor while I trip forward and go down hard.

The place is mostly empty, but it still goes dead silent when I hit the floor.

Well, except for Briana, who explodes on the twins. While she tears into them at top volume, someone grabs me under the arms and hauls me to my feet.

My shoulder screams.

"Shit, Junie, are you okay?" Mac asks, helping me to a chair.

"I'm so, so sorry, Junie," Briana says, abandoning the twins to check on me. "Where does it hurt?"

I'm seeing spots.

"I think it's her shoulder," says Mac. "Might be dislocated. Should we call an ambulance?"

"I'll take her to the hospital," Tallulah says. "Moonface, call her mom."

White Coral Best Actors Club
Today 4:03 PM

LUCY
What is that picture????? Is that you!!!??
You're in a sling!!!! Why!!!!

ME
Evil fucking klingman twins

MILO
Junie they're children

ME
I'M IN A SLING

GRAHAM
Scariest horror movies in the world have evil
children just saying

**Graham named the conversation
"Children of the Corn Support Group"**

MILO
Are you at home?

ME
I am bedridden
Oh the pain

MILO
Good to know you didn't injure your flair for the
dramatic

JUNIE

After we finish at the hospital, Mom brings me home to rest and then heads out to cover the rest of my afternoon shift. Almost as soon as she's gone, Milo arrives straight from work, smelling like sugar and waffle cones, armed with a cup of s'mores ice cream to cheer me up. I haven't exactly been subtle about my misery, which I guess is why Lucy and Graham show up not long after.

When they walk inside, Milo is kneeling on the floor by the couch, asking me in a dumb baby voice, "Do you need me to feed you?"

"I can handle holding an ice cream with—"

Milo shoves a spoonful of ice cream into my mouth before I can finish. He ignores my grunt of protest, and I smack him with my good hand.

I'm propped up against the pillows from my bed, which Mom helped me set up before she left. I've been sprawled on the couch watching *Proper Southern Ladies*, and the episode I'm on—from the first season of Lexington—is still playing.

"Could someone pause that?" I ask, motioning to the TV. The remote is behind Milo, and I can't reach.

Graham swipes it from the coffee table as he passes to the armchair and clicks off the episode.

It's still raining, and my friends are all a little damp. Milo's hair is slicked back from his face, and Graham's is wild from the humidity. As Lucy moves to perch on the chaise, she drags a huge satin scrunchy from her bag and ties back her braids.

"So, if I sprain my shoulder, I get spoon-fed by this stud?" Graham asks as he sprawls in the armchair. "I gotta rethink my summer plans."

"Be careful what you wish for," I say as Milo nearly fumbles the spoon and a glob of s'mores ice cream drips onto my shirt. "For a varsity athlete, he's lacking some dexterity."

Milo sighs, passing me a napkin so I can wipe the ice cream off. "Is this how it's gonna be until you get that sling off? You have hours to just sit here and work on your best comebacks?"

"Well, that's not *not* what I'll be doing." I toss the used napkin onto the coffee table.

"Awesome," Milo says. "Would you rather feed yourself?"

"Could you maybe just hold the cup for me?"

Milo offers it to me, and I take the spoon with my good hand.

"How long do you have to wear the sling?" Lucy asks.

"Three weeks." I take another bite of ice cream. "The doctor said it's a mild sprain."

"*Mild?*" Graham grins, leaning forward to brace his forearms on his knees. "That's interesting. This setup has you looking like an eighteenth-century tuberculosis patient."

I glare. "In that case, lean a little closer so I can cough on you. You can join me."

His eyes crinkle at the corners. "Desperate to spend more time with me? I get it."

Lucy snorts. "You don't think she's gotten enough of you at rehearsal?"

Graham puts a hand to his chest. "I've been too busy at rehearsal to socialize with anyone. Remember how I spent three hours fixing the AC units the other night? I might be the most valuable crew member."

I consider this. "I guess that's fair. I can admit it."

Milo chokes out a noise of outrage. "Hey! I'm in the crew."

I reach up and pat his cheek with my good hand. "And you are so helpful, too."

"Speaking of," Lucy says, glancing at her phone, "we have to get to rehearsal."

"You know, it feels kind of unfair that the person who roped us all into this gets to skip tonight," Graham says, shooting me a baleful look.

"Hey, it feels kind of unfair to be bedridden after being done bodily harm by a couple of possessed middle schoolers," I reply. "But the world is an unfair place."

"If I'd known that was all it'd take to get out of community theater, I would've paid the twins to maim me first," Graham grumbles as he gets to his feet.

"Should we grab Slices on the way? I haven't eaten," Milo says.

I groan. "Are you kidding me? I want Slices."

"You can order delivery," Graham says, leaning over the back of the couch to tap me on the nose.

I snap at his finger with my teeth and nearly catch him, but he jerks away in time.

He bends down toward me, his look severe. "Watch it."

"Or you'll do what?"

Lucy and Milo are chatting by the door, but their words are white noise. All I can see is Graham as he dips closer, his eyes dark and hot. "Try again and find out."

I glare at him, the dare heavy between us.

When I don't move, Graham smirks and straightens, his expression lightening as he turns to our friends.

I swallow, but it's like trying to drink sand. And as they file out, all I can do is call a dry, raspy, "Get a slice of margherita in my honor."

The door snicks shut behind them, and I collapse against my pillows, breathless and burning hot.

Chapter Twelve

VIOLA
Do you not know I am a woman? When I think,
I must speak.

ORSINO
Yes, it's the thinking part I was hoping you'd do a
little more of. Preferably before the speaking.

VIOLA
You have been spending *far* too much time with that
wretched Benedick!
                        —Act 2, Scene 12, *Midsummer Madness*

It's a well-known secret among locals that of the three Fourth
of July fireworks shows visible from the island, Bayfront
Beach has the best view. Because we split our budget between the fireworks show at Manatee Point and the one on
West Beach, the White Coral–sanctioned fireworks shows
that get advertised for weeks leading up to the Fourth are no
match for the show by Emerson across the bay. Being that
we can see their fireworks barge from Bayfront Beach, that's
where most of the locals spend the Fourth. It's one of Dot
Slip's great complaints as the former mayor that our locals
watch another town's fireworks show.

I head to Bayfront Beach armed with a drink carrier of lemonades from P&J's and Mom's warnings pinging through my brain like an army of Ping-Pong balls. *Don't forget to reapply your sunscreen every hour. Wear your hat. Be careful going in the water with your sling. Don't forget to take ibuprofen!*

I'm surprised she didn't make me bring a long-range baby monitor.

When I get to the beach, Lucy is already there, lounging on a towel. She's spread a few other towels around her, claiming the space.

She does a wolf whistle when she sees me coming. "Wow, that sling looks hot, Junie."

I do a little twirl, balancing the drink carrier in my good hand. "Where is everyone?" I ask as I pass her the carrier. "Milo said he'd bring me an umbrella."

I couldn't bring my own, considering my injury. I already had to walk here. My bike is just a pretty yard ornament these days.

"Milo has other plans today."

My head snaps up so fast, I hear something crack. "Exsqueeze? I think I misheard you."

She smirks. "Junie."

"Milo would never make other plans and not invite us. That would be rude."

"It wouldn't be rude if he was invited to something and we weren't."

The lack of inflection in her voice makes me wonder if she heard what happened at P&J's the other day. I haven't told my friends yet. I'm too worried how they'll react. I knew it'd get around eventually, but it's possible I underestimated just how quickly.

"Well, that's impossible," I say, testing the waters a bit to see if she'll crack. "No one would intentionally not invite *us.* I mean, Graham Isham alone is beloved."

"She's right, I am." Graham tosses a beach umbrella onto the group of towels and throws himself down beside it. He rolls onto his side so he can pluck a cup from the drink carrier and takes a long pull of lemonade. His gaze flicks over me, and he grins around his straw. "Hey, Lemonade Girl. Nice pigtails." He reaches out and tugs one of my braids.

I swat him away.

"Personally, I'd rather be here for the best fireworks show available." Lucy flings an arm toward the water and the strip of land visible across the bay—Emerson. "Not like you can really see the fireworks from someone's backyard."

"Plus, why would you give up this paradise on Earth?" Graham asks as a toddler tears by in a soggy-looking diaper, screaming. A harried dad follows close behind.

They're both being a little too blasé, like they can trick me into thinking I'm not mad that Milo ditched us. Graham seems determined to joke his way through the tension, as usual.

"Would've been nice for Milo to mention it, at least." I don't know how to sum up my annoyance with him in a reasonable way—especially without giving up what happened the other day—so I say, "I would've only brought three lemonades."

Graham's mouth twitches like he's trying not to laugh. "I'll drink his."

"Gee, I'm so relieved," I reply, deadpan.

Lucy chuckles as she stands and strips off her clothes. "I'm going in the water."

"So eager to get away from me?" I call after her.

She twirls around, stepping backward over the legs of a

sunbather as she twinkles her fingers at me. Then she spins and jogs into the surf.

I'm having trouble quashing my irritation. We're supposed to be spending time together this summer, all four of us. Last summer was a mess—Graham and me sneaking around, and Milo and Lucy in relationships. This summer was going to fix everything for us, superglue our friend group together so I don't have to worry when I'm not living as close to them. How am I supposed to do that if Milo doesn't even show up?

"Don't be too mad, Junie. He texted me." Graham reaches over and pats the beach umbrella. "I'm on babysitter duty."

I glare at him. "I don't need a babysitter. Don't be a dick."

His jaw drops into a wide, shocked smile. "Interesting. To the guy who's about to set up your umbrella."

I suck on my teeth, annoyed. "Leave it, then. I'll be fine." He snorts. "Yeah, right. We're here all day. You'll leave the beach looking like Mr. Krabs."

"My confidence is absolutely soaring right now. Thank you." I grab my phone from my bag to start what will certainly be a slow, one-handed text to Milo about his abandonment.

"Nope." Graham reaches over and plucks my phone out of my hand. "No way."

"Hey!" I make a swipe at him with my good arm and miss. I roll onto my knees and push myself up to glare at him. "Give it back."

He shakes his head. "No. You're not bothering him. Let him hang out with Cora in peace."

"What I let Milo do is my business. Give me my phone!"

I shuffle forward until I'm right beside him, and he nearly rolls off his towel into the sand to keep away. I half straddle him, pressing my knee into his leg and bracing my shin across his thighs to hold him in place. He stretches his arm far behind him, holding my phone as far away as he can.

"Junie," he says, warning in his voice. "Stop."

I make another grab, but as I close my hand around his wrist, I lose my balance, and we both go down. I land with my injured arm trapped between us and my face in his neck.

"Ow." Pain radiates from my shoulder. I ache all the way to my teeth, and when I open my mouth, all that comes out is a whimper.

Graham's arm curls around me, his hand settling in the center of my back. "Are you okay?"

I shake my head.

"Okay, give me one second," he says, an edge of panic in his voice. "I'm gonna move you."

"No, no, no—"

His hand slides up to cradle the back of my head as he rolls us both. He braces his knee between mine as he settles me on my back. I squeeze my eyes shut against the sun, which is suddenly too bright to bear.

"Is that better?" He brushes my hair away from my face, his touch featherlight. My head swims. "Junie?"

I cover my eyes with my good hand. "I'm okay," I say, my voice faint.

He sighs, his breath warm against my neck. I peek through my fingers at him. His head hangs low, his hair nearly touching my chin. He's still kneeling over me.

Then someone calls, "Get a room!"

Graham's head shoots up, and his gaze meets mine through my fingers before he shifts away. As he settles beside me, he lifts his middle finger in the direction of the voice, which earns a scandalized gasp from someone nearby.

While I peer at him, he reaches one hand up and rumples his hair.

"Here," he says, tossing my phone into my lap. "Do whatever you want."

He sounds mad. As I leverage myself up on my good arm, he turns away and pulls his shirt over his head. My gaze snags on golden skin—the curve of his spine, and the shift of his shoulder blades. I feel hot and itchy and out of my head.

"What's your problem?" I ask, my voice coming out more hostile than I intend.

He moves behind me to dig a hole in the sand for the umbrella. I twist to look at him, but he keeps his head down, his back to me.

"You aren't careful," he says, his voice strained.

I scoff. "Seriously? You really think you're the one best equipped to lecture me on being careful?" Graham might be acting more responsible lately, but I've seen him do some of the absolute dumbest stuff—like taking his skateboard into an abandoned pool a couple years ago, which resulted in a broken arm, or cannonballing off the Abadianos' boat while it was still moving, or scaling someone's balcony on a dare. Graham has always been a little reckless. Even if he's calmer now, I still sense it—something chasing the rush.

He lets out a humorless laugh at my accusation. "Not really. Which is exactly my point. Your mom already thinks I'm a giant child."

"What my mom thinks doesn't—"

"*Yes*," Graham says, desperation laced in his voice. "Yes, it does. It matters to me. So, the last thing I need is you getting hurt when I'm the one here. You want to do something stupid? Fine. I can't stop you. But save it for Lucy. Or better—save it for Milo."

I grip my phone so tight, my fingers ache. My mouth has gone terribly dry.

He leans back, bracing a hand against the towel so he can look at my face. "I shouldn't have done that, okay? If you need something today, just ask. I'll do whatever you want."

There's a pleading in his words that sends a shot of warmth ricocheting through me, burying shrapnel deep inside. My skin burns, and my heart thuds somewhere in the center of my throat.

"Okay," I say when I finally manage to speak. I nod at the umbrella. "Thanks."

He gets back to work setting up the umbrella, silent behind me.

As I dig my hat out of my bag and fit it over my now disheveled braids, I spy my sunscreen wedged under my e-reader.

Asking Graham would be a terrible idea. I'm definitely not putting myself in that position. I'd rather get a third-degree sunburn than let my thirsty brain run away with itself.

Which is why, when Graham finishes setting up the umbrella and swipes the sunscreen from my bag, I yelp in protest.

"I'm fine!" I make a grab for the sunscreen, and he lets me take it. "I can do it."

He stares down at me, his expression flat. "Your back? You can do your own back? Are you a contortionist?"

"Wouldn't you like to know," I say, and then want to drown myself in the tide. Why did I say that? Why? Why must I self-sabotage?

Graham snorts. "If you can put sunscreen on your own back, I'm putting out a hat so we can start making some money."

I roll my eyes. "Maybe I'm trying to get a tan."

"Sure, or sun poisoning, whatever." He snatches the

sunscreen away. "Do you need me to go get Lucy, or can you handle a little skin contact?"

I want to say no, I cannot handle the skin contact. But that would be the worst possible idea, so I go with the second worst possible idea, which is agreeing to let him put my sunscreen on for me.

Instead of speaking—mostly because I'm not sure I can at this point—I hunch over my knees, giving him full access to my back. I'm wearing a halter one-piece with a high neck. It was meant to minimize any strange tan lines from my sling, but it leaves half of my back fully exposed—a lot of area to cover. I hear Graham uncap the tube, and anticipation coils in me so tightly that I jump when he brushes a hand across my shoulder blade.

"Sorry." There's a wince in his words. "I should've warmed it up first."

"It's fine." My voice comes out high-pitched and ragged. The truth is, I didn't even notice the cold. All I can feel are his rough, calloused hands on my skin. That's new, too—Graham's rough hands. His hands used to be soft, but his new job has changed him. Like everything else about him that's changed, it's subtle. But I had half a summer to memorize the feeling of his hands on my bare skin—I remember enough to notice the difference.

"Milo would probably be way better at this," he says quietly, his fingers featherlight across my bad shoulder. I suck in a gasp when he touches a particularly tender spot.

"Milo has ham hands," I say, my teeth gritted against the ache. "I have no idea how he plays basketball."

Graham huffs out a laugh, and his breath skims across the back of my neck. I feel its warmth pour through me like honey. Then his hand moves to the other side of my back, away from my injured shoulder, and the pain eases. I relax a little.

Graham doesn't waver as he works the sunscreen across my back. When his fingers slip just beneath the edge of my suit, a shiver tears through me. My muscles feel like guitar strings tightened to breaking point. One more strum, and I'll snap.

"Arm," Graham says, hands withdrawing from my back.

I half turn toward him, confused. "Huh?"

"Your arm," he says, motioning to my good arm. "You can't do this one yourself, right?"

"Oh. Right." I try not to sound like my heart has lodged itself in my mouth.

He keeps his eyes down, his gaze focused on the tube of sunscreen. He squeezes a glob into his hand, then takes my wrist.

Graham has always been sure of himself, everything he does easy and second nature. He never hesitates. But the steadiness I've been noticing in him is stark now. It's not just that he knows what he's doing—it's that he doesn't second-guess himself. His fingers around my wrist feel like an anchor. I watch his face for any sign of a crack in his composure as he rubs the white sheen of sunscreen from my skin, but his expression is smooth.

His thumb brushes over a freckle on my shoulder, and my breath catches, as though a door has slammed inside my chest.

I thought my back was the most dangerous place to let him touch, but now that I feel his hands dragging up and down my arm, I realize I was wrong. His fingers grazing the underside of my wrist makes my stomach clench with anticipation. If he didn't have such a strong hold on me, I might sway.

I feel a staggering rush of disappointment when he's done, capping the tube without looking at me and tossing it into my lap. He stands and stretches, and I watch like a creep until he drops his arms and shakes them out. When he looks back at me, I'm very busy applying sunscreen to the rest of my body.

Nothing to see here. Extremely normal behavior. Just don't look at my face.

"You wanna swim?" he asks, his voice light.

I shake my head, words failing.

Graham shrugs and takes off. As I watch his retreating form, I get the feeling I don't need to wait for the grand fireworks show tonight. Because nothing will rival the riot of explosions happening inside my chest.

The day after the Fourth of July, we have rehearsal. Even though I only missed one practice after my injury, I'm woefully behind my castmates—even Will, which is really upsetting. I've had to reference my script three times already during a particularly difficult scene involving Benedick and Beatrice, the wedding band, and the melancholy Jaques, whom Benedick and Beatrice are attempting to set up as a date with other single wedding guests. There are a lot of moving bodies, and when I miss a line for the fourth time, Miss Liu calls for a break.

"Well, if it isn't my disloyal best friend," I say when I reach the cooler at the same time as Milo. He's drenched in sweat from their work on the train, which is the most complicated piece in the set.

Milo glares at me. "Nice. Real nice."

I flap my script at him. "Just telling it like it is."

"It's not like you gave me any warning," he says, his eyebrows drawing down low. "When they asked me not to bring you, I thought it was that stupid thing with Zephyr and the beer. I figured if I went, I could talk them out of being so pissed off about it. I didn't know what I was walking into. As soon as I brought it up, they shut me down. No one told me exactly what you said, but the words *life-altering rumors* were thrown around."

I scoff, tossing my head. "*Life-altering rumors.* They're so fucking dramatic."

"Do we need to talk about stones and glass houses?"

"I'm not dramatic!"

"She says dramatically."

I reach out with my good arm and shove him.

"Anyway," he says, "you really can't be that mad at me. I was there, like, an hour and a half, tops. And I told Cora I'm not planning on spending my summer separated from my friends just because you said some stuff to hers."

"An hour and a half? What did you do all day, sit at home?"

"What are you talking about? I had to work. You were probably already home by the time I got off."

I blink at him. "Wait, what?"

He gapes at me. "You thought I was there all day, at a party you weren't invited to? Jeez, JN, I thought you knew me better than that."

"But—but Lucy said—" I stop short and bite down on my lips.

Milo raises his eyebrows.

I frown. "She said you had other plans."

"I did," Milo says. "*Working.* And then McKayla's party to see Cora."

"Oh."

Milo grins. "I bet you feel pretty dumb now, huh?"

I scowl at him. "Don't look so happy about it."

"So, wanna tell me what happened that's got everyone so pissed off at you?" He perches on the arm of a pair of theater seats.

My cheeks burn. "Not particularly."

"Hey, come on." He puts a hand on his chest. "It's *me*. I promise I won't be too disappointed in you."

I feel a rush of outrage. "Oh, that's nice. You just assume I'm the one who did something wrong? Me, your best friend of seventeen years?"

He stares at me, unaffected.

"Wow. Okay." I smack him with my script.

He laughs, holding his hands up in surrender. "Easy, killer. I was kidding!"

I smack him once more for good measure. "For your information, they were giving Tallulah a hard time. All I did was step in."

"All you did," he repeats, sounding unconvinced.

I purse my lips. "I may have been less than kind."

"There it is."

I glare at him. "They deserved it."

"I'm sure they did. And you, who claims to not even like Tallulah, decided to play judge and jury?" He sounds incredulous.

"Just because I don't like her doesn't mean I think people should be allowed to treat her badly." I pause, considering. "I mean, I can treat her badly. But that's reciprocal."

"And it has nothing to do with you not liking Cora," he says. "Or you not wanting me to date her?"

I stare at him. "What are you talking about?"

He holds up his hands. "Just a thought."

"*What?* You think I'm trying to sabotage your relationship?"

"I'm not in a relationship."

"Because that's what matters here!" I step back from him, wounded. "I don't care who you date. It has nothing to do with me."

Milo watches me, and I can tell he's piecing together a response.

I don't want to know if it'll devastate me or not, so I turn and walk away, holding up a hand so he won't follow. As I move past a small group of my castmates huddled near the stage, Ireland Tuohy, who plays Puck, stage-whispers, "If I weren't off book yet, I'd probably spend my break working on my lines. But I guess that's just me."

I glance over sharply, and James Soltenberg, our Duke Orsino, flicks his gaze away with a smirk.

Sophie breaks away from them, tossing a glare over her shoulder as she links her arm through my good one.

"What's their problem?" I ask.

She gives a careless shrug, but the move is practiced, like she's been waiting to use it. "She's probably mad you got a better part than she did."

A startled noise jumps from the back of my throat, and I move to hush her. "Sophie," I whisper harshly, "I'm trying to win an election!"

Sophie purses her lips, and I catch a flash of discomfort before she covers it with a smile. "I know! But it doesn't change the facts." She leans in and cups a hand around her mouth. "Some people just can't handle their own bitterness. And James is a suck-up. He'll agree with anything Ireland says."

My nerves ease briefly. But then we pass Camila, who wrinkles her nose when she sees me, and Abe Rivera, who pretends to be busy on his phone when we sit near him. He gets up almost immediately and walks off.

"Do I smell?" I ask Sophie, lifting the collar of my T-shirt to do a stench test.

Sophie sighs. "Not exactly."

Peter wanders up and flops into the seat on Sophie's other side. "You've been burned."

I sit up like I've been zapped. "What are you talking about?"

He nods toward the stage, where I catch the stink eye from a few members of the Drama Club before they glance away.

"Babe," Sophie says imploringly.

"What? She'll find out eventually."

"Find out *what*?" I ask, an edge in my voice.

Sophie sighs. "The Vince Effect," she says, a term we've used for the way Vince is the social heart of the Drama Club. Even now, months after his graduation, knowing he won't ever come back, I understand the meaning.

I'd been hoping to gain Vince's favor to earn some points with the rest of the club for the special election. But instead, he's ensured exactly what he said at P&J's the other day: I'll never be Drama Club president.

Chapter Thirteen

BEATRICE
(To Olivia.) Why, I don't understand your anger.
I have never caused trouble to any person a day in
my life.

BENEDICK
A lie if I've ever heard one! You cause trouble for me
once an hour, at least!

BEATRICE
(Smiling.) I do admit to have troubled dogs occasion-
ally.

BENEDICK
Well! One may smile, and smile, and be a villain!
—Act 1, Scene 4, *Midsummer Madness*

By the time Founder's Weekend rolls around, I'm back on the
hook at Piper and Junie's. Mom is too short-staffed to spare
me, even with one arm out of commission, and Founder's
Weekend is the biggest event of the summer. It runs a full
three days—a festival for lady pirates, death by pie, and all
things clementine-flavored.

Over a hundred years ago, White Coral Key was settled
by Robert Bailey, Sr., who had just lost the Sarasota mayoral

election and retreated to the uninhabited island to build up a small but prosperous town. He brought the whole Bailey clan with him, including his eldest son, Robert Bailey, Jr. and Robert Bailey, Jr.'s new wife, Clementine.

It became clear in the following years that Clementine couldn't have children, and Robert Bailey, Jr. began taking his frustrations out on her physically. Clementine had been the doll of White Coral Key, yet no one stepped forward to help.

Eventually, after a decade of marriage and nearly as many years of abuse, Clementine baked her husband a pie laced with poison and killed him. It didn't take long for the local authorities to figure out what she'd done, and she was sentenced to death by hanging. She was jailed alongside Captain Nesi Quillam, a famous pirate captain who headed her all-female crew well into the late nineteenth century, long after piracy had mostly died out in Florida.

But they never got around to hanging Clementine. While they were holding her in jail, the whole town burned to the ground. Neither Nesi Quillam's nor Clementine's remains were ever recovered.

Skeptics say the fire burned so hot, there was nothing left to find. But most of us choose to believe the legend—that Captain Nesi Quillam's crew came to rescue her and lit fire to the whole town on their way out. That before they left, they gave Clementine a choice—die by the hands of the people she'd once trusted or come with them to sail the world.

Either way, whether it was a lightning strike or something as rare as one, the town had to be built anew. That was the real birth of the White Coral Key we know today.

The weekend starts on Friday, when local restaurants start putting out clementine-flavored desserts as a nod to Clementine the murderess and her husband's deadly sweet tooth.

Saturday is the Founder's Relay, and Sunday morning we have a float parade, followed that night by the closing ceremony. A group of women dress as pirates and sail out on their boats for the ceremonial releasing of Clementine to her freedom. And after everything is done, a portion of the revenue the island makes during Founder's Weekend goes to a local women's shelter, a tradition Dot Slip started when she became mayor.

Tallulah and I are both too busy with work to help with Market Day, which I can tell is irritating Dot. She doesn't like to deal with people on her own. She says she met her quota when she was mayor, and now she wants to relax.

I take pity on her during the long break in the middle of my double shift and head to the shop to help. The only surprise is that Tallulah follows.

"What are you doing?" I ask as she trails me through the crowd, ducking around a couple with a stroller.

I expect a snippy comeback, but she only says, "I have to help, remember? Part of my punishment."

We're living in a strange new world, Tallulah and I. We've seen each other a few times since I sprained my shoulder—at family dinner the other night, during our shifts at P&J's, and in passing at rehearsal—but she's been uncharacteristically pleasant. I haven't had to deal with one barbed comment or perfectly aimed insult all week.

It's almost unsettling. I have the urge to poke at her until she tries to bite my head off, just to experience some normalcy. It'd be the only normal thing going on lately. I haven't spoken to Milo since he accused me of trying to sabotage his relationships, and truthfully, I've been avoiding Graham since the Fourth. I just can't deal with a deep dive into old feelings.

"What are you gonna do about that arm tomorrow?" Dot asks as we approach her flower stand. She's wrapping up a bouquet for a girl who's clearly on vacation.

I pout. "Sore subject, Dot."

Tallulah tucks herself into an open space beside the flower display before she can get flattened by a family coming down the aisle.

"She's volunteering," Hal says from the table beside ours.

"It's the only way to participate without participating," I say. "Besides, I'm working the giant Jenga town history game, so it'll be educational."

Dot grunts. "The town history quiz was good enough the way it was. Why'd they have to add Jenga into it? Over the top, if you ask me."

"No one did," I say lightly as I lean down to rearrange the bucket of sunset-colored begonias.

Dot reaches out and smacks me with a long-stemmed rose.

"Hey! If you want to decide what goes on at the relay," I say, "maybe you should run for mayor."

Dot pulls a face. "Let me enjoy my retirement. If you all can't take care of this town without me, what's gonna happen when I die?"

"Dot! Don't talk about that. What's wrong with you?" I glance in Tallulah's direction. She's the only person I know who's ever been closely affected by someone's death, and it's occurred to me recently that I have no idea how she deals with it—if she's in therapy, or on medication, or both, or neither.

Tallulah catches me looking, and her expression flattens in annoyance.

"Begonia?" I ask, offering one to her.

It's a terrible recovery, but Tallulah accepts it with minimal glaring. Which is par for the course now that we've got a tentative truce between us—one I don't even remember signing.

"I'm just saying," Dot continues, "if I did my job right, this town shouldn't descend into ruin as soon as a new mayor takes office."

"It's not in ruin," Hal says, leaning over from her table after the people she was talking to walk off. "I like that they're changing some of the old games. Makes it more fun."

Dot shoots her a narrow-eyed look. "You would."

Hal grins.

"Hey, you." Dot snaps her fingers at me. "Since you can't wrap up bouquets, why don't you make yourself useful and grab me a coffee? Don't tell Moonface it's for me, or she'll make it decaf."

Even after all these years, Dot underestimates Moonface.

Dot pulls a wad of bills from her pocket. I've never seen her use plastic to pay for anything; just bills and barters. I don't even know if she has a bank account. I imagine she has cash buried all over her property, like mad money.

"That's because your doctor said you're not supposed to have caffeine," I say.

"Well, my doctor isn't here. What she doesn't know won't hurt her."

I frown and take the cash.

The line in the café is at least twelve people deep. A week ago, this would have been a nice reprieve from Tallulah's company. But today, it's just crowded and kind of boring being on my own.

"This is interesting. Don't you work here?"

I whirl, my body going tingly and weak from shock. Graham stands behind me, his work shirt splattered with water even though it's not raining. He's carrying an empty bucket in one hand, and a tool belt is slung around is hips. My heart gives a stupid, excited flutter at the sight of him.

"I do, yes," I say, an embarrassing shake in my voice. "But I'm on break, which means I stand in line with the commoners. What are you doing here?"

"One of the sprinklers was going off on its own. Drenched some tourist family eating outside. It sprayed me in the mouth, which is about on par with my luck this week."

I motion to my shoulder. "I think we can agree who had the worst luck this week, and it sure wasn't you."

"Ah. Good point."

I want him to leave and yet don't, both with equal intensity. "Nowhere else to be?"

"I've got a minute," he says, his gaze lingering on my face. I don't want to know what he can see in my expression. "I could use a coffee."

"You won't sleep tonight."

He gives me a half smile. "I never sleep anyway."

"Ah." I nod.

"The baby," we both say.

Somehow talking about Owen has become the safe space compared to every other thought zipping through my brain like it's the freaking autobahn.

I chew on the corner of my mouth. "Not getting any better about sleeping through the night?"

"They're supposed to start around three months," Graham says. "But we're going into month four, and he's a menace. I get maybe three hours of sleep at a time, on a good night."

"Was last night a good night?"

Graham shoots me a look. "It was not."

I frown in sympathy. "Well, if you ever want to get away,

you can come to our house. The couch isn't great, but at least you'll get a full night's sleep."

It feels like a dare. Like night swimming. Like finding a cliff and diving off into choppy waters. I don't know why I offer, except to prove that I can. Like having Graham sleeping on the other side of my wall couldn't possibly send my brain down the express track to Horny Town with no return ticket.

Graham huffs out a small laugh. "Wow, is the trundle only for Milo, then?" He gives me a sideways look. "You don't trust me in your bedroom?"

My stomach lurches up into my chest. "Oh—well, no—I just. Milo doesn't sleep on the trundle." My face heats. "Because it's short. Your feet might hang off."

He smirks. "I'm not that tall."

I'm having some trouble composing myself. "Well, I guess if you want it that badly, the trundle's all yours."

I feel hot and frazzled as I step up to the counter, Graham's gaze heavy on my back.

"Hi, Moonface," I say, breathless. I hold up Dot's cash.

Moonface slides a mug across the counter to me. "It's decaf. Don't tell her."

Like I said. Never underestimate Moonface.

Graham gets a to-go cup, and when he's finished filling it, I follow him to the front door. Being near him right now makes me feel like I just stuck my tongue in an electrical outlet, but I can't seem to tear myself away, even though I desperately need to cool down.

The blistering hot sun is no help.

"I guess I'll see you later," I say lightly, both hands clasped around Dot's coffee. The warmth bleeds through the ceramic to my palms. I'm going to be drenched in sweat soon.

Graham lingers, glancing toward the street, and I wonder if he doesn't want to leave yet, either.

He meets my gaze with a small smile, and the prolonged eye contact makes my skin tingle. That's when I spot Marissa Whalen, Milo's ex-girlfriend, across the street with a group of girls. She's watching me with an agitated look on her face. I expect her to glance away, but instead she holds my gaze, which is super unsettling.

Marissa lives on the South Shore, so it's uncommon to run into her so often outside school. Of course I'd see her now, so soon after I told off her and her friends at P&J's.

"What's up?" Graham asks, following my gaze. "Oh."

"Yeah," I murmur.

"This should be fun," he says as Marissa steps away from her friends and starts to cross the street toward us.

Shit, shit, shit.

My dread forces out every bubbling, electrified feeling inside of me, replacing it with sludge. "I should probably get back—"

"It's a little late for that," Graham says. "Unless you want to look like you're running away."

Well, obviously I don't want to seem like a coward. I plant my feet, steadying myself.

Marissa stops in front of us, her hands on her hips. "I have something to say."

I swallow and try to put on my best disinterested face. "Yes?"

"I don't think you have any right to comment on my new relationship. It's not my fault things didn't work out with Milo."

I frown at her. "You literally broke up with him."

She scoffs. "Are you serious? Look, Juniper Nash, I get you're an airhead and all, but you can't be that dumb. You need to start playing fair. You already ruined things for me—don't do it to Cora, too."

Her words strike, burying deep in my chest. "What—*what* are you talking about?"

Out of the corner of my eye, I see Graham wince.

Marissa lets out a long-suffering sigh. "I broke up with Milo," she says slowly, like she's speaking to a certified idiot, "because I will not be second best when it comes to my boyfriend. Not to some other girl, not to his boys. I'm number one, maybe number two, but only behind his mother."

I huff out a small laugh. "Don't you think you're being a little dramatic?"

"Oh, that's rich coming from you, drama queen." She's looking at me like I'm something gross she found on the bottom of her shoe. "And you know what? You might think I traded down when I started dating Braden, but he's never ditched me for Zephyr. He's never brought Zephyr along on what was supposed to be a date, never left my house early to bail him out of some stupid drama. He pays attention to *me*."

I shift uncomfortably. Has Milo been doing all that for me?

"Great," I say, my voice a dry rasp. "I'm really happy for you."

"I'm not *finished*. Cora is a good person, and she's a great girlfriend. If you aren't going to throw your hat in for him, then step out of the way. Quit your quirky little games, quit goading him into paying attention to you. Play fair, Juniper Nash."

I feel like I've been slapped. "I'm not playing games, Marissa. He's my best friend."

"Then act like he's your *friend*," she says, "instead of something else."

This time, I look at Graham. He's staring across the street, his mouth in a tense line.

Marissa gathers herself and pulls her shoulders back. "That's all. Don't feel the need to respond. I don't really care what you have to say. I just hope you heard me."

She turns and crosses the street, jogging the last few feet to her friends. She rejoins them with an easy smile that makes my skin crawl.

I clear my throat. "Well . . . that was . . . um . . ."

Graham nods. "Yep."

I stare at him, feeling tingly with nerves. "I don't—I don't know how else to be with Milo. I don't know why I can't just . . . be the way I am without everyone else putting their expectations on it."

Graham doesn't say anything for a long time. I'm so hyperfocused on him, every second that passes feels like a year.

Then the front door opens, and Tallulah sticks her head out. "Hey, Dot wants her coffee. She's getting mad."

I don't miss the look of relief on Graham's face as he steps away from me. "I should go. I have to check in with Rita."

I stare after him as he leaves, retreating down the congested sidewalk until I can no longer see his lime-green NEIGHBORHOOD HERO shirt in the crowd.

Tallulah eyes me as I follow her inside, but whatever she wants to ask, she keeps it locked up tight.

I'm not so lucky with Dot.

"What's wrong with you?" she asks as I hand over her coffee.

"You're all red, Junie," Hal says, reaching over from her table to put a hand on my forehead.

I wave her off. "I'm fine. Just hot."

Tallulah watches me, silent and assessing, but I'm too overwhelmed to worry about what she might see on my face.

Marissa's words have sent me spiraling into a wormhole of confusion.

Step out of the way.

Is that what Marissa really thinks? What Cora thinks?

Is that what Milo meant at rehearsal the other night, when he suggested I was trying to ruin his relationship before it started?

The thought makes me feel like bugs are crawling under my skin. I've never tried to sabotage Milo. I don't want to stand in anyone's way. The way I am with Milo has always felt separate from his relationships. He's my best friend. I treat him the same way I treat Lucy, or—or—

Well, there's the snag. Because there is someone I think of differently. Someone who I look at the way everyone seems to believe I'm looking at Milo. Someone who is so totally off-limits, it feels like he lives in the tallest tower, with no doors or windows, guarded by bars and chains and maybe even a fire-breathing dragon.

I realize belatedly that I wasn't waiting for Graham to fill that long, stretched-out silence between us. *I* wanted to say something—words that would assure him and everyone else who's made the accusation that Milo isn't on my mind. That the feelings I thought I'd taken care of months ago haven't gone away—they've been lying dormant, like a latent virus waiting for the trigger to infect me all over again.

I like someone else.

The thought falls like a guillotine through every neatly ordered piece of my life, shearing them clear in half.

This is the first year Milo and I won't be competing together in the Founder's Relay. We've been a team for as long as they'd let us play, as far back as elementary school. He's athletic and book smart. I'm a fill-in-the-gaps competitor, excelling in things like pop culture quizzes and eating contests. When we were thirteen, we won—the only year we've ever won—because I was the first one to name six of Cher's most popular songs of all time.

But even though I'm well enough to work, the relay organizers wouldn't let me compete, though they were happy to rope me into volunteering. Not that it matters much, since Milo and I still aren't speaking. As I trudge up to the volunteer check-in table, I spot him in line with Cora at the Mud Shack tent, where they're handing out complimentary coffee.

It's so unnatural to see him partnered up with someone else. I hate fighting with Milo, and this one feels like an oil spill—slick and devastating. This entire summer is sliding out of place now, and the last thing I expected was that it'd be Milo and me making things weird. And if he's willing to partner up with someone else for the relay, when I'm still living behind him and basically inescapable, what's going to happen next year when I'm living on the South Shore? Thinking about it makes me feel ill.

As I ease off my sling so I can slip my stiff volunteer shirt over my tank top, Milo glances my way. He opens his mouth like he's going to say something, and my heart gives a hopeful kick. But I startle and turn as hands close around the strap of my sling, helping me pull it over my head.

"This is so bad for the environment," Tallulah says as she hooks the strap of my sling over her shoulder like a purse. She takes my volunteer shirt and shakes it out, then scrunches it up and slips it over my head while I clutch my arm to my stomach. "They could've just asked us all to wear the same color or something."

"What are you doing here?" I ask, my voice a shocked

croak as she helps me ease my injured arm into the sleeve of my T-shirt and resecure my sling.

"Oh, these aren't free for everyone?" she asks as she grabs a volunteer shirt from the table.

I stare at her, and she smirks.

"I'm volunteering." She pulls her shirt over her head, revealing a bikini top underneath, and tucks it between her knees. Then she slips on the volunteer shirt.

"Since when?"

"Since I volunteered." She motions to the Mud Shack tent. "Can we stop there? I need coffee. It's way too early for this."

"You want me to come with you?"

She frowns. "We're working the same event."

I trail her to the Mud Shack tent, practically stumbling in my confusion. "Wait, for real?"

"Why do you seem so surprised?" she asks as she plucks up one of the complimentary coffee cups.

"You didn't say anything at work yesterday when we talked about it."

"I hadn't volunteered yet." She shrugs, and her gaze snags on something over my shoulder. Her brow visibly relaxes, and she lifts a hand in a small wave.

I turn, unsurprised to see Lucy skipping toward us. Graham isn't far behind, dragging his feet.

"Morning!" Lucy says brightly as she falls into line behind us. Even though she clearly doesn't need the coffee, she grabs one anyway.

Graham presses his fingers into his eyes, nails painted black and a streak of ink down his wrist. Then he reaches for his own cup. He doesn't look like he slept at all last night.

I didn't really, either. But not because I have a four-month-old baby brother at home keeping everyone awake. I tossed and turned, hearing Marissa's and Milo's words over and over in my head, remembering the look on Graham's face, like he's starting to believe what everyone else says.

I realize I'm staring when Graham lifts his gaze from his coffee cup, and his eyes catch mine.

I look away quickly, my heart sputtering in my chest like an engine that won't turn over.

"Looks like the first event is an ice bath," Lucy says, perusing her event schedule. "Then we can either go to the history quiz or the karaoke challenge."

"Just what we all need," I say to Lucy. "Your singing voice on a microphone."

Lucy smacks my arm, looking embarrassed. "I can carry a tune!"

"Yeah, into its grave," says Graham.

"Do I need to remind you that I made it into the ensemble of a musical recently?" Lucy asks, putting her hands on her hips.

Graham smirks. "I don't know, I heard they were pretty desperate."

Lucy glares at him. "I hope you have a lovely time in the ice bath."

Graham snorts. "Mm, no," he says, shaking his head. "I don't think so. That's all you."

"Absolutely not," Lucy says on a laugh.

He yawns. "Guess we better withdraw. No chance we'll win if we don't do the first event."

Lucy purses her lips. "I'll play you for it. Loser does the ice bath; winner gives up a level-two favor."

"Expiration date?"

"Three weeks."

Graham eyes her. "Fine." He bites down on the rim of his

empty coffee cup, lifting his fist. They go through a quick round of rock-paper-scissors, which Graham wins.

He drops the coffee cup into his hand and flattens it. While he asks to borrow a marker off one of the Mud Shack baristas, Tallulah turns to me with a question in her furrowed brow.

"Favor trading," I explain. "Best way to get what you want."

We watch as Graham scribbles his initials and *2–3W* on the coffee cup. He passes it to Lucy, who tucks it into her little strawberry-shaped crossbody bag.

"Just give a warning text when you get to the karaoke challenge," I say, patting Lucy on the arm. "I want to be ready when all the birds burst out of the trees from fear."

"I didn't even bring earplugs," Graham complains.

Lucy tips her head back and asks the sky, "What did I do to deserve such assholes for friends?"

"You're a victim of circumstance," Graham says with a grin.

My phone buzzes in my pocket, and I suck in a breath when I see the name. "It's my dad. I'll be right back."

I feel their eyes on me as I duck away and stop under the shade of an old oak tree, its limbs bent so low, they nearly touch the ground.

"Hi, Dad," I practically sing.

"Hi, baby." He sounds happy, which is a good sign.

Please don't be bad news. Please, please, please.

"What are you up to?" he asks.

"It's relay day. I'm working an event, since I can't participate."

I glance toward the coffee tent as the warning bell rings, and someone on a megaphone announces that the relay is starting in five minutes. Tallulah lingers, waiting for me as Lucy and Graham start toward the first event. They turn their heads in my direction, and I plaster on a smile.

"Why can't you participate?" Dad asks, already sounding halfway gone, even though he's the one who called.

My smile slips from my face before I can save it. Lucy is already distracted, peering at the event list, but even from fifty feet away, I feel Graham's gaze like a touch.

I turn my back on them, but it's too late.

I'm constantly trying to convince my friends that my dad isn't bad news. That he cares about me. Shielding them from the worst of him. Because their judgment of him feels like judgment of me, as if not being a priority in my own father's life is somehow a mark against me.

"I'm in a sling," I say, my voice coming out high and tight. "Remember?"

Mom called Dad from the emergency room when I got my sling, but we kept missing each other. We texted briefly about what happened, but it's been weeks since we spoke.

"Oh, right!" Dad chuckles. "I don't like thinking about you being hurt."

I bite my lip. "I'm okay," I say at last. "It doesn't even really hurt that much. I'll be better by the time you get here. Primed to kick your butt at mini golf."

He laughs. "Oh, you think so? You know I'm the master of the windmill."

"Oh yeah, we'll see—"

"We'll have to give Tracie a few pointers, though," Dad says. "Her aim's pretty bad."

Distantly, I hear a woman's laugh and a protesting, "Hey!"

I pull the phone from my ear and stare at it. "Wait, who?" I ask, pressing it to my ear again.

"Tracie," Dad says. "My girlfriend. She's real excited to see this play of yours."

I swallow. "You have a girlfriend?"

Dad doesn't answer, and I hear him saying something in a low voice to someone else. Tracie, probably. *His girlfriend.*

"I gotta go, baby."

"But Dad, wait—I don't know if we have room for both of you at the house."

"Don't worry about us. We'll figure it out. Hey, I'll catch you later, okay? Keep that wrist elevated."

Wrist?

"It's my shoulder," I say to the abandoned end of the line. Dad and Tracie, whoever she is, are gone.

I'm still standing there when Tallulah puts her hand on my arm, glancing in the direction of our event. "You good?"

I nod, stowing away my sour feelings.

We head off toward the history quiz, and my stomach twists with regret as we pass the ice baths, the karaoke stage, and the cookie taste-testing challenge. I should be there, running through these events with my best friend.

If we were speaking, that is. Which we very much aren't.

A sick feeling swirls in my stomach. Between my dad and Milo and whatever is happening with Graham, all I feel is dread.

"You look like a kicked puppy," says Tallulah.

I swallow down a burning sensation in my chest. "I just wish I were playing. I love the relay."

She peers at me, lifting her sunglasses so I can see her narrowed eyes. "Seriously?"

"I know you don't get it," I say bitterly. "You hate this place and everyone in it. But I love the island, and I love the relay. I love Founder's Weekend. I love everything about living here."

Tallulah drops her sunglasses. "I don't hate this place and everyone in it."

I shoot her a sideways glance. "You don't?"

"No." She says it like it's obvious, as though her piss-poor attitude has somehow been a giveaway about how much she's loved hanging around this summer. "I like Piper and Junie's, and I like your mom. And Moonface. I like Hal, and Dot. I like Market Day."

I turn to look at her in surprise. "Really?"

She shrugs. "And I like your friends." She sighs heavily, but I don't miss the pink creeping into her cheeks. "I guess you're growing on me. Kind of."

"Stockholm syndrome," I say. "You've spent too much time with me."

She laughs. "That's the most probable explanation."

Chapter Fourteen

(The closet door shuts on BENEDICK and BEATRICE, locking them together inside.)

JAQUES
Some Cupid kills with arrows, some with traps.

BEATRICE
(Offstage, screaming.) I'M GOING TO WRING YOUR NECK FOR THIS!

ORSINO
Some Beatrice kills with her bare hands. Should we get going?

—Act 2, Scene 15, *Midsummer Madness*

I'm in my bedroom after a long daytime rehearsal, preparing for what will surely be an exhausting family dinner at Paul and Tallulah's, when Mom leans in my bedroom doorway and says, "I heard your dad called."

I frown. "Who told you that?" Normally Milo is the grand tattler, and I feel a brief spike of hope that he found out somehow. That he saw me on the phone and knew—the way Milo always knows—that something was wrong. That he asked our friends about it because he was worried. Maybe this means he's ready to get past this weirdness between us.

"Tallulah. She was worried something happened."

I have only a second to feel the rush of disappointment before her response hits, and I blink. Tallulah? Worried about my feelings?

Clearly we have entered an alternate reality.

"It's fine," I say, trying to keep my voice even, like I'm not upset. I motion for her to come in, and she helps me extract myself from my ratty rehearsal T-shirt. I sniff under my arm and cringe.

Deodorant. Must get deodorant.

As I swipe it on, Mom asks, "What did he have to say?"

"Just checking in." My voice is light as cotton candy. It should get Mom off my back, but she frowns.

"Your dad? Was just checking in?"

The skeptical thread in her voice sends an embarrassed heat across my face.

"What, is that unheard of?" I ask, my voice sharp. "A dad checking in on his daughter after a serious injury?"

Mom's expression goes soft and a little wounded. "No, of course not. I was just expecting the worst, I guess. Tallulah said you looked upset."

"Tallulah doesn't know everything about me." I pause, considering this. "Or anything about me, actually."

"Juju," Mom scolds.

I slide off my cotton shorts and replace them with a clean pair. "I'm just saying, clearly she saw wrong." I hold up a tank top, and Mom helps me into it. I still feel gross, but a shower is a distant dream for me. "He called to say hi."

I can't tell Mom about Dad's girlfriend. Not because she'll go into a fit of jealousy or something equally ridiculous, but because she'll assume he's going to flake. It's The Girlfriend Factor. Anytime he has a girlfriend, the odds he'll flake on me triple.

I don't want Mom to start doubting him more than she

already does. When Dad and Tracie show up next month, I'll figure out where to put the girlfriend. She can sleep on the trundle. Or the chaise. Or on a lounger outside.

Mom opens her mouth, but she stops when the front door swings open and a high, cartoonish voice calls, "Hello, hello, Abrehearts!"

"Back here, Isabel," Mom says, half turning in my doorway to greet Milo's mom as she comes down the hall.

She's carrying a bottle of wine. "Can I interest you in half a bottle of the finest pinot noir Publix had on sale for the use of your fancy cheese slicer?"

"I'm surprised there's half a bottle left," Mom teases, accepting the bottle.

"Apparently my husband doesn't appreciate how the wine pairs with my huitlacoche quesadillas."

My mouth waters instantly. If she had huitlacoche, that means she got it fresh from the Oaxacan market her parents frequent religiously on the mainland. Isabel grew up going there, and I've been with Milo's family a hundred times. It's a little shop with the best food, made to order at the counter.

"Better for me," says Mom. "I'll take it to dinner tonight."

Isabel shoots me a playful look. "Thank goodness your mom found a man with taste."

"Paul doesn't have taste," I reply. "He just does whatever my mom tells him."

"Smart man," Isabel says.

As I follow them to the kitchen, Isabel ruffles my hair in the same way Milo usually does. He's so much like his mom, from the freckled face to the wide, ever-present smile to the magnetic personality. The only thing they don't share is the voice—Milo's is pitched very deep like his dad's, while Isabel operates in a much higher, animated register.

"So, what's going on in the world of Junie?" Isabel wraps an arm around me, giving me a squeeze. "I haven't seen you much this summer."

"I've been busy. Work, rehearsal." I half lift my injured arm. "This friggin' thing."

"It's always something with you," says Isabel.

"I'm sure that's all you hear from Milo, but don't let him fool you. He's just dramatic." I hop onto one of the stools at the counter. "That's why I roped him into community theater. He needed an outlet."

Isabel chuckles as Mom hands her the cheese slicer. "I feel like I never see *him* anymore, either. Between the two of you, we're getting real practice for our empty nests."

Mom opens her mouth to respond, but I beat her to it. "Oh, she won't have an empty nest for a while. She's replacing me with Paul and Tallulah, remember?"

Isabel's eyes widen, and when I glance at Mom, her mouth is hanging open.

"Juju," Mom says when she recovers, but whatever she wants to say, the words seem to have escaped her.

Isabel quickly glosses over the uncomfortable silence. "I can't even keep Milo at home on the weekends. As soon as you finished rehearsal today, he was off to Crystal River with Graham."

I jerk in surprise. "Crystal River?"

"Yeah, fishing. Apparently they fish now." She holds up her hands and shrugs. "I bet they don't even know how to clean a fish, let alone cook one."

"They're too soft for that," I say. "You know they couldn't kill a fish. Milo won't even kill a spider."

This makes Isabel practically glow with pride.

I follow her to the door, where she waves the cheese slicer at Mom. "Thanks, Piper," she says, grinning like she can will away the awkwardness that's settled over us. "I'll bring it back tomorrow."

Mom lifts a hand and waves, forcing a smile. As soon as Isabel is gone, she says, "Juju, what was that about?"

"I was just kidding." Then, before she can protest, I grab her keys and toss them to her. "Aren't we running late?"

Mom lets it go, but I can tell she's going to want this to be A Conversation.

I'm too distracted to focus on Mom, though. I'm stuck on Graham and Milo, and Crystal River, and how neither of them mentioned it at rehearsal today. Milo and I still aren't on normal speaking terms, but it's odd that I didn't hear about it.

On the way to Paul and Tallulah's house, I text Lucy.

> **ME**
> Did Graham and Milo say anything to you about going to crystal river this weekend?

> **LUCY**
> You mean to the affair house? UMMMM no.
> Graham would never.

> **ME**
> So tell me why Milo's mom just said they're in CR right now

> **LUCY**
> Little liars

> **ME**
> And Milo doesn't have a car. But you know who does.

> **LUCY**
> You can't hear my sexy whistle but I'm doing a sexy whistle right now

After I found out Graham's dad was Rooney's unavailable man, the rest of the story fell into place. The days on end she'd disappear, the overnight bag she'd ask me to stash at my house. With Angela at her apartment and Macaulay's family at his house, they had nowhere to go—except for the old, mostly unused vacation home the Ishams have in Crystal River.

Graham calls it the Affair House. And after everything came out, he vowed he'd never go back.

Which means there's no way Graham is in Crystal River with Milo. And if Milo is gone for the weekend, then it's extremely likely he's with Cora. She does have a car. And Crystal River isn't too far for a single night getaway—as we all learned.

So the next morning, I decide to find out the truth for myself.

I haven't visited Graham's house in almost a year. In the same way I've avoided it because of Rooney, Graham has seemed to want to keep us all from it. But I'm too keyed up to worry about seeing her. I need to know if I'm right.

Besides, if I catch him and Milo in a lie, I might be able to score a favor out of one or both of them. And I'm low on favors this summer. A level-three favor for my silence would be a delight.

Graham's family lives in a beach cottage on the bayside, the kind of house that looks smaller from the front than it is inside. It's a muted blue with white trim and a flowery welcome mat that says, HEY, CUTE SHOES.

It's very clearly a Rooney touch. Graham's mom, Joy, has much more traditional taste. Their old welcome mat said just that: WELCOME.

I knock before I can chicken out, because even though the driveway is empty, that doesn't mean Graham is home alone. Or home at all. And Rooney doesn't have a car, though that could have changed anytime in the last year. I have no idea what I'm about to walk into.

The door swings open, and relief rushes through me.

"Hey, liar," I say with a grin.

Graham groans, turning to press his forehead into the front door like he's wishing he could make me disappear with his mind. "What do you want?"

"What a lovely welcome, thank you."

"Excuse me, I need to see your ticket," he says as I push past him into the house.

"Hey, buddy, I'm a VIP. Don't you know who I am?"

"Oh, the tabloids are gonna love you when you're famous."

I glow with pride. "I love that you say *when*." I pause in the entryway to slip off my sandals.

"You don't have to do that," he says, some of the warmth leaving his voice.

I glance over at him in surprise. "What?"

He motions to my shoes.

Of my friends, I'm the only one who doesn't live in a no-shoe household. The last time I was here, there was a shelf by the front door for the family's shoes.

Now as I glance around the entryway, I notice a lot of changes. The shoe shelf is gone, and there are no sneakers and sandals and loafers piled by the door. The photos I've seen a thousand times have been replaced—pictures from their vacation to the Philippines to visit Joy's extended family in Luzon, the ski trip they took to Colorado where Graham sprained his ankle, and the old photo of Graham, Milo, and me onstage during our *Wizard of Oz* performance are all gone. Now their frames are filled with photos of a pink-cheeked baby with round blue eyes, and one tense family photo where Graham looks ready to bolt at any second.

My gaze snags on Rooney in that one—her wide smile and bright blue eyes, dark hair scraped back in a low bun, the baby in her lap. Instead of the peach blush and bronzer that always made her look young and sun kissed, she's made up to look older here—alabaster skin missing its usual tan, cheeks contoured to sharp edges.

I guess it makes sense. If she looked like the Rooney I know, this photo would have a different feel—a dad and his three children.

In their old family photo, a middle school–aged Graham sat between Joy and Macaulay, a perfect mixture of both—his mom's golden-brown skin, his dad's wavy hair, his mom's dark and narrow eyes, his dad's full mouth. It was an outtake, but his mom loved it more than the final product. You could see his dad's arm reaching around Graham to tickle his mom behind her ear. Her shoulders were hunched up, catching her mid-laugh. Graham had a half-pained look on his face like he was embarrassed but loving it.

In this new photo, he's smiling, but I know Graham. I can see the tightness in his mouth, the discomfort in his gaze. Like he thinks he doesn't belong there.

Something cold seeps through my chest and pools in my stomach. I feel so achingly sad for him.

Graham must see it on my face, because his expression tenses. "So, what are you doing here?" he asks, a forced lightness in his tone. Graham wears a lot of masks to hide his pain—the daredevil, the idiot, the clown. He's careful about how much he lets people see.

I slip off my other sandal, ignoring his protest, because it feels strange to be in the Isham house with shoes on. Even if every trace of Joy has been erased, she still lives in every corner and crevice for me.

"Just wanted to catch you and Milo in the world's worst lie," I say, steering him to safer territory.

Graham grimaces, wrapping a hand around his nape and tilting his head back. I'm momentarily distracted by the long column of his throat, the way his Adam's apple juts out, and his taut forearm.

"It just seems a little messy to say you're both out of town." I slip my free hand into my pocket to keep it honest. At least my sling has the other one under control. "What if you go out and run into the sheriff? Or literally any single one of his deputies? I bet they all know where you're supposed to be. It's gotta be tough being the alibi for the sheriff's son."

"And that's why I'm not going out." He motions to the house. "Part of the deal."

I grin. "So there *is* a deal."

He rubs his forehead, then points toward his bedroom and starts walking. I follow him through the rearranged living room with its new couch, reupholstered armchair, and massive TV over a fake fireplace.

"Wow," I say, the word slipping out before I can stop it. "It's, like, *really* different in here."

Graham glances over his shoulder. His gaze sweeps over the furniture, and he lets out a derisive snort before turning away. "Yeah, I think the name of the game was making sure nothing my mom liked stayed. It's probably better she couldn't figure out a way to stay on the island. She'd shit if she found out they're repainting the house."

I raise my eyebrows. "Seriously?" I follow him down the short hallway once filled with Graham's school photos, some of which are now replaced with pictures of Owen. I do a quick count and realize it's exactly half—like someone wants to prove that they're both equally important to this family.

Graham pauses at the threshold of his bedroom, glancing back. "Yeah. *Sea-foam green.*"

We both make identical fake-barfing noises as he steps into his bedroom.

I stop just inside the door.

At least one thing in the Isham house is the same. Clothes are heaped on the floor in front of Graham's closet, his dresser piled with what looks like a treasure trove of garbage—old receipts, coins, some thread bracelets I'm pretty sure Lucy made him in an elementary school art class. There's an old skate deck leaned up against the wall, cracked on one end. Beside it is a pile of used sketchbooks.

One wall is graffitied in permanent marker—doodles from all of us over the years, quotes we've liked from songs or movies, things we wanted to remember. A little stick figure I drew giving peace signs, which Graham calls Edward Scissorhands. His art stands out on the wall—perfect renderings of video game characters, and cartoonish versions of people in town, like Dot with the face of a sunflower, and Castor Clemmons, owner of the bike shop and meanest man on the island, holding an axe over his head and chasing an army of kids.

His sheets are twisted at the end of his bed, three pillows strewn across the mattress. The sight of it kicks up my heartbeat. Graham never makes his bed, but even after years of being alone in this room with him, it feels too intimate after what happened last summer. I spent a lot of afternoons making out with him in this room—on that bed.

Graham clears his throat. He reaches over and starts organizing his bed, shoving the pillows against the wall and pulling the blanket up over the twisted sheets. His sketchbook lies open on the ground next to his bed, pens scattered around it, and he quickly toes it shut before I can see anything but a few half-finished panels of ink.

Kind of like a comic.

It's not the first time I've caught a glimpse of Graham's sketchbook, but it is the first time I've seen something so distinct. I try not to look like I'm focusing too hard on it, but I know I fail because Graham leans down and picks it up, tucking it neatly under a pillow.

Well, okay then.

Graham doesn't have a desk, and even though sitting on his bed was never an issue before, I linger at the door. I'm not about to sit on the floor and look up at him the whole time.

"Do you think your mom will move back?" I ask, studying the marks on his doorframe that measure his height. They stretch a few inches above my head, the last one marked AGE 16—last year. Graham turned seventeen in April, long after everything fell apart. I guess no one was thinking about marking his height at that point. I get an overwhelming urge to shove him against the doorway and mark it for him. To prove that someone is thinking of him, that we don't have to stop at sixteen, even if he's stopped growing.

"I don't know," he says, a thread of exhaustion in his voice. I wonder if he's run the question into the ground already. If I'm just asking the things he's constantly asking himself. "She didn't want to leave, but now that she's there . . . She got some seasonal gig at another firm, and they want to keep her on. Right now, I don't think leaving my lolo's is an option. She needs the job for the health insurance, and all her money is tied up in divorce stuff."

Graham's grandfather's house is teeming with people these days—his aunt and her family after they lost their house to foreclosure, another cousin whose parents wouldn't take him back in after he quit college, and now his mom amidst her divorce. It's a landing spot for people who have fallen on hard times.

"My dad's trying to screw her out of everything." Graham's mouth tightens, his gaze sharpening with irritation I'm worried is directed at me until he speaks again. "No alimony, no house. He's making her pay for his crime—it's so fucked up. He's *so* fucked up. He gets everything he wants and makes sure no one else gets anything they need."

The way he says it makes me wonder if that's something happening with more than just Joy. If it's bleeding into Macauley's relationship with Graham, too.

My gaze flicks toward the open door across the hall, where an empty crib sits in the corner.

Graham steps around me to shut his bedroom door. "So, why are you here?"

The room shrinks, and there is a brief exodus of thoughts from my brain. My face burns, and I pray I'm not as red as I feel.

"To find out what Milo gave you," I say when I recover.

Graham's brows pull together. "Why the inquisition? Obviously it was a favor."

"I assume a level five." I put my free hand on my hip in an attempt to look calmer than I feel. "For something this big."

"You mean taking the key from the drawer and staying in my house for a day?" He shoots me a flat look. "Yeah, it's a real chore."

"What if your dad finds out you took the key?"

He snorts. "He'd have to go looking for it first, and they don't go to the Affair House anymore. That would require them to speak."

Surprise jolts through me. "What?"

A ghost of a wince passes across his face, like he regrets saying it. Instead of answering, he asks, "Anything else I can help you with?"

I let the subject change pass. I'm not eager to talk about his dad and Rooney, either. "You're being awfully cagey about the whole thing. Since when do we keep secrets from each other?"

His face lights up in a way that tells me I'm about to regret saying that. Whatever discomfort he felt talking about his dad and Rooney, he's buried it now.

"Oh yeah?" He grins, a calculating look in his eye. "I've got a few questions then. Should we trade? Secret for secret?"

Because of course, everything is tit for tat with us.

When I don't answer, he prowls closer, his eyes narrowed in amusement. "Like, why do you care so much that we lied?"

I back up against the closed door. "That's not a secret. It's dangerous. What if you—I don't know—fall off your bed and hit your head, and you go into a relatively not-serious coma—"

"Relatively. How generous."

"—and you're the only one who knows he's there!"

Graham tilts his head. "He has a phone."

"Sure, but what if they get in a boating accident and lose their phones in the water?"

Graham chews his lips like he's trying to hold in a laugh. "It's an interesting thought, but I don't think they're going boating." He gives me a meaningful look.

I grimace. "Gross."

"What's the big deal? Seriously, I don't get it." His smile loses some of its warmth, like something else is pushing to get free. "Is it just too much for you that he has another girl in his life?"

Cold races down my spine. "What's *that* supposed to mean?"

He raises his eyebrows, his expression icing over. "You know what it means."

He starts to turn away, but I grab his arm, forcing him to face me. I don't like when he has his back to me. It's too easy for Graham to hide his real feelings when I can't see his eyes.

"No, I really don't," I say. "I'd love for you to explain it to me. Because Milo, and Marissa, and now you all seem to think I'm some master saboteur. So what is it? You think I'm in love with Milo, too?"

Graham shakes his head, his lips pressed tightly together.

"You don't look so sure." My voice has a razor-sharp edge to it, barely recognizable to my own ears. "And considering you've been the one throwing him at Cora all summer—at the bonfire, the Fourth, this little weekend getaway—I don't know, it sounds like maybe I'm not the only one trying to sabotage something."

He frowns. "What are you talking about?"

"Well, Graham, if I'm in love with Milo, and you're so set on pushing him and Cora together, what does that sound like to you?"

His head dips lower. "If you're accusing me of something, just say it." His voice is deadly serious, all the humor drained from his face.

I start to speak, but the words scrape to a stop in my throat when he presses his hand over my mouth.

"But remember, once you say it, you can't take it back."

I jerk my face away from his hand, and as I do, my gaze snags on something I didn't notice earlier.

It's the *Wizard of Oz* photo, sitting on Graham's dresser amongst the mess. It's got a new, smaller frame now. I glance around quickly, taking stock of the room, searching for other changes like a game of I Spy. But it's the only photo in his room—no family vacations, no other friends. Just me and Graham, eight years old. Me with my arms thrown in the air, annoyed. Graham gazing up at me like he'd just seen the sun for the first time after days of rain. It's a photo I've seen a thousand times, yet never really *saw* until now. Maybe because before, Milo hadn't been folded out of it completely. His absence throws all the details into new light.

Graham follows my gaze and swallows audibly.

My heartbeat snags like a fishing line caught on a rock. I reach up, brushing my fingers against his cheek, and Graham freezes.

He turns to me slowly, and my gaze drops, landing on his mouth. I drag my fingertips down the line of his jaw, gently urging him toward me.

He reaches up and catches my wrist, his grip gentle but firm. But when I look up in surprise, his expression is ice-cold. "Juniper Nash," he says, his voice low, "don't start something you can't finish."

I suck in a breath, tugging out of his grip. He lets me go without any resistance, which stings for some reason.

"I'm sorry," I whisper, taking a step away. "Oh my God. I'm sorry. I don't know—I don't know what—"

"It's fine," he says flatly.

Panic rears up. "It's—it's being in this room. I don't know what I was thinking."

"It's fine, Junie."

I swallow down a hysterical sound. "I should go." My voice comes out so soft, I can barely hear it. Or maybe that's the blood rushing in my ears, drowning out everything else.

I turn and leave his room, covering my mouth with one shaking hand as I burst into the hall.

I almost kissed Graham. *I almost kissed Graham.*

What am I doing? What was I *thinking*? Of all people, it can't be him. Things between us are too fragile. After last summer, I swore I took care of this—that no matter my feelings, I would never, ever kiss Graham Isham again. We have the potential to ruin everything, and not only for us—for Milo and Lucy, too. This was reckless and thoughtless and the worst kind of selfish.

I shove my feet into my sandals and open the front door right as someone on the other side twists the knob.

And there's Rooney.

She's pushing a stroller, chubby-cheeked Owen snoozing under the shade, a fish-printed bucket hat on his head.

Her eyes widen. "Junie?" She blinks like she might be hallucinating.

The stroller is blocking the door, and I step to one side, then the other, trying to figure out the best way to escape.

A hand moves past me, grasping the front of the stroller and pulling it over the threshold. I whip around as Graham maneuvers the stroller around me, then reaches in and extracts a sleeping Owen.

It's the most surreal sight. Graham's flat expression, his downcast gaze, and the baby cradled against his shoulder. His hand looks huge splayed across Owen's back, dark-painted nails stark against Owen's onesie.

"Hey," Rooney says as I turn and step past her, hurrying down the front walk. But it's not so much a greeting as it is a signal to stop.

I keep walking.

"Junie." I hear her shoes crunching through the pebbles. "Hey. Stop a second. Are you okay?"

She catches my good arm, and I whip around to shake her off.

"What do you care?" The words fly out before I can stop them. It's been almost a year since I last spoke to Rooney. One day, everything was fine, the two of us joking around like usual. The next time I saw her, she didn't even look at me. She picked up her final check from my mom and left P&J's forever.

Which is why it feels so agonizingly unfair that she has the audacity to look hurt right now.

"Seriously, Roo, I don't know why you'd even ask," I say with a harsh laugh. "You know I'm not. You know I couldn't possibly be. I've had to live with what I did for you for a year, and I'll have to live with it for the rest of my life." I motion back to the house with a quick jab of my hand. "That's just a byproduct. So no, I'm not okay, and I don't think you have any right to ask me about it."

Her mouth hangs open in shock.

As I turn to leave, I don't chance a look at the house. I won't be able to handle whatever I'll find on Graham's face.

Chapter Fifteen

OLIVIA
I know that Sebastian would never leave me on his
own. He loves me! There is mischief afoot here—I'm
sure of it.

BEATRICE
(Sighing.) It must be true that when we are born, we
cry that we have come to this stage of fools.
—Act 2, Scene 13, *Midsummer Madness*

Rehearsal is hellish now that the rest of the Drama Club hates
me. The Vince Effect is in full force. It's sent Sophie into crisis
mode.

"We need to do something," she says. "Something big.
Something that'll ingratiate you to the club again."

"We should just give up." I tilt my head in her direction.
"People love you, but you're no match for Vince. And I was
really mean to him."

I'm trying to act cool about the whole thing, but I'm sick
with worry. I was counting on Drama Club president for my
transcripts. If I don't get into Florida State, I don't know
what my other options are. Florida has a lot of great schools,

but FSU has the best drama program. And without drama, I'm nothing.

I'm not good at anything else.

"He's such a prick," Sophie says bitterly. "If you want to cheat on your boyfriend, don't be mad when you get caught." She turns and gives me a sad, pouty look. "I just hate that you're going through this, Junie. It's so unfair."

It's over the top, even for Sophie. We get along well, and she's my closest friend in Drama Club, but sometimes I think she seeks out situations to involve herself in. Like life isn't exciting enough if there isn't a little social chaos.

Still, it feels good to have her on my side.

The ensemble is in the middle of practicing one of the fairy dance numbers, so Sophie and I are taking a short break before I start working on my hardest scene. In this one, Will and I are in side-by-side hotel rooms. Beatrice is helping Duke Orsino disguise himself as Olivia while Benedick helps Viola disguise herself as her brother, Sebastian. As we do, we sing the musical's most difficult duet. Half the lines are different words sung in unison, and at the end of the song, we both leave the hotel rooms at the same time, causing another snafu. Now the most volatile couple in the musical assumes the other is having an affair.

"Hello, dearest wife," Will says as he approaches with a fresh bottle of water. "You're looking ferocious tonight."

"Oh, darling husband," I respond, reciting the next line from the musical, "you must mean *ferociously beautiful*."

Will gives an exaggerated frown. "No, cherished one, I don't think I do."

I elbow him lightly in the ribs, and he laughs, breaking character.

I'm relieved at how good Will has turned out to be. I was worried he wouldn't pull his weight—especially since we're his no-more-Cabo-vacation fallback plan—but he's really shown up. Even though we have smaller lead roles, we have some of the most complicated scenes, and I wasn't too confident he'd be able to do it.

"Don't look now, but your bestie's giving you the stink eye," Sophie singsongs, quirking one eyebrow in the direction of the stage.

"Oh, that narrows it down," I say.

Since my fall from grace with the Drama Club, Sophie could be talking about anyone. But I have a feeling, since Will is standing close enough that our arms are touching, that she's talking about Camila.

"It's Camila," says Sophie. She's the type of person who gives you your birthday gift as soon as she buys it, even if she's four months early. She doesn't like the suspense of holding on to something.

"Great." I ease away from Will, putting some space between us. "Sorry, darling husband, but I'm trying to repair my image, and you aren't helping."

Sophie glances between us, her eyes lighting up. Which makes me a bit worried, to be honest.

"My parents are going out of town for their anniversary this weekend," Sophie says. "And *we* should have a party."

Will eyes her. "A theater party?"

Sophie shoots him a playful scowl. "*No.* You can bring your friends." To me, she stage-whispers, "If he has any."

Will's mouth drops open in faux offense.

Sophie grins. "You could do us a huge favor and spread the word." She leans in, her gaze flicking toward the stage. "In fact, if you could ask Camila specifically . . ." She waggles her eyebrows at him.

He groans, shaking his head. "Do I have to?"

Sophie folds her hands. "Please? And then you can talk Junie up a little. Make sure Camila knows Junie still has your favor even if she doesn't have Vince's."

He frowns. "Who's Vince?"

Sophie shoots me a look. "I guess the Vince Effect only reaches so far." She turns to Will. "So, what do you think? Come on, be a team player. Do it for your wife."

I glance toward the Drama Club kids gathered at the edge the stage. Camila and Sophie both have a lot of sway with the others. If we convince Camila, maybe she and Sophie can persuade the rest. Finding time to talk during rehearsal is hard, but at a party, anything is possible.

Will taps his chin, grinning. "I don't know, Keller. What do I get out of it?" His eyes light up. "Bedroom tour?"

Sophie reaches out and shoves him. Even though she's laughing, the shove has more force behind it than is entirely playful. "Watch it, Heinbach, or I'll tell my boyfriend."

He half turns, giving her an incredulous look as he glances between her and Peter, who is helping Graham carry a large set piece on the other side of the amphitheater. "That wimp? I could take him."

I'm momentarily distracted by the sight of Graham, Will and Sophie's back-and-forth turning to a low hum. Even from a hundred feet away, I can see the strain of Graham's muscles as the sleeves of his T-shirt slip back, the tense set of his shoulders, and the relieved smile on his face as they set the piece in the grass.

Graham reaches up to test its stability and says something

that makes Peter laugh. I feel a stab of jealousy. Graham has barely glanced in my direction since rehearsal started. He arrived a few minutes late, once Miss Liu had already dispersed us to work in our breakout groups, and went straight to helping the crew.

I've been hyperaware of his presence on the other side of the amphitheater all night. The weirdness between us is too familiar, like the early days after our big blowup fight, when I couldn't even get Graham to look at me, and kind of didn't want him to. Except now I do—I want him to. I want any sign that we're okay.

I am so ungodly mad at myself.

"Okay, Keller, I get it," Will says, dropping his arm around my shoulders and drawing my attention back to him and Sophie. "Makes more sense that Junie would pay up for me helping her out anyway."

Even though my sling is coming off soon and I'm almost healed up, I wince in anticipation of pain in my shoulder. But it only twinges a little, and as Will eases up on the pressure, the pain dwindles quickly.

I can hardly focus on whatever Will is saying to me, my eyes drawn back to Graham like he's fitted with Junie magnets.

But when I look his way, he's already staring at me, his gaze fixed on Will's arm around my shoulders. His attention feels heavy as his eyes move down my arm to where Will's fingers dangle against my bare skin. Graham's expression darkens, and I feel a thump low in my belly.

He shifts in our direction like he's about to cross the amphitheater to us, and anticipation squeezes my insides like a pressure cooker. But he freezes right when I hear Milo's voice.

"Hey, watch her shoulder."

Will jerks beside me as Milo grabs him by the back of the neck and drags him off me.

"Easy, buddy," Will says. "She was just asking me for a favor."

"I wasn't. Sophie was," I point out.

Sophie nods. "That's true, it was me. For a good cause." She turns toward Milo, grinning. "Hey, you could help. I'm throwing a party Saturday. We're trying to get Junie back in the Drama Club's good graces." She folds her hands under her chin and gives him a big, cheesy smile. "Maybe you could talk to them? Remind them Junie is the reason you're all even here?"

"Camila would be playing a talking plant if it weren't for me," I say with a dark look, avoiding Milo's eyes. We still haven't really spoken, just light greetings and passing small talk.

It occurs to me that Lucy is the only one of my friends I'm still on good terms with. Between my argument with Milo and my—my—whatever happened with Graham, I seem to be on the outs with just about everyone. I'm on better terms with Tallulah at this point, which is really saying something.

"Yeah, of course," Milo says, his voice so light and normal that my head jerks up in surprise. When he catches my eye, his expression softens. It's halfway to an apology, and something inside me eases at the sight. "I'm an expert at reminding everyone how great my best friend is."

Will gives a little huff. "Hey, man, that's my wife you're flirting with."

It's nothing we haven't heard before, and for a second, I feel a shot of nerves that this might tip Milo and me over again.

But Milo smiles at me, his gaze knowing, and I get it.

Without even speaking, in the same way we've traded words and secrets our whole lives.

Milo knows I'm not in love with him. And he isn't in love with me. Whatever he's accused me of, it isn't because of this—the thing everyone else expects of us. We may be beyond the understanding of other people, but other people don't matter. Milo and I know the truth—of ourselves and of each other.

The relief comes rushing in so strong, tears prick my eyes.

"I'll do whatever you need," Milo says, reaching up to ruffle my hair until it's in tangles. "We can strategize on our way home."

At the end of rehearsal, Lucy meets Milo and me by the stage, the three of us sweat drenched.

"If I never hear the words *pivot turn* again, I will die happy," Lucy says. "And I'm getting a headache from this bun."

As she lets down her braids, I glance around for Graham. I want to see him so badly, I ache inside. But I'm simultaneously dreading it so much, my legs feel like they've gone completely boneless.

"He took off already," Milo says. "He said Rita needed him for a late delivery. Someone called out tonight."

"Oh." I nod, trying to keep my face an expressionless mask. I don't need him or Lucy catching on that something's up between Graham and me. It's too soon after our last fight nearly ruined our friendship, and I don't want them to panic. "Okay, let's go then."

Lucy skips between Milo and me. "Hey, did I hear Sophie's throwing a party?"

On our way home, Milo and I fill her in on Sophie's big plan to nix the Vince Effect. But when she breaks off to head toward her house, the two of us go quiet. The rest of our trek home is silent, gaining tension the longer it goes on. His accusation still hangs heavy between us, and it's clearly not going away on its own.

"So," I say as Milo follows me past his street, "I guess we need to talk."

He blows out a breath. "Yeah."

"I don't want you to think I have a problem with you dating."

Milo makes a small, thoughtful sound. "It's not that I think you have a problem with *me* dating."

"Then what— You said—"

He rubs the back of his neck. "Yeah, I know. What I meant is, I don't think you like when *anyone's* in a relationship."

We're approaching my house, so I linger at the end of the driveway. If Mom spots Milo, she'll be all over us.

"I think to you, relationships mean bad things." He hesitates. "You know how your dad is."

I let out a sharp laugh. "So it's all down to my daddy issues."

"Your dad has ditched you a lot in your life, and he's never shown up for you when he has a girlfriend." His expression softens. "You're my best friend, JN. You mean the entire fucking world to your mom. He's the only one who considers you expendable."

My stomach twists, and tears prick my eyes. "Nice. That feels really good to hear, that you think I'm expendable to my own father."

"He treats you like a convenience," he says, an edge creeping into his voice. "And you never tell him when he's hurt you, like you're afraid if you voice one single complaint to him, he'll give up on you and take off again."

It's the *again* that really drives in the knife.

When my parents split and Mom left town to come to White Coral, my dad didn't try to get in touch until I was in first grade. I went from someone who'd only ever watched dads from afar to finally having one of my own. He drove in for three blissful weeks while he was on a job in Sarasota, and we did all the fun stuff—summer carnivals, pier fishing, beach arcades, ice cream every day.

When the three weeks were up, he left. He called once a couple weeks later, told me about his new girlfriend and their place in Naples. And then radio silence.

That's how it is with Dad. When he's single, he calls. He unloads his stresses, tells me about his dickhead bosses, chats about whatever is going on with me in school. Then a new girlfriend comes along, and the calls come less frequently, until I only hear from him every few months.

When they break up, the calls start again. New stresses, new dickhead bosses.

"I know why you do this," Milo says, drawing me out of my head. "It's the reason you insert yourself in my life more when I date someone. Why things get a little more dramatic and chaotic. You get yourself in more trouble. I know that's why you don't want to move in with Paul. The North Shore is always gonna be here for you, and you know that. You're worried about being second best."

I put a hand over my eyes like I can hide my tears, but my wet sniffle gives me away.

"Don't cry," Milo says, sounding pained. He reaches around to hug me, carefully avoiding my bad shoulder. "Come on, JN, it's okay. I didn't—I never wanted to say this because I knew it'd upset you, but listen— Are you listening?"

I nod, the top of my head bumping his chin.

Milo sighs. "Whatever your dad does, or has done, has

nothing to do with the rest of us. We're always gonna be here for you. You're stuck with me forever. No girlfriend is ever gonna change that, and anyone who thinks they can isn't gonna be my girlfriend for long. You're my family, Juniper Nash."

My hand slides down over my mouth as a small sob escapes.

He squeezes me tighter, forgetting my shoulder and that I need air to breathe. I wrap my arm around him, my free hand gripping the back of his shirt, which is damp with sweat. It's way too stifling outside to hold on to each other like this, but we don't let go—not for a long time.

When Milo finally releases me, it's to wipe his own eyes, which are wet and red in the dim light from the solar mushrooms Mom has staked in the ground around our mailbox. I'm surprised they haven't been packed away yet. She's been in a packing frenzy the last few weeks.

I have, admittedly, slacked a bit in the packing department. I blame my injury.

Milo gives me a shaky smile, his gaze flicking over my face. "You okay?"

I swipe my forearm across my eyes. "Yeah. Sorry for blubbering."

He chuckles. "Come on, from the Juniper Nash Cry Fest? I'm used to it."

"Hey, the Fest has only been here a few times this summer!" I reach out and shove him, and he keeps laughing.

There's still a thread of a laugh in his voice when he asks, "So, we're good?"

I nod, glancing away as my cheeks heat. It's embarrassing to be seen so clearly, even by Milo, who's seen every single one of my flaws—even the ones I didn't know about.

He waits for me to open the front door before he turns and starts in the direction of his house.

As the front door swings wide, it hits a stack of boxes leaning against the living room wall, and they topple, sliding across the hardwood.

Mom glances up from where she's wrapping some of our framed photos in old newspaper. "How was rehearsal?"

I stare the half-full box beside her. "It was fine. What are you doing?"

There's a frown in Mom's voice as she asks, "Have you been crying?"

I blink rapidly, reaching up to rub my eyes. "No. Sneezing."

But when I finally lift my gaze to Mom's face, I can tell she doesn't believe me. She tilts her head, her expression softening as she moves toward me.

"Do you want to talk about it?" she asks, gently ushering me toward the couch.

I collapse onto the cushions, sinking low. "Not really."

I can never, ever tell my mom that I'm worried about becoming second best to Paul, or Tallulah. I saw the look on her face when I made the mistake of joking about it the other night, and I don't want to hurt her.

But maybe it wasn't so much a joke as my real fear beating to get out. Because the truth is, I am afraid. I'm freaked out about moving, about leaving for college, about her being alone with the Breemans and me coming home to find them curled on the couch watching *Dateline.* Of finding out Mom is behind on *Proper Southern Ladies* by six episodes, then twelve, then whole seasons because suddenly she doesn't care about keeping up with the things we've always done together.

First it's Piper and Junie's, our place, infiltrated by Tallulah. Then it's our house, traded for that monstrosity on the South Shore to live with the Breemans. After that, it'll be all our things—*Proper Southern Ladies* and Thursday night gyros from the Greek place on the mainland and picking out bouquets for each other from Dot's selection and visiting the antique car show every August to commemorate my birthday and the stranger whose car I was nearly born in.

I've never thought I was afraid of change. I'm the type of person who updates their phone software as soon as a new version is available. When they changed us over to block scheduling at school, and when they got rid of German as a language elective and I had to switch to French, and when they stopped selling soda on campus, I took it all in stride.

But maybe it's because those things don't really matter to me. Maybe it's that most people hate change when it's something that really matters.

And maybe it's my job to make it clear what's important to me, because no one will know if I don't.

"Hey, Mom?" I say, my voice coming out small and more tentative than I knew possible.

Mom raises her eyebrows, head tilting slightly.

"Could we watch *Proper Southern Ladies*?" I ask.

Mom's smile is edged in confusion. "How about one episode? And then we work on packing?"

I glance toward the pile of boxes by the door, and my stomach dips and then rises like a cresting wave. "Two episodes?"

"I don't want to rush through them," Mom says. "What are we supposed to watch when we're caught up?"

I tug at the hem of my shirt, twisting it around my fingers. "I don't know. You could watch those true crime documentaries Paul and Tallulah love."

Mom pulls a face. "I don't think so. I don't like all that murder stuff—the news is bad enough. They can have their murder documentary nights without us, don't you think?"

The clenching around my heart loosens slightly. "You don't think you'll drop our trashy reality TV for all their serious stuff?"

Mom laughs. "Am I a serious-stuff watcher, Juju? Please. You're the one who's gonna need to keep up with me. You'll be off at college in a year, and I'll be calling you every Tuesday night to see if you watched the latest episode of Baton Rouge, and you'll be like, 'Mom, come on. I'm busy having a social life.'"

"I would never." I lean into her, tucking myself under her arm. "Some things are sacred."

Mom smiles, nudging me. "I think so, too." She brushes her hand over my hair and down my arm. "How's that shoulder feel? Ready to get your sling off?"

"It feels fine. I could probably take it off right now."

Mom makes a protesting noise. "Let's wait until we see your doctor tomorrow."

I groan. "*Fine.*"

She reaches for the remote. "So, one episode?"

I hold up two fingers.

"One and a half," Mom says. "And we watch the other half after we finish sorting through the living room stuff we want to keep or donate."

"Deal."

Chapter Sixteen

OLIVIA
(Distraught, speaking out the open window of Sebastian's empty hotel room.) Good night, sweet prince, and flights of angels sing thee to thy rest.

VIOLA
Olivia, he isn't *dead*! Only missing!
—Act 1, Scene 8, *Midsummer Madness*

There isn't much to the amphitheater's backstage—just two dressing rooms and a bathroom, all cooled by the pathetic box AC units that still sound about a day away from death, despite emergency repairs by Neighborhood Hero earlier this summer.

We're called in one at a time for our first fitting while the rest of the cast runs through different scenes, and by the time my turn comes around, Tallulah looks sweaty and irritable. Which is only a slight change from her normal look of just irritable.

But she isn't complaining. And considering she'd normally complain under the best conditions, I can't tell if she's sick or maturing.

"I attached the beading myself," she says, her focus on the

flapper dress I'm wearing. "Could you try moving around a lot so I can make sure it won't fly off when you dance?"

I feel ridiculous dancing the Charleston by myself in a room with just Tallulah, but I do it. At least I get to use both arms with my sling off.

When I showed up to rehearsal tonight—only two minutes late, which means I'm improving!—Derek took one look at me and shouted, "The champ is back in action!"

I swung my arm around in a full circle, then did an imaginary pitch. Derek swung an invisible bat. We both shielded our eyes against the sun as we pretended to watch the ball soar.

It really ruined my stealth mode, though, because as soon as Miss Liu got done laughing, she gave me hell for being late again. But really, what do I care about being on time when the Vince Effect has ruined my shot at Drama Club president anyway? Sophie is convinced this party will fix it, but I'm not sold. We've both witnessed how Vince can make or break someone when it comes to Drama Club.

Tallulah picks up her clipboard and marks her sheet. "Okay, you're good. Tell Miss Liu I'll take the next person."

It should be Will. We're both scheduled to do our final fitting one after the next since most of our scenes are together. But he's late to rehearsal today, and no one has been able to reach him.

I'm trying to be very chill about it, especially since I'm chronically late to everything. But as time ticks on, dread pools like sludge in my stomach.

I'm stepping out of the dressing room when Milo appears at the end of the hall, his expression grave.

"What?" I ask, already feeling the anxiety twist my insides.

"He's not coming."

"Like he's sick?"

Milo shakes his head slowly.

Tallulah appears in the doorway. "What's going on?"

Milo glances from her to me. "Will quit."

We have two and a half weeks of rehearsal left before opening night. That's supposed to be two and a half weeks of fine-tuning and perfecting. Making sure our costumes don't fall apart during dance numbers, that we're timed to the orchestra, that everything is in place.

And now Will is gone.

"Who told you that?" I ask, marching past Milo and out onto the stage.

Milo follows. "He did. I just talked to him. Kyle Forrester invited him on a Bahamas cruise. His cousin got sick or something, and they had an extra ticket. So Will bailed on us." He sighs, hanging his head. "I'm sorry, JN. I knew he was like this. I should never have asked him to begin with, but I figured with his parents canceling their vacation, we were in the clear. I didn't think he'd do something this shitty."

From the stage, I can see everyone gathered out in the grass, Miss Liu standing at the front of the group. She has her hands on her head, like if she squeezes hard enough, she might pressure cook her brain into a solution. But it's the distressed look on her face that really drives it home. Miss Liu is normally unflappable. If she looks worried, then this is real.

I hop off the stage and jog across the grass. Lucy and Graham stand near the edge of the group, and when I reach them, Lucy grabs my hand and squeezes.

I glance at Graham, and for the first time in days, he makes full eye contact with me. I just wish he didn't look so sympathetic, like everything has been ruined. It makes the dread in my stomach pool even thicker.

We have to be able to fix this.

"Maybe we move AJ to Benedick," Sophie suggests, studying her phone and what I assume is the cast list. "Then push someone from the ensemble into AJ's role."

AJ shrugs. "I can probably learn the lines in time."

"We'll have to cut the kiss," says Camila, peering over Sophie's shoulder. "Since Junie's underage."

"They can pull a fake," Sophie says. "We've done those before."

"Do any of you know the lines for Jaques?" Ireland asks, turning toward the ensemble gathered. But the ensemble is mostly basketball players and Milo's Space Science Club underclassmen. Lucy definitely can't fill the role since it's a solo singing part, and Lydia Kochani, the only regular community theater member in the ensemble, has horrific stage fright. She's normally a crew member but agreed to be in the ensemble to pad our numbers. When I even glance in her direction, she shies behind two basketball players.

Which leaves Peter.

Sophie turns, batting her lashes at him. "Babe," she says imploringly.

"No." Peter shakes his head, holding up his hands. "Definitely not. Come on, you know I can't do it."

"If you can memorize the entire periodic table, you can learn the lines!" Sophie protests, making a grab for his hand. "*Please?* For me?"

Peter groans, tipping his head back.

"It's all right, Peter," says Miss Liu, dropping her hands. "You don't have to do it if you aren't comfortable. Community theater is supposed to be fun." She takes in a deep breath and lets it out. "Take a break, everyone. Tallulah, you keep working on the costumes. In the meantime, I'm going to see what I can figure out for Benedick."

It occurs to me that as someone making a bid for Drama Club president, I should probably try to contribute to the problem-solving. But there are only so many ways to shuffle the cast around to fill the roles, and the more adjustments we make, the more room for error when we finally perform.

The worst part is, I'm not even sure what I'm fighting so hard for. The musical is probably ruined no matter what we do—either from Benedick's abandoned role, or a shuffling of cast members leaving holes all over. Meanwhile, I've already lost the election before I can run, and my dad has gone completely radio silent.

It all feels a little bit hopeless.

But as I stand here, wallowing over what I'm sure to lose, someone nudges their knuckles against mine. I glance over in surprise. While I wasn't paying attention, Graham eased between Lucy and me. He stares ahead as Lucy and Milo launch into problem-solving mode, the way all good students do. But his hand wraps slowly around mine and squeezes, just once.

A rush of warm relief floods through me, and I feel tears in my eyes.

Maybe everything else is ruined, and maybe I made a terrible mistake in his room the other day, but Graham is still here. One thing, at least, isn't beyond repair.

Children of the Corn Support Group
Today 11:39 PM

ME
Sophie just texted me
Party's still on
Milo tell your posse

GRAHAM
Posse . . .

ME

Shut up

MILO

I have to second the 👀 at the use of posse

ME

Oh my God please give me a break

GRAHAM

No lol

Graham named the conversation
" ✦ just posse things ✦ "

LUCY

How are we getting home? Not to be a whiner but I
don't want to walk all the way from the south shore

TALLULAH

We can stay at my place. I'll drive.
I'm definitely not drinking.

ME

After what happened last time? I'd sure hope not.

TALLULAH

You better sleep with one eye open.

Chapter Seventeen

(OLIVIA and SEBASTIAN arrive at the hotel to find the guests in a trancelike state, and VIOLA and ORSINO in their respective disguises.)

SEBASTIAN
I think they went through with it.

OLIVIA
With the wedding? *(She gasps.)* They're married?!

> *(SEBASTIAN lifts the entranced couple's hands, showing off paper-crafted rings. SEBASTIAN and OLIVIA look over the chaotic ballroom.)*

OLIVIA
This is very midsummer madness.
—Act 2, Scene 18, Midsummer Madness

Sophie lives in a massive house on the South Shore that dwarfs every other house on the street. It's so big, I once heard her refer to the part of the house where her bedroom is as "the east wing."

Even though her mom Reba is one of the most successful attorneys in Spoonbill County, I've wondered more than once what her mom Kerry does for a living. I have a hard time believing Reba "We'll Get You Off!" Keller keeps this place on her salary alone—and yet, I've never seen Kerry do anything but wander the house in athleisure.

Almost the whole cast of the musical is here, minus anyone over the age of nineteen. Even AJ showed up, bringing along a girl I don't recognize. There are some non-cast members from the basketball team, a few girls I know as basketball girlfriends, and some other people who are friends of the rest of the cast.

Sophie and Peter mingle with arms around each other's waists, wearing smiles that would make their orthodontists very proud. They greet each person individually, but I'm not sure if it's so much about being polite as it is about taking stock of every face in case something gets stolen.

Tallulah and I come straight from work. I nearly gave my mom a heart attack when I asked if I could sleep over at the Breemans' tonight.

I hadn't given much thought to how the rest of our friends would get here, but when I spot them sitting around the empty fire pit outside, I shouldn't be surprised that Cora is with them. I guess I just never expected to see Cora Kalisch at a Drama Club party.

Then again, I never thought I'd see Joel, Derek, Vanessa, Harrison, Porter, or Alana at a Drama Club party, either. Or half their friends they invited along. In fact, as Tallulah and I make a stop in the kitchen for drinks, I notice the Drama Club is pretty outnumbered. If it weren't for Sophie going around making sure everyone knows she's the host, it might feel like we're attending a different group's party entirely.

"This feels unsafe," Tallulah says, eyeing the giant cooler of bright red hunch punch as I fill my cup.

I hold it up and pretend to cheers. Then I take a long swig and make the loud noise of someone thoroughly refreshed by their drink, which is difficult to pull off when it tastes like sweetened acetone. My only comfort is that the amount of alcohol in there probably killed any lingering bacteria from the cooler.

Tallulah isn't as confident. "If you're planning on catching some kind of stomach infection, please don't get sick until you're home. I don't need anything on my conscience."

She opts for a soda, since she swears she's never drinking again. And also because she values her life a little more than I value mine, apparently, with the mystery cooler.

Outside, Tallulah drags one of the chairs around the fire pit right up next to Lucy's. Milo and Cora have already shoved their chairs together, too. There are three empty seats in a row between Cora and Graham, and I hesitate at the edge of the circle. Even though Cora and I haven't spoken in weeks, if Milo brought her here, then I should meet her halfway in the effort to make peace.

It has nothing to do with avoiding Graham. It's all about making Cora comfortable.

As my presence has been known to do.

Cora eyes me as I sit down, and I know I'm not imagining the tension in her expression.

I clear my throat. "Hi, Cora."

She smiles, but it's tight at the corners of her mouth. "Hi, Junie."

I feel Graham's eyes on me, and I twist in my seat to face Cora, letting my hair block him from view. It doesn't matter—the heat of his gaze is scorching.

I glance over Cora quickly, taking stock of her outfit. My

gaze lands on her platform sandals. "I like your shoes. They're very . . ." The word *cute* dies on my tongue—too fake—and I end up settling for, "tall."

Cora's nose scrunches. "Thanks?"

Milo angles toward us, catching my eye over her shoulder. *Be nice,* he mouths.

Cora starts to follow my gaze, but by the time she glances back, he's tipping his can of soda to his mouth, eyes on the sky.

"I'd probably ruin those in a week," I say, stretching out my leg to show her my sandal. "Mine are like one scuffed sole away from death. I really need to learn to pick up my feet when I walk."

Cora hesitates, like she doesn't know what to say. And truthfully, what do I expect? "That sucks," she says at last, and I have to credit her for it. We're both making an effort here. "These are pretty sturdy, though. If you ever wanted to try them."

The look of relief on Milo's face is enough to make the exchange worth it.

The chair beside mine moves, and I twist around as Graham drops into it. He's dragged it close to mine, and I momentarily panic. But when I shift, he closes a hand around my elbow and holds me in place.

I glance around, worried the others are watching us. But Milo and Cora are talking quietly, her legs slung into his lap and his hand rubbing up and down her calf. On the other side of the fire pit, Tallulah and Lucy have all but forgotten the rest of us are here. They have their heads together, looking at something on Tallulah's phone and laughing.

"How are you doing?" Graham asks quietly.

My chest tightens. "I'm fine. I just want you to—I just want us to be fine, you know? I'm sorry I—"

Graham clears his throat, his cheeks reddening. "I meant—I was talking about the Will thing."

My stomach lurches. "Oh."

Graham sighs, his mouth quirking into a smile that's more exhausted than amused. "So, how are you doing?" he asks again.

"I'm okay," I say quietly, embarrassed heat rushing through me. I push a hand through my hair and shrug. "I mean, it's just community theater, right?"

Graham watches me. "Wrong."

I give him a look. "I'm not, though. It's *just* community theater. We aren't saving lives or anything. This is barely important to anyone but the half of the cast that showed up that first night. If this didn't happen at all, it wouldn't matter to hardly anyone."

"But it'd matter to you. If it matters to you, that makes it important."

I flatten my mouth into a line. "Thanks, but it doesn't really work that way."

Graham puts an arm around me. It's tentative, like he's giving me the chance to pull away, but I sink into him instead. It feels so nice, even as my heart pounds in my chest.

"Junie," he says in a low voice, "you're allowed to call it a big deal. You've worked your ass off all summer, and now one dickhead might ruin it for you. That sucks. You can be mad."

I duck my head. Am I mad at Will? I feel like I haven't even had a minute to think about it, my brain consumed with half-assed solutions that will never save *Midsummer Madness*. Like having someone shout lines from offstage as though Benedick is a figment of Beatrice's imagination, or having different people play the part depending on who isn't onstage in each scene. Each idea is more ridiculous than the last.

Graham clears his throat. "I'm on your side, okay? That's all. No matter what happens, I'm always on your side. If you need me to . . . I don't know, to learn the lines, I'll—" He blows out a breath, and I lift my head to stare at him in shock.

"You don't have to do that. You've done so much for me already."

He looks off to the side, his jaw tense. "I'll always do whatever you need."

I blink at him, a tidal wave of want and need and gratitude rising in me. My voice comes out a small squeak. "Thanks, Graham."

He nods, his Adam's apple bobbing as he swallows.

But I don't have long to get lost in the moment, because across the patio, where Derek and Vanessa are dominating the opposing team at beer pong, Derek calls, "Man, we better get some real competition up here soon. This is getting embarrassing." He points at me. "Hey, champ, you want to take that arm for a spin?"

Milo barks out a laugh. "Sure, if you want to see the worst aim in the state of Florida."

I shoot him a fierce scowl. "That is incredibly rude!"

From the beer pong table, Derek belts out a few lines from "That Beautiful Frown." It's a song Benedick shares with Sebastian and Orsino. While Sebastian sings of Olivia's grace and beauty, Orsino sings of Viola's humor and smile. Then Benedick, the only married one, chimes in about all of Beatrice's terrible qualities. When Sebastian sings about how Olivia volunteers with orphans, Benedick responds that Beatrice might eat orphans for breakfast. When Orsino croons about Viola's lovely singing voice, Benedick replies that the last man who heard Beatrice sing didn't live to tell the tale.

When they hear the song, Abe and James join in, singing

their parts from where they're dangling their feet in the pool with Ireland.

I watch the three of them volley their lines back and forth in perfect time. Graham's arm falls from my shoulders as I push up from my seat, staggering across the patio with my jaw dragging on the ground.

"Derek!" I shout, raising my voice above the din of the party. "You know Benedick's song?"

Vanessa, who's poised to toss a ball across the beer pong table, purses her lips. "He knows the lines, too. He's just too chicken to tell you."

Derek stares at her, appalled. "Babe! What kind of betrayal?"

Vanessa shrugs, letting the ball fly. She lands it in a corner cup, then turns to me. "He practiced with Will. He knows the part, but he's too scared to step up."

I turn to Derek, and I imagine I have bright, twinkly stars in my eyes. "You know the lines?"

Derek groans. "Look. Listen. I promise, you don't want me trying to act."

"Oh, quit making excuses," says Vanessa while the other team makes their shots. They miss one, and when the ball pops off a rim, Vanessa snatches it from the air with lightning-quick reflexes. When the other lands, Derek picks up the cup and drains it. I think he's grateful for the distraction.

As Derek finishes and belches loudly, Vanessa turns to him. "You wouldn't have sung that song right now if you really didn't want to do this. You just want someone to tell you that you don't have a choice, because you're too big a chicken to say you want to do it. That way if it goes wrong, you can pull the whole *I said I wasn't good enough* bullshit. Well, Derek, no one's gonna take this bullet for you."

Derek tries to speak several times, but it comes out as a spluttering noise.

"Hey, are we playing, or what?" a boy from the other team calls.

Vanessa shoots him a glare, holding up both hands. She makes a simultaneous toss, both balls sailing through the air and sinking into the remaining two cups.

Everyone around the table goes wild.

Vanessa gives Derek a bland look. "You want to do this, and we both know you *can* do this."

"But I'm not good!"

"Derek," I say seriously, "come on. I just heard you sing. You're good."

Derek screws up his face, cheeks puffing out. He pushes out a breath through puckered lips and looks at Vanessa. "You know I'll be romancing another girl, right?"

She barks out a laugh. "Like I'm worried!"

Derek points at her. "Okay, then I'm saying it right now! If I agree to do this, you can't come back at me later and say I was trying to cheat on you! You know Benedick and Beatrice kiss at the end, and I won't hear a single word about it if I do this!"

"Oh, please! I don't see Junie being overcome by passion in a musical I'd be okay taking my grandma to see."

They continue to bicker as they set up their cups for the next round. The longer I watch, the more I see what Vanessa sees—that Derek wants to do it, but he's scared of messing it up. He wants someone to say he has to, or to say he can't. He doesn't want to make the decision himself when the whole musical is riding on him.

I set my drink on the edge of the beer pong table so I can hold up prayer hands, giving Derek my best sad-puppy look.

"You'd be our buzzer beater, Derek. Don't you want to be a hero?"

Derek groans, looking up at the sky. Then he picks up one of the cups before anyone has even made the first toss and chugs it.

The other team whoops, and Vanessa shoots them a flat look. "Don't get excited," she says. "You need the handicap. We're gonna wipe the floor with you."

Derek rubs the back of his hand over his mouth. Then he looks from me to Vanessa and back before letting out a small yell, crushing the cup in his hand. "*Fine!*" He slams the smashed cup onto the table. "Junie, will you marry me?"

Vanessa smirks, turning to the game to land her shot.

I'm so overcome, I throw my arms around Derek and squeeze. He belches loudly.

I shove him away with a grimace. "Gross. That sounded wet."

He swallows hard. "It was kinda."

Vanessa pulls a face. "Disgusting. Don't even think about kissing me for the rest of the night."

Derek's mouth drops. "Babe, I'm a hero. You don't want to kiss a hero?" He reaches for her, puckering exaggerated fish lips at her.

She shrieks and ducks away from him, laughing. I snatch my drink before either of them can knock it over.

Someone grabs my arm, and I turn. Sophie beams at me, her eyes bright. "Did Derek just agree to play Benedick?"

"He said he knows the lines," I tell her.

Sophie screams a cheer, then darts away from Peter to climb onto the edge of the fire pit. She holds her drink in the air.

"Excuse me, excuse me!" she calls over the noise. "A special announcement about the fate of our fair musical!"

Peter sighs beside me. "She really was born to do this, wasn't she?"

I grin.

When the noise doesn't die down to a Sophie-approved level, Peter puts his fingers in his mouth and whistles sharply.

The noise cuts off, and Sophie blows him a kiss. "A special announcement about *Midsummer Madness,*" she calls. Someone pushes open the sliding glass door so she can be heard inside. Through the large windows, I can see people turning toward the patio. "We have acquired a replacement Benedick."

Some people near the beer pong table start to cheer.

Sophie throws her hand out to Derek. "Please give a big round of applause for our hero, our brand new Benedick, Derek Johnson." She claps in his direction, and everyone cheers, even the people who aren't in the musical and probably have no idea what's going on.

"I hope you're ready to tutor me," Derek shouts to me over the noise.

I put a hand over my heart, raising my cup to him. "Night and day. We'll practice so much, you'll be sick of me."

Derek gives a smile that's half cringe. "Great, can't wait."

"Hey, sign us up for beer pong," someone calls, coming out onto the patio. "We'll play next!"

I turn, freezing when I realize it's Sloan and a girl I don't know. Annoyance flares up in me at the sight of her.

I feel a strange protectiveness over Tallulah now. I think she's having fun, and I'm worried seeing Sloan will ruin her night. She doesn't deserve that.

She didn't deserve any of what Sloan did to her.

I tip back my cup and chug the rest of my hunch punch, screwing my eyes shut at the bitter alcohol taste under the super sweet Hawaiian Punch. Then I crush my cup in my hand, the plastic biting into my palm as I cross the patio to intercept her.

Sloan skids to a stop when she nearly collides with me. She grabs her friend's hand, pulling her up short.

"What are you doing here?" I ask, my voice coming out even harsher than I intended. Which was, admittedly, pretty harsh.

Sloan flushes. "Hey, Junie. Nice to see you, too."

Her friend glares at me, then looks at Sloan. "Who the hell is this?"

"It's fine," Sloan says quietly. She plasters on a smile. "Junie, this is Elise. Elise, this is Junie. She's friends with Tallulah."

Elise doesn't smile at me, and I'm not feeling all that warm and fuzzy toward her, either. She's pretty, with the sharp eyes and pointed nose of a bird of prey, and she's looking at me like I'm a mouse.

"Nice to meet you. But that doesn't answer my question."

Sloan flushes. "Are we not allowed to be here? Sophie invited me."

I feel a sour curl in my stomach. I didn't know Sophie and Sloan even knew each other. I bite down on my annoyance. "Fine. Great." I blow out a breath. "Enjoy the party."

I start past her to the patio door, hot with irritation. It's a stark contrast to the cool relief of Derek taking over as Benedick, and I'm wondering if it's possible to get emotional whiplash for real. Or maybe the hunch punch is doing its work.

"Hey, Junie— Hold on, El, sorry, just one sec."

I glance back.

Sloan ducks around a few people to reach me. "Um, look,

it's not that I'm not over her or anything. I'm really happy with Elise. I just—is she okay? Tallulah?" She wrings her hands together. "I know what everyone's been saying about the bonfire at Cora's. Is she really upset?"

"She's fine. I took care of it."

Sloan frowns. "Yeah, I heard. How you took care of it." She doesn't use air quotes, but her voice sounds decidedly air quote-y.

"Look, don't worry about Tallulah. You're absolved or whatever."

Sloan grabs my arm when I turn to go. "I'm not trying to be absolved," she says. "I didn't do anything to be absolved from. I'm just making sure she's okay, which is far beyond the bounds of what I need to be doing, but I can't help myself, I guess."

I glare at her. "She's *fine*. She has friends who won't drop her as soon as shit goes sideways now."

Sloan looks hurt by that, and her eyes fill fast.

"What the fuck are you doing?"

I turn. Tallulah stands behind me, gritting her teeth like she's ready to murder me where I stand.

"What?" I say, confused.

She jostles me away from Sloan, until we're separate from the crowd. When I try to dart away, she grabs my arm, yanking me toward the front door. I drop the crushed remains of my cup.

Out on the porch, the noise of the party dies away. I feel flushed, my mouth tingly and everything a little hazy at the edges. In hindsight, it probably wasn't the best idea to chug that hunch punch.

"Don't talk to Sloan about me," Tallulah says roughly as she releases my arm. She moves to the balustrade, where she pulls a pack of cigarettes from her pocket and lights one. It's the first time I've seen her smoke in a while, but clearly she's still carrying them around, so it's not like she's kicked the habit. But maybe she's trying.

And I just pushed her to breaking.

"What is your problem?" I cross my arms, feeling hot with shame and sour with disappointment, all of it boiling together into frustration. I want to cry, but I'm too embarrassed to let her see me do it. "I was sticking up for you—as usual, I might add."

"I don't need you to stick up for me." She sounds exhausted, and it just makes me angrier. "Sloan didn't do anything to me."

"Then why do you look like someone punched you in the stomach every time you see her? If you aren't mad at her, and she isn't mad at you, can't you just be friends again? I don't get it." It makes me think of Graham and me. If we worked through what I did, then why can't Tallulah and Sloan work through what happened between them?

Tallulah takes a long drag of her cigarette, as if every word out of my mouth pains her. She turns to face me like her bones are rusted gears, grinding together as she moves. "Juniper Nash," she says slowly, her voice low, "I have tried to be patient with you. I have given you plenty of chances to not be so fucking far removed from reality. Sloan was not my friend. We weren't *besties*. She was my fucking girlfriend." She stubs out her cigarette on the glass table sitting between the two porch chairs and stuffs the butt into the little silicone bag she carries around in her pocket.

I exhale a long breath and close my eyes. "Wow. I'm, like, the world's biggest moron. You dropped every possible hint, right? I'm so sorry. No wonder you hate me."

She looks up, her eyes red and cheeks wet with tears. "I don't hate you." She sniffles and wipes her nose on her wrist. "It's not a big deal. I'm being stupid."

"It is a big deal, though. I made assumptions. My brain is a heteronormative black hole. And I don't have the excuse of not knowing any better when one of my best friends is bi and my godmother is a lesbian. I mean, we're literally on the front porch of a queer couple's house right now." I motion to the front door. "You don't have to let me off easy. God knows you wouldn't usually."

Tallulah snorts. "Okay, fine. You're a big fucking fool." She glances over at me, brushing the tears from her face with a sardonic half smile. "But I forgive you."

I twist my mouth up, matching her half smile. After a beat of silence, I ask, "Can I say something without you making it weird?"

Tallulah shoots me a flat look. "Because I'm the one known for making things weird here."

I ignore the jab. "I don't know what went down between you and Sloan, and I don't want to add salt or whatever, but if she left you while you were going through—you know, what happened to your mom . . . I mean, at that point, she doesn't deserve you."

"Well, that's a nice sentiment," she says thickly, "except I broke up with her."

I imagine my eyes spinning in my head like a cartoon. Even when I thought they were friends, I always assumed it was Sloan who ended things, not the other way around.

It's becoming abundantly clear that I don't know anything about anything.

"Well, God, *why'd you do that?*"

The corner of her mouth kicks up, even as she sighs. "I was going through some shit."

"Yeah, obviously. Wouldn't you want your girlfriend around for that?"

She shrugs. "I could tell it was too much for her, but she was too nice to say anything. I cut her loose because it's what she needed."

"You seriously pulled the *I don't deserve you* card?"

"Well, it's true," she says, indignant. "I was not easy to be around after"—she falters, blanching briefly before recovering—"well, *after*. I was like . . . barely a person, and we were only in middle school. She deserved something easy, and I was the furthest thing from easy. I still am, honestly, but I'm—I'm better." She huffs out a laugh. "It's amazing what therapy and medication can do."

I take a second to absorb this. I always assumed Tallulah was getting some kind of help, but having her confirm it is a shocking moment for me. We've never talked about anything this deep, much less her mom. I feel like she's giving me a gift, even though I just tore into her ex for no good reason except that I didn't know any better.

"I guess I owe Sloan an apology then," I say. "Ugh, that sounds like the worst."

"It's fine," Tallulah says. "I'll take care of it. I'll—I'll text her or something."

"You're not doing that." I eye her. "Unless . . . you *want* to do that? Maybe clear the air and—"

Tallulah holds up a hand. "Stop getting ideas. I'm not interested in dating Sloan anymore. I've moved on, and obviously she has, too. I mean, you met her new girlfriend."

The revelation hits me like a bus. *Sloan's girlfriend.* "Oh, right. Duh. You know, everything makes a lot more sense when you have some context."

"I'm sure."

Elise, I think. She was gorgeous, like a polished diamond. She was similar to Sloan that way. Remembering the two of them standing side by side reminds me of looking at a pair of expensive earrings in a glass case. They were a matching set.

"Sloan deserves that," Tallulah says. "She deserves to be happy."

I glance over at her, frowning. "You deserve that, too, you know."

Tallulah exhales a soft laugh. "Sure. I don't know if you remember that bonfire, but I think the words *catch and release* were used."

"That was your warped sense of yourself and Zephyr, the biggest idiot in our entire town. I don't think that counts. You've got stuff going for you. I'm not planning to, like, bathe you in compliments or anything. But you're very pretty."

She stares at me.

"Even though I know it doesn't matter how pretty someone is," I say quickly. "And you've got, like, a personality . . ."

She gives me a flat look. "Wow. Thanks."

"You *care* about stuff! That's something. I bet Elise drinks bottled water and uses plastic straws."

This time, she smiles. "I'm sure you're right."

"I bet I am. Honestly, Sloan should be so lucky to get a second chance with you."

"Uh-huh. That's not really how it works though," she says. "It's not about how pretty you are, or what your personality's like, or if you *recycle.*" She rolls her eyes at me. "Those things all factor in, but it's the chemistry that matters. How you click."

She links her hands together, fingers entwined, and holds them up.

"Sloan and I were like this. But when something breaks in you, you get screwed up. You become different. You don't fit anymore."

She pulls her fingers apart, bends one, and tries to fit them together again. When she's demonstrated how that doesn't work, she drops her hands.

"It kind of works, but it's not the same. We weren't gonna last, because she was in love with a totally different me."

"I think love is about finding a way to fit together even after the hard stuff happens," I say. "I don't think it's supposed to always be easy. It's about choosing someone in spite of the obstacles."

I think of Graham, and all the obstacles between us— Rooney and his dad and the part I played in that, the risk of not just our friendship but what would happen with Milo and Lucy if we were to blow everything apart a second time.

Tallulah raises an eyebrow, like she can read every thought on my face. I flush.

"You should go back in," she says, taking a seat. "I'm gonna hang out here. Just let me know when you're ready to leave."

"I'll stay, too."

"Please don't—" She sighs as I settle into the other chair. "Fine, sure. Make yourself comfortable."

I shoot her a sideways look. "You should be a little nicer, or I might think you don't enjoy hanging out with me."

Tallulah smirks, kicking one long leg out to rest her heel on the balustrade. "And what a tragedy that would be."

After a few minutes, my phone buzzes, and I pull it from my pocket.

GRAHAM
Where are you?

ME
Sophie Keller's house

GRAHAM
Interesting joke. Tell me where you are for real.

ME
Porch with Tallulah
Ready to leave whenever you are

Tallulah and I sit in silence, swatting at mosquitos and sweating in the balmy night. But it doesn't take long for the front door to swing open.

Lucy bounds out, grinning. "I beat Derek and Vanessa at beer pong!"

I smile, because Lucy's happiness is contagious. When I glance at Tallulah, her expression has softened.

Milo trails out after her, holding Cora's hand. "We're heading out. You all gonna stick around?"

I look from him to Cora and back. "You're not coming to Tallulah's?"

Milo's cheeks grow pink. "Nah." He doesn't elaborate. Cora clutches his hand, but she doesn't look embarrassed.

"Right. Okay." I nod, my eyes skipping past them as Graham comes out the front door. My heart thumps out of rhythm at the sight of him. "I guess we'll see you later, then."

I wake with a start, breathing heavily. I blink the sand from my eyes while my vision adjusts to the dark room, bringing everything into hazy focus. We're in the den at Tallulah's house, everything washed in moonlight. The blackout curtains Tallulah was bragging about hang open, forgotten.

When I fell asleep, I was on the air mattress between Tallulah and Lucy. Lucy was snuggled into my side with one leg slung across me. Tallulah was stiff as a board on my other side, perfectly still on her back with her hands clasped on her stomach, like a corpse. I've never seen anyone sleep like that.

Graham is still sprawled on the sectional, one leg bent and his arm thrown over his head. He has a hand on his stomach, his shirt riding up.

I tear my eyes away as I take in the rest of the room.

Empty.

I slide to the edge of the mattress. My mouth feels heavy and dry from the alcohol, and I have a headache that seems too intense for how little I drank—probably a result of all the sugar in the hunch punch.

I tiptoe to the bathroom, where I rinse my mouth out and then stare at my reflection for too long. My eye makeup is smeared, my eyelashes caked together. I wash my face with hand soap, hoping the cold water will help calm my erratic heartbeat. I can feel it pulsing in my stomach.

On my way back to the den, I pause and peer across the room at the back doors. Through the glass, I can make out two shadows on the deck.

I tilt my head, taking one step in their direction, but a hand closes around my shirt. I gasp, spinning to face Graham.

He puts a finger to his lips and tugs me toward the den. I frown, shaking him off as I turn again toward the back doors.

"Hey, Junie, come on. Give them some privacy," he whispers, putting a hand on my back. "Come back to bed."

263

My stomach dips at the words, low and so intensely inti-mate. I swing around to look at him. "What?"

Graham's face gives away nothing as his hand drops to his side. "Go back to sleep. Let them do whatever they're—*Junie.*" I've started toward the doors, but he grabs my arm and pulls me against the wall. "Just leave them."

I turn my head away, staring past the glass, where I can no longer tell the shadows apart. In the dark, my eyes adjust, pulling in enough light that I finally see what's happening.

Lucy and Tallulah are sharing a chair on the deck, and they're kissing.

"Oh," I whisper.

Graham sighs. "This feels a little creepy, I gotta say."

I twist to around to face him, startling when I realize how close we are. His face is inches from mine, maybe less. My gaze drops briefly to his mouth, and something in me squeezes with want. It takes me a second to draw myself out of my head.

My voice cracks as I ask, "How long has that . . . ?" I jerk a thumb over my shoulder.

Graham takes my hand, pulling me toward the den again. His skin is warm, and the shaky feeling left over from drink-ing makes my knees wobble. My heart pounds.

In the safety of the den, Graham says, "A while. And also not long at all."

I lean against the wall, tugging him to a stop as I sink to the tile floor. I close my eyes and rest my head back.

"Are you okay?" he asks, crouching in front of me.

"Fine. Probably shouldn't have had the hunch punch." I lift my gaze to his face. "That wasn't really an answer, by the way."

Graham shrugs, a tightness around his mouth. "They've liked each other awhile," he says. "Or Lucy's liked Tallulah awhile. I won't ever pretend to know what's going on in Tallulah's head." He motions to the other room and the backyard beyond. "That's new. Pretty sure it's the first for them."

If Lucy and Tallulah have kissed before this, Graham would know. Lucy tells him everything. When she got her first period in middle school, she told Graham even before she told me. I asked Milo if he was upset I didn't tell him first when I got mine, and his response was, "I wish you hadn't told me at all." But Graham got a bunch of tampons from his mom and gave them to Lucy like a flower bouquet, and she still has the photo I snapped on my phone hanging in her bedroom.

It reminds me that Graham might be different now—subdued, responsible, less reckless—but he's still the same Graham—funny and thoughtful. And maybe that's why I feel this way. The reason I want him so badly is because he's the boy he's always been, but not so much a boy at all.

I realize belatedly that I'm staring at him, probably with scary serial killer eyes, like I want to take his skin off and make it into a suit. Graham bites his lip, and my gaze snags there, hyperfocused on sharp white sinking into lush pink.

I reach out and touch his shirt, the fabric soft as I fist my hand in it, his stomach firm against my knuckles. His eyes go hazy, half-lidded, and hot.

At that look, every rational thought in my brain slides away, like the whole thing has been flushed. All I know is want.

I lean up and kiss him.

Graham's mouth is warm, and he tastes like the spearmint toothpaste he used before bed. I lick the sweetness from his lips, and his mouth opens in surprise. His hand tightens on my lower back, pulling me closer, and I wrap my arms around his neck. I lean into him, pushing him backward, until he's sprawled on the cool tile.

He pulls me down on top of him, our mouths barely separating. I brace a hand against his chest, but it's not close enough, and when I move my hand down and slide it under his shirt, he takes in a surprised breath that makes me jerk back.

I sit up. "Oh my God—you're—I'm sorry." I take my hand out of his shirt. "You were drinking."

He catches my hand before I can stand. "So were you."

"Only one drink," I say. "I'm not—I'm not drunk. Not even a little." And it's true. The hunch punch had me warm and buzzing when we arrived at Tallulah's, but even with my headache, I feel like I've downed an entire pot of coffee. My whole body is a live wire. Everything has hardened to crystal clarity around me.

Graham's eyes practically glow in the low light from the window. "Neither am I."

I have no idea what we're admitting right now, but it makes my skin burn. My cheeks must be tomato red. My hand was up his shirt, touching his bare skin—his bare chest. I can still feel the ridges of muscle and dip of his belly button under my fingers.

I cover my face with my hands. "Shit."

Graham is silent. When I peek at him through my fingers, he's pushed up onto his elbows, watching me with an intensity that makes my heart beat even faster. It feels like a bass drum being played from both sides.

"I'm sorry," I say.

He drops back onto the floor and nods, his gaze fixed on the ceiling. "Great."

"Graham."

"I told you—"

"I know."

"—don't start something you can't finish."

I don't say anything. Somehow I don't think *I couldn't help myself* or *I just want you so badly I can feel it in every single nerve ending in my body* are going to fly. Because I don't know what comes after that, and it's unfair to ask him to figure it out for me.

In the stretch of silence, Graham lets out a soft, exasperated laugh. "Fine. Okay. So, we should just forget about this, right?" He sits up, shaking his hair out of his eyes. "We're great at forgetting stuff, aren't we?"

"Are you mad?" My voice cracks as it comes out.

"No, I'm not mad, Junie." He pushes to his feet, turning toward the couch. "I'm not mad you don't want to kiss me. I just don't want you to do it if you don't want to."

"Graham—"

"We'll just forget it," he says again. "It never happened." He sits on the couch, letting his head fall against the cushions. I stare at his exposed throat and try to think cool, calming thoughts, but every part of me is burning, inside and out.

And guilt gnaws at me, sinking its teeth into my bones, because I'm confusing him. I know I am. I'm confusing *myself*. But I don't want him to think that anything that's happened between us is meaningless to me, or that it could be anyone else but him.

"I do want to kiss you." I should sit on the air mattress, but I can't do the smart thing right now. Instead, I take the spot beside him on the couch, pulling one leg up so I can face him.

"Junie," he says, a warning in his voice.

"I do." I touch his wrist, my fingertips brushing the soft skin at the base of his palm. He watches me like I might bite. "I want to kiss you so badly, it's basically all I think about."

Graham sucks in a breath.

"But you're also *you*," I say.

He winces. "Nice."

"That's not—you know that's not what I mean. I'm trying to be good, okay? I already messed this up once." I swallow. "I told you, I'm turning over a new leaf this summer."

His lashes flutter as he exhales a laugh. "Right. A real hard-working one." I start to pull away, but he catches my hand, closing his fingers around mine. "What do we do then? Wait for this to go away?" His eyes flash in the dark. "What if it doesn't?"

It's the closest Graham has gotten to admitting he's having the same feelings about me as I am about him. Whatever those feelings might be. But if it's just kissing—if it's just wanting my hands on him—maybe it's like a craving. And once you have enough of it, you're satisfied. Sometimes you never want it again.

"Maybe we should get it out of our systems," I whisper, my voice shaking.

Graham eyes me warily, like he's anticipating something painful. I lean in until we're nearly touching. I think he's holding his breath. I wait, watching him, our eyes locked. He blinks once, a slow sweep of his lashes against his cheek.

When he opens his eyes again, he closes the distance and kisses me.

Whatever is happening between us roars to life like a fire doused in alcohol. It blazes hot and strong and fast.

Graham's hand closes on my waist, pulling me in. His mouth is soft, but his kisses are hard. Desperate, matching mine. Like if this is the last chance we ever get, it's going to count.

It all comes freshly rushing back, kissing him last summer. I remember everything, like the way he's a little ticklish where his neck meets his shoulder, and how he sometimes forgets to breathe. But there are new things, too, like the rough feel of his hands after months of work, and the risk of where and when we are making us both frenzied. We used to kiss like it was our favorite pastime, like we had all the hours in the world. Now it feels like trying to outrun a wildfire.

We kiss until we're both breathless—until I'm straddling his lap, and my hand has crept under his shirt again like an obsessive little weasel, but he liked it enough that his hand made it up my shirt, too.

I sit back, watching his shirt slide down as I retreat. His hands move to my hips, and he squeezes lightly, his head falling back.

His voice is pained as he whispers, "I don't know how to get you out of my system. But this definitely wasn't it."

My mouth is kiss-swollen, and I feel feverish. I press the backs of my hands to my cheeks.

Graham watches me, eyes gleaming in the dark.

"Maybe we should keep trying," I whisper back.

Graham doesn't say anything, but when I lean forward, he meets me halfway.

And we kiss, and we kiss, and we kiss. Until there's barely breath left in my lungs, until my head is swimming with want. Until I have relearned the stretch of his bare skin with my fingers, and he's recharted my neck with his mouth.

We keep kissing even though we know we shouldn't. No matter how much I want to get him out of my system, all I'm doing is filling myself up with him—his saltwater scent, the softness of his hair, the perfect pressure of his mouth against mine, every dip and ridge of muscle under his shirt, and the noises he makes. Everything is becoming not just what I craved, but my favorite. The thing I will want every day, like chocolate or coffee or sweet watermelon or—or *water.* The thing I crave the most, that I need to survive.

Oh no, oh no, oh no.

The back door opens, and the moment shatters. Graham and I pull apart as whispers drift toward us, bare feet padding across the tile.

I tug my shirt down and slide off him, returning to the air mattress. By the time I've curled onto my side, he's lying on the couch, stretched out facing me.

We stare at each other in the dark as Lucy and Tallulah climb into bed. This time, Lucy is in the middle, leaving me closest to Graham.

The room quiets, and as their breathing evens out, Graham reaches across the empty space between us and brushes his fingers over my cheek, tucking my tangled hair behind my ear. His thumb skims over my puffy mouth, and his expression is agonized. Like he's afraid of what just happened.

And the truth is, I am terrified.

Chapter Eighteen

BENEDICK
For which of my bad parts didst thou first fall in love
with me?

BEATRICE
All the ones that were worse than mine.

BENEDICK
You must be joking, darling wife. I'm quite sure none
of my bad parts are quite as terrible as yours.

> (*BEATRICE shoves him playfully at the same time the
> closet door opens. BENEDICK tumbles out into the hall.*)
> —Act 2, Scene 15, *Midsummer Madness*

"Why are you acting so weird?"

I glance over at Milo as I rearrange the boxes of cookies I
brought for rehearsal today. It's our first rehearsal since Will
bailed, and one of our long rehearsals—eight hours of blistering sunlight with a full orchestra. Though I'll be spending
most of rehearsal getting Derek up to speed on Benedick's part.

I emailed Miss Liu about Derek as soon as I woke up. She
responded almost immediately.

Great work, Junie! That is a very big relief!

Her praise filled me up like a balloon, but it wasn't quite

enough to drive out the leftover jitters from sugar and alcohol and whatever that was between me and Graham last night. When I wandered out of the empty den after sending off my email, Lucy and Tallulah were blissfully making pancakes, and Graham was gone.

"Rita picked him up," Lucy said when I asked. "He took the early shift so he can make it to rehearsal later."

I've thought of almost nothing else but the moment I'll see him, and how we'll both act. Whatever I said last night, I know I didn't get him out of my system.

But I can't tell Milo that's the reason I'm acting weird.

"I'm not," I say, picking up a cookie and shoving it into his half-open mouth. "Eat that and stop talking."

Milo glares at me as he chews. He's one of the only people brave enough to venture near the cookies. I'm starting to wonder if Gatorades would've been a better choice. I don't think any of us thought through a party last night paired with eight hours in the heat today. The air smells like hangover. Even Derek and Vanessa, for all their beer pong victories, look wan.

"Uh," Milo says around a mouthful of cookie, "when were you gonna tell me about that?"

I follow his gaze. Lucy and Tallulah are coming down from the parking lot. They're walking so close together, it takes me a long time to realize they're holding hands.

When Lucy spots Milo and me, she smiles so wide, it eats up her whole face. Her pink braces sparkle in the sun.

Joel, who has wandered up to peruse the cookies, possibly against his better judgment, says, "I gotta tell you, I had a feeling we'd get a couple out of this group, but I never would've guessed Tallulah Breeman would be half of it."

"Don't let her fool you," I say. "She's just like every other prickly thing in the world—soft on the inside."

Joel shoots me a grin that's a little wilted compared to his usual smile. Then he takes a bite of cookie, freezes as his face pales, and spits the bite into his hand. "Yeah, wasn't ready for that." He tosses the cookie into the trash. "Definitely wasn't ready for that."

When Lucy and Tallulah reach us, we try to act natural. Milo picks up the box and offers them a choice from the selection, and I twiddle my thumbs together and pucker my mouth innocently.

Joel fishes a water out of the cooler and takes a tentative sip, then groans. "I'm really gonna barf."

As soon as he staggers off, I motion to Lucy and Tallulah's clasped hands and say, "Seems sweaty in there. You wanna let go?"

Tallulah glares at me.

Lucy just laughs. She reaches for a cookie. "What's the occasion?"

"Celebrating the play's newest couple," I say, tilting my head at them. "Or . . . *are* we?"

Lucy and Tallulah exchange a glance, and Tallulah's cheeks go red.

"We could say that," says Tallulah, looking away. Her flush reaches the tips of her ears.

Lucy beams.

Miss Liu takes the stage and claps her hands twice to start rehearsal. "We'll be working through every song without Beatrice and Benedick to start," she calls. "Junie and Derek, you two will work on your parts separately."

I give her a thumbs-up.

"Where's! My! Wife!" Derek yells, lurching to his feet. He bangs on his chest like Tarzan, then immediately hunches over, grabbing the back of the nearest seat for support.

Vanessa watches him with a mixture of love and disdain. She kicks him lightly in the hip, and he staggers out of the row, looking sick.

As I head toward him, I spot Graham coming down from the street. His shirt is sweat-soaked, and he has his skateboard clutched in one hand as he jogs across the grass. The sight of him sends excitement sparking through me. As he finds the rest of the crew, he pushes his damp hair back from his forehead, scanning the amphitheater. He catches my eye through the crowd, and his gaze is so knowing, so blazing hot, I feel it through my entire body.

I duck away, focusing on Derek. I can't spend the day thinking about Graham, and his mouth, and his hands. The way he looked at me, his eyes burning in the dark.

Nope, no, absolutely not. I'm sweating enough as it is. I don't need to be over here fanning myself like some verklempt Victorian woman.

I've nearly reached Derek when my phone buzzes.

GRAHAM
Meet me after
Just us

My heart skips out an erratic beat, my hands shaking.
Just us.

By the end of rehearsal, I'm jittery with nerves, like I've downed six cups of espresso. Which is why, when someone catches my arm on our way up to the parking lot, I nearly scream.

Camila staggers back a step. "Whoa, sorry." She holds up her hands. "I was just going to ask if we can talk?" She stares at me with wide eyes, like she shook a sleeping animal and it snapped at her.

"Oh yeah," I say, my voice coming out high as a whistle. "Sure. What's up?"

I glance at my retreating friends. I'm looking for Graham, but it's Milo who catches my eye. He raises his eyebrows in a silent question, and I give a small shake of my head for him to go on without me. After the hard time Camila has given me this summer, I'm not expecting a friendly chat about the weather, and I don't really want whatever embarrassment is coming to be witnessed.

Camila bites her lip. "Look, I've been unfair to you."

On second thought, maybe I should call everyone over to see this.

"Vince was saying all this stuff," she continues, "and, like, Vince and I are friends, so I felt like I should listen to him. He said you're too unpredictable and you'll end up running the Drama Club into the ground just because you feel like it one day."

Okay, I take that back. This was better just between us. The last thing I need is someone agreeing with that.

"Gee, thanks, Camila." My voice comes out flat and annoyed. I'm beyond ingratiating myself to the rest of the Drama Club these days, and I'm too exhausted to worry about how I sound. "Anything else?"

Camila flushes. "I'm sorry is what I'm trying to say. I don't think he's right. I mean, we'd be doing *Little Shop of Horrors* again if it weren't for you. I'd be playing the talking plant with my luck. But in this, I've got a really good part. I don't think anyone has given you enough credit."

"Well, that's only because of Milo," I say, because I am a very modest person.

"And Derek. The only way he'll pull this off is with you helping him. Plus, you're the reason Milo got them all here in the first place. Give yourself some credit."

I don't admit I paid Milo to be here. Getting credit feels nice after a summer of dirty looks and snide comments.

"You've done a great job. So, for what it's worth, you'll have my vote, Miss President." She smiles and pats my shoulder, like we're pals now. It feels nice, but after I've written off the special election as a bust, it's just going to get my hopes up.

As soon as Camila is gone, I realize my friends are nowhere in sight—not even Graham. I've been left behind. The parking lot is empty.

"Oh, cool," I say to myself, plastering on a fake smile as I wave at Camila, who is climbing into her car a few spots away. "I guess I'll walk alone, then. Don't worry about me or anything."

"So dramatic."

I jerk around, my heart giving a surprised thump.

Graham leans against Miss Liu's car, arms crossed over his chest as he rolls his skateboard back and forth under one foot. When he sees me coming, he snaps it up, catching the end of the deck in his hand.

"Where'd everyone go?"

He shrugs. "Home."

"And it's just," I point between us, "me and you here?"

Graham smiles a little. "I did say *just us.*"

"Right," I say, my voice a squeak. "Right, that's right."

Graham raises his eyebrows, a smile pulling at the corner of his mouth. He swipes a hand over it like he can make it disappear. "Does that make you nervous?"

"No!" I answer too quickly.

Graham ducks his head to hide his stupid grin. Then he reaches for my hand and tugs me along, heading toward my house. "Come on."

I follow, my feet trailing him without my brain having any say in the matter. As we fall into step, he releases my hand, and I feel a rush of disappointment.

"What'd Camila want?" he asks.

I try not to think about how badly I want to feel his fingers slotting between mine. "Just to thank me for being the savior of our great production," I say lightly, hoping it masks every other feeling coursing through me. "Nothing major."

"Ah, must be that time." He checks an invisible watch.

"What time?"

"Bullshit hour," he says, shooting me a sideways look.

I scoff. "Oh, come on! I've worked my ass off this summer!"

He shrugs. "That's true. But I really think *I'm* the savior here. The phantom behind the scenes."

"I don't know if you really want to compare yourself to him. He was kind of a creep."

"What?"

"*Phantom of the Opera?*"

Graham blinks at me.

"Never mind. You were saying, oh great phantom behind the scenes?"

"Well, without me we'd have no AC backstage. No set either, really. No one Milo brought even knows how to use a power tool."

I smirk. "Not everyone can be a neighborhood hero."

"Not even Milo?" He shoots me a look out of the corner of his eye, his gaze flicking away when I return it.

"Milo doesn't even count," I say quickly, batting my hand at the air. "He's getting paid."

Graham stops walking. "What?"

I turn to him, eyes wide. "What?"

"Milo's getting *paid*?" He says it like an accusation.

I realize I have no room to backpedal, and I panic. "Well, I had to do something! I was desperate!"

Graham laughs. "Now this is interesting. Milo's getting paid. Milo's getting *paid*? And what are you paying the rest of us?"

"My endless love and friendship?" I say hopefully.

Graham inches closer. "Try again."

I flounder. "Hey—listen! Milo's the one who convinced you to come. Maybe you should be talking to him about payment."

"Milo didn't convince me."

"What—what do you mean? I asked him to convince you, and he said he would, and then you showed up."

"He didn't have to convince me. I'd already decided to do it. For you."

"Oh." I swallow thickly. "Well. Thank you."

A heavy beat passes before Graham says, "So what'd Milo get for all his trouble?"

I grimace. "I don't like this line of questioning."

Graham eyes me. Then something seems to dawn on him, and he stops. I make it three steps before I realize, and I twist around to look at him.

"What?" I ask.

He stares at me, his mouth lifting in a loose, open smile. "A level-five favor."

"*What?*" I nearly choke on the word.

"That's what you paid Milo. A level-five, non-expirational favor."

"How could you possibly—"

"Now this is ironic." He grins as he reaches into his pocket and pulls out a slip of fabric I recognize. Purple. The same size and shape as the piece missing from my favorite lounge shorts. Scribbled with the letters *JNA,* the *A* made into a star, and *5N.* Level five, non-expirational.

"Why do you have that?" I ask.

Graham smirks. "I bought it from him."

"*How?* What would even be worth it to him?"

Graham gives me a look.

"Ah. The vacation house." I sigh. "So, what, you've just been carrying that around, waiting to use it on me?"

Graham's brow creases. "No. I brought it tonight because I planned to use it."

A breathless laugh skitters out of me. "What could you *possibly* want from me?"

"A date."

I feel like someone stuck a vacuum cleaner down my throat and turned it on. "You're using your favor for a *date*?"

He shakes his head. "No. I'm asking you on a date."

I blink at him. "Are you serious?"

Graham licks his lips, and I'm momentarily distracted by the sweep of his tongue. My whole body heats. "Yeah, I'm serious. Jesus, Junie, I wouldn't have kissed you if I wasn't serious."

He says it like an accusation. Like he's waiting for me to pull the rug and say, *Well, I was just messing around!*

"God, stop looking at me like that!"

Graham drops his gaze.

I sigh. "I want to say yes."

Graham's cheeks go pink. "I'm sensing a *but.*"

"It's not fair of us to do this, is it? After what we put Milo and Lucy through all year."

Graham's gaze flicks up to meet mine, and he steps forward, capturing my hand. He presses something soft against my palm.

"If we hate it, then we never have to talk about it again," he says. "We can pretend it never happened."

He releases my hand, and I clutch what he left behind—a slip of purple fabric. The favor token.

"That's it?" I ask hoarsely. "You think we can pull that off?"

"If we can go back to normal after last year, we can get past anything."

I close my fist around the fabric. My nails dig into my palm.

"But if you like it—if *we* like it—you have to go on a second date with me."

I huff out a laugh. "Does this keep going? If we hate the second date, we never talk about it again, but if we like it, there's a third, and then a fourth, and a fifth, on and on until it starts to suck, and then we drop it and never talk about it again? We just date until we hate it, and then we go back to being friends?"

"Is that what you want to do?"

I grimace at the lightness in his voice and the playful look on his face. "Graham, I'm being serious. If we mess this up, it's not only us on the line—it's everything. We'd be taking Milo and Lucy into it with us."

"I'm being serious, too," he says. "Go out with me."

I hesitate. Silence stretches out between us.

Graham swallows. "Look, I'm not gonna force you. If you want to say no, then say no. I won't push it. But if you say no now, this is it. I'm not gonna try again."

I scoff. "Oh, nice, an ultimatum."

He shakes his head. "No, that's not what I mean. If you say no, I'm respecting the no. I'll go back to being your friend, and I won't push it, because I'd never pressure you. If you're uncomfortable, if it's not worth it to you, then please say no." He reaches for my hand, dragging his fingers lightly up my palm before he closes his hand around mine. "But I think you want to say yes. I know you're freaked out and worried about what might happen, but why assume the worst before we've even started? Don't say no because you're scared. Only say no if you don't want me."

I look down at our clasped hands. "I do—" The words catch at the back of my throat. Embarrassment traps them there. I take a deep breath and try again, screwing my eyes shut. "I do want you."

A breeze ruffles the palms overhead, and I wait, and wait, and wait. Graham doesn't say anything.

When I open my eyes, he has his lower lip caught between his teeth, a smile pulling at one corner of his mouth and his gaze cast across the road.

"Don't look so pleased with yourself," I say.

At that, he grins, meeting my eyes.

I take a deep breath. "I'll be busy with rehearsal."

His smile droops.

"That's not a no!" I say quickly. "I'm just saying, I'll be tied up helping Derek. I don't have a ton of free time right now."

He nods so fast, I worry he might scramble his brain. "Then after. We have a day off before opening night."

I hesitate. "That's true."

It's a tight window. One day between our last rehearsal and opening night. I should be preparing for my dad to get here. I should be running lines with Derek, even though we're expressly forbidden to rehearse on the day off. We're in an extenuating circumstance. There's even a party that night—the last of the summer, which I know everyone will be using to blow off steam.

But the truth is, I don't want to do any of that. I want to be irresponsible and a little reckless and take what might be the biggest risk of all this summer.

"So?" Graham prompts. The hope in his eyes makes my stomach turn over with excitement.

I chew my lip. "One date. On our day off." I hold up the favor token. "And if we hate it, we never talk about it again. Nothing has to change."

He nods. "Nothing has to change."

But as we agree to this, I get a sensation that feels like sinking and soaring at the same time.

Everything is about to change.

Derek and I practice every moment we have free. But between my job at Piper and Junie's and his at the Jet Ski rental place down at the marina, that doesn't leave a ton of time. On his days off, he follows me around the café while I clear tables and deliver food, both of us trading lines. I spend my free mornings at the marina, running through our scenes together while he cleans the Jet Skis and makes gas runs to the marina pump.

Sometimes Vanessa comes and sits with us, checking Derek against the script and reminding him to move. He tends to deliver a lot of his lines with lead feet, though I'm just thrilled he's getting the lines right. Other times, it's my friends, bringing doughnuts from Hot Dough or ice cream from the General Store, the four of them filling in for other characters in our more complicated scenes. Milo and Graham proving they belong on the crew, because their acting skills are pretty dismal. Lucy proving the ensemble can make anyone sound good when she tries to sing one of Sophie's parts on her own. Tallulah proving love really can conquer all when she still looks at Lucy with big, fat heart eyes.

One night while Tallulah and I are closing P&J's and Derek is helping sweep up while we sing through our difficult duet, half the cast shows up to work on the bigger scenes—Sophie and the other Drama Club kids, along with AJ. Peter tags along, too. We push the tables back and run through as many scenes as we can. Isaac and Elden hang out and watch, and when I tell her why I'll be home late, Mom shows up with boxes of pizza from Slices.

I finish every day so exhausted that I'm practically asleep before I fall into bed.

By the time our final rehearsal rolls around, Derek and I have practiced every scene a dozen times over, sung every song twice as much. I've been shower-singing my songs so often, Mom is threatening to buy earplugs.

Tonight is our last rehearsal, one final run-through with the orchestra. Derek misses a line at one point, but James saves him by ad-libbing, pulling the whole scene back on track. At the end, Derek dips me for our big, dramatic kiss but misses my mouth by a long shot. His lips land on my eyelid, and I have to hold back my laughter so we don't ruin the scene.

"Sorry," he says once we've finished, both of us breathless from the final dance number. "My aim was way off."

I grin. "It's cool. Not the worst kiss I've gotten from my darling husband. One time Will mashed his mouth against mine so hard, I cut my lip on my tooth."

Derek sags with relief. "That makes me feel better."

"It shouldn't," Vanessa says as she approaches, clapping him on the back. "Why are you so nervous?"

Derek holds up his hands. "I'm *not*! I swear!"

Vanessa's serious expression drops as she bursts into laughter. "Oh my God, you're too easy." She loops her arm through his and drags him closer to her height. "Wanna go home and practice that scene with me?"

Derek gives her a serious look. "Baby, if you think I'm gonna kiss Junie the way I kiss you, you must think I don't value my life at all."

She tosses her head back and laughs.

As she drags him off, I glance around, noticing the rest of the cast has begun to disperse. My friends wait at the edge of the amphitheater. Milo is on the phone, and Lucy and Tallulah have their arms around each other, talking quietly. Graham stands beside them with his hands tucked in his pockets, watching me.

"Junie," Miss Liu says, placing a hand on my shoulder as she passes, rolling her cooler behind her, "you did a great job this summer."

"Oh! Thanks, Miss Liu."

She smiles. "Get home and rest. *No* practicing tomorrow—I'm serious. One day won't make a difference."

"Don't worry, Derek won't even tell me his address because he's afraid I'll show up."

She tugs her cooler over a bump in the grass. "Somehow I think his instincts are correct."

She splits off from me with a wave, and I cross to my friends. Everyone else is gone.

"I'm supposed to drop you off at home," Tallulah says. "Your mom said no pit stops."

I pull a face. "What is she, my jailer? Am I in trouble?"

"She said you've been slacking on your packing," says Milo.

I glare at him. "How do you know?"

"She was telling my mom earlier," Milo answers. "She said you haven't even started on your room."

Lucy groans. "Jeez, Junie, you move in a week!"

"I've been busy!" I protest.

We reach the parking lot, and I spot Cora idling at the curb, her windows down even though it's stifling hot.

Milo glances at Graham. "Hey, we can drop you off."

Graham glances at me, not quite smiling but his expression soft like he's on the brink of it. "Sounds good."

They climb into Cora's car, and Lucy tugs me toward Tallulah's, talking about checklists and daily packing goals and how she can really turn this packing thing around for me.

Behind us, the amphitheater is empty, quiet.

And like that, it's over. Rehearsals are finished. There's only one night left before our first performance.

But before we get there, I have to do something even scarier.

I have to go on a date.

Chapter Nineteen

JAQUES
Well, you know what they say. The course of true love never did run smooth.

WEDDING PLANNER
The groom is missing, the band is terrible, the bootleggers are trying to kill each other, and now I can't find the bride. Are we even on the course at this point?

—Act 2, Scene 16, *Midsummer Madness*

"Ooh, someone's awfully dressed up," Mom singsongs as she comes into my bedroom.

I'm at my dresser mirror with a mascara wand poised at my eye like a threat. "Not . . . really . . ." I answer slowly as I try not to poke out my own eye.

"You're wearing a skirt."

I lower the mascara, my gaze sliding to hers in the reflection. "I might have a date." She opens her mouth, but I hold up my hand and cut her off. "Don't ask with who, because I'm not telling."

"A secret date?" She eyes me. "Juju, all I ask of you in this life is that you not make me into a *Dateline* mother."

I groan. "No, Mom, please, it's—he's fine. He's good. I'm just worried we might not be compatible in a date setting." I accidentally jab myself with the mascara, smearing black under my eye.

Mom grabs a tissue, wets it in the bathroom, and comes back to help me wipe the mascara away. Her fingers are cool on my flushed cheeks. "Well, don't go into it thinking it'll go badly, or it will. Try to relax. Is he picking you up here?"

"God, no! I'm meeting him there at seven."

"I'll drive you."

"Absolutely not." I know she's angling to get a look at him, and the last thing I need is Mom running to Hal and Isabel. It'll be all over the island before midnight, and worse, Isabel will tell Milo.

"Check the time, Juju," Mom says. "Unless you want to be ten minutes late to your date, you're gonna want to rethink that answer."

She's right, of course. I really don't understand how people do this time management thing.

"Okay, fine," I grumble. "But no peeking to see who it is. Please respect my privacy."

"Why do I feel like I'm trouble when I haven't even done anything yet?"

"Because I know you."

She pauses in the kitchen to piddle around, as moms are known to do. I go to the front door to hurry her along, but I nearly have two heart attacks when I open it. The first, because it's startling to open the front door to someone who's about to knock. And the second, because the person about to knock is my date.

"*Whoa.*" I shut the door and flip around to face Mom. "Actually, I don't need that ride."

Mom glances over from the fridge, where she's filling one of the reusable water bottles Tallulah gave us. "You'll be late, Juju."

"No, I won't." I open the door a crack, peeking briefly at Graham's bewildered face. "Because he's here. Bye!"

I slip out the door and pull it shut, holding it a moment to see if Mom will peek. When she doesn't try the handle, I grab Graham's hand and yank him down the front steps.

"This is interesting," he says as I drag him out to the street, keeping a quick pace and glancing over my shoulder to make sure she isn't being nosy. "Did you just commit a crime? Why are we running?"

"We aren't running," I huff, because I'm a little breathless from the, well, from the running.

I slow as we near the stop sign, looking back once more before I finally relax.

"Okay. Whew." I blow out a breath. I'm already sweating in the heat, and I'd bet another level-five favor that my makeup is smudging. As my heart rate calms, I turn to Graham and ask, "What are you doing here?"

He stares at me like my hair has morphed into a second head—which, considering the humidity, it may have. "We have a date?"

"No, I know!" I flap my free hand at him in exasperation. "I meant here, at my house."

He blinks at me. "Picking you up. For our date."

"You walked all the way here to pick me up?"

"I skated here," he says, motioning back to the house. "I left my board on your porch."

I stop and let out a distressed wail.

Our entwined hands stretch out between us as Graham

makes it few steps farther, then turns to look at me in alarm. "What's wrong?"

"She'll *know.*" As he drifts back to me, I slump, letting my forehead fall to his shoulder. "She'll know it's you I'm on a date with—" I catch the scent of something so nice, I nearly lose my train of thought. I sniff at his shirt, practically huffing it. He smells sweet and salty, and I imagine peeling an orange with my feet in the ocean while the sun beats down on my back, pleasantly warm.

"—and then she'll tell Isabel," I continue, sniffing along his collar between words, "and at that point we may as well buy a billboard. You know Milo's mom can't keep a secret for anything. God, you smell really good. What is that?"

Graham huffs out a small laugh. "My super secret Junie trap. I wore it in case you decided you're too embarrassed to be seen with me. Sounds like I made a good choice."

I jerk back to look at him. "I'm not embarrassed!"

"You didn't even want your mom to know we're going on a date tonight." He tilts his head, his expression flattening.

"I just think the less people involved, the better. This could go very horribly." My gaze drops to his shoulder, where I've left a streak of makeup on his shirt. "Oh my God, see?" I try to clean it off with my thumb, but they don't call it long-wear foundation for nothing. I groan, closing my eyes. "I'm seriously just going to walk into the ocean and never return. That should be fine, right?"

When I open my eyes, Graham is peering at the shoulder of his shirt with a small smile that makes my heart give a little thump.

"Junie, I really don't give a shit about this shirt," he says, tugging my hand until I start walking. "I just want you to relax."

I take a deep breath. "I can relax. I'm great at relaxing. But I do give a shit about your shirt. I—I like it."

He's wearing a short-sleeved, blue Hawaiian shirt and a pair of khaki shorts he calls his Church Shorts. I've been so distracted by the shock of finding him on my porch and the worry that my mom might guess who I'm on a date with, I didn't even realize Graham dressed up for this.

He grins. "Thanks. I'm glad you said that, because I've been dying to tell you how much I like that skirt on you, but I thought you might get embarrassed."

I instantly go hot all over. "Oh, uh, thanks," I choke out, embarrassed but also very, very pleased.

"By the way," he says, squeezing my hand briefly, "for future reference, so I don't shock the hell out of you again—I will always be planning to pick you up for a date, wherever you're at. Home, work, Dot Slip's house, wherever."

"Wow, even when I live four miles away on the South Shore?"

Graham smirks. "So you're assuming we'll still be doing this then?"

I make a sound like a squeaky toy that's been stepped on.

Graham chuckles. "Nice."

The farther we get from my house, the more I start to ease into this. Maybe it's because Graham doesn't seem unnerved by anything that's happened so far. His calm is rubbing off on me.

We're nearly to the Bayou Diner when I spot something that makes me gasp. I yank Graham to a halt, already turning toward the street. "Waffles."

Graham whips around. "What?"

"Waffles."

The Waffle Counter is open. This almost never happens in the summer. The Waffle Counter only stays open as long as they have ingredients, and they're usually sold out by lunch. They do sweet and savory waffles, anything from key lime with graham cracker topping to tomato and burrata with prosciutto.

"There isn't even a line." I tug on his hand, pulling him across the street. "This is fate. We cannot pass this up."

Graham glances down the street toward the diner. "I figured you'd want to eat inside." He shoots me a teasing smile. "You know, less chance of being seen with me."

"Stop saying it like that." I pull him under the awning. "Besides, everyone's at the beach. Last party of the summer."

"Ah." He glances away, momentarily hiding his face. "I forgot about that."

"What's it like not suffering from extreme FOMO?" I ask as I peer at the menu.

Graham shrugs. "I'd want to be there if you were there. So I guess I have FOMO Lite?"

I stare at him. "Do you practice these lines at home in the mirror, or what?"

He grins. "If they're working, then maybe. Otherwise, no, absolutely not."

I roll my eyes and nod toward the menu. "Wanna go halfsies? Sweet and savory?"

Graham's eyes light up. "Do you practice these lines at home in the mirror, or what?"

I flip my hair. "I don't have to practice. I'm naturally gifted."

"Sure, right," Graham says, a small smile quirking the corner of his mouth. "What do you want? S'mores and . . . buffalo chicken?"

My mouth is already watering. "Ooh, ye—" I stop, considering. What will my breath smell like after a buffalo chicken waffle? Probably not primed for kissing. "Actually, what about mac 'n' cheese instead?"

If he notices something off, he doesn't show it. As he turns to order, I sag with relief.

The Waffle Counter being open suddenly feels like the universe intervening on this date. I'm relieved we didn't make it to the Bayou Diner. Why would he try to take me to a diner where every dish on the menu is made with garlic, onions, peppers, or an unholy combination of all three?

Maybe he's not planning to kiss me at the end of the night. He clearly didn't have any issue ordering a buffalo chicken waffle, so it's not beyond the realm of possibility. I don't know what Graham normally does on a first date— I've never asked. It seems stupid now to have never gotten this detail. Why didn't I ever press him about it? But we've already kissed before—a lot, even. With whatever kind of breath we had at the time, probably. We certainly weren't popping breath mints before we made out last summer. But a date feels bigger. There's more expectation behind a kiss now than there was back then.

Still, it's Graham. Maybe it didn't occur to him. Kissing is probably on the agenda. Maybe. More than likely. If I have any say in it, it's definitely near the top of the agenda.

When he finishes ordering, Graham produces his card to pay before I have a chance. I start to protest, and he shoots me a look. "It's a *date,* Junie. I'm paying."

I scoff as he takes back his card from the cashier. "It's not the sixties anymore, Graham. Women can even vote now. Isn't that something?" I start around the side of the building to find a spot to sit.

Graham follows. "If you're that upset about it, then you can ask me on our next date, and you can pay."

I glance at him, catching his triumphant grin before he manages to stow it. Graham isn't competitive like Lucy and Milo—in sports and elections and grades, the things people expect you to be competitive in. But he likes to win—in board games and bets and conversations you didn't even realize were a competition until it was too late—and it's most obvious in these moments.

I want to keep arguing, but Graham holds out a hand to help me onto one of the stools at the long metal counter along the side of the building, and I'm momentarily distracted. Partly because it's such a polite move from someone who has definitely bodychecked me to get to Milo's extra-comfy beanbag chair on more than one occasion, but mostly because I noticed his nails are painted my favorite shade of pink.

I bite down a pleased smile as I take his hand and climb up onto the stool. I don't let go, turning his hand over in mine to run my thumb over his nails.

"Is this for me?" I ask, peering up at him.

Graham grins. "I thought you'd like—" He sucks in a breath through his teeth, jerking away from the counter, where he leaned his forearm against the burning hot metal. It's a rookie mistake—something almost every local has learned the hard way.

"You okay?" I ask, reaching for his arm.

Graham nods, bending his arm to peek at the red mark on his skin. Behind me, they call his name from the counter.

"I'll get it," I say, moving to get down.

Graham holds out a hand to stop me. "I'm good. Stay."

I glance over my shoulder as he starts toward the counter,

rubbing absently at his forearm. Then I turn away, covering my face with one hand.

Is this date turning into a total disaster?

I lean heavily into the counter without thinking, and the metal sears my elbow. I jerk back, clasping my hand around the tender spot, and groan.

"I guess that's a yes," I mutter. "Thanks, universe."

Graham returns with both waffle baskets and a handful of napkins.

"Watch your arm," he says, a too-late warning. He unfolds a few napkins and spreads them across the counter like a tablecloth, setting the waffle baskets on top. Then he flicks his gaze to me, smiling. "I'm a genius, right?"

"I'm calling Harvard right now," I reply as he hops onto the stool beside me.

He gives an exaggerated shiver. "No thanks. I don't think I could handle New England in the winter." He cuts the waffles in half, making quick work of transferring them between baskets. A little chocolate from the s'mores waffle gets onto my mac 'n' cheese waffle, but as I take a bite, I don't hate the combination.

"That's fair," I say, cutting a piece of s'mores and a piece of mac 'n' cheese and spearing them both together for a bite.

"And that's disgusting," Graham says, eyeing me as I chew. "Cheese and chocolate?"

"Don't yuck someone else's yum. It's rude. Besides, you haven't tried it." I take another bite of both waffles together, shooting him a daring look. "Unless you're scared."

Graham immediately cuts off two pieces and tries them together. He glares at me as he chews. "I hate that this is kind of good."

"You shouldn't be afraid to admit when you're wrong."

He takes another bite, shooting me an annoyed look. "Gloating isn't cute."

"Now you're just lying to yourself." I spear another piece. "Hey, remember when Milo made that Cracker Jack ice cream?"

Two years ago, the General Store had a competition amongst the employees for coming up with a new flavor. Milo had just started working there, and he got really into it, making Lucy, Graham, and me his taste testers for the summer. It wouldn't have been so bad if his combinations weren't so shockingly awful.

"Are you kidding? I had popcorn stuck in my braces for a month. I swear my orthodontist pulled a piece out when I saw him before school started."

"Ew, Graham!" I shove him with one hand, and he laughs.

"It wasn't as bad as that blue-cheese chocolate one he tried," he says. "I still have nightmares about the way that tasted."

"Clearly I'm the only one who should be making the chocolate-and-cheese choices around here," I say, indicating our empty waffle baskets.

Graham starts gathering up our trash as he begrudgingly admits, "You got one hit one time. Don't start applying to culinary schools just yet. I've seen you try to cook—it's not a pretty sight."

I take his offered hand as he helps me off my stool, and as soon as I have both feet on the ground, I give him a light kick to the back of the leg. "My cooking is just fine."

"Yeah, if they've changed the definition of *just fine* to *perpetually burnt*." He dodges my next kick, our hands stretched out between us, before he falls back into step beside me. Without discussing it, we start walking toward the water.

"I'm completely offended," I say without any heat, because he's right. Mom might be an excellent cook, but I'm a mess. *Perpetually burnt* isn't far off. I tend to get distracted in the kitchen. It's just so much *waiting*. And when it's not waiting, it's doing ten things at once. Multitasking is a great enemy of mine. I have a feeling it's a very close relative to time management.

"The good news is that when you're famous, you'll never have to worry about cooking for yourself," Graham says, squeezing my hand.

I practically glow with pleasure. "I do love that you always say *when*."

We drift down the pier, talking about the musical, my birthday coming up, and school starting soon.

"I'm already signed up to retake my SATs in the fall. I'm really just not a test type of person." I pause, considering this. "Or even a school type of person, actually. But what am I supposed to do, right? It's like, college or . . . ?" I flap my free hand vaguely.

"Or the great unknown?" He smirks. "I don't think I'm going to college."

"Wait, what?" Shock lodges in my throat, and my voice comes out high. "Why?"

He frowns at me. "Why should I?"

"You don't want to go to art school?"

Graham flushes. "I can't afford art school."

"I'm pretty sure I've heard your parents mention your college fund."

"Yeah, my *college* fund," he says. "Not my art school fund. They'd never go for it. It's probably the only thing they'd agree on these days. It's a four-year college and some kind of business or finance degree, or bust for me."

"Business or finance?" It sounds like a different question altogether as it leaves my mouth. *Don't they know you at all?*

Graham shrugs. "My parents are very traditional. They both think life is about wearing business casual and padding your bank account."

With his parents both working in accounting, this shouldn't surprise me. I consider my mom, in her sack dresses and messy hair, who never went to college and now runs a café she has admitted she would have never been able to buy without the help and support of people like Dot and Hal and the Barajas sisters.

I imagine it's probably easier for me to decide I want to major in theater than it is for Graham to propose the art school thing.

"What about loans? You could go to Ringling and live at home to save money on housing."

Graham snorts. "That sounds like my fucking nightmare. The only bright light at the end of this tunnel is moving out when I turn eighteen."

I bite my lip, dropping my gaze to the old boards of the pier under our feet.

Graham nudges me with his shoulder. "Come on, don't look so beat up about it. I might not be any good, anyway. Why pay forty grand to have some stuffy art professor tell me I suck when I could just show my sketchbooks to my dad and get the same effect?"

I jerk my head up to glare at him. "What are you talking about? You don't suck!"

"You've never actually seen my art," he reminds me.

"I've seen what you'll let me see," I reply. "And what you do is incredible. If you can sit down and do that in only a few minutes, I can't even imagine how amazing the rest of your work is."

Graham's face reddens, and he turns his head away. A

breeze ruffles his hair. "I guess I'll have to show you some-time," he says into the wind.

Delight curls warm in my stomach, and I try to rein in my smile. "You'd show me your super-secret sketchbooks?"

He leans down, tipping his head against mine. "I'd show you anything you wanted."

I jerk away, elbowing him. "That sounded like a line. This better not be a trick to get me in your bedroom."

Graham laughs. "Hey, I don't do that kind of stuff on the first date."

"Ooh, a date," a little-boy voice calls from behind us. I hear the telltale sound of wheels on wooden boards, and then they're upon us—the Klingman twins, little demons on bikes. Technically bikes aren't allowed on the pier, but the Kling-man twins operate with their own set of rules—that is, no rules at all. Tiny anarchist shitheads.

They circle Graham and me like little sharks.

"A date, a date," one of them sings, giggling madly.

"Dude, do you need glasses?" the other one asks Graham.

"I'm gonna kick your little asses into the ocean, I swear to God." I make a swipe at the nearest one.

They start laughing, pedaling faster now.

Graham tugs me to a stop beside him.

"K-I-S-S-I-N-G," one demon sings, "the ugliest girl we ever did see." He sings it until his brother joins in, and then they're both circling us and singing.

"Guys, seriously?" Graham says to them. "Knock it off."

"If you think she's so hot, then kiss her," one of them says.

"Yeah, kiss her if she's so hot," the other one echoes.

"Fine, you little idiots," I snap.

But Graham startles when I lean up to kiss him, and my lips catch air.

The Klingman twins practically howl.

"She's ugly, she's ugly, she's ugly," they chant, whooping and screeching as they pedal to the end of the pier, turn sharply back around, and zoom past us. Graham grabs my shoulder, pulling me out of the way before one of them can take me out.

Their shrieking laughter rings in my ears long after they're gone, and I'm still standing here like the world's biggest idiot.

I stare up at Graham. "What. The fuck."

He gives me a look. "Come on, Junie. Don't start."

I shrug out from under his arm, burning all over. "Seriously? You do realize *you* asked *me* on this date, right? Not the other way around?"

"I'm not gonna kiss you for the benefit of some middle schoolers."

"Yes, that would be a tragedy. Every kiss should be for a good reason."

"It should at least be because you want to!"

I freeze, staring at him. "Seriously?"

He rubs a hand down his face. "That's not what I meant. Can we just slow down for a second?"

"Yeah, we can slow down," I say, my voice too bright to really be agreeable. I can tell from the wary look on his face that he senses it. "In fact, we can stop altogether."

He sighs. "Why are you getting such an attitude about this? We were having a good time."

I scoff. "A *good time*? Seriously? This date is a disaster! We've been on the same wavelength for about a total of ten minutes, and you *didn't even want to kiss me.*"

"I hate to tell you this, since you've so clearly wanted this to end badly so you could have your big *I told you so* moment, but this date hasn't been a disaster. You've been making up imaginary problems since the second you opened your front door. If you were second-guessing going out with me, you should've just said so."

"Well, now I am, and I'm leaving."

"Are you fucking kidding me?" He lets out a harsh, disbelieving laugh. "Junie, come on."

I point at him. "Don't forget the deal. When I see you tomorrow, it's like we were never even here."

He doesn't answer, his jaw tight and his gaze cast down the pier.

"Graham."

"Fine, Junie," he says, his voice quiet. "Whatever you want."

It's *not* whatever I want. But I don't know how to explain— how to slow this moment down.

So I walk away.

When I get to the end of the pier and finally look back, he's exactly where I left him, leaning against the railing with his head tilted toward the sky.

When I get home from the Disaster Date, all the lights in the house are on. I walk in to find Hal and Mom sitting on the living room floor, sucking down strawberry daiquiris, surrounded by newly packed boxes. They seem to be sorting through knickknacks, deciding what to keep and what to donate.

Mom looks up from the vase she's holding. "You're home early. How was your date?"

"Was it scintillating?" Hal asks, shaking her shoulders.

"Not really how I'd describe it," I say.

I don't want to talk about it, and definitely not when they've been drinking. I go to the kitchen counter, where they've left a huge mess of strawberries and alcohol. "Can I have a daiquiri?"

Hal snorts. "Nice try, kiddo."

Mom pats the floor beside her. "Sit. Tell your mama what happened." Sometimes when Mom drinks, it becomes painfully clear she's from the Panhandle. They say in Florida, the farther north you go, the farther south you get. Mom's voice gets particularly twangy when she's been drinking, betraying that she's practically from southern Alabama.

"No, thanks."

Out of the corner of my eye, I see the front porch motion-sensor light flick on.

"Is that him?" Hal asks, looking past me. "Did you forget a good-night kiss?" She waggles her eyebrows suggestively.

Doubtful, I want to say as I rush to the door. I hear footsteps on the stairs.

"Maybe he forgot to grab that skateboard he left," Mom says, a knowing look on her face as she gazes intently at the framed photo she's wrapping in newspaper.

She totally knows. But from the way realization lights in Hal's eyes, I don't think she'd mentioned it to her yet. Which means maybe she didn't tell Isabel. Maybe they won't tell anyone.

And she could be right that it's Graham coming to get his skateboard. I might get another chance to rewind what happened. With time and distance, I'm exhausted from our fight, and regret is building sourly in my stomach. Maybe we can talk it out—we can apologize. We're good at that.

I don't want to hash things out with Drunks 1 and 2 here, so I fling the door open and snap it shut behind me before either of them can see him.

But it isn't Graham.

"Hey," Milo says.

Cora eases out from behind him and lifts a hand in a tentative wave. "Hi, Junie."

Awesome. Just what I need.

"Why aren't you at the beach?" I ask, my voice flat.

"Well, Graham showed up without you, and he didn't look happy. Lucy said you guys went on a date tonight. I figured someone should check on you." He steps past me into the house, pulling Cora along behind him.

My heart tugs sharply in surprise, and I yank the front door shut with more force than I intend. "What are you talking about?"

Milo shoots me a look. "Come on, did you really think he wasn't gonna tell Lucy?"

I glare past him, trying to rein in my annoyance and failing miserably. "I really thought he'd keep his mouth shut, yes." But thinking on it now, we never made that part of the deal. Last summer was about sneaking around. I guess I assumed this would be, too.

But last summer we never went on a real date. And even though I liked him then, comparing those feelings to the ones I'm having now is like comparing Little League to Major League Baseball.

"What, you didn't tell one person you were going out with him tonight? I know it wasn't me, but . . ." I don't answer, but he must see it clear on my face, because he groans. "Jesus, JN."

"I didn't want to advertise it in case something went wrong," I whisper fiercely, glancing at Mom and Hal, who are definitely eavesdropping. They are dead silent on the other side of the room.

"So, you were calling it before it even happened."

302

"I was being realistic."

"No, you weren't giving it a chance," Milo says.

I feel a headache coming on. "Can we go outside, please?"

"Milo Abadiano, you are getting so grown up," Hal says as Milo and Cora follow me across the house to the back door. "Is this your girlfriend?"

Cora's face goes red. "Hi, I'm Cora. It's very nice to meet you."

I must have a face on, because Mom gives me a narrow-eyed *be polite* kind of look.

I swallow. "Do you want anything to drink?" I ask Cora.

Cora's smile is hesitant. "I'm okay. Thanks, though."

As I shut the door behind us, I say to Milo, "I can't decide if I should thank you for coming to check on me. You're already getting on my nerves."

Milo sprays down his legs with mosquito repellent, then passes the can to Cora. "Hey, I couldn't leave my best friend on her own after she ruined her date with the guy she likes."

I scowl at him as I perch on the porch swing while Milo and Cora take the chairs. "He's not just some guy I like. We're talking about Graham. And—wait, *I* ruined it? Is that what he said?"

Milo holds up his hands. "He didn't say anything. I swear. But I think Graham was psyched for this date, and it sounds like you . . . weren't."

"He couldn't have been that psyched about it. He didn't even want to kiss me. So there's the big secret."

Milo eyes me. "That doesn't sound like Graham."

I shrug. "Well, you weren't there. But you can ask those stupid fucking Klingman twins, because they'll probably be singing about it for the whole town until I die."

Milo holds up a hand. "Back up. Start at the beginning."

303

And because I can't lie to Milo—not because I feel some great wave of guilt or anything, but because he'll know if I do—I tell him the whole story.

At the end, Milo is quiet, his expression tight like he's trying to find a gentle way to break some bad news to me.

Which is what gives Cora her opening to blurt, "You totally screwed that one up, Junie."

My attention whips toward her. "Excuse me?"

Cora holds up her hands. "Sorry, but it's true. You messed that up."

I bristle. "Great, please tell me more about how I ruined everything. I was just thinking you were exactly the person I wanted to hear that from."

"Hey, come on," Milo says, waving his arm between us.

Cora glares at me. "I'm trying to help you out right now."

"The tone could use some work, if you're open to critique."

Cora sighs. "Graham Isham looks at you like you hung the fucking moon— *God,* I sound like my mother." She makes a grossed-out face, but doesn't pause long enough for me to get a word in. "If he didn't want to kiss you in front of some little twerp kids, then you let it go. It's not like he wasn't planning to kiss you at all."

"He suggested a buffalo chicken waffle for dinner."

Cora cringes. "Well, that's because boys don't think." She jerks a thumb at Milo. "He had hummus on one of our dates. I tasted garlic for a week."

Milo looks at her in surprise. "Seriously?"

"Boys have no shame," Cora says.

Milo catches up to the conversation in time to add, "And it's not like you two haven't kissed before."

Cora gives me a look. "Are you kidding me?"

"Only once," I say weakly. It's really a half-truth, because kissing at Tallulah's that night felt like more than one kiss or even two. It felt too big to just call it kissing.

I guess it's even less than a half-truth, because Milo says, "And all last summer?"

Cora's eyes widen. "*What?*"

I point a hand at her, glaring at Milo. "Thank you for putting all my business in the street for everyone to see. Yes, Graham and I hooked up last summer. But that doesn't apply here. There were . . . circumstances."

"But you've kissed since those circumstances?" she asks.

"Once. Or, a lot, I guess, if we're being honest, but it was one night."

Cora sighs. "So you kiss, *he* asks *you* on the date, and then you get mad when he doesn't kiss you in front of some middle schoolers that called you ugly?"

I frown. "When you put it like that, it sounds really immature."

Cora gives me a pointed look.

"Not to mention you were just waiting for something to go wrong," Milo says. "You didn't tell *anyone* you were going out with him. You didn't even think he was gonna pick you up, and that's Dating 101. Of course he was gonna pick you up."

"He doesn't have a car."

"Neither do I." Milo looks at Cora. "Do I pick you up for our dates?"

Cora smiles. "Only when I don't pick *you* up."

Milo holds out a hand like, *See?*

"Well, I haven't been on a lot of dates." My voice comes out high and defensive. "Or, like, any dates. The last guy I was involved with was that Russian exchange student, and we just made out behind Publix a few times." Alek was my attempt at getting over Graham. I've known most people at school since my bike had training wheels. Fresh blood was a welcome reprieve. And Alek wasn't really into talking, which was a big plus for me.

Cora makes a face but tries to smooth it over.

I glare at her. "Listen, he was hot."

Cora's conceding smile still looks like a grimace.

"I don't need your judgment, Cora."

"It's just—behind the Publix. There's, like, a dumpster and stuff. It's kind of gross."

I look at Milo. "Is that judgment? It sounds like judgment, and I think I just said—"

Milo sits up suddenly and pulls his buzzing phone from his pocket. He looks surprised. "Hey, Luce. What's up?" His expression shifts to panic. "What?"

"What's wrong?" I ask.

Cora looks from Milo to me and back, expression tightening with worry.

"Okay, yeah," he says, standing and pulling Cora with him. "We're coming." He motions for me to get up.

"What's going on?" I ask.

"I'm with her," he says to Lucy, right as Mom opens the back door and holds up my phone.

"Juju, your phone keeps ringing."

I jump off the swing and grab it from her. It's still buzzing, and I answer without even looking. "Hello?"

"It's me." Tallulah's voice is never full of much emotion, but right now it's completely flat.

My heart hammers. "What happened?"

Milo grabs my arm. "We have to go."

Mom's eyes go wide. "What—what's going on?"

"It's Graham," Milo and Tallulah say in unison.

Cora takes my hand and squeezes.

"I'll tell you on the way," Milo says, plucking my phone from my hand. Into it, he says, "We'll be there in ten minutes."

"Where are we going?" My voice sounds faraway, like someone else is using it.

"Spoonbill General Hospital," says Milo.

"We'll all go." Mom grabs her keys, holding them out to Milo, but Cora snags them first.

"I'll drive," she says, giving Mom a reassuring nod.

We leave every light in the house on.

Chapter Twenty

(Locked in the closet, BENEDICK and BEATRICE sit in silence, exhausted from fighting.)

BENEDICK
(Sadly.) Perhaps it is a different husband you deserve.

BEATRICE
Oh, you continue to be the fool! I'll have no husband, if you be not he.

—Act 2, Scene 15, *Midsummer Madness*

It's still tourist season, so the emergency room at Spoonbill General Hospital is packed. We pick our way through to the back, where Lucy and Tallulah sit side by side, not touching. Tears run down Lucy's face, and she looks like she's been crying for a long time. Tallulah stares blankly ahead. She's soaking wet, a thin hospital blanket wrapped around her shoulders. Her hair hangs in tangles around her face.

I spot Milo's dad right away, towering over everyone else. He stands at the front desk with Graham's dad and—

I swallow. Rooney.

She's holding Owen against her shoulder, the stroller parked beside her.

"I don't know what happened," Lucy says when we reach her. "He was passed out, but he was breathing. We made sure. He woke up as they were taking him in the ambulance, but— I don't know. He wouldn't look at me."

Milo repeated the story he got from Lucy while we were on our way to the hospital.

They decided to go night swimming—Graham and a few others from the party. He got caught in a swarm of Portuguese man-of-wars that had blown in. He wasn't the only one stung, but he got the worst of it. By the time the rest of the swimmers realized Graham wasn't with them, the whole party was in a panic.

Tallulah was the one who went in and pulled him out while someone else called 911.

"They said he'll be okay," Lucy says through a hiccup. "They can treat him. They wouldn't lie, right?"

Tallulah stands up, the blanket slipping from her shoulders. I notice she's been clutching a cloth-wrapped ice pack to her arm, and when she drops it on the chair, I see a long red welt stretching up her forearm.

I stare at it, eyes wide. "Tallulah." I reach for her hand, but she jerks away. Her arm swings, and I recoil, afraid she might hit me, but she just staggers past.

Milo and Cora glance up as she goes.

I don't know why I follow her. I should leave her to deal with it on her own. She'd probably prefer that. But my mind keeps rolling back to the beach, and how she went into the water in the dark to pull him out. How it so clearly mirrored what I know is the most traumatic event of her life, and she didn't freeze up.

Gratitude swells in me, and I feel full enough to scream or sob.

Tallulah has a head start, and by the time I push open the bathroom door, I can hear her retching in one of the stalls. She hasn't bothered to close the door, and I find her kneeling on the floor with vomit in her hair.

I crouch down beside her. "You did good."

Tallulah winces.

"You did," I say. "You saved him. You—you saved his life, Tallulah." The words almost get stuck in my throat. I give a wet sniffle and brush my fingers under my eyes, hoping to stall the tears gathering.

Tallulah puts her hands over her face and stiffens like she's holding her breath.

"Breathe," I whisper, rubbing her back in slow circles.

She lets out a slow, shaky breath.

I reach past her to flush the toilet, in case the smell turns her stomach again.

"Come here." I pull on her wrist.

We go to the sink, and I rinse the vomit from her hair.

"I thought he was dead." She takes in an unsteady breath, and her eyes fill. "I thought he was dead, but I kept going. I just kept . . . I thought if anything, maybe . . ."

I reach down and take her hand. "You don't have to tell me."

She lowers her gaze. "I thought if I couldn't . . . then how fucked up will I be for it later? How many more prescriptions and appointments and nightmares? I was being selfish. I just kept thinking if he dies, I'll never be able to sleep again."

I don't say anything.

"I'm not a good person, Junie. So don't start kidding yourself thinking I did it to be good. All I thought about the whole time was myself."

"That doesn't change anything. You still did it."

I turn and hug her. She doesn't lean into me, doesn't even face me. I hug her from the side, with her bony elbow digging into my stomach, and rest my forehead against her knobby shoulder. I can feel her taking longer, steadier breaths.

Then someone knocks on the bathroom door and cracks it open.

"Mush? It's Dad."

Tallulah jerks away from me. When I turn around, she's torn open the bathroom door and thrown herself into Paul's arms. I can hear her sobbing even after the bathroom door swings shut.

I wait a few seconds before I follow, but they're still standing there. I try not to look at Paul, because he's crying now, too, but he catches my eye over her shoulder and gives me a grateful nod.

Mom waits for me at the end of the hall, looking really put together for someone who cries during Disney movies.

"Macaulay just went back," she says. "They said Graham's okay—he's awake. But you won't be able to see him for a while, maybe not until morning. Do you want to go home and wait there?"

"No. I'm not leaving until I see him."

I look past her at my friends. Milo and Cora sit on the floor between Lucy and Hal. He has his arm slung across Cora's shoulder and his head resting back against Lucy's knee. Lucy's parents have arrived, too. Her dad paces in the small space between the rows of seats. Her mom is returning from the vending machine, holding a ginger ale, which she cracks open and offers to Lucy.

"They want her to go home and get some sleep," Mom says.

"She won't be able to sleep tonight."

Mom lets out a long breath and smooths her hand over my hair. "I know."

I expect Tallulah to go home. I can tell Paul wants her to, but he also brought her a change of clothes, like he expected she wouldn't want to leave. She waits with us, and as the ER clears out, our group starts claiming more seats. Tallulah takes one beside Lucy and reaches for her hand, and I think Lucy may burst into tears all over again.

Paul gets a deck of cards from a break room somewhere, and the parents and Hal start up a game.

Rooney sits at the end of the row, moving the stroller back and forth with her foot when Owen wakes briefly and starts to fuss. As the waiting room clears, it becomes increasingly more uncomfortable to have her sit away from our group.

Even though Mom is still upset with her about last summer, she eventually turns and says, "Roo? Why don't you bring him over here? I'll hold him a while until he falls back asleep."

Rooney glances over, bleary-eyed. A small, soft smile inches across her face as she stands and makes her way over to us.

Mom takes Owen out of the stroller and cradles him against her chest, patting his back lightly with her card-holding hand. Then Rooney drops her head on Mom's shoulder and closes her eyes, and I think we all briefly tense up.

Mom looks at me, and I hesitate, then shrug.

And that's how we're all sitting when Joy Isham comes flying into the waiting room.

Graham's mom doesn't stop to speak to any of us. I have a feeling it's 75 percent about being anxious to get to Graham and 25 percent about the girl her husband cheated with sitting in the waiting room.

She disappears into the back, into that mysterious place none of us can go, where they're keeping Graham. I feel a rush of jealousy, even though *of course* she can walk straight back there. She's his mother.

I'm just his . . .

Well, now probably isn't the time to try to figure that one out.

When it starts to get really late, Cora's mom arrives to pick her up, and she promises to come back in the morning if we're still here. That's about the time we all start dropping—Rooney falls asleep on Mom's shoulder, Lucy and Tallulah drift off leaning on each other. Milo sprawls in the seat next to me, his head tipped back and mouth open.

Eventually only Paul and I are left.

"You should try to sleep," he whispers across the aisle to me.

I shrug. "I'm kind of wired." I'm also freezing. My legs bounce lightly, partially from nerves but also because I'm shivering. The whole waiting room has that dry, ice-cold air-conditioning feel.

Paul leans forward and shucks off his jacket. He half rises from his seat to drape it across my lap. "Sleep, Junie. I'll wake you when they come out."

The jacket is still warm, and I pull it up over my shoulders, dragging my legs up into the seat so it covers nearly all of me. "Aren't you tired?"

He grins. "I've pulled a lot of all-nighters in my lifetime. I'll be fine."

I chew my lip, sleep already tugging at my eyelids until they droop. Like the combination of the warm jacket and the reliable man across from me have given my body the signal that it's okay to rest.

"Thanks, Paul."

I lean my head on Milo's shoulder and finally shut my eyes.

"Junie? Junie, wake up."

A hand touches my shoulder, and I jerk up with a gasp.

Paul leans over me, his eyes round with surprise. "Sorry," he says, taking a step back. "Did I scare you?"

I swipe my hand over my mouth. I feel like I was asleep five minutes, but the sun is shining, so it must have been much longer.

Around me, everyone else is still snoozing.

"What's going on?" I whisper.

Paul nods toward the front desk, where Macauley stands, talking to the nurses. I lean forward, blinking the haze of sleep from my eyes. Then the door beside the desk opens, and Joy holds it as Graham steps out.

I stagger to my feet, and he stops as I move toward him. His mom says something I can't hear. Everyone could be saying something all at once, and I wouldn't be able to hear them. It's like someone turned the volume down on the whole room—everything is muted except the thudding of my heart.

I stop in front of him, not quite close enough to touch, because I don't know how much pain he's in. He's wearing different clothes than he did on our date—a pair of soft-looking sweatpants and a white T-shirt his dad or Rooney must have brought from home. He has angry red welts up one arm, disappearing under the sleeve of his shirt and curling back out from his collar. One welt winds up over his jaw, stretching onto his cheek. There are dark circles under his eyes, and his skin has lost its color. He's covered in a light sheen of sweat, like he might have a fever.

Looking at him makes my heart feel like the husk of a juiced lemon, squeezed flat and scraped clean of pulp. I lift my arm and press my face into the crook of my elbow as I let out a sob.

He exhales a soft laugh. "Geez, I hope they've got the Scrambler at the Cry Fest this year."

I drop my arm to swat at the air. "It's not funny."

His smile is tired, and his gaze is wary, like he isn't sure how to act.

"You're so stupid." My voice comes out wobbly and wet as I sniffle. "I can't believe you did that."

He sighs. "Yeah, I know. I got the whole lecture from my mom already. She covered all the bases—you don't need to repeat it."

I glare at him. "You could have died."

"I know."

"That was just—that was *so* stupid."

"Junie, I know."

"And *why*? Why would you do that? You know how dumb night swimming is—you know it's dangerous. Why—"

He catches my hand and squeezes. "*Junie.*"

I drag my gaze up to his face.

"I know," he says. "I'm an idiot. Trust me, I've had a lot of time to think about it."

I brush my free hand over my eyes. "I was really worried."

"I'm sorry."

I glance over him, taking in the welts and bandages and the gray tinge to his skin. "You better be glad you didn't die. I would've been at Moonface's house so fast for a séance to call you back here just so I could kick your ass."

315

"I'm glad I didn't die, too. But for other reasons."

"Oh yeah?"

Graham's gaze is hot and serious and frustrated as he grabs me by the back of the neck and pulls me in roughly. "Yeah," he says just before our mouths meet.

I expect it to be a hard, bruising kiss, but it's soft. Our matching relief sweetens everything between us. I don't know how to touch him, so I settle for fisting my hands in the front of his shirt, because it's the closest I can get.

Graham wraps his fingers around my wrists and moves my hands up, pressing one to a spot right above his heart and the other to the uninjured side of his neck. When my palm touches his bare skin, he sighs against my mouth, tension bleeding out of him.

When he pulls away, he rests his forehead against mine, breathing harder than he should be after a short kiss.

"Hey, don't overdo it," I whisper.

"Call it a compromise," he says, his voice ragged. "That wasn't even the half of it."

I duck my head, cheeks burning.

Graham pulls away. "You shouldn't be here."

"What?" My voice comes out like a hiccup.

"You have the play tonight." He reaches up and tucks my hair behind my ear. "You should be at home sleeping. Why would you stay here all night?"

I set my jaw, narrowing my eyes at him. "You think I would've been at home *sleeping* while you were in the hospital? Are you kidding me?"

He closes his eyes, letting out a slow breath through his nose. "I just meant it's been the most important thing to you all summer, and you—"

"You idiot." I clutch the front of his shirt and push myself up to bump my forehead against his. "*You* are the most important thing to me."

His tired eyes light with the barest spark. "Did you just headbutt me?"

"Seemed safer than anything else."

"Hey, I hate to break this up," Lucy says from behind me, "because I think the waiting room is really enjoying the show. But could I, like—" She breaks off with a small sob, losing all of her bravado at once.

I step away, giving her room to move in. She whispers something to him that I can't hear, and Graham reaches around to pat her back lightly as she starts to cry.

I don't realize Tallulah is standing next to me until Graham glances over and says, "You know, I've owed a lot of favors in my life, but—"

Tallulah holds up a hand. "Don't."

"It's already done." He reaches into his pocket and pulls out a piece of what looks like torn hospital gown. On it in black marker are the words *The Big One* and his initials. "Probably goes without saying that this one doesn't have an expiration date."

Tallulah doesn't move to take it. "I don't want it. You don't owe me."

Graham steps closer and presses the fabric into her hand. "Just keep it. You might need it one day. That's got a lot of trading power. Junie already has her hungry eyes on it."

I drop my gaze. "I don't know what you're talking about."

"Graham," his mom says, her voice stern. "It's time to go."

Graham winces, his eyes drifting toward his parents standing a foot apart, stiff-backed at the front desk. He starts toward them, but as he passes me, he reaches out and gives my hand a quick squeeze.

Later, as Mom and I are pulling into the driveway, my phone buzzes with a text.

DAD
Running behind. Won't make it 2nite sry.
Will b there 2mrw

Chapter Twenty-One

QUEEN TITANIA
I promise you all, my fairies will be dealt with. These games and schemes have gone on long enough.

PUCK
But your majesty, it was all for you!

QUEEN TITANIA
Am I not queen? Do your orders not come from me and me alone?

SEBASTIAN
(To Puck, smugly.) And thus the whirligig of time brings in his revenges.
—Act 2, Scene 18, *Midsummer Madness*

Opening night runs without a single issue. Derek remembers all his lines and dance moves, and even manages to land our kiss somewhere near my mouth—this time on the side of my nose—which is good enough for the audience. I'm starting to think his missing my mouth is less about Derek having bad aim and more about him not wanting to kiss another girl. Which is actually kind of cute.

Afterward, while half the cast heads off to Slices for pizza, my friends and I are shepherded home to sleep.

"Wait, but Mom," I complain as she ushers me toward Isabel's car with Milo and his parents. "I need to schmooze. I'm trying to win an election here."

"Schmooze tomorrow," Mom says.

I look to Milo for help, but he practically has his eyes closed already.

"You need to rest up, little one," Isabel says, putting an arm around my shoulders to give me a shake. I nearly fumble my armful of flowers—from Mom, Hal, and Milo's parents.

I guess our parents have a point, because on the two-minute ride home, I fall asleep with my face mashed against the window, which leaves a really cute sweat mark on the glass. In my room, I strip down to my underwear and fall into bed without showering, even though I am basically wearing old sweat like a second skin.

I don't wake until my phone starts buzzing on my nightstand. I feel around for it without sitting up. When I finally grab it, my heart gives a wild thump of anticipation.

GRAHAM

"Juniper Nash," he whispers when I answer.

"Hmm?"

"Juniper Nash. Juniper Nash." His voice is low and gravelly. It makes me want to curl under the covers and go back to sleep while he whispers my name in my ear.

I take in my dim bedroom through bleary, half-open eyes. Early morning light filters in through my closed curtains. "What? What? What's up?"

"You said if we say your name three times, you'll be there. Like Beetlejuice."

I rub my eyes. "Huh?"

"At the bonfire."

The bonfire. It feels like a million years ago.

I sit up, my quilt falling into my lap. "You remember that?"

Graham makes a small, hesitant sound. "I remember everything you say."

I cover my face with one hand, trying to smother my stupid smile.

"So, is it gonna work?" Graham asks, a nervous edge in his voice.

"You want me to come over now? It's so early."

He makes an embarrassed noise. "Right. Sorry, I should let you rest. I don't know why I—"

"No, that's not— I'm glad you called."

The line is quiet for a moment. Then Graham says, "I miss you."

My heart jumps like I've been electrocuted.

"I know that's stupid," he continues. "We just saw each other, but—"

"I miss you, too," I whisper.

He lets out a heavy breath, and I hear the relief in it.

"I'll be over in ten minutes."

It's more like twenty, because only after we hang up do I remember that I'm basically crusted in old sweat. I take a fast, hot shower, scrubbing myself pink, throwing on the first clean clothes I can find after. Then I bike to Graham's at breakneck speed, the skateboard he left on my front porch balanced on the basket of my bike.

He opens the door before I knock.

"Shouldn't you be in bed?" I ask, running a hand through my wet hair. The back of my T-shirt is damp.

Graham raises an eyebrow. "This is interesting. Trying to

get me in bed already? Geez, Junie, I was just in the hospital." He takes his skateboard from me and leans it up against the wall in the entryway.

"*Resting,*" I say. "You should be resting."

"That's what I keep telling him," comes a woman's voice from inside.

It's not Rooney, which can only mean . . .

A hand comes around the edge of the door, pulling it open. Joy stands behind her son, several inches shorter but somehow looming. She looks stern and tired, but her expression softens when she sees me.

"Hi, Junie," she says, beckoning me inside. "How are you doing?"

I glance at Graham as she hugs me. So we're all going to pretend it's normal for Joy to be standing in the entryway of the house she no longer lives in, with her ex-husband and his new girlfriend perched awkwardly on the sofa.

Rooney catches my eye and smiles tightly. Macaulay doesn't look at me at all, his focus on his phone.

"I'm good," I answer at last, my voice coming out stilted and uncomfortable. "It's nice to see you. Well—not—not *nice.* I mean, it'd be nicer if . . ." I glance at Graham for help.

"If I hadn't almost died," he says. "Mom, come on, give her a break."

He shoots me a flat look, flicking his gaze toward the living room like he's saying, *Yeah, imagine how I feel.*

Joy pulls back, runs her hands over my hair, and smooshes my face between her palms, then releases me. "You're all getting so grown up."

At this, Macaulay speaks. "Yeah, grown up enough to be kissing in the middle of the emergency room."

I flush all the way to my hairline.

"Dad," Graham says balefully.

"Jesus, Macaulay," says Rooney.

He looks up from his phone. "What? We all saw it."

Joy sighs. "Do you have to be such an ass?"

I take a step away from Graham, putting some space between us.

Graham tips his head back and says to the ceiling, "Do you guys have to fight right now? Seriously?"

"I'm just saying, when I was your age, I probably would've thought twice about kissing a girl in front of my parents like that."

Graham glares at his dad. "Yeah, you're a real pillar of modesty."

"Graham," Joy says, at the same time Macaulay stands up from the couch, his expression furious.

Rooney turns red and drops her gaze to her lap.

Graham grabs my hand. "We're going to my room. I'm tired."

"Door open," Macaulay says sharply.

I barely manage to squeak out a shocked sound before Graham drags me away. It has the feel of getting the vaudeville hook. I've been unceremoniously yanked offstage before delivering any of my lines.

In his room, Graham makes a point of loudly closing his door. Not a slam, but a very firm shut. He flips the lock for good measure.

I glare at him. "Hey, don't drag me into—"

He wraps his arms around me, enveloping me in a hug. His weight sinks into me, like all the strength has left him.

"Graham, you're hurt," I remind him.

"I don't care." He walks me to his bed without letting go

samantha markum

and pulls me down with him, rolling us until we're lying with him half on top of me.

It would be an extremely compromising position, except that it doesn't feel that way. Even though he has one leg pressed between mine and his arms holding me tightly against him, his chest is heaving.

Whoa.

"Hey," I whisper, rubbing a hand up and down his back. "Doesn't this hurt?"

He shakes his head, his hair brushing my cheek and his labored breath warm against my neck. "Feels better than it hurts."

"What's wrong?" I ask, cupping my hand around his nape.

He sighs, nuzzling into my neck. "Nothing now."

"Do you think your dad will bust down your bedroom door and drag us out of here?" I ask, a nervous edge to my voice.

Graham huffs out a laugh. "My mom would murder him before he made it halfway down the hall. She's got a lot of sway right now since I almost died on his watch." He pushes up onto one elbow, loses his breath, and rolls quickly onto his back. "Fuck."

"I knew it," I say, sitting up to lean over him. "You're in pain."

He puts a hand over his eyes and takes in a deep, steadying breath. "It hurts no matter what. I can take it if it means I get to touch you." He peers at me from between his fingers. "Are you uncomfortable being in here with me? We can open the door."

I shake my head, stretching out beside him. I set my head on his pillow, so there's barely an inch of space between us, though we don't touch. I'm nervous about hurting him.

Graham drops his hand and rolls to face me. He reaches

up and takes a lock of my hair between his fingers, smiling. "You showered before you came over?"

"Well, I was basically wearing a second skin of dried sweat."

Graham smirks. "Is this your version of dirty talk?"

"Yeah, do you like it? Wait, let me tell you about how stiff my shirt was when I took it off last night."

Graham chuckles, hooking an arm around my waist and dragging me into him. "That's probably more dangerous than you think."

My breath leaves me in a whoosh, my heart racing.

Graham's eyes settle on mine. "Hey. It's just me."

"I know. I'm very calm right now."

"Your heart's beating like a little rabbit's."

I blush. "That's your heart, not mine."

He ducks his head and laughs. His fingers stroke my hair, dragging down my back. When he lifts his head again, his nose nearly brushes mine. I feel a thrill of anticipation run through me.

I swallow. "Are you about to kiss me?"

He grins. "Junie, I'm always half a second from kissing you. I've just been holding myself back."

I give a small smile and lean in, and Graham meets me halfway.

We kiss slowly, and even though I'm holding myself back for Graham's benefit—he was just in the emergency room, after all—I'm savoring it at the same time, a series of long, gentle kisses, keeping our hands to ourselves even though I'm dying to touch him.

When he loses his breath, I pull back, and he settles against the pillow, chest heaving.

"Are you okay?" I ask, worried. "Was that too much?"

He grins and closes his eyes, moving his hand to my thigh, his skin warm against mine. "Too much? You're kidding," he says with a rough laugh.

I watch him while he rests, his breathing evening out and the pinch of pain in his face easing. I smooth my fingers over the inside of his forearm, where there are no welts.

"How was opening night?" he asks when he catches his breath. "I guess you all made it through without me. Somehow. Pretty shocking, really."

"Yeah, it was a real struggle without our—what'd you call yourself? Our phantom behind the scenes?" I say with a laugh. "Derek remembered all his lines, which is really all I cared about."

Graham turns his head to look at me, brow furrowed. "What happened?"

I blink at him. "Nothing?"

"You sound weird."

I roll onto my back. "I'm fine. It was nothing important."

"Junie."

"We should be worrying about you, not me."

"I'll worry about whatever I want," he says, turning on his side. "And you haven't mentioned your dad yet."

The assumption he hasn't made aloud hangs in the air, unsaid but clear.

I frown at his ceiling. "He couldn't make it last night. But it's fine. He'll be there tonight—he said so when he texted me."

Graham hesitates, watching me. "Are you okay?"

I swallow, thinking of my dad and his last-minute text yesterday. I haven't heard from him since. He didn't even call to ask how it went.

But he still didn't cancel.

"He said he'll be here." I pick at a loose thread on my shorts. "I can't write it off yet, so I'm just . . . trying not to get ahead of myself."

Graham reaches for my fidgeting hands and flattens his palm over them. When I turn one hand over, he laces his fingers through mine.

"What about you?" I whisper, rolling to face him. "Your mom being back . . . That has to be hard."

"It's not hard having her back." He lifts my hand to his mouth and presses featherlight kisses across my knuckles. "It was harder having her gone."

I hold my breath against the wave of guilt. Graham must see it in my face, because he squeezes my hand, then shifts forward to kiss my forehead lightly.

A long beat passes before he says, "She asked me again. To go to Jacksonville with her and stay with her and my lolo."

"Oh," I say, aiming for lightness. "So, you . . . you're leaving?"

He tenses, his brows curving together, a crease forming between them. He sits up, and our hands pull apart. "I don't know. I haven't given her an answer yet."

I sit up, too. "Do you want to go?" I ask, forcing it out past my hesitation. I'm not sure I want the answer, but I need to know. "If it's hard for you here—if the thing with your dad is too much—"

"It is." He swallows audibly. I watch his Adam's apple bob from the force. He reaches up to cover his eyes. "It sucks. It really, *really* sucks. I'm fucking miserable."

I feel the tears rush up, but I try to hold them back. The absolute last thing Graham needs is to worry about the Juniper Nash Cry Fest. But watching him in pain—not just physical pain, but the other pain I've been seeing since last year, that has claws. They dig into my heart, an ever-present reminder of my fault in this.

"Maybe you should go?"

Graham's hand slides slowly from his face. His eyes are wet and red-rimmed, and the claws in my heart dig even deeper. "Do you think I should?"

"I'm not selfish enough to tell you to stay. Even if I want to. Like, really badly." I close my hand around his. "I don't want you to stay if you aren't happy."

Graham squeezes my hand. "I just don't know if I can handle another year in this house. No matter how happy I am outside of it. And I really—" His voice cracks, and he pauses before trying again. "I don't think I can say no to her again. Not after last time. It's been so hard without her. I don't think I realized how hard it would be until she was gone."

I swallow down the lump in my throat and try to put on a brave face. I don't want him to be thinking about me and my feelings when he's deciding—not when he so clearly needs to be with his mom.

"Hey, it's only four hours, right?" I press my shoulder into his. "Maybe one of us can get a car. We can do weekend trips. Four hours—it's nothing."

"It's even closer to Tallahassee," Graham says. "When you go to school."

I let out a sharp laugh. "Right. If I get in."

Graham nudges his shoulder against mine. "You will. And I'll come visit every weekend. Your roommate's gonna love me."

"Well, she'll have to get in line. As we know, Graham Isham is beloved by all."

Graham grins, leaning in to wrap his arms around me. He

pulls me down beside him, tucking my head under his chin. "That's just my burden to bear, I guess."

I close my eyes and sink into him.

I don't know how much longer we have. Days, maybe. A week at most. If he leaves for Jacksonville, he won't be here much longer. My throat squeezes with tears, my stomach aching with regret.

I did this. I did it to myself—to us both. I played my part last year, and this is the consequence. Not our fight or the weirdness that followed or anything else that's happened. It's this—that I have him, and he's mine, and he's probably going.

I can't ask him to stay. These are my chickens. They've come home to roost.

That night, I stand behind the heavy black curtain, peering out at the crowd and periodically checking my phone. It's the second night of the musical, the biggest of our three performances. Like last night, I spy Mom and Paul in a row with Milo's and Lucy's parents, Lucy's grandmother, and Ruby. Dot, Hal, and Moonface take up three seats behind them. Cora and some of her friends are on the other side of the main aisle. Rita Delgado and her husband are near the back, and I notice her sisters and their husbands at our little snack counter, buying candy.

Then I spot Graham coming in from the parking lot, his mom trailing him. Mom motions for Joy to take the empty seat next to her, and Graham falls in on his mom's other side. He should be at home resting, but no amount of telling him that could stop him from coming tonight. He's even carrying flowers—two bouquets, because of course he thought of Lucy—and my eyes prick with tears.

His mom keeps glancing at him, like she's checking that he's okay. He says something that makes her laugh. Their faces light, and I feel the tingle of my anxiety in my stomach.

It's only been a few hours since I left his house. He probably hasn't decided yet about going with his mom or not. Leaving White Coral and the rest of us behind. The thought mixes with the rest of my anxiety—namely that my dad hasn't showed yet, and we're only a few minutes from curtain. The orchestra is getting ready to play the warning notes for everyone to get into their seats.

I send Dad another check-in text.

ME
Starting soon. Are you running late?

I stare at my empty screen for what feels like an eternity, waiting for any sign of a response. The orchestra plays the warning notes.

I grip my phone tighter.

ME
I'll tell the stage manager to leave your ticket at the snack bar.

I turn and run headlong into Tallulah, who has been standing behind me for who knows how long.

"What are you doing?" I gasp, slamming my palm against my chest.

She glances down at me, unaffected. "I was looking for my dad."

"Oh." I swallow. "Me, too."

"You were looking for my dad?" She raises an eyebrow.

"No." I shoot her a flat look. "I was looking for mine."

Her expression softens. "Right. Is he . . . ?"

I glance around, hoping Milo isn't nearby. He doesn't need to know my dad isn't here yet. Hopefully no one but Mom will notice.

"Yeah, he's just running late. No big deal."

Tallulah frowns. "Yes, it is."

"What?"

"Yes, it is a big deal." She stares at me like half my brain is coming out of my ears. "You've worked your ass off all summer for these three nights, and he couldn't even be on time? That's bullshit, Junie."

I swallow. "Please, I don't need to hear this from you."

Tallulah shakes her head and reaches past me, pulling back the curtain. "Look."

I don't turn. "Tallulah, seriously, I don't want—"

"*Look.*" She points past me to the crowd. "You see those people out there? Your mom, my dad, your boyfriend—"

I nearly choke. "My what?"

"Fine, your soon-to-be boyfriend. Whatever you two are calling yourselves. Just look."

I turn reluctantly, my head lolling to the side in annoyance.

Tallulah uses her hands to gently force my gaze forward. "Those people are here for you. Dot, Hal, Moonface, the Barajas sisters. If none of us did this with you this summer, they'd still be here. We'd all be out there, watching you." She puts her hands on my shoulders, turning me to face her. "You don't need anyone who doesn't want to be in your life, Juniper Nash. You have so many other people who are ready to be there for you. You might have grown up wishing you had what all the other kids with dads have, but guess what? People would kill to have the family you've made here. You don't have to stick with what you're born into, just because it's what you think you need. A dad who doesn't show up isn't a dad. He's just a father."

I sniffle. "Are you trying to make me ruin my makeup before the first act?"

She tugs my shoulders, pulling me in, and hugs me tight.

It's the first time we've ever hugged, like *really* hugged. Hugging her back, I suddenly understand the term bird-boned. She feels featherlight, like I could pick her up without any effort. But her hug is strong, locked around me like a vise. Somehow, it eases every tight feeling in my chest.

Tension bleeds out of me as Tallulah rubs a hand up and down my back.

When she pulls away, she's teary-eyed. She swipes the back of her hand over her eyes, sniffling. "Jesus. I better be careful, or they'll start asking me if I'll have a Ferris wheel at the Tallulah Cry Fest."

I tip my head back and fan my eyes, trying to dry my tears before they track down my face. "You'd have to cry a lot more than this to get your own Fest. Trust me, I've built this reputation over many meltdowns." I take and then release a long breath, finally dropping my chin. "How do I look?"

Her gaze flicks over my face, and she nods. "Good. Only a little smudging." She reaches into her pocket and produces a tissue, which she dabs under my eyes.

"Thirty seconds," Miss Liu calls. The rest of the cast starts spilling out from the back. It's stifling in the wings, the breeze blocked by the temporary curtains that were hung up for the performance. The AC units in the back are not strong enough to reach us up here.

I shouldn't be worried about tears ruining my makeup—I'll sweat it all off by the second act anyway.

Derek claps my shoulder. "Ready, darling wife?"

I think of the people on the other side of the curtain—my friends, my family. My maybe-sort-of-kind-of-possibly boyfriend. Everything is changing so quickly, I can barely catch my footing.

Maybe my dad won't make it. Maybe he was never planning to. But Tallulah is right. I have people who are here to see me, who love me and support me every day.

For them, this is like anything else—like *The Wizard of Oz* in elementary school, or my eighth-grade graduation, or my first high school play. They were there for those. They're here for this. They'll be here for everything, because they're my family. And I won't have to beg, and I won't have to wonder. Because that's what family is about—not wondering if they'll be there, but knowing they will be. Whether it's the family you're born with, or the friends who feel that way.

I spot Milo behind Derek, dressed in his all-black crew outfit. Lucy in her wedding player costume, holding someone's dress closed while Tallulah pins the zipper that just snapped open. Warmth bubbles in me as I realize how grateful I should be, and how grateful I am.

"Darling husband," I say to Derek, "I've been waiting for this moment all summer."

Chapter Twenty-Two

ROSALIND
We should wander and wander in this forest until
when? With mischievous fairies afoot to ruin
the wedding they will not allow us to reach? With
my father lost to us? I cannot allow it.

ORLANDO
You wish to fight against the fairies? Rosalind, be
reasonable. You may as well attempt to defy the
stars.

ROSALIND
For my father, and my dear friend Olivia, I would do
both. I would fight the fairies, and I would defy the
stars!

—Act 1, Scene 9, *Midsummer Madness*

My dad doesn't show all weekend.

He doesn't text, and he certainly doesn't call. But I'm no longer worried. It feels strange to have let go. I expected it to feel like losing a part of myself, but instead, I feel lighter. Like I've freed myself from a burden.

It helps that when I walk into the cast party after Sunday night's performance, I get cheers from every corner of Mayor Choi's house. My mood lifts considerably.

"Oh wow," I say, stopping to give an exaggerated bow. "Thank you. Thank you. No flash photos, please."

"Never let anyone say she loves attention," Tallulah mutters as she inches away from me. "We can't stand for that kind of slander."

Lucy laughs.

"That's our JN," Milo says. "Born to make a scene."

Graham slides an arm around my waist as I straighten. Though his welts have faded slightly, he's still easily fatigued, so he had to beg his mom to let him come tonight. He's been staying with her in a cheap vacation rental near No Man's Land. It's a pink motel called the Pink Flamingo, but prices are steep since we're still in season. According to Graham, Joy is making Macaulay foot the bill. Which I think is more than fair, all things considered.

No one has asked us about—well, about anything. About the casual way he touches me, or the kiss we shared in the hospital. Like we're all waiting to see where the chips fall before we start asking and answering questions.

Right now, we're in limbo. That means our only choice is to enjoy the party and that exhausted, giddy feeling of finishing a performance weekend without any major glitches.

I can tell Camila has been working her magic on the rest of the Drama Club, because Ireland hands me a cold soda before I've made it to the patio, James gives me a thumbs-up when I pass him, and Abe brushes some leaves off a chair outside before I sit.

A few months ago, winning the special election felt like life or death. Now, my goal of becoming Drama Club president feels like it belongs to someone else's life. The same way I've let go of constantly running after my dad's approval, I no longer care about that, either.

So much more has happened this summer, and the possibility of Graham leaving has eclipsed everything else. Not because I might lose him right when I've made him mine, but because he's Graham. Losing any of my friends would be a killing blow. That it's him feels twice as bad, like a guillotine that didn't cut through my neck on the first try, so they'll take another whack.

That's what I'm thinking about when my phone buzzes with a call.

DAD

I look up at my friends in alarm. "Um."

Milo glares at my phone. "Send him to voice mail."

I sigh. "Milo."

Tallulah holds out a hand. "No, let me answer. I have a few things to say."

I pull my phone out of her reach.

"Don't answer if you don't want to," says Lucy, putting her arm out to hold Tallulah back. "But if you want to, that's okay, too."

I look at Graham.

He gives me a small smile. "You know I always agree with Luce. She's the voice of reason."

I stare down at my phone. The call ends. A second later, my phone starts buzzing again.

I swallow and slide to answer. "Hello?"

"Hi, baby! Hey, I'm running real behind, but we're getting on the road now."

In letting go of my need to please him, I allow myself to think the thing that's haunted me most of my life: I hate that he calls me *baby*. It's a nothing nickname. It means nothing to me, and just proves the thing I haven't wanted to admit all this time. That my dad knows nothing about me.

In the background, a woman says something, and a radio blares to life and is quickly lowered. "You think you'll be awake in three hours?"

"No."

"Well, that's fine," he says. "We'll just call when we get there. You won't mind getting up to unlock the door, right?"

"No, I'll be awake."

"Oh, goo—"

"I meant no, you aren't coming here."

"What are you talking about? I'm already on my way!"

"You said you'd come for the musical."

Dad sighs. "I know, baby, and I'm sorry I missed it. But we can still do stuff this week. I want to hang on the beach, take a boat out. Jet Skis. All that stuff."

I clench my teeth. "And I wanted you to come here for my musical."

Distantly, I'm aware of my friends hanging on every word. Graham wraps his hand around mine and squeezes.

"Hey, give me a break, okay? I'm doing the best I can here," Dad says, an edge creeping into his tone.

And that's the worst part. He probably is doing the best he can, and it's so subpar.

"You know what I wanted to hear, Dad? That you're sorry you missed it, but you still want to be here to see me. To celebrate my birthday. To do whatever I want to do—not what you want to do."

"Hey, it's not all about you, Juniper. I work my ass off, and I deserve a vacation."

"You can take a vacation. That's totally up to you." My

nose feels extra wet as I try not to sniffle. I don't want him to know I've started to cry—that he can make me cry, even when I say I no longer care. Maybe that's why I'm crying—because I don't care, and that sucks. "You can even come here. I'm not trying to stop you. But I'll be doing what I want this week, with the people I want to see. If you want to see me, you'll have to do what I want to do."

He lets out an indignant little huff. We have never fought before. I've never wanted to disappoint him or make him angry. My hands are shaking, and I'm shivering like I'm freezing, even though it's stifling hot outside. My teeth nearly chatter as I force out my next words.

"And you'll have to find a hotel, because we don't have room for you at the house. We're in the middle of moving, and it's just—it's too much right now."

This time, he laughs. "Oh, I know. You and your mom and your fancy life with her doctor boyfriend. I get it—no room for two dads, huh?"

He's wrong there, too. Proving once more that my dad has no idea what my life has been like all these years. Because of course I don't have room for two dads. I've barely had room for one dad. Mom has been filling both spaces my entire life.

Some people don't understand that single parents are like water—they fill the space available to them as best they can. I miss my dad, and I want the things other kids have with their dads. But I've never felt the absence of a parent; my mom has filled all that space to brimming.

"Look, I'll always have a place for you in my life if you want it," I say. "How big that space is—that's up to you." I glance up at my friends. Graham and Milo, Lucy and Tallulah. All four of them watching me with worried eyes. "I'm really busy right now, Dad. I have to go."

I hang up, and Milo holds out a hand. I pass him my phone without argument, and he tucks it into his pocket.

Graham puts an arm around my shoulders, and I lean into him as the party comes screaming back into focus. Through the windows, I can see some of the adults holding a poker game inside, playing for potato chips, while AJ deals like it's a real Vegas table. Derek and Vanessa are slow dancing on the other side of the patio while Ireland and Camila belt along to an eight-ies ballad playing over the speakers. Jamil and Joel are trying to build a pyramid of plastic cups, which I can tell is making Tal-lulah's eye twitch from the waste factor. Beside them, Bridget from the Space Science Club is putting up a card pyramid with Alana, and I think the four of them might be racing.

Everyone else is scattered around, the Drama Club and Space Science Club and basketball team all intermixed, friend-ships forged over a summer of sweating together to pull off this single weekend.

"Hey," Graham says, his breath warm on my ear. "You did that."

I turn my head to look at him. "I paid for it."

"You still did it."

I bite my lip, my gaze drifting toward Lucy, Milo, and Tallulah. Sophie leans over the back of Milo's seat, saying something to them. Peter stands at her back, smiling as he sips from a can of soda.

I glance at Graham. "Have you . . . decided? What to do?"

He takes in a breath and lets it out slowly. "No, but . . . I'm leaning."

The way he says it, I know he means toward Jacksonville. My heart squeezes. "Got it."

"Just focus on tonight, okay?" he whispers. "Enjoy this. You earned it."

I don't know how to tell him that I don't feel like I can enjoy anything with the possibility of him leaving looming over us. But I don't want to make him feel bad, so I plaster on a smile and squeeze his hand, and I do what I'm best at. I perform.

I'm dead on my feet by the time I get home from the cast party. Sweaty, clothes stiff, hair a tangled mess. And there's a chip crumb in my bra that somehow evaded all my digging around for it and has been irritating my skin for the last hour. I drag myself inside and nearly trip over the threshold.

Mom is standing in the center of the living room with her hands on her hips, her back to me. She turns with a gasp at the sound of the front door hitting a box left too close to the entryway.

Her face is wet, eyes red.

"Mom?" I drop my bag and rush to her. "What's wrong? What happened?'

She swipes her tears away. "No, no, nothing. It's nothing. I was just . . ." She sniffles and glances around the room, her eyes filling again. "I was just thinking I'm going to miss this house."

My throat tightens. "Me, too."

She reaches for me, pulling me down beside her on the couch. "Do you remember when we moved in?"

I hum. "Vaguely. I remember putting stickers on everything I wanted to keep, because I thought you were going to throw it away if I didn't." It's the reason there's still a superhero sticker on our oldest living room lamp. Mom never even tried to remove it.

Mom chuckles. "I remember that. I also remember when Isabel called to tell me this place was going on the market."

She sighs, leaning into me. "I know you don't love the idea of moving to the South Shore. It doesn't feel the way the North Shore feels, does it?"

"Unless Tommy Bahama starts selling hand-knit clothing and serving breakfast burritos, no, I don't think so."

"But the North Shore isn't just a place. It's our community, and it'll always be here for us." She slides her hand into mine, slotting our fingers together as she rests her head on my shoulder. "No matter where we live, if it's the South Shore or the Panhandle or Mars."

"We're going to Mars?"

Mom nudges me with a smile. "I just want you to know things don't end when you leave a place like this. These people are our family." She brushes her thumb over my knuckles, and adds quietly, "I'm sorry your dad didn't make it this weekend, Juju."

I flap a hand. "It's fine. I talked to him."

Mom hesitates. "Oh?"

"Yeah. He called me tonight. I let him have it."

Mom sits up and twists to look at me. "You did?"

I nod. "I don't care what he has to say. If he can't be here for me when I need him, then I don't want him when it's convenient."

Mom's face crumples. "I'm sorry, Juju."

"Mom, don't be sorry." I wrap my arms around her. "*Don't* be sorry. You can't control what he does. Besides, you've already done the most. There are no gaps left in my life for him to fill—you've filled them all. So don't apologize to me."

Mom sniffles.

"You're the reason I have all those other people, too. I get to have a godmother and a grandmother and aunts and uncles. You brought those people into my life. And I can count on them for everything, the way we already have—Milo's parents finding us this house, and the Olivers selling you P&J's, and Hal finding us a place to stay and Dot actually letting us. I'm lucky." I think of Tallulah, and what she said backstage the other night. "People would kill to have what I have."

"We're very lucky. That's how it is here," Mom says thickly. "It's what we do for each other."

An idea strikes me then, staring at our emptying house with its bare walls and much of the furniture already gone.

I sit up. "Mom."

"Hmm?"

I turn to face her. "Could we do that for someone?"

"Do what?"

"Help them. How everyone has helped us."

Mom frowns. "Of course. But who?"

"Joy Isham."

Mom straightens. "Joy. Why— What—"

"She wants Graham to come back to Jacksonville with her." I motion to the house. "What if we let them stay here? She can rent our house until she gets on her feet."

Mom hesitates. "Well, it's not that simple. She'd need a job, too."

Not just any job, either. She needs one with a good health-care plan, or the cost of her insulin would bankrupt her in a month.

I pull my phone from my pocket. "So we start calling. Right?"

Mom scratches her cheek, considering.

"Mom, come on. She could come home. They could stay. We just leave the rest of the furniture for them—the stuff that isn't gone yet. It's not much, but it's something, right? And someone on this island must know of a job somewhere. What about Paul? The hospital might have something. Whatever the job is, it just has to have benefits. She's diabetic."

Mom picks up her phone. "Let me start calling around. But don't get your hopes up, okay, Juju? She might not want to stay, and a job with good healthcare isn't easy to come by."

"We should try, though, right?"

Mom scrolls through her phone and taps a name. *Tony Delgado.* The White Coral Key real estate king. The man who knows everyone. The husband of a Barajas sister is like the tip-top of the phone tree—the word will trickle down from Tony and Rita.

I type out a text to Sophie anyway. Just in case.

ME
Hey. Could you have Peter check with his dad about any job openings on the island?

SOPHIE
You bored with the family business?

ME
For Graham's mom
And it has to have healthcare!! GOOD healthcare!

SOPHIE
OH!!! Yeah I'm on it!!

Chapter Twenty-Three

ORLANDO
Sir, please see reason. You cannot stay alone in Fairyland.

DUKE SENIOR
But Queen Titania, in my respect, is all the world. Then how can it be said I am alone when all the world is here to look on me?
—Act 2, Scene 17, *Midsummer Madness*

Mom and I spend most of the night on the phone, so when I wake late the next morning, I'm shocked to find her gone. I figured she would've called Elden in to cover her shift, but as I shuffle through the house, it becomes abundantly clear that it is just me and the many moving boxes.

I'm in the bathroom brushing my teeth when the knocking starts.

I spit foam into the sink and rinse my mouth. "I'm coming!" I shout when the knocking continues, louder now. "I'm coming, *God*! Have some patience!"

I pull open the front door, and I barely have a moment to register that it's Graham, skateboard abandoned in the grass, chest heaving, sweat dripping from his temples, still covered in fading welts—before he grabs my face and kisses me.

I let out a squeak of surprise as he pushes me into the house, kicking the door shut behind him and pressing me into the wall. I'm still trying to de-haze my brain and convince myself this isn't a dream when he drags his mouth up my jaw, pressing kisses up to my ear, and I realize he's saying something.

"You are a fucking miracle girl."

"What? What's going on?" I push at his shoulders, but he wraps his arms around my waist, splaying both hands against my back to pull me right up against him. He nuzzles into my neck, his mouth warm, his teeth grazing my skin.

"What happened?" I ask, breathless and burning hot.

"You," he answers, finally lifting his head. He leans me back into the wall, his weight pressing into me. "You happened." He cups my face and kisses me again.

I laugh against his mouth. "Graham—could—I need—*hey.*"

He pulls away, breathing heavily. "Your mom called mine this morning. She's over there now with Dot Slip and *the fucking mayor.*"

I blink at him. "What?"

"Mayor Choi offered her a job," he says. "Your mom offered her your house. I'm—" He drops his head, and the next sound that comes out of him sounds like a whimper.

I put my hands on his face and pull him back up to find that he's crying.

He lifts his shirt to wipe his eyes, and I'm momentarily distracted by the sight of his bare stomach, which feels wildly inappropriate but, I mean, he was *just* kissing me up against the wall, so it's not my fault, really.

Then he drops his shirt and braces his hands on the wall, bracketing me between his arms. "I love you," he says, the words rushing out like he can't say them fast enough.

I bite my lip, tucking my fingers into his front pockets to keep him close. "I love you, too."

"No, I mean, I'm *in* love with you, Juniper Nash." He shakes his head, swallowing hard. "And not because of this, but because you're you. Because you do shit like this—you would've done it for anyone, but it happened to be me. You're incredible. You're the fucking miracle girl."

I duck my head, blushing fiercely. "You gotta stop saying that. I'm gonna get a big head."

"I don't care." He presses his lips against my neck, leaning his body into mine again. "You are. You're the miracle girl, and I'm in love with you."

I wrap my arms around him, pressing my hands against his back and holding him close. "I'm in love with you," I whisper. "I was in love with you the first time you kissed me. Probably even before that, but I didn't know it then."

He squeezes me tighter, and I laugh.

"You're wrong, though," I say. "I wouldn't do it for just anyone. I'm not that great." I slide a hand up into his hair, letting my fingers drift through it. "I did it because it was you. I'm actually really selfish—I wanted to keep you here with me."

He lifts his head, his mouth so close, it ghosts against mine as he says, "You can always be selfish about me. Please never stop being selfish about me."

I grin. "Now we're venturing into toxic couple territory."

"Fine by me," he says, nuzzling into my neck again. Then

he leans back and looks at me, his gaze roaming over my face like he's taking stock.

"What?" I ask. "Do I have toothpaste . . . ?" I swipe at my mouth, though if there were toothpaste there, odds are Graham already cleared it away with his lips.

He smiles. "Just committing this to memory."

"What? Please don't. I'm a mess—I can smell myself right now."

"I have to," says Graham. "Today's the day Juniper Nash Abreheart told me she's in love with me."

I purse my lips, turning my face away. "Well, when you put it like that, I wish I would've showered last night."

He puts his hands on my face and turns me toward him. "Stop, I'm still memorizing."

My gaze snags on the welt curling onto his cheek, a light pink now that it's healing. "Hey! You skated here? You're supposed to be resting!"

"Junie, I don't know how to tell you this, but I'm not resting today. I couldn't if I tried." He drops his hands, clasping one around my wrist and tugging me toward my bedroom. "Come on, I want to see where I'll be sleeping."

"You mean my bed that you've seen a thousand times?"

"Right," he says, pulling me down onto my twin mattress with him. "Actually, I guess it'd be more accurate to call it the bed where I won't be sleeping."

He settles on top of me, bracing himself on his elbows. Something he couldn't do two days ago, now fueled by adrenaline and whatever is making his eyes so hot.

"Not sleeping?" I ask, tilting my head as I gaze up at him.

"I don't think I'll ever be able to sleep if I'm thinking about you."

"Better than the newborn method, I guess." I grin up at him. "Should we call it the Junie method?"

He presses his mouth to my ear. "Sure. As long as I'm the only person who ever gets to use it."

I wrap my arms around him, holding him close. "Obviously. I'm only meant for you, Graham Isham."

Chapter Twenty-Four

(Lower noise on the wedding reception as the two newlywed couples, VIOLA and ORSINO, OLIVIA and SEBASTIAN, move to the center of the stage to have their first dances.)

ROSENCRANTZ
How lucky they were that Queen Titania arrived just in time.

GUILDENSTERN
How lucky we were to be invited to a double wedding.

QUEEN TITANIA
(To the ghosts.) Do the two of you really have no idea you're dead?

> *(ROSENCRANTZ and GUILDENSTERN stare at her in wonder.)*

QUEEN TITANIA
(Turning back to Duke Senior/King Oberon.) If this were played upon a stage now, I could condemn it as an improbable fiction.
—Act 2, Scene 18, *Midsummer Madness*

It's a cloudless, robin's-egg blue sky over the summer's antique car show. And like every year, it's so hot I can feel the blacktop through the soles of my sandals, and I'm already getting a headache from the glare of the sun.

"Do you want frozen lemonade?" Mom asks as we pass a line of vintage trucks.

I push onto my toes to peer through the crowd, shielding my eyes with one hand. "Is there strawberry?"

"Oh, that sounds good," Paul says from Mom's other side. "I could go for strawberry lemonade."

"I don't want frozen, just with ice," says Tallulah as she digs through her bag on my other side. She finally produces an extra pair of sunglasses and passes them to me. "Here you go, Mess."

I pluck them from her hand and slide them on. "Do you think I can trade back those reusable straws you got me for a new nickname instead?"

"No refunds or exchanges, sorry." She reaches into her bag again and pulls out the box of straws she gave me for my birthday earlier this week, which I distinctly recall were sitting on my dresser this morning. "I washed these for you, so you can use them today."

I shoot her a flat smile. "Very thoughtful. Thank you."

"Saving the world starts at home," she says, a phrase I've heard from her many times since moving in. In the last week, Mom and I have made the switch to reusable Ziploc bags, wool dryer balls, and eco-friendly paper products. Tallulah is even teaching Mom to compost. In return, Tallulah has quit smoking—something she was already working on when she started dating Lucy, but Mom got her to fully commit to in the composting deal. As it turns out, no one was quite as oblivious to Tallulah's bad habit as I thought, and Mom is the original master of the favor trade.

As I stow the box of straws in my bag, my phone buzzes

in my pocket. I pull it out, hesitating when I see the name on the screen.

DAD

Mom glances at me as I silence the buzzing. I type out a quick text, then slip my phone in my pocket.

Mom raises an eyebrow. "You don't want to talk to him?"

"I told him I'll call him later," I say, leaning into her. "I'm busy right now."

Mom wraps her arm around me and squeezes.

I haven't entirely cut my dad out of my life. It's not that I think he's a bad person. I just think he's a selfish person. But I can be selfish sometimes, too. So it's not like I can hold that against him.

My new method of handling my dad is inspired by Tallulah's hard edge but softened by the love I have for him. I won't put him first anymore—not before Mom or anyone else, and especially not before myself. But I'll always have a space for him in my life, whenever he's ready to fill it. The size of that space is up to him. And if he leaves it empty, it'll be a loss, but not a monumental one the way I used to believe. Because I hate to admit when Tallulah is right about anything, almost ever, but she was right about the biggest thing: that I have a family that cares about me already, and the spaces those people fill are big enough for me.

"Is it too early to head to the house?" Paul asks a while later, glancing at his watch as we start toward the parking lot, trading vintage Thunderbirds and Tudors for the modern age of Civics and Malibus.

"I don't know if time is the issue here," I say, patting my stomach. "I might be eighty percent funnel cake right now. I don't know how I'll be any help."

"You weren't gonna be much help anyway," Tallulah says. "Or did you forget how unhelpful you were when we moved you out last week?"

I gape at her. "You would bully me? On my birthday?"

"Your birthday was four days ago."

"Don't worry, Juju," says Mom. "I'm sure you'll recover on the drive over. Besides, Joy said they don't have much to move in."

As we pull up outside our old house, now Graham and Joy's, I'm stunned at the number of people already here. The Neighborhood Hero truck and Hal's pickup are parked on the street, and Joy's crossover with the small U-Haul hitched to the back is in the driveway, the door rolled up to show it's still half-full. As we head up the front steps, I spy Lucy's roller skates abandoned by the front door.

"Hello, hello!" Isabel calls as she swings open the front door for us, letting out a cacophony of sound. Milo and his dad are in the middle of moving a dining set into the space where our kitchen table used to be, and Lucy and Cora are helping Rita hang photos on the wall outside Mom's old room. While Dot argues with Moonface over how the kitchen should be organized as they unload a box, Hal positions a sculpture that is clearly her own work in the corner of the living room.

"Art makes the home," she says as Joy comes out of the bedroom, and they both pause to survey Hal's work.

The house is missing some vital pieces—some of the furniture sold well before we knew they'd be moving in—but they've got a couch, one barstool, and most of the furniture from the bedrooms. Graham insisted on keeping my glittery pink dresser, but I took the heart-shaped mirror with me to the new house—the one I'm trying very hard to call *home*.

I only make it two steps inside before arms snake around

me, yanking me into the hall. Graham is quick to cover my mouth, smothering my shriek of surprise against his hand.

He huffs out a laugh against my neck. "So dramatic."

"You scared me!" I twist in his arms to smack him lightly, still careful since his man-of-war stings haven't totally healed. They've mostly faded, though I wouldn't be surprised if they leave behind more than a couple scars.

"I missed you," he whispers, tugging me into a hug.

"It's only been a week," I say into his shoulder.

"Way too long. Never again."

After Joy agreed to stay in White Coral and rent our house, she and Graham went to Jacksonville to pack up her stuff and move her things out of storage. He spent most of the week catching up with his mom's side of the family, and was so chaotically busy, we barely got to talk.

It's safe to say a week apart was a little long for me, too.

"I have something for you." He pulls me toward the bedroom—once mine, now his.

"This feels a little risqué," I say as he shuts the door behind us. "Is this the type of birthday gift I should get when everyone's gone home?"

He shoots me a look. "No, perv."

I gape at him. "*Me?* A pervert?"

"Yes, you. A pervert." He pulls his sketchbook from the backpack on the floor and passes it to me.

I take it but don't flip open the cover. "What . . . ?"

He motions to it. "Open it."

I eye him. "This feels like a trick."

He runs a hand through his hair, and I catch a flash of yellow-painted nails. "It's not a trick. It's a gift. Kind of. If you consider my art a gift, which—okay, well, don't tear it," he says as I whip the sketchbook open.

I stare at the first page.

Miracle Girl and the Magic Island

Underneath is a black-and-white cartoon drawing of a girl with wild hair and hearts in her pupils, a town sketched behind her with a huge wave rising over it.

As I flip through, I see people I recognize—a boy with stars in his hair who is so tall that his head sometimes disappears in the clouds, a girl with roller skates for feet and an ever-present smile, a woman with flower petals for hair and vines growing up her arms, and another whose head is a crescent moon. There's a magic tea maker, a talking wishing fountain that eats coins, and jellyfish that drift across the sky.

In the first few panels, Miracle Girl finds a message in a bottle that warns of a man-made hurricane destined to destroy the island if she can't stop it.

"I started writing it last summer."

I lift my head to stare at him, stunned. "Last summer?" I flip the title page around to him. "You started *this* last summer?"

He glances away, clearly embarrassed. "I've always thought you were a miracle girl, Junie."

I look down, staring at the version of me in his head.

"It's not finished," Graham says. "I just cleaned up the first few chapters so I could have it ready before I start applying to art school, but—"

"Art school?"

He glances away with a sheepish smile. "Yeah, well. My parents might not agree, but it's my life, right? I'm the one who has to live it. I've been talking to Hal about it, and she said she has a friend I can apprentice with, too. I might not get into school or get to go right away, but that's . . . that's what I want."

I set the sketchbook on the dresser and wrap my arms around him.

He chuckles. "If I'd known college was this important to you, I would've done this sooner."

I shake my head, pulling back to look at him. "I don't care if you go to college. I might not even *get* into college."

"From this year's Drama Club president? Really?"

I roll my eyes, trying to rein in my smile. "Hey, that's not official yet."

Graham scoffs. "As good as. Didn't your campaign manager say she's gotten eight confirmed votes?"

I snort. Sophie, of course, took it upon herself to move straight from community theater into election mode. She's been hounding the other members of the Drama Club basically since the curtain dropped on *Midsummer Madness*. Even the club members who didn't participate in community theater have had to deal with Sophie over the last week.

"Well, yeah, if you trust Sophie's work, I guess it's basically official." I smile, nudging him with my shoulder. "But either way, I want you to do whatever is gonna make you happy."

"I'm happy with you," he says, reaching up to cup my cheeks.

I grin. "Well, that's a start."

I lean up and kiss him, savoring the feeling I've been missing for the last week.

"Where the hell are Graham and Junie?" Dot shouts from the other side of the house, starting up a chorus of our names being called.

"Ignore them," Graham whispers, squeezing me closer.

I laugh. "We can't hide forever. The house isn't that big."

"Not forever. Just one more minute."

I grin. "What if we go out there now, and later I show you how to open the bedroom window without it squeaking?"

Graham scoffs. "I work for Neighborhood Hero. If the window squeaks, I can just fix it."

"Ooh, big man have tools. Big man fix window." I grab his hand and pull him toward the door. "Big man unpack lots of boxes."

Graham groans. "How about big man kiss his girlfriend one more time?"

I twist back around and kiss him quickly, and I can tell by the noise he makes that I surprised him.

"One more time," I murmur against his mouth. "Because you called me your girlfriend."

"Interesting. I can keep saying it if this is the reaction."

"You better keep saying it anyway." I tug him toward the door again. "Because it makes me happy."

I fling the door open and drag him toward the living room, where our friends, who feel more like family, are waiting.

Acknowledgments

There are many people I have to thank for making this book what it is, but first, I have to thank my editor, Vicki Lame. This book would be sitting in my trashed manuscripts folder if not for you. I am eternally thankful to you for not just believing in Junie and Graham but for *seeing* them, and for trusting me to make it happen.

To Ashley Blake, thank you for championing my career. I count myself very lucky to have gotten your eye and your guidance for two books, and I've taken every piece of advice you've given me to heart.

To my agent, Lauren Spieller, thank you for always being available to brainstorm, and for pushing me to keep improving. I'm so lucky to have landed with you.

To the amazing Kerri Resnick who quite literally never misses, and the incredibly talented Guy Shield, for giving me the summery, beachy cover of my wildest daydreams. I have lost so much time just gazing lovingly at it, but it feels like time extremely well spent. Thank you to Alexis Neuville and Brant Janeway for promoting the stuffing out of my books, and to Meghan Harrington for all that you do and especially for dealing with my extremely!!!! excited!!!! emails!!!! I'm so honored to work with everyone at Wednesday Books, and I want to hugely thank everyone who has helped bring up this baby book—Vanessa Aguirre, NaNá V. Stoelzle, Melanie Sanders, Lena Shekhter, Eric Meyer, Jonathan Bennett, Sara Goodman, and Eileen Rothschild. I'm honored to work with such a wonderful team.

Friendship is a big part of all my books and especially this one, and I only know how to write friendship the way I do because I have such amazing friends in my life. To the Nervous Girls—thank you for reading every version of this book as I wrote and scrapped and wrote and scrapped, and for never once saying it wasn't worth fighting for. To Whitney, for talking me through every problem, day and night, no matter how small or irrational. To Sonya, for always hyping me up. And to Ashley, for being Graham's number-one fan from the very beginning. You saw him first, and if not for the seed you planted in my brain, I might never have. I couldn't have written this or probably anything else without the three of you.

Thank you to Ellen for reading the first, very terrible draft of this book, and for never being afraid to tell me the truth. To Helena Greer, thank you for reading this early and yelling about it fully at every chance. A huge thank-you to Rachel Katz for using the word *perfect* to describe this book, and for all your kind words over all these years. I'm so happy we get to do this together. And to Kasee, thank you for making my debut year so amazing, and for being a friend. I'm so glad this wild time brought us together, and I appreciate everything you are and everything you do.

To Marielle, thank you for answering every teeny-tiny question I had while working on this. And to Julianne, who has taught me so much about the T1D community—I hope Joy's story brings a little more awareness to what you deal with every day, and what you fight for always. To Joe, thanks for being the president of the Markum Militia, and for the eternal tagline #takenolovers that, for better or worse, will never die. To Shyenne, thank you for letting me turn you into a reader. There is no greater compliment in the world than when someone reads your book and it inspires them to read more. Having both of you so invested in this journey I'm on means more than you know.

To my second family, the Barrons/Houghs, thank you for being mine, and for being the type of people who have always opened your hearts and homes to the ones who need you. I am inspired by all of you always, and by Hope most of all. Thank you for bringing me to the place that inspired this book, and for making Florida always feel like home whenever I come back and especially when I'm away.

To my first family, thank you for being for others what others have been for me. I'm so lucky and grateful to have such loving, generous people in every corner of my life. I cannot express enough how much I love you all, and how much I appreciate your belief in me.

And of course, to my mom. This book has a little love letter to single moms in it, and that's all because of you. No one has done more for me, or ever will, than you have. Thank you for filling all the space, all the time.